Praise for the Mary Crow Novels

Deadliest of Sins:

"[A] smart and well-paced mystery with a gutsy protagonist and a touch of romance." —*Kirkus Reviews*

Music of Ghosts:

"Bissell's fifth Mary Crow novel is an eerie tale that skillfully weaves folklore, Cherokee tradition, and familial angst." —*RT Book Reviews*

Legacy of Masks:

"A grim but well-written adventure that skillfully interweaves Cherokee lore and human nature at its best and worst." —*Booklist*

"[Mary Crow is] a kickass Atlanta prosecutor." —*Kirkus Reviews*

"Mary proves a captivating protagonist. The mystery and suspense are eerily entrancing, and there's even a touch of the supernatural." —*RT Book Reviews*

"Readers will take a few deep breaths ... A fascinating mix of Cherokee customs and folklore play an important role ... Sallie Bissell has created a set of characters that are realistic and full-bodied." —*Mystery Scene*

"Vividly described ... The interweaving of the Cherokee culture with the investigation should attract readers ... it adds colorful texture to this smoothly written mystery ... a pleasant read." —*Deadly Pleasures*

A Judgment
of Whispers

The Mary Crow Series

In the Forest of Harm

A Darker Justice

Call the Devil By His Oldest Name

Legacy of Masks

The Music of Ghosts

Deadliest of Sins

SALLIE BISSELL

A Novel of Suspense

....

A Judgment of Whispers

MIDNIGHT INK
WOODBURY, MINNESOTA

First Edition
First Printing, 2015

Book format by Bob Gaul
Cover design by Lisa Novak
Cover photo: iStockphoto.com/5334736/©spxChrome
        iStockphoto.com/5878944/©Canoneer
Editing by Nicole Nugent

Midnight Ink, an imprint of Llewellyn Worldwide Ltd.

Library of Congress Cataloging-in-Publication Data
Bissell, Sallie.
    A judgment of whispers: a novel of suspense/Sallie Bissell.—First edition.
        pages; cm.—(A Mary Crow novel; #7)
    ISBN 978-0-7387-4361-5
1. Crow, Mary (Fictitious character)—Fiction. 2. Women lawyers—Fiction. I. Title.
    PS3552.I772916J83 2015
    813'.54—dc23
                            2015018563

Midnight Ink
Llewellyn Worldwide Ltd.
2143 Wooddale Drive
Woodbury, MN 55125-2989
www.midnightinkbooks.com

Printed in the United States of America

For Debra Fisher

Acknowledgments

My thanks to:

Jim and Dorcus McBrayer, who introduced me to Rugby, Tennessee. Your hospitality is amazing!

Robbie Anna Hare—superb agent, fellow granny, friend, and champion.

My colleagues at Midnight Ink—Terri Bischoff, Nicole Nugent, and Beth Hanson. I so appreciate your enthusiasm and hard work.

Finally, to those whose lives have been touched by autism—I salute your courage and admire your heart.

PROLOGUE

It came into his bedroom unbidden, through the screen of his open window. At first he rolled over and pulled the covers to his ears, thinking it was a dream. But then it came again—a sound, a smell, a shadow that flitted across the field of moonlight that puddled on his sheets. It was all of those and none of those. It was something he hadn't felt in a long time.

He reached—a habit of fifty-two years—for his wife. But Jan's side of the bed was empty, her sheets cool. *Minnesota*, he remembered. *Jan is in Minnesota now. I'm in charge of the cat and the chickens.*

He turned his back to the window, deciding that whatever he'd felt had been just the strangeness of Jan not sleeping beside him. Then it came again—unidentifiable, inadmissible in a court of law, but there nonetheless. For some reason, he thought of his daughter Lisa, rehearsing her role as the second witch in a college production of *Macbeth*: *By the pricking of my thumbs, something wicked this way comes.*

He sat up, studied his thumbs. They seemed all right. A breeze fluttered the sheer curtains, making them puff out like ghosts. He got up and went to the window. The half moon was low, about to sink behind a thick bank of clouds. In the dimness he could see his garden, the two rows of corn standing like sentinels guarding the squash and tomatoes. Faraway he heard a menacing growl of thunder.

"Just a storm," he whispered. "Nothing to worry about."

And yet he knew it was more than rain. It was a sense of something returning. He could smell it, thick as the ozone wafting in from the south. As lightning sparked and turned the cloud bank a sick shade of yellow, he realized what it was. Something wicked *did* this way come.

———————

It scared him so badly that he threw on his robe and went into the kitchen. He turned on the lights and put on a pot of coffee, the cat brushing against his legs, mewing for its breakfast. Though he usually considered the furniture-clawing Ivan a pain in the ass, at that moment he was glad to have his company. He was something warm, something alive.

"You want chicken or tuna?" he asked, peering at the cans of cat food Jan had left in the pantry.

Ivan did not indicate a preference, just kept yowling. He opened a can of tuna and scraped it into his bowl. The cat took one bite then stalked off into the den, its rigid tail an exclamation point of disdain.

"Must have guessed wrong," he said. He considered opening another can, perhaps the chicken, but decided against it. He'd grown up on a farm, where cats lived in barns, fending for themselves. He couldn't imagine any of them turning down a can of anything.

He poured a cup of coffee. This early the morning news would be nothing but a rehash of the night before, so he went into the little bedroom Jan had turned into his study. Mostly he just kept his junk—the golf clubs he used weekly, a treadmill he never used at all. In the corner stood a desk that sported his old nameplate—Jack Wilkins, Detective, Pisgah County Sheriff's Department.

He sat down, turned on the light, and looked at the array of mementos piled on the desk. A couple of citations for valor, a news photo of him comforting a child whose mother had survived a bad wreck, and his gold detective badge leaning against the lamp. "Those were the days," he whispered.

Mostly, he'd done okay. Though he'd taken two bullets (one in the upper arm, no big deal; the other in his calf, which pained him to this day), he'd cleared thirty years' worth of cases and slept untroubled by the people he'd sent to prison. There was only one case that still haunted him—that would, he guessed, haunt him until the day he died. Teresa Ewing—a little ten-year-old girl who'd gone out to deliver a casserole to a neighbor and never returned. Or never returned alive, at least. Had the memory of Teresa Ewing awakened him? Had something to do with that case come back?

He hesitated before he unlocked his bottom drawer. The case had become an issue between him and Jan. He, along with everybody else in Pisgah County, had grown obsessed with it. Teresa Ewing had taken up residence in the back of his mind, and he often found himself thinking about the dead girl when he should have been thinking of his alive and very pretty wife. Jan had finally given him an ultimatum: that case or her. He had, wisely, chosen her, but he had never thrown his case files away. Sometimes when Jan was out shopping or having lunch with friends, he would sneak in here and touch the locked drawer, as if it held some memento of a wildly extravagant affair. Today, though, it seemed like more than just visiting an old obsession. Today something felt changed.

3

He unlocked the drawer and took out the tattered, coffee-stained file. For an instant he hesitated, like a sober alcoholic weighing the cost of just one drink, then he started turning the pages, reading the reports, looking at pictures of himself when his stomach was flat and his hair was the color of sand instead of snow. And the girl … the little girl.

———

Two hours later he closed the file. Though the thunder growled more loudly, he hurried to put on his clothes. He needed light, human voices, the bustle of normalcy. He got in his car and drove to the Waffle House, an early morning stop for tourists and truckers and retirees like himself. Today the place was mostly empty, the weather, he guessed, keeping everyone in their own kitchens. His favorites were at their duty stations—Mike scrambling eggs on the grill, Linda shouting orders like a drill sergeant. They knew he'd been a cop; both called him Chief, though officially he'd never risen higher than Detective.

"Don't tell me you're playing golf today, Chief." Linda frowned. Outside, the yellow sky had turned a sickly ochre.

"No, just woke up early and couldn't sleep." *Couldn't sleep or wouldn't sleep? How did that old song go?*

"Aw." She was already pouring him a cup of coffee. "Mrs. Chief out of town?"

"Minnesota with the grandkids." He smiled at her perceptiveness. "How'd you guess?"

"You got that hubby-at-loose-ends look about you. You want your regular?"

Usually he came for a breakfast hamburger before he played nine holes at the municipal course. Today, though, was different. "No, I think I'll have eggs. Over easy, with sausage."

Linda raised a penciled-on eyebrow. "No hamburger? Chief, are you hungover? Mike's got some hair of the dog, if that'll help."

He laughed; he hadn't had a drink in years. "No, I'm okay. Just in the mood for eggs."

"I'll fix you the special and charge you for the regular," she whispered as she put a spoon and napkin down beside his cup. "You'll get a free waffle."

He sipped his coffee. He was admiring Mike's ability to fry bacon, cook waffles, and scramble eggs all at the same time when he felt someone put an arm around his shoulder. He looked up as Irving Stubbs slid onto the seat beside him.

"No golf today, eh, Jack?" Irving was his next-door neighbor, and, like him, retired. Unlike him, Irving had been an accountant and a member of the chamber of commerce.

"Not unless we play in swim trunks." Jack looked over his shoulder. Cars were now traveling with their lights on, as if it were midnight instead of 8 a.m.

"I hate days like today," Irving grumbled as Linda poured him a cup of coffee. "You wake up early, then you look outside and realize you got nowhere to go."

"Can't you go back to sleep?" asked Jack.

"My eyes open at 6:17 regardless. Been that way since the day I turned seventy."

Linda put Jack's order, along with his free waffle, down in front of him. Stubbs ordered hash browns and eggs.

"You boys cheer up," she told them. "This might blow over by noon."

Jack made a little sandwich—sausage on a piece of toast, covered by an egg, finished off with a splash of Tabasco. As he ate, Irving grew chatty, asking if he and Jan had vacation plans, were they going to the Rotary Club picnic, had they seen the new play in Flat Rock. Jack answered in monosyllables, his thoughts returning to Teresa Ewing's sad, thick file. Finally he wiped his mouth with his napkin.

"You were here in 1989, weren't you?"

"We moved here in '86," Irving replied. "Why?"

"Oh, just woke up thinking about some old cases I'd worked on. You remember Teresa Ewing?"

"That little girl who was killed over on Salola Street? I was talking about that poor little thing not a week ago."

"I remember her." Linda paused as she refilled their coffee cups. "I worked at the Donut Den then. We went on double shifts to keep the volunteers in crullers. I bet we passed out five thousand donuts." She gave Jack an odd look. "You work that case, Chief?"

He nodded.

She put the coffee pot down and leaned close. "So, who do you think did it?"

"I don't know," he said softly.

"Remember how one psychic said she was in water? And then another one said two men had taken her to Winslow, Arizona?"

"We got a lot of false leads."

Linda went on. "After all the psychics crapped out, everybody decided that big retarded boy killed her."

"It was a tough case."

Mike looked over his shoulder, eavesdropping from the grill. "They got any new leads?"

Jack emptied his coffee. "Not that I know of. It's still a real cold case."

"And somebody got away with murder," said Irving.

Jack stood up and left enough money to cover his breakfast and Linda's usual two-dollar tip. He said good-bye to Irving and headed for the door, back out into a morning that looked like midnight, his left thumb suddenly twitching like mad.

ONE

AT FIRST SAUNOOKE THOUGHT the dog was going to bite him—it growled at him from under the big rhododendron that spread across Mrs. Whitsett's yard. But Saunooke knelt down and whistled softly, avoiding direct eye contact, his hand open and unthreatening. Then the dog bounded from beneath the bush gratefully, as if he'd found an old friend. He came to Saunooke, tail wagging, trying to lick his face. Why he'd gotten a vicious dog call on him at eight in the morning, Saunooke couldn't say, except for the fact the animal had no tags on its dingy red collar and the people of Elk Mountain Estates liked their property free of strays. That coons and bears and wild turkeys had roamed here for centuries made no difference; the upscale home owners were voters and taxpayers who wanted their neighborhood kept safe. Raccoons carried rabies. Turkeys shit on their driveways. Bears turned over garbage cans and destroyed expensive bird feeders.

"Come on, buddy. Let's go for a ride." Saunooke opened the door of his cruiser. The dog looked at him questioningly, then hopped in.

He was male, long-legged, of indeterminate breed—dirt-colored with a white chest, floppy hound ears, fifteen pounds too thin. Saunooke guessed he'd once belonged to someone; he had no fear of people and jumped in the car as if he'd ridden in them all his life. A runaway, thought Saunooke. Or maybe just dumped. When people ran out of money, pets became expendable. Animal Control would at least fill his belly before they put him down.

Saunooke radioed dispatch to tell them he was on the way to the pound. Boots Gahagen's cackle came through the static. "10-4, Saunooke. Don't let your prisoner get the drop on you."

He signed off and turned his cruiser around, stung by the derision in Gahagen's laugh. Two years ago he'd been Sheriff Jerry Cochran's fair-haired boy, brought up from the Highway Patrol, seemingly on the fast track to detective. Then he'd blown his part in the Fiddlesticks case—taken Joe Slade's word about his brother's whereabouts on the night a girl was murdered. His blunder had almost cost attorney Mary Crow her life. Certainly it had cast him out of the inner circle of Pisgah County detectives and back into the chilly darkness of Pisgah County patrol.

"Guess I'm the dog catcher now," he said to his passenger, who looked at him with sad, old man eyes. Saunooke sighed. He needed a break—a good case to work his way back into Cochran's good graces. Otherwise, he'd be catching dogs and writing traffic tickets for the rest of his life.

He kept his radio on but drove to the Sonic drive-in, where waitresses delivered your food on roller skates. He ordered an egg sandwich and coffee, then added an extra sandwich to his order. "May as well make your last ride a good one," he told the dog, who still watched him with sad eyes. A few minutes later, a waitress named Sandra rolled up to his cruiser.

9

"Hey, Rob." She smiled, then saw his passenger in the backseat. "Aw, what a cute dog. What's his name?"

"Rover."

"When did you start working with the Canine Squad?"

For an instant he was tempted to tell her he now worked narcotics and this was a drug-sniffing hound. But he was a bad liar and the dog looked more like he'd been *on* drugs rather than sniffing them out.

"I haven't," admitted Saunooke. "He's a stray. I'm taking him to the pound."

"Aw." Sandra stuck out her lower lip. "But he looks so sweet. Here, give him this." She handed him an order of bacon destined for some other customer. "I'd take him home with me, but my landlord would have a fit."

"You're still nice to give him the bacon," said Saunooke. He watched her as she rolled back to the kitchen, wondering what it was like to strap on roller skates the first thing in the morning. He ate then, feeding the dog little bites of egg and bacon through the mesh of the cage. They'd almost finished when the radio squawked again.

"Saunooke? What's your 10-20?"

"Soco Road," he replied vaguely, not wanting admit he was at the Sonic Drive-In, feeding bacon to a stray dog.

"You been to the pound yet?"

He winced. "Not yet."

"Okay. I need you to stop off at the Lone Oak Acres construction site. I got a call about somebody up there trying to hot wire a bull-dozer."

"10-4." Saunooke started his engine. "On my way."

———

10

Lone Oak Acres was a newer development than Elk Mountain Estates. Pricey green houses were scheduled to be built along winding Salola Drive, with bike paths to the university, walking paths to town, and a shared green space for a playground and community vegetable gardens. Most of the old '50s ranch houses had been leveled, their lots now just mounds of red Carolina clay. But four families remained, today having a yard sale, junk piled high on card tables. Saunooke drove past the shoppers trudging from house to house and turned towards the construction site, where a number of bright yellow bulldozers and backhoes surrounded the huge old oak tree his people called *Undli Adaya*. His heart gave a funny jump. Twenty-five years ago, this was where little Teresa Ewing had disappeared. The whole county had gone nuts searching for her, then a month later, a jogger found her body between the roots of that big tree. Though the police had half a dozen suspects, they weren't able to pin the murder on any of them. Saunooke, who'd been in diapers when the girl died, had studied the case at the police academy. It remained unsolved, and every Halloween dispatch would get calls from people wildly claiming to have seen a pretty little girl in a green jacket standing wraith-like beneath the tree, until she vanished before their astounded eyes.

He pulled up next to one of the bulldozers. Suddenly the dog began to whine, pawing at the back window. Saunooke hesitated a moment, wondering if he ought to let the animal out. If he did, he might run away and annoy a different neighborhood. But if he didn't, the dog might crap in his backseat. He'd eaten a lot of bacon at the Sonic.

Not wanting to clean dog crap out of his cruiser, Saunooke got out and opened the back door. "Okay, Rover. Go do your business."

11

The dog hopped out and trotted off, lifting his leg against one of the backhoes. Saunooke made a circuit of the construction vehicles, slipping through the rutted clay soil. Considerable excavation had gone on back here—they'd carved up the earth for underground utility lines and staked skinny little orange flags down to mark off the boundaries of the yet-to-be-built houses. Saunooke glanced over his shoulder at the dog, half-hoping the animal might grasp his last chance at freedom. But the dog ambled along behind him, nose to the ground, making little forays to explore the churned-up dirt.

"Must be part bloodhound," Saunooke muttered. He walked over to the biggest bulldozer. Two empty Coke cans had been left in the driver's seat, but the engine cowling was locked down and there were no scratches around the gas cap. He ran his hand along the dozer's massive fender, thinking how he would have loved to climb up on one of these monsters when he was little. He wondered if some kids bored by the yard sale hadn't felt the same way.

He'd just turned back toward his cruiser, when a gray-haired man appeared from behind the backhoe. He was tall and lean, dressed in khaki pants and a blue FOP windbreaker. He startled Saunooke so that he almost reached for his weapon.

"Easy, officer." The man lifted his hands. "I'm unarmed."

"You have business here?" Saunooke felt silly, almost drawing on an old man. But everyone carried guns these days, even at restaurants and playgrounds. You had to be careful.

"Just looking around." The man stepped forward but kept his hands raised. "Detective Jack Wilkins, Pisgah County Sheriff Department, retired."

Now Saunooke felt even dumber. Almost drawing on one of Pisgah's own. "Sorry," he began. "I got a call about somebody hot-wiring one of these things. I didn't see you there."

12

"It's okay," said Jack. "I was just taking a little walk down memory lane."

"You lived here?"

"No. I just spent a lot of time here."

Saunooke looked at the man. He was the right age, had the right air of regret about him. "Teresa Ewing?"

Wilkins nodded as he lowered his hands. "I was the lead detective. Worked with a rookie named Buck Whaley. He still on the force?"

Saunooke squelched a groan. He despised Whaley, who detested him in equal measure. "He is."

"Really?" Wilkins seemed surprised. "I didn't figure he'd last that long."

"He's senior detective now," said Saunooke. "You guys really went all out on Teresa Ewing."

Wilkins gave him a bitter smile. "In thirty years, it's the only one I didn't clear."

Saunooke looked at the man's muddy sneakers. They were beige, fastened with Velcro straps—exactly the kind old men with bad bunions wore. "You come here a lot, to think about it?"

"I haven't been here in years. I just wanted to see the neighborhood one last time, before they tore it up completely." He turned and looked at the bulldozers, the mounds of dirt. "The only things I really recognize now are those houses and this tree." He turned to the massive oak towering over them. "Teresa and the other children played here. The soil had eroded around the roots. They had a great network of hidey-holes here."

"Didn't they find her in one of those holes?" asked Saunooke.

"Yeah, we did."

Suddenly the dog bounded up, a cast-off tin of chewing tobacco in his mouth, his tail wagging as he dropped the item at Saunooke's feet.

"Go on," Saunooke said, growing irritated. "I'm not here to play fetch with you."

The dog looked at him disappointed, but then ran back into the scrubby vegetation that had once comprised someone's back yard.

"He belong to you?" asked Wilkins.

"He's headed for the pound," Saunooke replied. "I got this bulldozer call on my way there."

"Too bad," said Wilkins. "He seems like a nice dog."

"I should probably check the rest of this site out," said Saunooke. "Want to come along?"

"Sure." Wilkins shrugged. "Be like old times."

They walked slowly around the edge of the development, Wilkins explaining how they'd worked the Ewing case. The SBI had come in; some anonymous benefactor had two cadaver dogs flown in from New York.

Wilkins turned and scowled back at the tree. "We searched under that tree more times than I can count. Teresa Ewing's body was not there."

"And then it was," said Saunooke, the case etched in his brain as indelibly as the paragraphs of the Miranda rights. "A jogger found her there. He thought somebody had put a jacket under the tree. Turned out to be a body."

"And we've all looked like fools ever since." Wilkins kicked at a clump of dirt.

"You know, people still talk about her," said Saunooke.

Jack gave a bitter laugh. "Last week somebody on the golf course asked me if I knew who did it."

"What did you say?"

"Nothing. Oh, I've got some ideas. But I can't prove 'em. No point in talking about what you can't prove."

"I guess not."

The two men turned. They'd just headed back toward the bull-dozer when the dog began to bark, loud and frantic.

Wilkins said, "Sounds like your pal's found something interesting."

Saunooke looked around. "Where did he go?"

"He's over there."

They walked toward the ancient tree. The Spanish Oak was famous in its own right, having supposedly saved the Cherokees from Desoto's conquistadors. Lately someone had nailed on a little bow tie of a label, proclaiming it a "Quercus Alba" and had dumped new manure and potting soil around the old roots. Flowers and some kind of ground cover had been planted around it, all protected by a perimeter of low plastic fencing. On the forbidden side of the fence was the dog, digging at the tree's roots, barking like mad.

"Shit!" said Saunooke. "He's messing all that landscaping up."

He ran over to the fence, whistling for the dog. "Come on, boy. Come on over here."

But Saunooke's command only made the dog dig faster.

"Damn it!" cried Saunooke.

Jack said, "He's probably got a chipmunk trapped. Come on, I'll help you pull him out."

They stepped over the fencing. The dog was still digging, still throwing dirt in the air, when suddenly his tail started wagging like a buggy whip. As he backed out of the hole, his front legs and paws were caked with dirt, but his eyes were shining. He turned to Saunooke with what looked like a greasy plastic sandwich bag in his mouth.

Jack Wilkins laughed. "Looks like he dug up someone's lunch."

"Drop it, dog," ordered Saunooke.

The dog refused to drop the bag, but he did allow Saunooke to pull it from his mouth. Saunooke held it up, thinking he would find some construction worker's moldy sandwich. Though the outside of the bag was smeared with grease, it held a piece of clothing, folded neatly inside.

"What the hell?" said Saunooke. Turning to Wilkins, he opened the bag, pulling out a pair of girl's underpants, pink flowers printed on a field of dingy white. As strange as that was, what stopped his heart was the faded letters of a laundry marker that spelled out, along the waistband of the garment, *Teresa E. Cabin 8.*

TWO

"LADIES AND GENTLEMEN, IT's my special pleasure to introduce our second candidate, Hartsville attorney Mary Crow." Yvette Wessel adjusted the microphone that stood in the corner of the Chat N Chew Restaurant. Fifty Pisgah County voters had just consumed a breakfast of rubbery eggs and cheese grits, now they were going to hear from the people running for District Attorney.

"Not only is Mary a graduate of Emory law school and former special prosecutor for Governor Ann Chandler," said Yvette, "but she's the first candidate for any Pisgah County office who's also an enrolled member of the Eastern Band of the Cherokee Indians. She serves on the Domestic Violence Committee for the North Carolina Bar Association, the Health Initiative for the Quallah Boundary, and the board of directors of Pisgah-Cherokee Sports Park." Yvette paused to smile at Mary. "She's also a very good tennis player and makes a mean peach cobbler."

The audience laughed politely and started to applaud. Mary rose from her seat. As she made her way to the microphone, she looked out at the crowd. Most were female and white, though there were a couple of tables of Cherokee ladies. At the back of the room sat the people who'd gotten her into this—Ginger Cochran, Emily Kurtz, and Anne Babcock. *You'd make a great DA,* they'd said. *You could do so much good in that office. People are so over Turpin. Go for it, Mary. The time is right!*

That she could do better than George Turpin, she had no doubt. Convincing the voters at the Chat N Chew was something else— particularly since Turpin was sitting just one table over, ready to give out free bottles of his prize-winning barbeque sauce.

She thanked Yvette for her introduction, smiled at Victor Galloway, who had sneaked into the back of the room, then began. With only ten minutes to speak, she decided to tell the voters who she was and why she thought she'd make a good DA. Negative campaigning had turned her off since the days of the first George Bush, and she was determined to keep things positive.

"First, let me say how proud I am to be here," she began. "It reflects highly on the voters of Pisgah County that they would consider a Native American woman as a candidate for District Attorney. When my mother was born in the late forties, North Carolina had only recently guaranteed us Cherokees the right to vote, so I consider it a particular honor to be here running for office."

The audience clapped, pleased to be considered progressive in their political thinking. She went on, telling them about growing up on the Quallah Boundary, working as an ADA in Atlanta, and being dubbed "Killer Crow" by the Atlanta newspapers because of her perfect record in capital murder trials.

"That nickname may seem a bit harsh," she said, "but when I was a senior in high school, my mother was the victim of a homicide. That incident marked me for life. Never have I forgotten what it feels like to lose someone you love to violence. Though the courts can't return the person who was taken from you, they can ensure fair trials and stern punishments for those found guilty. As DA, that would be my goal and my total commitment to the voters of this county."

She ended her speech quickly after that. The audience looked at her questioningly, shocked, she guessed, that an eighteen-year-old kid would make avenging a murder her life's work. She nodded her thanks to enthusiastic applause, taking her seat as Victor gave her a thumbs-up from the back row. *So far, so good*, she thought. *My first stump speech. And nobody threw any tomatoes.*

Next up was perennial candidate Prentiss Herbert, a small, slender man who wore bow ties and reminded Mary of an earthworm wearing glasses. He had a small defense practice in town, advertising on billboards that he was the man to call next time the cops collared you for DUI. To Mary's knowledge, he'd never worked a capital case. She tried to look interested as he rambled on about how the framers of the Constitution believed in liberty and justice for all. From the glazed looks on the audience's faces, they were as bored with Herbert as she was. She caught a flicker of motion from the corner of her eye. She turned to see Victor hurrying out the door, cell phone to his ear. *That's a business call*, she thought. *Somebody must need the SBI, double quick.* Unless, of course, Victor had just called his own number so he could escape Prentiss Herbert.

Finally the little man finished. Though everyone clapped, there was an unspoken sense of relief in the room. Maybe the audience figured almost anything George Turpin had to say would be more interesting than Prentiss Herbert's yammering about the Constitution.

Turpin was out of his chair almost before Yvette was finished introducing him. A big, broad-shouldered man with an ever-widening gut, Turpin wore a blue suit with an American flag pin and so much cologne that Mary could smell him from six feet away. He raised the microphone to accommodate his height, booming his thanks to Yvette and his opponents who flanked him on either side.

"I've known Prentiss for a long time," he said jokingly, as if he and the wormy little man played poker every Friday night. "But Mary Crow, not so much. She usually gets her clients set free before I can get ahold of them." He looked at her with a sly grin. "How many is it, now Mary? Two? Three?"

She was surprised, never dreaming that Turpin would bring up old cases. But she also saw the trap he was setting for her—trying to force her to defend her own record. She just sat there and returned his smile.

"Let's see, I know there was the Indian boy who was accused of murdering that teenager. Then there was the bird rescuer who we tried to convict for killing Governor Carlisle Wilson's daughter. Were there any more?" He made a show of scratching his head. "I can't remember." He turned back to the audience.

"It really doesn't matter. Ms. Crow's a fine attorney, although I was surprised to learn that she believes so strongly in law and order. My own dealings with her have been more along the line of catch and release."

The audience chuckled, casting glances at Mary. Though she was dying to stand up and tell the asshole that all her clients had been innocent, she said nothing. She wondered if Turpin was going to add that she'd once applied for a job in his office and he'd turned her down. But no, Turpin had apparently taken all his shots at her. He moved on to how crime rates had dropped ten percent since he'd been in office.

She listened along with the rest of the audience. Turpin was expansive, welcoming. No woman need be afraid while he was in office. He had a wife and two daughters; he knew how they felt when their children came home late, when they were bullied in school, when their girls lingered too long on the Internet. "I promise you that I will enforce every law on the books in this county, and I will advocate for harsh punishment for those who put women and children at risk."

He went on, ringing the bell for family values and a return to the morality that the country had been founded on. Mary watched the audience for their reaction. Half seemed comforted by his words; the other half looked unimpressed. Mary couldn't help but wonder what the Cherokee women thought of the morality of the Founding Fathers. It hadn't done their ancestors a hell of a lot of good.

Finally Turpin began passing out barbecue sauce, and Yvette ended the meeting with thanks to all the candidates. As everyone rose to leave, Mary shook hands first with Yvette, then with Prentiss Herbert, and finally with Turpin himself.

"Interesting speech," she said.

He shrugged, his jowls quivering. "Just using my talking points."

"But you did it in such a clever way," said Mary.

"Those are the facts, Ms. Crow. You were the attorney of record in those cases."

"I know. I just hadn't heard them related with such a twist at the end. But it was great." She pinioned him with a look, then gave him a big smile. "I learned a lot, George. Thanks for giving me my first lesson in politics."

For an instant, his gaze faltered. She knew she'd struck a nerve.

"Well, I'm sure we'll be doing this a lot before the election."

"Good." She shook his fleshy paw again, now squeezing a little harder. "I'll look forward to it."

She left Turpin and headed for her table of supporters in the back of the room. Ginger Cochran was there wearing sunglasses and a straw hat pulled low over her face. As Sheriff Jerry Cochran's wife, she wasn't supposed to get involved in politics. But as Mary's best friend, she'd been heavily involved since day one. She split the difference by coming incognito.

"So how'd I do?" asked Mary.

"Fantastic!" Ginger gave her a hug. "That story about your mom was incredible."

"It was a stroke, Mary," said Anne Babcock, a former beltway lobbyist now retired to the Carolina mountains. "Having a candidate who was also a victim gives a whole new level of voter identification. We can really run with this."

Anne's words made Mary uncomfortable. She'd told of her mother's death to explain who she was as a person, not to add an extra coat of gloss to her burgeoning political career. "But ... "

"And just look at what Grace Collier brought over." Emily Kurtz pushed an older woman forward. Like Mary, she had black hair and olive skin, but with dark eyes and a stockier frame. She carried an artist's portfolio that she unfolded across the table, displaying an array of artwork for political signs. Each design was beautiful, with stylized mountains in blue and green. Mary Crow's name was always prominent in black letters, but with a tiny crow sitting atop the O in her last name.

"Grace!" Mary cried. "These are beautiful!"

"I hoped you'd like them," she said, pulling at one of the long-sleeved shirts she always wore buttoned at the wrists. "I didn't know what your campaign slogan would be, so I left a lot of white space between your name and the mountains."

Mary put an arm around her shoulders. "They're just gorgeous. Cherokee, but not totally Cherokee. Just like me."

Smiling, Grace turned to Anne and Ginger. "Did you all ever decide on a slogan? I had to leave the last campaign meeting early."

"Equal Justice for All," said Ginger. "The main plank of her platform. Turpin's way too lax on domestic violence. Did you know he doesn't keep the sex offender register up to date? And he considers spousal abuse a victimless crime! It's so unfair, it's just ... "

"Ginger." Anne put a hand on the woman's arm. "You're preaching to the choir."

"Oh." Ginger looked at them. "I guess I am."

"Listen," Mary said. "I want to thank everybody for all their hard work. Grace, your posters are amazing; Ginger, your research is superb; Emily and Anne, you two have done an incredible job getting me started."

"It's our pleasure, Mary," said Emily. "You'll make a wonderful DA." Always the taskmaster of the group, she looked at the women gathered around her. "When shall we meet again? Monday night at Mary's office, just like always?"

"I'll order pizza," said Mary.

"And I'll bring the wine," Anne volunteered.

"Great. Then I'll work out a campaign schedule and we'll talk about that on Monday." Emily smiled. "Thanks for coming, ladies. Mary, you were terrific!"

Anne and Emily bustled off, politicos who had another candidate in neighboring Swain County. Mary and Ginger helped Grace pack up her artwork, then they all left the restaurant together.

"Gosh, Mary," Ginger said as they stepped out into the bright morning light. "How does it feel to be a real candidate?"

She thought of Turpin and her old disappointment when he hadn't hired her, and of his snide remarks today about catching and releasing criminals. She had hated him for an awfully long time. "It feels great," she said. "Like I'm finally going back where I belong."

THREE

Jerry Cochran took a set of calipers and pulled the underpants to the top of the bag. "Are you kidding me? *Teresa E. Cabin 8?*"

"Maybe she'd gone to summer camp," Saunooke said, almost breathless. "Maybe she wore those there."

"A lifetime ago," Cochran replied. He dropped the pants back inside the bag. "This sandwich bag doesn't look like its been in the ground more than an hour or so."

"That's what I thought," said Saunooke. "Makes you wonder if it didn't get here, like, today."

"You get anything else?" asked Cochran.

"A cigarette." Saunooke held up the broken cigarette he'd placed in another evidence bag. "The dog might have shredded it, digging up the underpants."

Cochran turned to Wilkins, his eyes cold. "This one of your smokes, buddy?"

Wilkins shook his head. "I quit years ago."

"Then tell me again who you are."

Saunooke said, "He says he ... "

"Jack Wilkins, Pisgah County Sheriff Department, retired." Jack handed the sheriff his wallet. It held all his IDs—driver's license, Medicare card, an FOP membership card. "I worked this case when it was new."

"He claims he worked it with Whaley." Saunooke sounded like a kid tattling to his teacher.

Cochran looked up from the wallet. "That true?"

Jack nodded. "Whaley had just been promoted from patrol. I already had fifteen years as a detective."

"So what brings you back here this morning? You come to check out the yard sale?"

Jack felt his cheeks grow hot. What should he say? That his wife had gone to Minnesota and he didn't know what else to do with himself? That this morning he woke up early because something evil was in the air? "I've never forgotten this case. I wanted to see the neighborhood one more time, before they built all these new houses."

"Go sit over there by the bulldozers," said Cochran. "I'll talk with you later."

"Yes sir." Jack nodded, hiding a smile. This young police chief had mastered the command stare pretty well. His gaze was flinty, without a trace of humor. The patrol kid still had some work to do. He stood there sweating, obviously excited, still holding the dog by its collar. Jack turned to him. "Would you like me to get the dog out of your way?"

Cochran turned his attention to the animal, which was wagging his tail, as if he were part of the team as well. "Why have you got a dog here anyway, Saunooke?"

"I got a 10-91," he replied. "I was taking him to the pound when Gahagen said somebody was trying to hotwire a bulldozer over here."

Cochran turned back to Wilkins. "That wouldn't have been you, would it?"

"No sir," said Jack. "I'm way too old to drive a bulldozer."

Again, Cochran gave him the cop stare, but then he nodded at the dog. "Then take Rover over there and wait for us."

"Yes sir." Jack took the dog by the collar and walked over to the huge vehicle. The dog trotted beside him, lying down by the front tire while he sat down on the running board. Jack, even more than Saunooke and the chief, was dumbfounded. This dog had dug up a pair of Teresa Ewing's underpants! How had they gotten there? Could they be evidence they hadn't found?

"Good boy," he said softly. He rubbed the dog between his ears, then settled down to watch. Over the hill, shoppers were haggling over vinyl record albums and old water skis; here, a murder investigation had sprung back to life.

At first Cochran and the patrol officer stood talking outside the plastic fence that surrounded the tree, Saunooke pointing at various spots while the chief's gaze intermittently returned to him. Then a green Mustang pulled up beside the officer's squad car. A muscular, dark-haired young man dressed in dark trousers and a white shirt got out of the car. He carried a large, aluminum briefcase. CSI, decided Jack. Maybe SBI.

"This better be good," the young man called as he hurried over to Cochran. "You pulled me out of a speech by Prentiss Herbert."

The sheriff laughed. "Then you owe me a beer, Victor. Maybe a six pack."

Jack crept closer, eavesdropping. His hearing was still good, and this Victor sounded interesting.

"Mary made her first speech this morning," the young man went on. "At the Chat N Chew."

"How'd she do?" asked Cochran.

"Great," said Victor. "Laid Prentiss Herbert low." He pulled out a pair of latex gloves from his back pocket. "So what have we got here?"

"A case so cold it was frozen," said Cochran. "Until Saunooke's dog came on the scene."

Victor glanced over his shoulder at him and the dog, then back at short, broad Saunooke. "Who's that holding the dog now?"

"An old guy who was just up here," said Saunooke. "Claims he worked this case years ago."

Victor looked at Cochran. "Seriously?"

"His IDs check out," said Cochran, "though I've never heard of him."

Victor shrugged. "Whatever. Tell me what's up."

Cochran turned his back and brought Victor up to speed. Jack caught the words "a nine year old white female … casserole to a neighbor. Found her … under that tree."

"Her name was Teresa Ewing. She died of blunt force trauma to the left frontal squama," called Jack, suddenly wanting to prove that he was not just some old fart revisiting his glory days. He wasn't stupid. He was just retired. "Her jeans were unzipped, and she didn't have on any underpants, but there was no evidence of sexual assault. No semen, and her hymen was intact."

The three younger men gaped at him. He kept going, repeating details only an investigator would know. "Logan had just gotten his first DNA kit. He thought it was total bullshit, but he knew we'd be in trouble if he didn't at least make a stab at using it. But the scene was polluted before he even opened the kit. Everybody in the neighborhood ran over to peer at the dead girl under the Spanish Oak."

"Did you have any suspects?" called the sheriff.

"We questioned plenty of people, took blood and hair from six. But Logan had messed up the DNA sampling so badly that they couldn't come up with any matches. It wasn't like it is now."

The one named Victor frowned at the sheriff, as if wondering if he should really be talking to him. Jack was thinking now would probably be a good time for him to shut up when a second car pulled up. A heavy, red-faced man pulled himself out of a white Crown Vic and waddled toward the group under the tree. Jack chuckled. He would recognize that slew-footed walk anywhere.

"Hello, Whaley."

The man stopped, stared, blinked. "Hamburger Jack?"

"None other." Wilkins got up, started to walk over to Whaley, then remembered he was a quasi-suspect. He looked at the sheriff. "May I go greet the detective?"

Cochran nodded. Jack went over, gave Whaley a brusque, masculine hug. He saw immediately the toll that years of law enforcement had taken on the man. He was thirty pounds overweight, with bloodshot eyes and a network of red capillaries on his nose that screamed *I drink way too much. I've drunk way too much for years.* Still, Jack was glad to see him. Though their partnership had been like a bottle of oil and water, he was glad that Whaley was still upright and breathing.

"How you been, old buddy?" Whaley clapped him on the back. "Still chomping the burgers?"

"I'm doing okay. Got four grandkids and a little mini-farm out Azalea Road."

"How's your wife?"

"Fine."

"Still playing golf?"

"Shooting in the low eighties."

"That's great." Whaley frowned over at Cochran. "So how come you're out here with these jokers?"

"Like I told them—I wanted to see this neighborhood one last time. You know, before they bulldozed it into something new."

"You may be too late," said Whaley. "Most of the houses are already gone."

"The Shaw and the Russell places are still here. And you can tell where the Ewing house was."

Whaley's eyes narrowed, making him look even more porcine. "Still got a jones for Teresa, don't you?"

"Don't you?"

"Not me, brother." Whaley laughed. "I know who did it."

"Collier?"

Whaley shrugged. "He still can't look at me without shitting his pants."

"So why don't you charge him?" Jack spoke sharply, feeling as if he'd rejoined an argument they'd debated twenty years ago.

"You know why as well as I do."

Jack nodded toward the tree. "Well, I think you just got some new evidence. Maybe you can make your case this time."

Whaley started to say something else, then stopped. "So are you just going to sit on that bulldozer? With that dog?"

"I am until your boss says I can go. I think I'm being politely detained."

"Well," said Whaley. "I'll go see what I can do." They shook hands. "Nice seeing you again, Jack. Give my best to Jan."

"Will do."

Jack sat back down on the bulldozer, patting the dog but still shame-lessly eavesdropping. He was curious to see what Whaley would add to the investigation. So far not much, beyond watching the young patrolman put up a wider perimeter of crime scene tape while the one named Victor rummaged in his briefcase. It was only when the sheriff pulled Whaley aside that he knew they were talking about him. He imagined the conversation as the two conferred, casting sly, over-the-shoulder glances back at him.

"This guy for real?" the sheriff would ask.

Whaley would nod. "He used to be our best detective, but this case pushed him over the edge."

"How far over the edge?" Cochran would ask, meaning *Is he loco? Do I need to worry about him?*

"Not crazy far." Whaley would start out generous, then turn nasty. "But you never know about these old guys. You know—most of 'em are on a lot of meds."

"You think he could have planted these underpants?"

Whaley would damn him with a shrug. "Who knows? Like I said, you never know what's going on inside an old head."

The one named Victor ended their private conversation. He pulled a camera from his briefcase and asked for the exact location of the underpants. For the next hour, the four of them worked like bees around a hive, Cochran directing them like a field marshal. He sent Saunooke to canvass the yard sale people, to ask if anyone had seen anyone around that tree. "Tell them we're investigating some vandalism." Whaley was to go back to the office and get a list of ev-eryone who'd worked on this construction—from the architect to the crew bosses. "Get me the names of anybody who's got more than a traffic citation."

Saunooke headed for the yard sale, then caught sight of him sitting on the bulldozer, the dog now flopped across his feet.

"What about him?" he asked Cochran. "And the dog?"

"The what?" Cochran turned, irritated.

"Mr. Wilkins and the dog I'm supposed to take to the pound."

For a moment Jack thought Cochran might tell Saunooke to take them both to the pound, but instead Cochran relented.

"Detective, you're free to go. Whaley, you take the dog to Animal Control on your way to the office."

Jack looked down at the dog, lying next to his feet. He hadn't misbehaved, not once. He'd stayed right beside him, watching the activity and snapping at an occasional fly. He reminded him of himself—old, but not washed up. Still with something to contribute. "Could I take the dog?" Jack asked the sheriff.

"To the pound?" Saunooke looked surprised.

"No. Home, with me."

Saunooke turned to Cochran. "That okay, sheriff? He's just a stray."

Cochran shrugged. "Leave your phone number and address with Saunooke, and the dog is yours."

"Thanks," said Jack, again taking the dog by the collar. "And good luck with your investigation." *You're going to need it,* he thought. *You're going to need a whole lot more than a pair of underpants to put this case to bed.*

FOUR

"Where have you been, Mama?" Zack Collier paced up and down the living room, shaking his hands as if they were covered in spiderwebs. Grace recognized the nervous, agitated signs of an impending meltdown; she only hoped she'd gotten home in time to stop it.

"I'm sorry, Zack. I had to go to a meeting, then I had to get some gas." She looked up into her son's gray eyes. His pupils still looked normal—they hadn't dilated into the black orbs that usually presaged his fits. "Cars won't run without gas, you know."

"But it's one thirty. Clara left at one. You're always back by one fifteen. Now we'll be late!"

"The yard sale goes on for three more hours, Zack. We'll get some tapes today."

"Promise?" He looked at her, his hands stopping in mid-shake.

"Yes. Take a bathroom break and we'll go."

"Awwriiight!" Zack lifted a triumphant fist. "New videos today."

Grace watched as her two-hundred-pound son ran to the bathroom. She knew he would strip naked before he used the toilet, then wash his hands ten times before he dressed himself again. His ablutions would cost them far more time than her stop at the gas station, but Zack couldn't see it that way. His clock ran differently than everybody else's.

Still, she guessed she should feel lucky. She'd averted a meltdown that could have left a new set of bruises down her arm. Earlier she'd noticed Emily and Ginger looking at her oddly, no doubt wondering why someone would wear a long-sleeved shirt in August. "They probably think my husband beats me," Grace whispered, holding up her arm to examine the splotchy purple marks. "Wonder what they would have said if I'd told them my son put those there?"

She pulled her shirtsleeves back down and walked out to the mailbox. People could think whatever they wanted. Like most everything else in her life, it was out of her control. She opened the mailbox, flipped through the mail. Two bills, a flyer from the hardware store, and a political ad from DA George Turpin, grinning smugly as he stirred a vat of his barbeque sauce. Nothing for Zack, nothing from Mike, nothing from Hillview Haven, the communal living home for autistic adults. She'd taken Zack for his entrance interview weeks ago; now she was waiting to hear if he'd made the cut. She closed her eyes, offering a small, guilty prayer that Dr. Keyser and his crew would take him. Zack would need a place to live when she got older and could no longer manage him. Better to get him accustomed to that place now, while she could visit regularly.

"Mama!"

She looked up from the mailbox. Zack stood on the front porch, fully dressed and smiling. *He looks so normal,* Grace thought. *Handsome even, with my dark hair and Mike's eyes. Until you tried to talk to him, you'd never guess anything was wrong.*

"Did I get any tapes?"

34

"Not today, sweetheart. But we'll get some at the yard sale. Have you got your money?"

From his pocket he pulled the money she'd given him for mowing their grass. "Fifteen dollars."

"Then we're ready." She walked toward the house. "Where shall we go for lunch?"

He thought a moment. "McDonald's. They've got robots in the Happy Meals."

———

The rainy morning turned sunny as they ate in the far corner of McDonald's parking lot, Grace ordering two Happy Meals for Zack and a salad for herself. As Zack played with his robots, Grace wondered if she could distract him away from the Salola Street yard sale. Though it might be a good place to find tapes, Salola Street was the last place she wanted to go. They'd lived there when Teresa Ewing was murdered. Her death had cast a shadow on their lives that lingered to this day.

"Hey, Zack," she said, starting the car as he grew bored with his toys. "How about we drive over to Sarge's Flea Market? I hear they've got a lot of videotapes there."

"I want to go to Salola Street."

"But that'll be mostly clothes and furniture, Zack. Those people are moving out. Sarge's has a whole section for videotapes."

"We went to Sarge's last week," he replied. "I want to go to Salola Street."

"But if you want videos, Sarge's might…"

"Salola Street, Mama!" he cried. "I want to see our old house."

"They tore our old house down, Zack. It's not there anymore."

"But I want to see where it was. Adam might be there."

"Adam won't be there, Zack. Adam lives far away." Zack's one and only friend Adam Shaw had been sent away years ago, just after they found Teresa's body. Now he was 39, some kind of special photographer working in New York. His parents, though, had remained on Salola Street, resolute in their stand against police harassment, steadfast in their hatred of her and Zack.

"I-want-to-go-to-Salola-Street!" With every word he hit the side of the door with his fist. Next he might turn his rage on the window, or worse, her right arm.

"Okay, Zack." She caved in, as usual. "If you can calm down, we can go."

He sat back in the seat, his hands limp in his lap. He sat like that for a few minutes, then he said, "I'm sorry, Mama. I'm calm now."

Grace backed out of the parking spot, dreading the prospect of seeing either Leslie Shaw or Janet Russell. Leslie, she'd heard, had become such a bad alcoholic that Richard had sold her car. And Janet had become some sort of priestess in a cult that believed everything from caterpillars to coconuts emitted vibes that controlled the destiny of the world. *At least I haven't gone that crazy,* she told herself, trying to pluck up her courage. *At least not yet.*

They left McDonald's and drove to the neighborhood where Zack had grown up. A trendy new green development was going up, and most of the old ranch houses had been razed to make way for the new construction. To Grace's dismay, tables of yard sale merchandise stretched across the front lawns of the Shaws and the Russells—the two homes she wanted most to avoid. Nonetheless, she pulled to the shoulder of the road a little way down the street and reminded her son of his manners.

"I know how excited you get, Zack. But you can't push people out of the way. And remember to say *excuse me* if you bump into anybody."

"Excuse me," Zack repeated, fumbling with the latch of his seat belt. "Excuse me, excuse me."

He bounded out the door before she got the car parked, running to Adam Shaw's house as fast as he could. She hurried after him, thinking this was like letting a big, rambunctious dog run loose. Like most dogs, Zack was not truly mean or vicious. He just lived in his own world, obeying urges that often defied his control.

She watched him as he perused the tables, searching for VCR tapes. In his excitement he brushed against one little girl, sending her armload of computer games to the ground. "Excuse me," Grace heard him say, as if on cue. "Excuse me."

"What's the matter with you?" the girl's mother cried. "You almost knocked her down!"

But Zack did not help the girl pick up what she'd dropped; Zack just ran on to the next table. Grace hurried up to the woman. "I'm so sorry," she said, kneeling to retrieve the games. "He didn't mean to be rude."

"Is he with you?" The woman's upper lip curled in disgust.

"He's my son," explained Grace, handing the games back to the child. "He's autistic."

"Well, he needs to be more careful." The woman turned to her daughter. "Are you alright, Jenna?"

"I think so," the little girl whined, turning injured eyes on Grace.

"Come on." The mother grabbed her hand. "Let's just pay for these and get out of here."

"I'm sorry," Grace called as the woman strode off, her daughter following like a wounded duck. She looked around for Zack. He was

37

now several tables away, rummaging through a laundry basket of videotapes. As much as he liked cartoons and exercise videos led by bikini-clad women, what he prized most were family videos—total strangers toasting the bride at weddings or belly-flopping into swimming pools at back yard cook-outs. He would watch them for hours, sometimes rewinding the same scene over and over. *That's not uncommon for autistic people*, his therapist once told her. *We think it's how they figure out behavioral cues. You know, how people react to each other.*

Though Grace found it unsettling and slightly creepy, Zack took endless pleasure in the antics of strangers. Never did he talk about the people, or express any desire to meet them. He just dissected little slices of their lives, over and over again. She watched as he rifled through the basket, discerning as an oenophile seeking an aged bottle of port.

While Zack shopped the videos, she stepped back to look at what was left of her old neighborhood. In the distance she could see the top of the Spanish Oak, still standing majestically behind the Russell house. After Teresa had turned up dead beneath it, Leslie and Richard Shaw had led a drive to have the tree cut down. "It holds too many horrible memories," they said. "People will say it's haunted. It will lower our property values." But the Cherokees had risen up in protest. Though it was no longer on tribal land, they called the tree *Undli Adaya,* or Big Brother Tree, and regarded it as holy. Ultimately it had been spared, much to the delight of the new developers, who were now using its stylized silhouette as their logo.

Grace turned away from the tree to watch Zack as he finished looking through the one basket of VCR tapes and began making his way through the other merchandise strewn along the tables. She followed him at a distance. His initial excitement had cooled, making his movements slower and his passage through the crowd less disruptive. Still, she noticed that once people realized they were standing beside a forty-two-year-old man ogling exercise videos, they quickly moved away.

What's going to happen to you, Zack? she wondered, rubbing her arms against a sudden chill. She was almost sixty, an adjunct art professor living on a small salary and child support from her ex-husband. Though she made enough to keep them afloat now, what would happen to them when she retired? What would happen to Zack when she grew too old to drive him to these stupid yard sales? Or when in a rage, he might strike out and break her arm or hip?

Don't think about that now, she told herself. *Today's a good day. He's happy. He's* trying. *Just be grateful for that.*

She watched him, hoping some new item might catch his eye and make him forget all about the Shaws, but as soon as he crossed the Russells's driveway, he headed straight for their house. They had done considerable remodeling—turning their side porch into a sunroom and paving a circular drive across their front yard. What had not changed was the look that Leslie Shaw was aiming at Zack. Though her hair was now gray and she'd gone from svelte to dumpy, the hatred in her gaze glowed like an ember. Grace decided she'd better hurry and get between the two of them. Richard and Leslie Shaw had always blamed Zack for Teresa's death. It was clear that time had not altered that opinion.

"Hi, Ms. Shaw." Shy about speaking to people, Zack bobbed on the balls of his feet, his eyes downcast. "Is Adam here?"

"No." Leslie's reply was final.

Zack stared at her as if he'd been struck mute.

"Hello, Leslie." Grace came up and stood beside her son, the fruity smell of alcohol wafting across Leslie's table. "How've you been?"

"Fine." Leslie's mouth was a pinched slash across her face.

"Zack wondered if Adam might be here."

"Adam lives in New York." Leslie spoke as if her words were coins that she hated to part with. She glared at Zack, who'd stooped to rummage through another basket full of old VHS tapes, then turned to Grace. "You got some nerve, bringing him over here."

"To a yard sale?"

"To this yard sale," said Leslie. "I just hope Richard doesn't catch you."

"For God's sake, Leslie. He's just looking at your old tapes."

"He cost me my son." Leslie's dark eyes narrowed.

"That was your call. All the other boys stayed here."

"And look at them—freaks and misfits." She pointed at Zack. "And all because of him!"

Her face burning, Grace walked over to Zack. "Come on, honey. We need to get out of here."

"No!" he cried. "I want to buy some of these!"

"Pick two, Zack," said Grace, cursing herself for bringing him here in the first place. "You can't buy the whole box."

"I don't know," he started to flip through them. "I have to look at them."

"Leave now and I'll sell you the whole box," said Leslie.

"The whole thing?" Zack frowned, as if she were making fun of him.

"How much money have you got?"

Zack stood up and pulled bills from his pocket. "Fifteen dollars."

"Fifteen dollars it is, then," said Leslie, grabbing the money from his hand. "Now take them and get out of here."

"Zack, that's all your lawn-mowing money," said Grace.

"I don't care." He grinned, easily lifting the heavy box. "I can make more money. I might never get another box like this!"

FIVE

"You get a new dog?" Irving Stubbs strolled into Jack Wilkins's carport, keeping well away from a galvanized tub that held a smelly wet dog lathered in shampoo.

"I did." Jack washed behind the dog's ears. Though he'd wanted to open his Teresa Ewing files as soon as the cops turned him loose, he knew Jan would kill him if he brought a dog this filthy into the house. So he'd stopped on the way home and bought a new collar and leash, plus a bag of dog food.

"You tell Jan about this?" asked Irving.

"Not yet."

"What do you think she'll say?"

"She won't mind." Jack scrubbed some kind of tar off the animal's chest. "As long as he doesn't bite the cat."

Irving asked, "Where'd you get him?"

"Over on Salola Street. A cop was about to take him to the pound."

"What were you doing over on Salola?"

"Went to a yard sale," Jack lied, scrubbing the dog harder.

"You sure you weren't investigating Teresa Ewing?"

Irving's question took Jack by surprise. "What do you mean?"

"We were talking about it the other day, on the golf course." Irving looked at him as if he'd suddenly come down with Alzheimer's disease. "Then again this morning at the Waffle House."

Jack stopped his dog washing. This morning seemed weeks ago, but of course bean-counter Irving would remember everything. "No, I went over there to see if anybody was selling a pair of decent hedge clippers."

Irving kept digging. "But why was a cop over there?"

"He had a 10-91," Jack explained. "A stray dog call. He was taking this guy here to the pound. I felt sorry for him, so I brought him home with me."

"So no news on Teresa Ewing?"

"Teresa Ewing's still a real cold case, Irving." The lie came with amazing ease, but he didn't care. Irving gossiped like one of his hens. If Jack told him about those underpants, everybody in the county would be talking about it tomorrow. He was still cop enough to know to keep his mouth shut.

For a long moment, Irving just stood and watched him wash the dog, his accountant brain running the numbers. Finally he said, "Want to play golf tomorrow? Get up a foursome with Norman and Hank?"

Jack shook his head. What he really wanted to do was get the dog dry and go back to the files in his den. "Thanks, but I've got some chores to do. Maybe next week."

"Suit yourself." Irving started down the driveway toward his own house, then stopped. "Hey, what's your dog's name?" he called.

Jack looked at the dog, whose coat was turning out to be a rich chestnut brown instead of a dirty, muddy gray. "Lucky," he said. "I'm going to call him Lucky."

Jerry Cochran sighed as he looked at the cold case files spread across his desk. However addled old Jack Wilkins might be, he knew the Teresa Ewing case dead on. On February 13, 1989, at approximately 5:24 p.m., ten-year-old Teresa Ewing's mother sent her across the street to deliver a tuna casserole to Melanie Sharp, a neighbor who'd recently had a baby. At 7:16 p.m. a missing person call came into dispatch. On March 8, after a manhunt that included cadaver dogs, wildly varying readings from psychics, and sightings that ranged from California to Canada, John Ferguson was out for a jog and found the child's body not a hundred yards from her house.

Cochran shook his head, flipping through the old black-and-white police shots, feeling as if he were turning the pages of an old school yearbook. Sheriff Stump Logan, with sideburns and a white cowboy hat, stood arms akimbo as Jack Wilkins and an amazingly skinny Buck Whaley pulled the body from beneath the tree. Though Logan had put it out to the press that the little girl looked more asleep than dead, the photos showed a grimmer image. Her skull had been fractured, her hair matted with dried blood. She wore a T-shirt, jeans, and a green nylon jacket. Her clothes bore minimal traces of red clay soil, and her body did not look like it had been decomposing for almost a month.

"Underpants?" Cochran looked at the evidence inventory. She'd been found wearing unzipped jeans, but no underpants. He stared at a school picture of the girl someone had clipped to the file. She was a

44

gorgeous child—dark hair framed a pale face with startling blue eyes. Her features were small, her mouth a perfect little bow that turned up on the ends, somehow promising more than it truly revealed. *She would have been trouble,* Cochran thought. *Had this girl lived, a long string of broken hearts would have followed behind her.*

He flipped to the autopsy report. Death was due to blunt force trauma to the anterior left skull. *Almost instantaneous,* the coroner, a Dr. A.W. Core, had penciled in the margin of the report. The girl had not been raped, either vaginally or anally, and they found no other wounds on her body. Her stomach contents revealed a chocolate bar. Cochran looked to see what DNA panels they'd gathered, but he found only two pages with very sparse data. Then he remembered: criminal DNA sampling hadn't even started until '87, and that was in the big, well-funded police departments. In 1989 Stump Logan was still working out of a jail heated with a Franklin stove.

"So much for forensics," he whispered. He closed the autopsy report and opened the thick binder of case notes. Wilkins and Whaley and three SBI agents had seemingly interviewed everyone in the county. By all accounts, Teresa Ewing was a precocious child who dressed as a gypsy every Halloween and took acting classes at the Flat Rock Playhouse. Father Bob sold insurance and mother Corinne worked two mornings a week at the county nursing home. Until the night Teresa disappeared, the police had never received a call from the Ewing home.

Cochran read through pages of interviews with dozens of possible suspects. With the sex offender registry seven years in the future, they ranged from the janitor at Teresa's school, to a funny old bachelor who sat on his porch, giving candy to passing children, to the Ewings themselves. The prime suspects ultimately evolved into six people—

the four neighborhood boys (Zack Collier, Devin McConnell, Lawrence Russell, and Adam Shaw), a Cherokee ex-con named Two Toes McCoy, and Arthur Hayes, a college sophomore by day and Peeping Tom by night. Logan and Whaley had actually gotten the Collier boy to confess to the crime, but his lawyer had his confession thrown out, on grounds that the kid was mentally incompetent. After that, they didn't have enough evidence to arrest anyone else. Still, Jack Wilkins hadn't given up. His notes indicated that he'd worked the Teresa Ewing case until the day he retired.

"The only case he didn't clear," said Cochran, turning to Wilkins's employment record. He earned a BS from the University of Minnesota, then a stint with the 82nd Airborne brought him to North Carolina. Logan hired him in '79; he retired in 2004. With several commendations, his record indicated that he was a smart cop—probably smarter than either Logan or Whaley. So why did he drive in all the way from Azalea Road to wander around that old tree? To bury a pair of fake underpants and get the only case he couldn't clear ginned up again?

"Possibly," said Cochran. But a lot of other scenarios were possible too. Practically everybody involved in the construction of Lone Oak Development had tromped around that tree—from architects to site planners to backhoe drivers. Any of them could have heard about the murder and buried those underpants as a prank. And the yard sale was a factor too. Yard sales started at daybreak. Who knows how many shoppers could have gone up there before Saunooke arrived.

He uncapped a pen and started an outline on a yellow legal pad. On the first line he wrote *Jack Wilkins*; on the second line *Sick joke*. On the third line he scribbled the thing he dreaded most: *Trophy/warning*.

That would be the worst. That would mean that whoever killed Teresa Ewing was still alive, still in town, and still taunting the police. Maybe even planning to abduct another child.

He thought of his own daughter, Chloe—eleven months old, red-haired like her mother, an angel he'd loved at first squawk. The idea of some stranger touching her made him sick to his stomach, and his first inclination was to bring all the old suspects in and let Whaley grill them until they screamed. But he could not do that. He had to tread carefully. Pisgah County had once gone on a witch hunt; Cochran was not going to let that happen again. He would not officially re-open the Teresa Ewing case until he found out more about those underpants.

He started to gather up all the old photos. He'd just put the cold case file back in its box when he heard a knock on his door. Wondering if Whaley had found something, he said, "Yeah? Come in!"

The door opened. His wife, Ginger, stood there in a yoga outfit, holding Chloe on one hip. "Ready for a surprise?"

Cochran loved surprises from Ginger. Sometimes she brought apple strudel, sometimes fresh coffee, sometimes, in the privacy of their bedroom, treats of a different nature. He closed the case file. "Bring it on."

"Get the camera on your cell phone ready."

Cochran reached for his phone. "Ready."

"Okay. Hit record!"

Cochran turned to the open doorway. Ginger put Chloe down and pointed her at Cochran, saying, "Go on, honey. Go see Daddy!"

As Cochran filmed, the chubby little red-headed baby walked toward him, wobbling as if she'd had too much to drink.

"She's walking?" Cochran cried. "All by herself?"

"She started when I got home from Mary's speech!" said Ginger. "She let go of the dining room table and walked into the living room, all on her own."

"Chloe!" Cochran called, keeping his phone trained on the child. "Look at you, sweetheart! You're walking!"

Chloe listed far to the right, but then regained her balance, heading straight for Cochran. "Daaa-deeee!" she cried. She walked a few more steps then fell laughing into his arms.

"What a big girl!" he cried, scooping her up, nuzzling behind her ear. How he loved her! The way she smelled, the way her hair curled when her neck grew damp, the way she slept, her little rosebud mouth quivering as she dreamed. He'd thought that Ginger had completed him; then Chloe came along and he wondered how they had ever lived without her. He lifted her high in his arms. As she squealed with delight, he brought her down, catching a glimpse of the Teresa Ewing file on his desk. He thought of the girl's father, Bob. He'd probably once held his arms out to his toddling daughter and thought that he would provide all the shelter and protection Teresa would ever need until she was grown and gone.

How wrong he had been about that, thought Cochran, remembering the picture of the little girl's body under that tree. *How very, very wrong.*

SIX

GRACE COLLIER WAS GRIPPING the steering wheel of her car so hard
that her fingers had gone numb. She and Zack had fled the Salola
Street yard sale immediately after their encounter with Leslie Shaw,
Zack cradling his box of old videotapes as another man might carry
a child. For a long time Grace just drove—over to the college, then
up into the Reservation, wanting to put as much distance as possible
between them and their old neighborhood.

"It's good they're tearing all those houses down," she said to no
one in particular. "That street's been cursed ever since Teresa."

Teresa. The name stuck in her throat—she hadn't spoken it in
years. Te-reee-saaaa. The syllables themselves seemed to give voice to
the tragedy—an explosive *T*, then a *reee* like a scream, then a lingering
soughing of sadness and mystery. Never had the little priss been Terry,
or Tee, or any of the sweet nicknames she might have engendered.
Always, she was Teresa. First shouted by the searchers, then cried by
her mourners, then whispered for what seemed like forever. *What do
you think really happened to Teresa Ewing? Where was she for those*

three weeks? How do you think Zack got away with it? He's retarded, you know. Dumb as a post but strong as an ox. And he loved her...

"Mama!" Zack cried from the backseat, interrupting the soundtrack playing in her head. "Watch out!"

Grace's attention snapped back to the highway. She was driving down Fodderstack Mountain on a narrow two-lane and had drifted over to the shoulder of the road. Her tires crunched in the gravel, veering to the edge of a fifty-foot drop. She jerked the steering wheel in the opposite direction, only to hear the angry blast of a horn. She looked up to see a red semi chugging up the mountain in low gear. She turned the wheel again and zoomed by the truck with only inches to spare, garnering another blast of the horn and a fleeting glance of the driver's angry, cursing face.

"Mama, are you okay?" Zack's voice was shaky.

"I'm fine, honey." She felt weak, her hands tingling now, thick and useless on the wheel.

"You want me to drive?" he asked, laughing.

"No, but thanks for offering." Zack had never driven. She kept her car keys hidden, to make sure he never would. She took a deep breath and tried to stop trembling. "Want to go to Hornbuckle's?"

"Sure!"

———

Hornbuckle's had been part of their lives since Zack was a baby. One of the curious little Tsalagi shops that sold everything from toma-hawks to hunting licenses, Fred Hornbuckle scooped up ice cream from behind a small counter in the back of the store. At two years old, Zack had eaten his first bowl of ice cream here, shivering at the sudden cold, then grinning as the sweetness melted in his mouth. By four, Zack's speech was still garbled, but he could gurgle "ice cream!" when they pulled up in the parking lot. By six, they'd gotten the official diagnosis of autism and Zack had settled on his dish of choice—Bear Tracks in Snow, chocolate ice cream with marshmallow sauce, topped with chocolate sprinkles. For nearly forty years, Hornbuckle had brought Zack a Bear Track and a tall glass of water, ice cream spoon placed precisely on a paper napkin perpendicular to the table. As Hornbuckle had gone from a middle-aged man to a senior citizen, Grace figured Zack's lifetime total for Bear Tracks in the Snow was around two thousand.

She came off the twisty mountain road and took a right, pulling up in Hornbuckle's small parking lot. Zack hurried into the store, heading straight for the ice cream counter in the back. Grace followed more slowly, nodding to the wizened Fred Hornbuckle, who stood behind the cash register wearing a tattered straw cowboy hat.

"*Sheeoh,*" he greeted her in Cherokee. "*Doehuhduhnay.*"

"Fine, thanks. How are you?"

He gave a noncommittal Cherokee grunt as he cut his eyes toward Zack. "A Bear Tracks in Snow and a caramel sundae?" Though their order never varied, he always checked, to be sure.

Grace smiled. "Same as always."

She threaded her way through the tight aisles to the little counter and took a seat next to Zack. As Hornbuckle scooped their ice cream, she noticed Zack frowning.

"Are you okay, honey?" Never did Grace know what Zack was ruminating about. Sometimes it was a bit of overheard conversation, sometimes the way someone had looked at him, sometimes a bird in the sky or the sequence of numbers on a license plate.

He shook his head, his eyes downcast.

"What's the matter? You got so many new tapes today."

He cracked his knuckles, a habit reminiscent of his father. "I miss Salola Street."

"You do?"

He nodded. "I had fun there."

"What was fun about it?" she asked, wondering what he would say.

"Playing with Adam. But Teresa was fun too. When she didn't squeal."

Zack's hypersensitive hearing had always been an issue. Certain noises—high-pitched sounds, loud voices—would send him either running away with his hands over his ears, or into a rage, where he screamed *Smackertalker* and lashed out at whoever was speaking. With a chill Grace looked at her son's big hands, now folded on the table. Had he bashed Teresa Ewing's skull in, just to stop her from squealing?

She pushed the thought away. Zack was compromised, true. But where strangers saw a hulking man obsessed with inappropriate videotapes, she saw a tender boy who kept their bird feeders filled and cried when they passed a rabbit killed on the highway. *He could not have killed that girl,* she told herself for the thousandth time. *It's just not possible.*

They ate their ice cream, Zack scraping the last bit of chocolate from the frosty little dish, then he stood up, ready to go.

"Hurry, Mama." He bounced on his feet. "We need to go home."

She paid Hornbuckle and followed Zack out to the car. As he began admiring his new videos, she headed for home. Despite Leslie Shaw's hatefulness and their near miss with the semi, it had been a good day. Zack hadn't had one meltdown, he'd apologized for bumping into that little girl, and he'd behaved respectfully toward Hornbuckle. She hoped his new tapes wouldn't disappoint him.

She turned down the shady, meandering lane that led to her house, wondering if Zack might get engrossed in his tapes long enough for her to get some work done. She had a landscape show coming up in an Asheville gallery, and volunteering for Mary Crow's campaign had put her behind schedule. If he got involved in a tape for a couple of hours, she could get back to her painting. Selling a couple of canvasses would do their bank account a lot of good. She and Zack might be able to go to the beach for a long weekend. It had been years since either of them had seen the ocean. She was dreaming of warm sand and seagulls when Zack began to scream.

"No!" he cried. "No, no, no!"

She jammed on her brakes, her heart pounding. "What's wrong now?" she cried.

With wide, terrified eyes, Zack pointed at their house. "He's come back! He's here!"

She leaned over to peer through the passenger window. Her house stood on a small hill, overlooking the street. Parked in her driveway was a white Crown Vic with a whip antenna and a state license plate. Her stomach clenched. Detective Whaley was here. The day that she had just deemed good was turning sour, fast.

She turned to her son. "Remember what you do when he comes, Zack? You stay in the car and sit still. That way you won't get hurt."

"Don't let him zap me, Mama. Please!"

"I won't, Zack. But you've got to sit still, okay?"

"Okay, okay, okay, okay, okay."

She turned into the driveway, trying to take a deep breath. The last time Whaley had come, Zack had run out of the car, flapping his hands and crying. Whaley had spooked and tasered him. Zack had lain on the ground, twitching, urinating on himself while the big cop stood there laughing. If she'd had a gun, she would have shot Whaley dead on the spot.

"Just stay in the car, Zack," she whispered as she parked beside the police car. "Sit there and look through your new tapes."

She got out of her car, lifting her hands high over her head. Whaley had never drawn a gun on them, but she'd seen too many cops on television, killing people of color for not much reason at all.

"Is there a problem, officer?"

Whaley looked at her as if she were an idiot. "You don't need to put your hands up. I've come to talk to your boy."

"Why?"

"I'm *asking* for DNA."

"But you took some, years ago." She remembered another long-ago nightmare, where three cops wrestled with Zack in a jail cell, trying to pull hairs from his arms and groin. They finally had to sedate him to complete the test.

"We need more."

"But why?"

"I'm not at liberty to say."

"So you just come out here and demand it? Do you know how traumatic that is for an autistic person?"

"A lot less traumatic than getting your head bashed in."

Grace closed her eyes. Always, it was Teresa Ewing; it would forever be Teresa Ewing. She'd made a big mistake in staying here. She should have followed Mike to Colorado. So what if he didn't want to be married to her anymore? She could have gotten a new start, in a new place. Painted the Rockies instead of the Appalachians.

She looked at her son. He was sitting in the passenger seat with his head down, clicking the tapes together. He was scared but trying to control himself. And it had been such a good day.

She turned back Whaley. For once, she was going to stand up to him. "Do you have a court order for this?"

"No." He straightened a little, as if she'd surprised him. "Right now you would be cooperating with an ongoing investigation."

"What would it be if I refused to let him give you any more DNA?"

"Then it would look as if you had something to hide."

"We don't have anything to hide, officer. You have badgered my son for most of his life and have gotten no more evidence against him than the day that little girl disappeared."

"So you're refusing to comply?"

Grace took a deep breath and nodded. "Until you come with a court order, Zack Collier will not be giving any DNA."

Whaley looked at her, his eyes flat with hatred. "You need to re-think this. If I have to come back with a warrant, it'll mean hand-cuffs, a cage in a squad car, the whole nine yards."

She turned and walked back to her car. "I'll take that chance, officer. Sorry you wasted a trip over here."

SEVEN

"What do you call this muscle?" Victor Galloway asked as he cradled Mary Crow's foot in his lap.

"That's my toe, Victor. It's not a muscle." Mary was sitting in bed, foregoing the Sunday *New York Times* for a thick report from Emily on George Turpin's tenure in office. Emily had done her homework—Turpin was twice as likely to go soft on domestic abuse cases, and twice as likely to double down on females charged with crimes. The statistics were so clear Mary was amazed that some judicial oversight committee hadn't already pointed this out to Turpin.

"Sure it's a muscle," Victor went on. "You have to move your toe with something. It's not just there, hanging on to your foot."

"I don't know what muscle it is," Mary said absently. She looked up from the Turpin report and stared at Victor's bare back. The word *Rosaria* was tattooed on his left shoulder blade, a youthful declaration of love he now claimed to regret. Suddenly she remembered that he'd ducked out of the League breakfast yesterday, and had crawled into bed long after she'd gone to sleep. "Where did you disappear to yesterday?"

"You working any criminal cases now?" He was always careful to make sure she wasn't playing defense in the great battle for justice.

"Nothing more criminal than the Hargood Burton estate. Properties in three different states, heirs who remind me of the suspects in Clue."

Victor laughed. "Professor Plum and Colonel Mustard?"

"All arguing with Mrs. Peacock." Mary flopped back on her pillow. "I wish I had a capital case. It would be more fun than the squabbling Burtons."

"Do you remember the Teresa Ewing murder? Back in 1989?"

She thought back. *1989. Fourth grade, Cherokee Elementary. Miss Batson was her teacher. Jonathan Walkingstick sat across from her. He wore jeans and black Chuck T's. Even then it was hard to keep her eyes off him.* "Everybody remembers that one," she said, willing Jonathan Walkingstick's image back into the ancient-history file in her brain. "Little girl vanishes while delivering food to a neighbor, then turns up dead under the *Undli Adaya*."

"Well, your officer Saunooke stopped off to check on some bulldozers on the girl's old street. The stray dog he was taking to the pound dug up a pair of underpants with Teresa's name on them."

Mary lowered her pencil. "You're kidding."

"No. But the capper is that the old detective who'd worked that case was wandering around that Ugly Adama tree ... "

"*Undli Adaya*," she corrected. "It killed one of Desoto's scouts. They say there's a Spanish helmet up in the branches."

He frowned. "The tree killed a Spanish scout?"

"So say my ancestors. Probably the Spaniard got drunk and ran into it."

"Yeah. Anyway, this old cop claimed he wanted to have a look at the neighborhood before they built that new development."

"And maybe plant some evidence he'd been withholding? Get something off his chest before he kicks the bucket?"

"That's Cochran's take. Whaley's not so sure."

Mary looked at him, even more surprised. "Hang 'em High Whaley's squirting the milk of human kindness?"

"Whaley and this old guy were partners back then. Lead detectives on the case. Grandpa could recite every detail of that homicide like it happened last week."

"So you took the underpants to the lab in Winston?"

He nodded. "Handed them over myself. They're trying to date them. If they're new, then it's probably some sicko's idea of a joke. If they're original, then it's a whole different ballgame."

"No kidding," said Mary. She was about to ask Victor when he expected results back when her work phone buzzed. "That's odd," she said, reaching for the thing. "Work doesn't usually ring on Sunday morning."

She cleared her throat. "Mary Crow," she answered in as professional a voice as she could muster. After a long pause, a soft voice came on the line.

"Mary? This is Grace Collier."

Mary sat up straighter in bed, looking at the campaign signs she'd brought home from the breakfast. "Grace, how are you? I'm sitting here admiring those incredible signs you designed."

"I'm okay," Grace said, then came another pause. "Well, actually I'm not so great."

"What's up?"

"There's a situation with a family member." Grace spoke in a hush, as if she were afraid she might be overheard. "It's been going on for a long time..."

Mary pictured the pretty woman who always wore her shirts long-sleeved and buttoned to the wrist. She'd seen it before, far too many times in Atlanta. Someone was abusing Grace and she didn't want the bruises to show. Maybe that was why she'd been so passionate about Mary's stand on domestic violence.

"The police were here yesterday..."

Mary was about to ask what exactly had happened when Victor's phone rang. He rolled off the bed and went into the bathroom to answer it, closing the door behind him.

"I really need to talk to a lawyer," Grace was saying. "Could you possibly come over to my house this afternoon?"

Mary had planned a slow day with Victor, but with both their work phones ringing, that now seemed unlikely. "Sure," she told Grace. "Where and what time?"

They agreed to meet at two. Mary scribbled the address down on the back of the Turpin report. "Okay," she replied. "I'll see you then."

She clicked off about the same time Victor did. He strode back into the bedroom, frowning. "Duty called?" she asked.

"Yep. How about you?"

"The same."

"Anything you can talk about?"

"I'm guessing domestic abuse," Mary replied.

"Right up your alley," said Victor. "You got a meeting today?"

"At two."

"I'm meeting Cochran at one," he said. "Here's a totally off-the-record newsflash for you. Those underpants Saunooke found? They were manufactured by the Carter Company from 1985 to 1990."

"Holy shit, Victor. Hartsville will go nuts all over again."

"I know," he said, shoving the *Times* to the floor as he took her in his arms. "But until then, how about you and I go a little nuts right now?"

Grace Collier lived in a small, nondescript ranch house made incredibly descript by its landscaping. Mary could see an artist's eye in the varying greens of the ivy and azaleas and rhododendrons that bloomed close to the house, accented by purple phlox and yellow impatiens, all pulled together with white alyssums. The effect was not studied, but natural, as if the house had just sprouted up in the middle of a bank of flowers. The only thing that spoiled it was a tall privacy fence that surrounded the back yard. Even there, though, beauty had been encouraged. Thick trumpet vines draped the fence, bees buzzing among the lush red flowers.

Aware that she was coming as an attorney more than a friend, Mary shouldered her briefcase as she walked to the door. She lifted a brass doorknocker in the shape of a Cherokee bear mask, and remembered that she and Grace were sisters in skin—both were part Cherokee, living in a world different from the reservation.

She heard heavy footsteps nearing then thudding away from the door. She knocked again and lighter ones came, growing louder. A lock turned, the door opened. Grace stood there in an oversized shirt with paint spatters down the front.

"Mary." She smiled. "Come on in."

Mary stepped into a small living room, bare of furniture except for a single sofa and a wingback chair. Grace's paintings hung on the walls, and the room held the scent of oranges. Distantly, Mary heard what sounded like a cartoon show on television.

"I really appreciate this," said Grace. "I know you probably don't work on Sunday."

"No problem." Mary smiled at the memory of her Sunday morning with Victor.

"Would you like some tea?"

"No, thanks." Mary replied, sitting on the sofa. "I just had lunch. So tell me what's going on."

Grace sat next to her. For a moment she gazed at her lap, picking red paint from beneath her thumbnail, then she said, "The reason I called you is my son, Zack."

"I didn't know you had a son," said Mary.

"He's autistic," said Grace. "A forty-two-year-old man who's emotionally still a child."

Mary heard the weariness in Grace's voice. "I'm afraid I'm not very knowledgeable about autism. It's a birth defect, right?"

"Not exactly. It has to do with the brain, but they're not sure how. Mostly it affects boys. People who have it can range from being near geniuses to being barely able to speak."

"And your son?"

"Zack's relatively high-functioning—he can read, sign his name, remember long series of numbers. He's also talented—he can draw and paint."

"Just like his mother," said Mary, wondering when the downside of this story was coming.

"What he can't do is live a normal life. Autistic people can't relate to other people as we do. They live inside themselves, struggling with social skills you and I would find easy."

"And Zack's world is what?" asked Mary.

Grace sighed. "This house and the back yard is Zack's world."

"He doesn't go to any kind of school?"

"He has anger-management issues. Not many programs will take someone like that. I've got an application into a new one right now, but if he doesn't get in, he'll have to live here, with me. A caregiver stays during the week, but nights and weekends, it's just the two of us."

Mary glanced at the long sleeve that had ridden up to Grace's elbow. Bruises dark as tattoos decorated her forearm. "Did he give you those?"

Grace quickly pulled her sleeve down. "Yeah. I saw Emily looking at these yesterday. I bet you all think my husband beats me, don't you?"

"I don't know what Emily thinks," said Mary. "I've just worked on a lot of abuse cases and connected my usual set of dots."

"I'm divorced. My husband, Mike, left me when Zack turned sixteen. He just couldn't take having a damaged child anymore."

Mary asked, "Did his leaving set off your son's outbursts?"

"No, Zack's had anger issues since he was a little boy." Grace looked down, her chin quivering. "He's always remorseful after one of his meltdowns, but in the moment, he truly can't control himself." She rose from the sofa and walked over to the front door.

"See this painting?" She pointed to a small landscape of their front yard, sunlight dappling the flowers, the blue mountains hazy on the far horizon.

"It's beautiful," said Mary. "When did you paint it?"

"I didn't," Grace replied. "Zack did. Zack also did this."

She took the painting off the wall, revealing a fist-sized hole in the plaster. "I don't have the money to have them all repaired, so I just started hanging pictures over the worst ones." She gave a deep sigh. "Sometimes I feel like I've spent my whole life covering up Zack's outbursts."

Suddenly a high-pitched yell came from the back part of the house.

"Excuse me," said Grace. "I'll be right back."

As Grace hurried to her son, Mary remained on the sofa, wondering how many paintings were there on display and how many just hid fist holes in the walls. Soon she heard Grace's footsteps returning.

"Sorry," Grace apologized. "The VCR chewed up one of his tapes."

Mary said, "He still watches videotapes?"

"He's obsessed with them—as are many autistic people. He orders them from all over the country. Getting a new video in the mail is like Christmas for Zack."

Mary didn't know quite what to say, so she asked the obvious. "So how can I help you?"

Grace said, "Have you ever heard of the Teresa Ewing murder case?"

Mary drew a quick breath. First Victor, now Grace. "Of course I have. The little girl under the *Undli Adaya*. Why?"

"My son was the only person they arrested. We lived on Salola Street then. He played with Teresa and the other neighborhood children. Everyone was convinced Zack did it, because he was older and bigger and, well, strange."

"But they didn't go to trial," said Mary.

"No. The police scared him into signing a confession. Then Cecil Earp got the thing thrown out." Grace rubbed her temples, as if she had a headache. "This reason I called you is that a detective came here yesterday. He said they wanted new DNA samples from Zack."

Mary frowned, confused. If Victor didn't know the date of manufacture of those underpants until this morning, why had the cops asked for DNA yesterday? "Did the detective give you his card?"

Grace gave a bitter laugh. "I don't need Buck Whaley's card. He comes by here every month or so. Zack's the puppy he likes to torture."

Mary stared at her. "Are you serious?"

Grace nodded, her words pouring out. "Mary, Teresa Ewing's murder was the worst thing that ever happened to us. We got constant phone calls, garbage dumped on our lawn, a rattlesnake in our mailbox. Once I was buying flowers at the hardware store when a man waggled a rope in front of me and said he was buying it to lynch my pervert son. After they threw out Zack's confession, it got ten times worse. I think that's what finally drove my husband away. It was awful for him—awful for all of us."

"I had no idea," said Mary.

Grace reached for Mary's arm. "I'm just telling you—we can't go through that again. After Whaley came yesterday, I realized I'd met someone—you—who might understand. Could you help us?"

Mary opened her briefcase, thinking that far worse than Whaley was going to come if they found DNA on those underpants. But now was not the time to go there. She pulled out a legal pad. "Tell me exactly what Whaley said. You may have a case against him for harassment."

"That they needed more DNA. If Zack didn't voluntarily give it, he would get a court order and take him down to the station in handcuffs. Mary, policemen just terrify my son."

"But Whaley didn't serve you with any papers?"

"No."

"Well, that's good news."

"So this isn't so bad?" Grace asked, the hope palpable in her voice. "This might just be Buck Whaley's idea of a joke?"

"No, he wouldn't come out here and ask for DNA for a joke."
Mary couldn't share what Victor had told her, but she still wondered why Whaley had jumped the gun by a full day. Maybe Cochran and Whaley knew something Victor didn't.

Tears spilled from Grace's eyes. "I don't know what to do. If all this Teresa Ewing stuff starts up again, we can kiss Hillview Haven good-bye. That's Zack's last chance—my last chance—for him to have a semi-independent life."

Mary wondered how well someone who pummels drywall might do in a group home, but that was not her call. "I'd advise you to do nothing right now," she told Grace. "If Whaley shows up with a warrant for DNA, call me. I'm happy to represent Zack, and I promise you nobody will bully him this time."

"Bless you." Grace wiped away tears, then said, "I don't have a lot of money. I teach art at the college, and occasionally sell a painting. It might take me a while to pay your bill."

"Don't worry about it, Grace. For now let's just trade—my legal advice for all that gorgeous artwork you created for my campaign."

"*Wahdoe,*" Grace whispered, for the first time speaking in Cherokee, the language she and Mary both understood.

EIGHT

Jerry Cochran stood in front of his white board, blue marker in hand. In front of him, Rob Saunooke, Victor Galloway, and Buck Whaley sat in a semicircle, looking at him, watchful as retrievers. "Okay, gentlemen, tell me what you've learned in the past twenty-four hours." He turned to the board. "Saunooke?"

The young patrolman stood up. "Nobody at the yard sale noticed any unusual activity. They said there were some kids playing on the dirt piles the bulldozers pushed up, but their parents yelled at them to come down. I bagged two cigarette butts people had thrown away."

"Good," said Cochran. "We'll run a check." He turned to Whaley. "Buck?"

"I got the employee rosters from the construction firm," reported Whaley. "Found some DUIs and a couple of assaults. No rapists or pedophiles, though a bunch of their workers are illegals with no records. Checked with the arborist who pruned and fed the tree back in February. He didn't notice anything buried in the roots."

Cochran nodded. "Galloway?"

Victor unfolded himself from a chair. "According to the SBI, the underpants were made by the Carter Company around 1988. The size would have fit a girl of Teresa's height and weight. The sandwich bag was made in Illinois in 2011 and contained traces of sodium nitrate, a chemical used to preserve meats like bologna and bacon. The cigarette is American Spirit—a Native American brand."

"Any DNA or prints?" asked Whaley.

"Prints on the bag, but they don't match anybody in the system. They're working on the underpants. The smoke was clean."

"There go your butts, Saunooke." Whaley laughed.

"Not necessarily," Saunooke replied. "Somebody could have strolled through the yard sale, smoking, casual-like. Then he sneaks off to bury the underpants. Maybe something scares him off and he doesn't notice a cigarette's fallen out of his pocket."

Cochran shrugged. "That's possible. One smoke could fall out of a baggy shirt pocket if you're bending over a hole in the ground." He drew a question mark on the board. "So what does all this tell us, gentlemen?"

"Somebody, possibly a smoker—possibly a Native American smoker—has kept a pair of little girl's underpants for a very long time," said Victor. "And very recently buried them in the spot where Teresa Ewing's body was found."

"After he finished his bologna sandwich," said Whaley.

Cochran ignored Whaley's sarcasm. "What sort of person might do that? Young? Old? Male? Female? White? Cherokee?"

"Somebody local and older," said Whaley, now serious.

"Agreed," said Cochran. "Someone would have to be at least in their mid-thirties to have any real memory of this case. Let's look at our old suspects."

He listed their names on the board—Zack Collier, Devin Mc-Connell, Lawrence Russell, Adam Shaw, Arthur Hayes, and Two Toes McCoy. Hayes is off the list—he fell off a fire escape and broke his neck while peeping into a woman's apartment."

"I thought Two Toes was doing twenty in Craggy Prison," said Whaley.

"He's out on parole. He now lives on the reservation, claiming to be a priest in some Native American religion."

Whaley laughed. "Two Toes behaves pretty good in prison. It's in real life that he fucks up."

Cochran went on. "The rest of the suspects were all neighborhood kids. Four males, between eight and twelve, except for Zack Collier, an autistic boy who was fifteen at the time. From the old interviews I read last night, they were about to get into some sex games."

"At that age?" asked Galloway.

"Shannon Cooper and Janie Griffin were two female witnesses. They claimed that on that last afternoon the boys dared the girls to play Bottom Up, a version of strip poker where you start betting your shoes and work your way up. They refused and went home. Teresa said she didn't want to play either, but the last time the girls saw her, she was still under the tree, talking to the boys."

"What did the boys say?"

"They all denied that anybody played anything."

"Same old shit." Whaley laughed. "He said, she said."

"Do those kids still live here?" asked Galloway

"Devin McConnell, Butch Russell, and Zack Collier do. Adam Shaw's father sent him to live with relatives in New York shortly after they found Teresa's body. Shannon Cooper and Janie Griffin moved away years ago."

"Have they stayed clean all these years?"

Cochran checked his tablet. "McConnell and Russell have a number of DUIs. Shaw and the girls are clean, and the Collier boy lives with his mother. He's not capable of living alone." He squinted at the screen. "Get this—Lawrence Russell, aka Butch, works campus security at the college."

Whaley snorted. "Hope they vetted his application for possible murder suspect."

Saunooke asked, "So where do we go from here?"

Cochran studied the board. "For once, let's get ahead of the curve here. Whaley, I want you to check in with the Salola Street boys. Saunooke, you take Two Toes. Just say we're updating our files and want to check their addresses. Do not be threatening, but pay attention if anybody starts to sweat. Galloway, see what DNA you can pull off Saunooke's cigarette butts. I'm going to talk to Jack Wilkins. He's the expert on this case and he was right there at that tree yesterday."

Galloway sat up straighter. "You think he might be involved?"

"No way." Whaley defended his former partner. "This case might be a monkey on his back, but he's no crazier than any other old guy out to pasture."

"I'll keep that in mind, Whaley," said Cochran. "Remember, gentlemen, to walk softly. If the press gets wind of this, they'll light it off like a rocket. Guess whose asses will be on the line then?"

"Jesus." Whaley shook his head. "The rumor mill worked double-time back in '89 with just the newspaper. Now we've got Facebook and Twitter and Instagram and God knows what other social media shit."

"That's why we need to proceed quietly," said Cochran. "It's a brand-new world of misinformation out there."

————

The meeting broke up, each man heading off in a different direction. Whaley drove toward Salola Street, thinking of the four kids who'd once been their prime suspects. He'd kept up with them over the years. Devin McConnell had been a tough little Irish mick, the eldest of his parents' endless litter of children. He now ran his father's used car lot and had racked up a couple of domestic assault charges. Butch Russell, a pudgy redhead, had delighted in blowing up chipmunk holes with olive jars stuffed with gunpowder. He'd tried to join the police force but washed out of the academy. That he was now a campus cop did not surprise Whaley at all. Collier, of course, was an idiot, but had strangely been friends with Adam Shaw, the smallest and smartest of the lot. He and Jack had interviewed all of them, several times. Butch Russell, Devin McConnell, and Adam Shaw had admitted, under intense questioning, that they'd asked the girls to play strip poker, but all of them had refused. Scared and stinking of little-boy sweat, the three had sworn that Teresa had gone home about five minutes after the other girls. All Zack Collier had done was cry for his mother.

With a heavy sigh, Whaley turned on to Salola and pulled up in front of the Shaw house. Empty tables were still set up across the front lawn, remnants of yesterday's yard sale. As he parked his car he thought of the Shaws. Richard had been the hard-nosed chairman of some department at the college. His wife, Leslie, was a pretty woman who scuttled around after her husband like an acolyte with a priest. The son in question, Adam, reminded him of the cocky little shits from his own school days—the cool, funny ones who snapped towels at his butt in the locker room. Any of those assholes could have offed a little girl and just talked their way out of it. And so could Adam Shaw.

He walked to the front porch and rang the bell. A small woman with bloodshot eyes pulled the door open. Though her dark hair was now gray and feathery age lines sprouted from her lips, he recognized her immediately. Leslie Shaw. Mother of Adam, wife of Richard. He looked behind her to see packing boxes lining the foyer of the house, along with huge, waist-high roles of Bubble Wrap. The hold-out Shaws were finally leaving too.

"Yes?" She squinted at his badge, as if the light was too bright. If she recognized him, she did not show it.

Whaley drew up his great bulk. "I'm looking for Adam Shaw."

"Adam … doesn't live here anymore."

"Do you know his whereabouts?"

"No."

Whaley felt a flash of impatience. Leslie Shaw wasn't stupid. Did she not realize you couldn't stonewall a cop anymore? Back in '89 maybe, but not today. These days the police were far too well connected.

"Do you know how I can get in touch with him?"

"No."

He gave her one of his cards. "Ma'am, we're updating our files. I'd like to ask Adam a few questions."

She straightened her shoulders, as if summoning all her strength. "You'll have to talk to our attorney, Robert Meyers. We no longer entertain questions from the police."

"You no longer *entertain* questions?" Whaley stared at her, anger warming his neck. "I didn't know you could *entertain* a question."

"Robert Meyers." The woman repeated the attorney's name as she lurched forward to close the door.

Whaley took a step forward and stuck one of his size-thirteen brogans into the doorway. "Let me tell you how this works, ma'am.

I don't need your or your husband's or your attorney's permission to talk to your boy. And I can find him, probably in about ten minutes. I was just checking to see if he might be here. A courtesy call, if you will."

"Robert Meyers," the woman repeated for the third time.

"I'll remember that name," said Whaley. "Also this conversation, when we have your boy by the short hairs again."

The woman paused in her closing of the door. "What did you say?"

"I mean, you cooperate with us, we go a little easier. If you don't, we don't. Goes to respect for the law."

She thought a moment, then said, "Wait—let me see if my husband..."

"Sorry." Whaley withdrew his foot from the doorway. "You had your chance. It's too late now."

He turned and left her standing at the door, talking to his back as he headed to the house across the street.

———

Unlike Leslie Shaw, Janet Russell recognized Whaley the moment he rang her bell. Opening the door wearing a gaudy, tie-dyed robe, she had tattoos crawling up both arms, eight rings on the fingers of both hands, and three different kinds of crosses resting between her copious breasts. If Leslie Shaw was a meek little acolyte in the First Church of Richard the First, Janet Russell was the high priestess in a faith of her own making.

"Detective Whaley. How nice to see you again." The woman's hair was white and wiry, her eyes chips of bright blue. She put her hands together in front of her chest and said, "Peace unto you."

"Peace to you, too," Whaley replied, uncomfortably. "Uh, we are updating our files, ma'am. I need to ask Lawrence a few question."

"What about?"

"It's police business."

"Then it must be about Teresa."

Whaley sighed. These women weren't stupid. They knew what was up when he knocked on their doors.

Janet Russell shook her head. "But you've asked him so many questions. He always answers them, but you never believe him." She fingered her jeweled cross. "You know, you once had Butch so scared he started wetting his pants. For years he slept at the foot of my bed, shivering like a dog."

"Murder investigations can be hard on everybody." Whaley took a deep sniff. The house smelled of some musky herb. Not weed—he would recognize that—but something akin to it.

"But he was just a little boy." Sighing, she walked back into her living room. It held the same kind of chaos as the Shaw house—half-filled packing boxes, Bubble Wrap, some carved decorative tree branches she was trying to fit into a too-small box. She turned to him. "May I show you something, detective?"

"Sure." He followed her through a maze of boxes as she weaved her way down a long hall lined with photographs. Pictures of her, Butch, Jesus, the Dalai Lama, and a group of people in white robes gathered around a wigwam. He stopped as one figure in that photo caught his eye. A Native American with long Apache hair, a silver disk the size of a poker chip embedded in one ear lobe. Whaley recognized him from his mug shot. It was Two Toes McCoy.

"Come tell me if this looks like the bedroom of a normal thirty-seven-year-old man," Janet Russell called, standing at the doorway at the far end of the hall.

Whaley hurried to catch up. As he did, she opened the door and stepped aside, as if revealing some grisly but compelling scar. Whaley looked into the room and saw a twin bed with a plaid bedspread, made up with military precision. In one corner was a barbell with a set of weights and a police scanner. On the walls hung posters for X-Men movies and a sad little diploma from a security guard training course. The only photograph was of Butch himself, red-haired as his mother had once been, standing serious and sober in his campus cop uniform. Over his bed was a gun rack, filled with semiautomatic weapons. Whaley took a deep breath, trying to catch the odor of cigarettes, but he smelled only the sharp aroma of gun oil and dirty sheets.

"I'm not even allowed in here," said Janet Russell. "If I was, it would smell far better than this. Bad odors invite bad karma."

"And you think Butch invites bad karma?" Whaley felt silly asking the question. He wasn't even sure what karma was.

"This is the room of someone profoundly afraid," she replied. "Someone shut off from the possibilities of the universe."

Whaley wondered if Butch wasn't trying to shut off the possibility of life without parole, but he said nothing.

"He's been like this ever since Teresa went into the light, so long before her time."

"I see." Whaley stepped inside the room to see a small security camera in the corner, its lens pointed at the door. On the opposite wall was another one, aimed at the window. A chill went down Whaley's spine. He imagined the bedrooms of the sickos who shot up schools and shopping malls probably looked a lot like this one.

"He watches those cameras on his cell phone," said Janet Russell. "He trusts no one. Not even me."

"So where is Butch now?"

She glanced at the red numbers of the digital clock on Butch's desk. "I imagine he's just left work. He's a security guard at the college. He likes to work the early shift, so he can get home before dark."

"Seriously?" Whaley frowned. Janet Russell made Butch sound more like seventy-seven instead of thirty-seven.

She leaned toward him, spoke in a whisper. "Do you know he's never been married? Never even asked a girl out? He goes to work, comes home, and watches television with me! No wife, no sweethearts, no friends at all."

"I'm sorry to hear that." Stepping back, Whaley pulled a card from his wallet. "Tell him to call me at his earliest convenience. Mostly, we're just updating our files, but I would like to talk to him."

"I'll see that he gets this." With one hand Janet Russell made some kind of sign at the threshold of Butch's room, then re-closed his door.

"I don't suppose you have any new leads on Teresa, do you?" she asked as she followed him back down the hall. "Not, of course, that you'd tell me if you did."

"Just updating our files," he repeated as he again passed the picture of her with Two Toes.

"Well, Butch will cooperate, as always." She opened the front door for Whaley to leave, then she put a hand on his arm. "Please find the killer this time. All this suspicion sucks the life out of people."

"That's what we're trying to do, ma'am."

"Then Godspeed." Once again she pressed her palms together, jingling her necklaces again. "And peace."

Whaley made his way back to his car, feeling a curious sadness for the families on Salola Street. Their lives had been blighted by

Teresa Ewing's murder. One mother couldn't stay sober, another had become a religious nut, and yet another had turned into a jailer, keeping her kid under permanent house arrest. "Jack always said this street was cursed," he whispered as he got back in his car. "Maybe he was on to something way back then."

NINE

WHILE WHALEY WAS TOURING Butch Russell's bedroom, Rob Saunooke was threading his way deep into the Quallah Boundary. Kenny Anderson, Two Toes's parole officer had told him that even though Two Toes's official address was Birdtown, he always met him at the Hartsville Burger King, because it was more "convenient."

"More convenient, my ass," Saunooke grumbled as he drove up the twisty road to Birdtown. "It's just safer. Anderson knows Two Toes won't slit his throat at the Burger King. There'd be too many witnesses."

But Birdtown was not where Two Toes resided. After searching the little village for more than an hour, a withered old crone at a convenience store said she thought Two Toes might live in a trailer up on Lickstone Ridge. "He's got some kind of sweat lodge up there, but don't tell him I told you," she said. "He might burn my store down."

"Don't worry," Saunooke assured her. "I won't tell."

"*Geyatahi*," she called after him. "Be careful. I hear he's become a witch."

So Saunooke drove down the coves and up the ridges, looking for the thin threads of white smoke that would indicate a trailer or a cabin. So far he'd heard that Two Toes had become a minister, then a witch. He remembered the man's reputation from his childhood, when his mother would warn him, *Don't forget to say your prayers, and keep Two Toes away!* His father told him that was nonsense, that he would keep Two Toes away with his shotgun. Though Saunooke said his prayers every night, he always slept better when his father was home.

He drove to the point that he'd almost decided the old woman at the store had been mistaken, when the road dribbled down to just a grassy sward that was swallowed up by a low-hanging cloud. As he stopped to put the cruiser in reverse, he heard a chorus of dogs start barking off to his left. Following their yapping, he turned down the long, mashed-down grass. At the end of the path, an arch made of willow branches spanned the road. From the center hung a sign that read RIGHT PATH RETREAT. Hoping the thing wouldn't fall on his cruiser, he drove under it. He continued a few hundred feet farther down the path, finally making a sharp turn to the left. In the middle of a small meadow a rust-streaked trailer sat on concrete blocks, surrounded by three teepees. A battered black truck was parked outside, next to a long, fifty-foot wire, to which four dogs were tethered. They looked like German shepherds, but with longer legs and thick, curly tails. Slowly he drove toward the trailer. With every turn of his wheels the dogs went crazier, saliva flying from their dark lips as they snapped first at their chains, then at each other. He realized that there was no way he could get out of his car and approach the trailer. The wire was not much stronger than a clothesline—if those dogs broke it, he'd be a dead man before he could draw his weapon.

He put the car in park and was reaching to announce himself with his siren when the door of the trailer opened. Saunooke held his breath, waiting to see if a minister or a witch or the devil of his childhood would emerge. He half expected someone wild-eyed, with their hair on fire. He was astonished when a barrel-chested man with long black hair came out, wearing nothing but a dingy pair of jockey shorts. The man yawned, glanced once at Saunooke, then began urinating off the front porch.

Saunooke got out of the car but stood behind the open door, his weapon drawn. The dogs went even more berserk.

"*Elawei!*" the man barked at the animals. They went silent in an instant but kept watching their master with sharp, bright eyes.

"Are you Two Toes McCoy?" Saunooke called, thankful that his voice didn't betray his nervousness.

"I might be," replied Two Toes. "Are you the *yonega* who pulls a weapon on an Indian with only his dick in his hands?"

Saunooke wanted to say that he wasn't *yonega*, he was Tsalagi. His was a family of chiefs and diplomats. But Kenny Anderson had warned him that Two Toes was clever with words. "Just stick to the facts," he'd said. "If you don't ask him what you want to know, straight up, he'll have your head spinning in circles."

"Approach the car with your hands raised," Saunooke ordered him. "You have to answer some questions."

"Can I put my *wadohli* back?" asked Two Toes. "Or do you want it for target practice?"

Saunooke didn't know what to tell Two Toes to do about his penis. "Take care of it," he finally said. "Then come down here."

Two Toes shook off his dick, then made his way down the steps. The dogs watched him silently, their ears pricked. As Two Toes came closer, Saunooke saw that his body was a landscape of his life. Knife scars crossed his torso, while both shoulders had the crater-like scars of old bullet wounds. Various tattoos decorated his arms—GWY for Cherokee, the old logo for AIM, the American Indian Movement, and some designs on his neck that looked like oddly shaped crosses. He'd apparently kept up the weight-lifting regimen of so many prison inmates. He had little old man flab, just bone and muscle. True to his name, he had only two toes on his right foot. The other three, rumor had it, had been bitten off by a wildcat, turning his given name of George forever into Two Toes.

He stopped even with Saunooke's front fender and held his arms out wide. "There," he said proudly. "*Ecce homo.*"

Saunooke didn't know what to say. He didn't know what Two Toes was talking about.

"It's Latin. It means 'behold the man.'" Two Toes explained, his dark eyes boring into him. "Jesus said it when they were crucifying him." His eyes flickered over to Saunooke's gun. "You about to crucify me, boy?"

"I need to ask you some questions."

Two Toes shrugged. "Ask away, then. I got nothing better to do than stand here in my panties and talk to you."

Saunooke began, asking Two Toes his long list of questions. All his answers were predictable—no. No, he hadn't been to Hartsville since his last parole meeting; no, he hadn't been near *Undli Adaya;* and no, he hadn't smoked any cigarettes in years.

"This is about that little girl, isn't it?"

Saunooke decided to play dumb. "What little girl?"

"The little white girl they found underneath *Undli Adaya.*" Two Toes folded his arms, rocking back on his heels. "Back when you were sucking your mother's tit."

Saunooke checked an impulse to plant his fist in Two Toes's face. "What would you know about that?"

"Which one?" Two Toes grinned, showing dark gums and incisors he'd filed into points. "The girl or your mother?"

Quivering with anger, Saunooke lifted his gun. "What do you think?"

"Considering the way your hand is shaking, I think I'd best say the little girl."

"And what do you know about that?"

"Only what *unole* whispers at night."

Saunooke frowned. This is what Anderson had warned him about. Two Toes talked, but like a rabbit. Hopping down one hole to pop up in another.

"Maybe you could hear *unole* better in Hartsville. In jail." He glanced at the dogs. "Your dogs have no rabies tags, and it's illegal to keep them chained in Pisgah County."

"This is not Pisgah County. This is Quallah."

"The same laws apply."

Two Toes pinioned him with a black stare for what seemed an eternity, then held out his hands in a gesture of giving. "I heard they found something to do with the girl. The cops are on it. I imagine that's why you're here."

"How did you know that?"

"If you knew your people, you'd know *Undli Adaya* tells us everything that happens there."

"Did the tree tell you who killed Teresa Ewing?"

He shook his head, slow and deliberate. "Not a Tsalagi," he replied. "And certainly not me."

Jack Wilkins was feeding his chickens when one of them came calling. He figured it would be Whaley on tamp-the-crank detail; he was pleasantly surprised to see the young sheriff emerging from a slick-looking black Camaro. *They must be taking me seriously,* he thought, puffing up with a little pride as he stood up from filling the chicken feeder with grain. *Or else they really do think I planted those underpants.*

"Detective?" Though Cochran was out of uniform in jeans and a plaid sport shirt, he still showed his respect by addressing Jack with his old title. Jack would have done exactly the same, had their positions been reversed.

"Nice to see you, Sheriff." Jack let himself out of the chicken pen and extended his hand. Cochran's handshake was firm, collegial. He smiled over at Lucky, who was tethered to a tree, wagging his tail. "How's the dog doing?"

"Real well. Gave him a bath, got him a new collar. I'm keeping him tied up for a few days, till he figures out the girls here aren't dinner."

"Good idea." Cochran looked at the six speckled hens pecking at their feed. "You get a lot of eggs?"

"More than enough for the two of us," replied Jack. "Wyandottes are good layers. My wife thinks they're pets. She says nobody can stay sad watching chickens."

Jack smiled, knowing Cochran had not driven all the way out Azalea Road to discuss the antidepressant quality of chickens. This was all about those underpants and that tree. "Get anything back from the SBI yet?"

"As a matter of fact, we did," said Cochran. "The underpants were made around the time of Teresa Ewing's death. The plastic bag was made in 2011."

"Teresa's pants," said Jack. "In a new bag."

"Right."

"Get any prints? Any DNA?"

"They haven't finished all the tests yet. The bag and the cigarette were clean. Somebody knew what they were doing."

"And you're thinking maybe that somebody was me."

Cochran just looked at him, one eyebrow lifting.

He knew this was coming, knew the minute the dog dug that thing up, he'd be on the griddle. But that was okay. Maybe his twitching thumbs meant he was supposed to be there. On the other hand, maybe he was just an old man at loose ends with his wife away from home. He didn't know what to think anymore. He looked up at Cochran. "Would you like to see everything I know about Teresa Ewing?"

Cochran gave a solemn nod. "I sure would."

"Then follow me."

He unhooked Lucky from the tether and led the dog and the sheriff inside his house. They walked through the kitchen and into the spare bedroom that served as his office/junk repository. Jan would be mortified at him bringing a stranger into such an ill-kept room, but he didn't care. The sheriff wasn't here to give him the Good Housekeeping Seal of Approval.

He crossed the room and turned on the lamp, illuminating the framed commendations on his wall. As Cochran and Lucky watched, he unlocked the bottom drawer and pulled out the five red notebooks that had almost cost him his marriage.

"This is everything I know," said Wilkins. "I left the department copies of all my files on the day I retired, ten years ago." He held up two more notebooks. "This is what I've gathered in the years since then. Have a seat if you'd like to look at it."

"Don't mind if I do," said Cochran, sitting down in an old rocking chair.

"Would you like some coffee? A beer?" offered Jack.

"Coffee would be nice," Cochran replied.

"Then you read and I'll go brew a pot."

He cranked up the Mr. Coffee using the special gourmet blend his daughter had sent him from Minneapolis. As Lucky's toenails clicked on the floor behind him, he got cups and saucers, found half a bag of Oreos in a cabinet, and put them on a plate. A few minutes later, he and Sheriff Cochran were eating cookies and drinking something called Bonecutter Brew.

"Whaley tell you I was obsessed?" he asked as he turned his desk chair to face Cochran.

"Whaley said you were a good cop who'd let this get under his skin," replied Cochran.

He nodded. "That's true. It's gnawed at me for years. My wife almost left me over it."

"Really?"

"Almost. Then I came to my senses. Realized that I had taken my best shot at that case, and it was time to move on."

"Where's your wife now?" asked Cochran.

"Up in Minnesota. Our daughter just had our fourth grandchild. A little girl."

"Congratulations." Cochran smiled. "Little girls are awfully sweet. I have one myself."

"Then you might understand how a case like Teresa Ewing can get to you."

"Is that why were you there poking around that old tree yesterday?"

He shook his head. "I just woke up early—couldn't go back to sleep. Weather was too bad to play golf," he said, leaving out the part about his twitching thumbs and strange sense of dread. "Beyond that, I can't say. I just wanted to see that tree again. Pay my last respects, I guess."

"Your last respects?"

"It'll be different once they start putting those new houses up. I know that tree's important to the Cherokees and they're building a little park around it, but it won't be the same. New people will move in—people who will never have heard of Teresa Ewing."

"And you think that's a bad thing?" asked Cochran.

"I don't know what I think. All I can tell you is that Logan and Whaley and I did our damnedest to find out who killed that child. It seemed her little life ought to have counted for something."

"So who do you think did it?"

He shook his head. "Logan liked Big Jim McConnell's boy, Devin. Whaley liked the retarded kid. I can make a good case for any of them. And we're not even talking about Arthur Hayes or Two Toes McCoy."

Cochran said, "But you must like one more than the others."

"Well, since her underwear is showing up, I guess we can discount the late Mr. Hayes—he's dead, as I'm sure you've discovered for yourselves. That leaves those kids and Two Toes. All were people she knew. They were in the neighborhood, had the opportunity, and managed to keep her hidden for three weeks."

"But where would kids hide a body? How could they keep a secret like that for nearly month?"

Jack shrugged. "You scare a kid bad enough, they won't talk. That's where Logan blew it, coming on to those kids like one of the Gestapo. Whaley was almost as bad, until I got him reined in. Anyway, I've got another theory."

"What?"

"The Eastern Band was having a big powwow that week. Indians came from all over the country. Vendors on the powwow circuit, roustabouts who put up tents and ran the pony rides. There were probably two or three hundred strangers in the area."

"And you think one of them killed her?"

"I think it's a possibility."

"But why would they come to Salola Street? And where would they keep her for a month?"

"That tree means a lot to the Cherokees," said Jack. "It would be like a pilgrimage. Look at this."

He got up, grabbed two maps from his desk, and unrolled them on the floor. The top one was a detailed map of Salola Street and three miles of the surrounding country to the south. "Here's their little neighborhood. All the back yards are thirty feet away from the Quallah Boundary line." He rolled up that map and showed Cochran the one underneath it. "This is an aerial map of that part of Quallah. Mostly thick woods, but these little lines here"—he ran one finger along a line that ran east to west—"are trails. Used for centuries."

Cochran frowned at the map. "So you're thinking some stranger saw her, killed her, and took her back up into these woods?"

"There are ten million places to hide a body up there," said Wilkins. "You could turn a hundred cadaver dogs loose and still not find her. Here's something else. You know that cigarette we found with the underpants?"

Cochran nodded.

"I've studied a bit on Indian culture. Tobacco is an offering to the Great Spirit. A peace offering, as it were."

Cochran was about to say something else when suddenly his cell phone chirped. He pulled it from his pocket, checked the screen, then looked at Jack. "Looks like we might need a bit more than a peace offering now, detective."

Jack frowned. "How so?"

"They just found DNA on those underpants."

TEN

GRACE USUALLY LOVED THIS time of day—daybreak, when the light was neither yellow nor blue but a soft, gentle gray. The various greens of trees emerged slowly from the shadows, and the birds began their chirping—little wrens raspy around the feeders and, hidden away, the flute-song of a wood thrush. As she sat at the kitchen table drinking coffee, she could also hear Zack's snoring, deep and rhythmic. She sighed. This was the longest he'd slept since Whaley showed up. For the past two days he'd paced in an endless circuit of the house, locking and relocking all the doors and windows, then washing the "cop germs" off his hands. Last night, when she thought she might scream if she heard the water at the sink come on again, she'd given him two Trazadones, the largest dose she'd ever administered. Fifteen minutes later, he clutched his toy dog Smiley and collapsed on his bed, asleep.

She, however, had not fared so well. While he had slept she lay awake, tortured by a thousand devils of possibility. *What if the newspaper found out about all this Teresa Ewing business? What would the people at Hill-view Haven say? What if everybody still thought Zack killed that child? What if Zack had killed that child? What if they put him in the criminal ward at Naughton Mental Hospital? He would understand so little of it—all he would do was cry and beg to come home.*

"That won't happen," she'd told herself, fighting a moment of real panic. Mary Crow was supposed to be brilliant, and Cherokee as well. Mary wouldn't let them take Zack away.

But in the morning light Grace realized that not even Mary Crow could make a miracle. Sighing, she padded into the living room to make sure some bear hadn't knocked over the bird feeder in the night. As two cardinals pecked at the safflower seed, she thought about how different her life would have been if Corrine Ewing had, that evening, simply taken the damn casserole over to Melanie Sharp herself. Teresa would still be alive. She and Mike and Zack might have made a go of it. The rest of her life would not have been just her and her son, convicted without trial, living in a penal colony for two.

"Oh stop it," she whispered, disgusted at her self-pity. "At least you have a job. Food on the table, a roof over your head. That's more than a lot of people."

She returned to the kitchen and glanced at the clock. 7:32. Clara would be here at eight, then she would be free to go out to the garage and work. She wanted to tweak a couple of paintings before she took them to the gallery in Asheville. She had high hopes for this new show—she'd done well there last fall and was actually starting to build a following.

Suddenly she heard a dull thump coming from the living room. "Oh no!" she cried. She'd heard that sound before. Usually a bird had lifted off the feeder and flown into the front window. Sometimes they were just stunned; other times they lay dead, their necks broken.

She hurried back to the living room, hoping it wasn't one of the cardinals. There was a smear of blood on the window, which was unusual for a bird strike. After fumbling with the front door lock, she stepped out onto the porch. A dead squirrel lay on the walk, bright red blood staining its white chest. She was staring at it, surprised to see such a thing, when suddenly she heard someone yell something from the street. She turned in time to see a beat-up black truck tear away from her mailbox, as someone in the passenger seat gave her the finger.

For an instant she could make no sense of it—a dead squirrel on her walk, someone making obscene gestures as they hurried away. Then it all fell into place. Someone in the truck must have thrown the squirrel against her window, fleeing when they saw her come out on the porch. She sighed. The news must have gotten out. The Teresa Ewing nightmare was beginning again.

She looked at the little creature, its tail still fluffy and waving slightly in the breeze. An hour ago, it had probably been alive. Just an hour ago. Tears came to her eyes, then she realized that she had to get it cleaned up before Zack got up. A dead animal might push him over some kind of edge after everything else he'd suffered in the past two days. She started to go back inside for the broom and dustpan when she heard another car pull into her driveway. She turned, wondering if the same bastard had come back to throw something else, but the car was different—big and white and sadly familiar. It stopped and a moment later, Detective Whaley emerged. As he lumbered toward her, she felt her hands closing into fists. She did not need to deal with Whaley right now.

He ambled up the walkway, stopping when he saw the squirrel and the blood on her window. "Somebody swing from the wrong tree this morning?"

"Somebody threw that at my window." Grace crossed her arms.

"Really." Whaley looked mildly interested. "Get a make on the car? A plate number?"

"Black truck, passenger with an active middle finger, heading west. You can't see plate numbers from this front porch."

"Male or female?"

"I couldn't tell," she replied. "I just hope they didn't put a snake in the mailbox."

Whaley's eyes grew sharp. "Excuse me?"

"Snakes in the mailbox, detective. Business as usual here, every time Teresa Ewing gets resurrected."

His face darkened to the point that she feared he would hit her. Instead, though, he turned and walked back to the driveway and down to her mailbox. She watched as he tore off a long forsythia frond and looped it around the mailbox latch. Standing a good four feet away, he pulled the door open. Looking up at her with utter disgust, he stepped forward, stuck in his hand, and retrieved her mail. Tossing the forsythia frond to the ground, he walked back up to the front porch.

"Thank you," she said, not bothering to hide her sarcasm. Why should she be grateful for one act of kindness after so many years of abuse? He was a cop; he was supposed to fish snakes out of people's mailboxes.

"Here's your mail." He held out the usual array of bills and advertisements, then he pulled something from his back pocket. "Also a subpoena for Zachary Collier's DNA. He needs to comply by Friday."

He turned and headed toward his car. She didn't know whether to laugh or cry. Nobody had put a snake in her mailbox, but the police had delivered something far worse. Whaley paused to glare at her one more time, then he got in and sped away, tires squealing as loudly as the black truck full of hate. She flipped through the subpoena, then she went inside and got the broom and dustpan. First, she would bury the little squirrel under some leaves in the back yard. After that, she would go inside and call Mary Crow to tell her that business had picked up. The Teresa Ewing circus had once again hit town.

———

Mary's phone rang as she stood in Victor's kitchen, spreading butter on a piece of toast. She'd just ceded the shower to Victor, who was singing an Argentinian soccer song as he bathed. "*Es un sentimiento,*" he bellowed, "*no puedo parar...*"

She closed the kitchen door against Victor's yowling and answered her phone.

"Mary Crow," she said loudly, wondering if she ought to tell Victor to hush.

"Mary? This is Grace Collier."

Mary took the phone outside to Victor's tiny patio, finding a space between his bicycle and barbeque grill. As she listened to Grace, she was not surprised that Zack Collier had been served with a subpoena—Victor had been working in a white heat after every communication with the Winston lab. What did surprise her was the dead squirrel hurled at Grace's window.

"Nobody knows they're reopening this case," said Mary. "I've been watching the paper's newsfeeds on the Internet—not a word of content about it."

"Well, somebody found out something." Grace's voice cracked. "When people start talking about Teresa Ewing, ugly things happen here. I'm sorry about the squirrel, but I'll get over it. If Zack saw it, he would cry for months. He's just now getting over Whaley's last visit—I don't know how he'll react to giving DNA again."

"Let me make a few calls," said Mary. "Maybe we can work out an easier way for Zack to comply."

———

She hung up from Grace, absently gazing at Victor's nubby-wheeled mountain bike. With a significant piece of fresh evidence, she knew the state would try to retrofit their old suspects to the new development. What needed to happen, if Zack Collier were to ever get off the hook, was for someone to find out who really killed that little girl. But how? Had the girl died a month ago, you could interview witnesses, talk to people who knew the child. As in all cold cases, most of the clues had vanished in the fog of memory, or were lost in evidence rooms of the police department.

She went back inside the apartment. Victor had stopped singing, though the shower was still running. Must be shaving, Mary decided. It's hard to sing and shave at the same time. She retrieved her toast and headed to the bedroom. She needed to get dressed and go to work. Not only did she have a Skype session scheduled with the squabbling Burtons, but now she also needed to call Jerry Cochran about Zack Collier's DNA.

She walked through the dining room, which Victor used as an office. Two computers, a printer, and several piles of different colored papers were spread out on a long table. Though she knew it was wrong, she couldn't resist taking a peek at what Victor had been working on. The name Teresa Ewing appeared on all the sheets of paper. Mary walked along the table, quickly scanning the first pages of the documents. Mostly they were SBI reports, comprehensible only to SBI agents, but as she came to the end of the table, she found a thick manila file with a Pisgah County Sheriff Department stamp. *Ewing, Teresa* had been typed across the top. *J. Wilkins and O. Whaley, dets.* This was it! Exactly what she needed! The original file at the time of the girl's death. She'd just turned to the first page when she heard the water quit running.

She jumped away from the table. Victor always came out of the shower like a man on a mission. A second later the door opened and he appeared in a cloud of steam, a towel wrapped around his waist. He was on his way to the bedroom when he saw her out of the corner of his eye.

"Hey," he called. "Whatcha doing in there?"

"Got a call from work," she answered truthfully. "You were singing 'Go Argentina' so loudly I went outside to talk."

"'Play Argentina,'" he corrected, looking at the papers spread out on the table. "Sorry about the mess. I'm taking all that to the office today."

"Don't on my account," she said. "I'm accustomed to work files at home."

"Yeah, but the SBI doesn't like it. They're pretty touchy about their cold case files."

He turned and headed for the bedroom. She followed him, but not before she sneaked a final glimpse at Teresa Ewing's case file.

J. Wilkins and O. Whaley she repeated the names to herself. Buck Whaley would die before he told her anything about this case. But this J. Wilkins might be more willing to talk. "Wouldn't Turpin just love that," she whispered with a soft chuckle. "I might find out as much about the case as he does."

ELEVEN

ADAM SHAW GAZED DOWN at the Appalachians from 15,000 feet in the air. From this height the old mountains looked like lumpy green carpet. Though they lacked the muscularity of the Rockies or the awesome majesty of the Himalayas, the Appalachians were a soupy, mysterious world unto themselves. Down there, he guessed, the cops had found a clue that might reveal Teresa Ewing's killer. How odd that it had turned up just as his parents were about to leave the place that had almost destroyed them. It was as if the mountains weren't going to let Mr. and Mrs. Richard Shaw go without a fight.

He sat back in his seat and closed his eyes, remembering the call from his mother. "The police came by today," she'd whispered, sounding like a creature afraid to come out of its burrow. "You need to come home."

He'd been asleep—newly arrived from a photo shoot in Vancouver—and at first thought he might be dreaming. Then his father came on the line, his voice crisp as a general assuming command.

"Adam, the police have found something under that godforsaken tree. Bob Meyers says you need to give them a cheek swab."

"I was coming next week to help you guys with the move," he told his father. "Should I get an earlier flight?"

"Get here as soon as you can, so we can put this lunacy behind us for good."

So he changed his flight and here he was, coming back to the home he'd left twenty-five years ago, remembering his long-ago words. *We were playing by the tree. Then Butch's mother called him and we all went home. I was eating supper when Mrs. Ewing called...*

He'd told that story so many times it was like a speech he'd learned by rote. He recited it first to the uniformed officers, then to the detectives. Endlessly. Before school started, then again when he got off the bus. Saturdays after basketball practice; Sundays after church. Always the same questions, the same two detectives. One reminded him of his science teacher, the other a football coach. *We've heard you guys wanted the girls to play strip poker that afternoon. Did you make Teresa take off her clothes? Did anybody touch her, try to kiss her? Was Zack there? How soon did he leave after Teresa? Which direction did he go? He claims you're his best friend. What does that mean? Tell us what really happened, son. We want to help you. We understand how things can get out of hand. We know you don't want to rat out a friend, but in this case it's okay. A little girl has been murdered.*

He wondered, as the airplane began its final descent, if the cops would ask him the same questions this time. Some new sheriff had probably gone through the cold case files, he told himself. Decided to make his mark by solving the great mystery of Teresa Ewing. Still, a request for new DNA was like a registered letter from the IRS— vaguely troubling and always mysterious.

He rented a car at the airport, amazed at the speed of the transaction. At Heathrow or JFK it would have taken at least an hour; here he was driving toward Hartsville just minutes after he got off the plane. As the highway made pleasant, banked curves through the mountains, he thought back to his childhood friends. He figured Zack Collier, the autistic kid, was probably dead by now. He knew Shannon and Janie had moved, but that Butch Russell and Devin McConnell still lived in Hartsville. He'd never reconnected with them on Facebook or Twitter. Being suspects in a murder case was nothing you wanted to post on your timeline. Still, he wanted to look them up, take them out for a beer. He felt like he owed them that. He'd gotten to leave and live in New York while they'd had to stay and eat shit at Pisgah County Junior High. None of the cool kids wanted to hang out with anybody who might be accused of murder.

He reached the city limits of Hartsville and cut his speed to thirty-five. Though the streets were familiar, the town itself looked strange. Video Land had morphed into a tattoo gallery. The Foto-Mat had vanished and the land was now part of the Olive Garden's parking lot. The hospital now had a helo pad and the police station, where he had spent a number of unpleasant hours, had expanded from a fieldstone building heated by a woodstove to a sprawling complex with a fleet of black-and-white squad cars, sleek as Orcas.

"Whoa," he whispered. "Looks like there's some serious crime-detection going on here." He gazed at the police station for a moment, then he turned toward Salola Street. Tomorrow he would give his DNA. Today he just wanted to go home.

If the new Hartsville had surprised him, then Salola Street left him amazed. Most of it was gone—the houses, the back yard barbecues, the vegetable gardens and swing sets. All had been replaced by mounds of earth and little orange stakes in the ground that marked off the lots in the new development. The only familiar thing left was the oak tree, presiding regally over all the upturned earth. He squinted up at the top of it, looking for a glint of the fabled Spanish helmet. Two Toes had told them if your heart was brave, you could see it, in the very top branches. Never had he seen it. He figured his heart wasn't brave enough.

Adam drove on, turned into their cul-de-sac, and found the last three remaining houses. They huddled together, a Custer's last stand against progress. The Russells, the Fergusons, and the Shaws. His mother had wanted them all to move to New York, but his father had drawn a line in the sand against Sheriff Logan and Detective Whale-Ass. *No cop is going to railroad me* had become his mantra, words he'd lived by for the past quarter century.

He pulled into their driveway, the memory of his father's voice so clear that it stunned him. Then another voice caught his attention.

"Oh my God!" His mother burst out the front door. "You're home!"

She ran to him, her arms outstretched, her heavy breasts jiggling. His father followed in tennis shorts, then his brother Mark and Mark's wife, Sharon.

He'd barely gotten out of the car before his mother engulfed him. "I can't believe this! I can't believe you're here!"

"Mom, I just saw you guys at the beach in June."

"I know," she cried. "But it's just so nice having you here."

His father clapped him hard on the back. "Welcome home, Adam."

Three years his junior, Mark was now a Charlotte banker who played golf and wore rep ties. He gave Adam a brusque hug while Sharon smiled, holding his little nephew Owen in her arms. "Yo-bro!" said Mark. "Welcome to the last dance on Salola Street! You're just in time to take over the packing."

He endured their exuberant welcome, then he stepped back to get a better look at the home he'd left so long ago. Though they'd painted it gray and planted azaleas in the front yard, his mother's bird bath still stood on the lawn and his old basketball hoop still hung over the garage. How many games of Horse had he played there? Hundreds, at least. Even now he could see them all—Butch's face as red as his hair, Devin with his Notre Dame cap backward, Zack usually missing the hoop entirely, throwing the ball either into the bushes or over the backboard.

"Come on in, honey." His mother pulled him toward the door. "I've made spaghetti for dinner. We can have a drink while the pasta cooks."

As Mark grabbed Adam's knapsack from the car, Adam allowed his mother to pull him inside the house. Again, he was shocked as he stepped through the front doorway. The home he'd remembered as being decorated with military precision was cluttered with books and clothes and furniture half-covered in bubble wrap. "Where's all our old stuff?" he asked.

"Either waiting to get packed or sold," his mother said.

He frowned, not understanding. "Sold?"

"We had a garage sale last Saturday," she explained as she hurried into the kitchen. "Got rid of all our junk and made almost a thousand dollars."

"Wow." He looked around the foyer, the living room stuffed with chairs and two sofas. "It looks so different. Smaller, somehow."

His father handed him a bottle of beer. "You recognize those pictures, don't you?"

He looked in the dining room. All the pictures on the wall were photographs he'd taken. A sunrise in Tibet, a mist-shrouded ferry in the San Juan Islands, Japanese lanterns floating out to sea. They'd been enlarged to gallery-sized prints and matted in expensive metal frames.

"They look terrific." He didn't know what else to say. In twenty years his father had never commented on his choice of profession—outdoor adventure photography. Even though he'd had pictures in *Outside* and had worked on every continent, his father only ever asked if his traveler's health insurance was up-to-date.

Mark came and stood beside him. "We hung your shot of that beach in Thailand in our living room. What are you going to do next?"

"Gorillas in Rwanda." He caught his father's frown. "But only after we get everything to Hilton Head."

An odd silence fell. He felt suddenly as if he were some non-English-speaking stranger his family was desperate to make feel welcome. Soon they would start pantomiming their conversation.

"Come on, Adam," his father finally said, "let's get you settled in."

While Mark went to rejoin Sharon, his father led him down the hall to the last door on the right. He stepped inside his boyhood room with a sense of relief. This, at least, seemed familiar. Though his basketball team pictures and his letter for junior high track were gone, his bed and his dresser and his desk all stood in the same place. He stepped over to the window. He could still see the back yard and the shed where they'd played.

"Look familiar?" His father dropped his knapsack on the bed.

"This does." He took a sip of beer. "Everything else sure has changed."

Typically, his father cut to the chase. "I called Bob Meyers. He said it's best to get the DNA thing over with. He'll go with you down to the police station first thing tomorrow."

"I'd rather go by myself, Dad. I've handled Turkish border guards and the Moscow cops. I think I can manage the Pisgah County police."

"I know." For an instant, his father's eyes grew watery behind his glasses. He seemed to want to say something else, but instead he reached again to clap him on the back. "It's good to have you home, Adam. Just relax and I'll go help your mother."

After his father returned to the kitchen, he went over to his old closet and opened the door. It held only flattened packing boxes, waiting to be filled. He ran his hands along the top shelf, wondering if any remains from his childhood lurked there, but the shelf was empty of everything but a thin layer of dust.

He wandered down the hall. All the other bedrooms looked as impersonal as motel rooms—they held beds and dressers but were empty of pictures, photographs, or books. Crossing the living room, he went downstairs, to the basement rec room where he and Mark had once reigned supreme. The Ping-Pong table was gone, along with the dartboard. The only thing left was the big entertainment center where they'd watched endless movies—stopping, rewinding, and showing their favorite scenes in slow motion. For his tenth birthday, he'd asked for his own video camera and tripod. A year later he was filming everything—bears with their cubs, Mark riding his skateboard, once a scripted drama about the Civil War, starring Devin as a Yankee, Zack as a slave, and Teresa in an old prom dress, playing a rebel spy. He turned and opened the cabinet in the bottom of the bookcase, looking for those old tapes. All he found were empty shelves. He stood there, unbelieving. Had they already packed those up? He'd planned on taking them home with him. Suddenly he heard his mother call, "Adam! Dinner's ready!"

He closed the cabinet and went upstairs to the kitchen. Though his parents had added a food processor and a juicer to their array of appliances, the same Tiffany lamp hung low over the wide oak dining table, and his mother's cookbook collection spilled from the shelf above the stove. He sat down between baby Owen and his father.

"I just can't believe you're home," his mother said, spooning marinara sauce over a plate of pasta.

"I can't believe how everything's changed," he replied. "What's this new development going to be?"

"Lone Oak Acres," his father replied. "Energy-saving homes—water furnaces, underground utilities, bike paths. They'd have gone solar, except they didn't want to cut any trees."

"Particularly the haunted one in the middle," Mark joked. Everybody just stared at him, not laughing.

"You'll like Hilton Head." His mother changed the subject. "It's nice—relaxed and homey."

"Tennis courts for Dad, 24/7," said Mark, trying to make amends for his regrettable joke. "They even have a pro who'll video all your strokes and tell you what you're doing wrong."

Adam took a bite of spaghetti. "Speaking of videos, what happened to our old tapes?"

His father said, "What tapes?"

"Our VHS tapes. You know, the ones we kept in the bottom of the bookcase downstairs."

His brother twirled pasta around his fork. "God, I haven't watched a tape since high school."

"I found those old things when I was cleaning up," said his mother. "I put them in a box and sold them at the garage sale."

"All of them?"

She nodded.

"But they were hilarious. Don't you remember Mark's skateboard show? My Civil War movie?"

She shrugged, apologetic. "I'm sorry, but I don't. But I can tell you who bought the whole box."

"Who?"

"Zack Collier. Spent every dollar he had. All fifteen of them."

"His lawn-mowing wages," said his father, giving a bark of a laugh.

His mother went on. "You should have seen him at the sale. He practically salivated over those tapes."

Adam frowned. "I'm surprised he's still alive. A lot of autistic people die young."

"He still lives with his mother." His father grunted his disapproval. "How she manages that I'll never know. He's big as an ox."

Adam could tell by his parents' acidic tones that they were still in the ranks of those convinced that Zack Collier had killed Teresa Ewing. Though nobody could prove it, it was the only theory that made sense. The boy had been a teenager playing with much younger children. With a hair-trigger temper and his hormones in full flower, Zack Collier simply had to be the one who killed that girl.

"He's not a monster, Dad," Adam replied, defending his childhood friend. "Or at least he wasn't when I left."

His mother huffed up. "We didn't say he was a monster, Adam. He's just so big and—I don't know—strange. You should have seen him going after those tapes."

"He always liked to watch tapes," said Adam. "Movies, cartoons, anything you could put on a screen."

His mother refilled her wineglass, sloshing a little on the table. "Do you want me to call his mother and buy them back?"

"No, I might stop over there. I'd like to see Zack again."

"There's no need for that," said his father.

Adam shook his head. "I want to see everybody once more. Butch, Kevin, and Zack."

"What on earth for?" cried his mother.

"Just to say hello," he replied, wishing that his heart was brave enough to say why he really wanted to see them. *I want to tell them I'm sorry. I want to tell them I'm not the chickenshit they think I am. I want to tell them that I didn't even know I was leaving town until we were halfway to the airport.*

TWELVE

GRACE COLLIER'S HAND SHOOK slightly as she held out the pills for her son. Sertraline for depression, Geodon for seizures, and Abilify for anxiety. Zack scooped them from her hand and gulped them down with a glass of orange juice. "Where's Clara?" he asked. "She usually gives me the pills."

"She took the day off," said Grace. "Remember? You and I are going downtown today."

"To the bakery?" Zack never forgot any place that dished out sweets.

"Sure, we can go there."

She'd agonized over telling him the real reason for their trip and had decided to spool out the information, slowly chumming him along with treats. By the time he was scheduled for the DNA test, the Abilify would have taken effect. He would be nervous, but not terrified. And Mary Crow said she'd arranged for him to get special treatment at the police station. Grace could only pray that was true.

"Ready!" Zack finished his juice.

She held out his escape from the world, a portable DVD player. "You want to watch a cartoon or just talk on the way?"

"Cartoons," he said, plugging in the ear buds. "You smackertalk too much."

She nodded. Sometimes his hearing was so acute that he couldn't tolerate even the sounds of vocalization—the hissing of s's, the percussive smacks of b's and p's. Though the enforced silence of their life often made her want to scream, today she was relieved. She could listen to a podcast on her iPhone and not think about what was to come.

————————

Amazingly, she found a parking space in front of the bakery. As she turned off the engine, she looked up and saw the Palladian windows of Mary Crow's office. She knew Mary was waiting for them, but she had to stop by the bakery first. Reneging on a promise to Zack was never a good idea.

"Come on, buddy," she told him. "Let's go see what they've got."

He withdrew his ear buds and followed her inside. The cases were filled with éclairs and cookies, tarts and pies. A few people sat at the little tables, talking over coffee. They would take no notice of him until he started to speak. Then they would look at him, then her, and share a knowing glance with their companions. *A mentally challenged adult. His soon-to-be-old mother. How sad. How noble.* If Zack behaved, they would think no more about it. If Zack went off the rails, then the bakery would empty in a heartbeat. She'd gone through it too many times not to know what would happen.

She walked over to stand at Zack's elbow. "What would you like, honey?"

"That." He pointed to a bear claw, then a crème horn, then a cherry turnover.

"Choose two," she said. "You can have one now, and another later." She held her breath, waiting. If the drugs had kicked in, he'd be happy with two; if they hadn't, he might want everything in the place.

He pointed to the cherry tarts and the crème horns. "I want one of those, please," he told the girl behind the counter. "And one of those."

Grace felt a wave of relief. Two was going to be enough.

She paid for the pastries, then they left the bakery through a back door. A sign for Ravenel & Crow pointed upstairs, so she started up a wide interior staircase. "Come on, Zack. Let's go see a friend of mine."

"Who?" he asked, his mouth already full of cherry tart.

"Mary Crow. She came to our house the other day. She's nice."

They walked into a small reception room. A diminutive woman in a pale blue business suit sat behind a desk decorated with a vase of fresh flowers and two miniature flags—Old Glory next to the Union Jack.

"Good morning," she said, her accent sounding straight off the BBC. "May I help you?"

"We're here to see Mary Crow," Grace replied.

Smiling, the woman checked her schedule. "Mrs. Collier, then. And Zachary?"

Grace nodded.

"Wonderful. If you'll take a seat, I'll tell Mary you're here."

Grace was backing toward the sofa when Mary herself opened an office door on the other side of the room. "Thanks, Annette," she told her secretary. "I'm ready."

"Shall I bring tea?" asked Annette. "Or coffee?"

"Nothing for us, thank you." Grace smiled.

"Then come on in." Mary held her office door open. "Welcome, Zack," she said softly as he lumbered into the room. "I'm Mary Crow."

"Nicetomeetyou," he mumbled.

They walked into a soft yellow office that overlooked Main Street. Law books lined the walls, interspersed with Cherokee baskets and a carved bear mask. Behind her desk hung an intricate tapestry woven in rich greens and deep, vibrant blues.

"*Uwodu*," Grace said, admiring the tapestry.

"Thanks," Mary replied. "From my *agiji*."

"Your mother's very talented," Grace said. "Does she work locally?"

"No," said Mary. "She passed away, some years ago."

"Of course," Grace said, noting the sadness in Mary's eyes. "You mentioned her at the breakfast the other day. I had no idea she was such a gifted artist."

"She had an amazing sense of color," said Mary. She nodded at the two armchairs that faced her desk. "Please, sit down."

Grace took one of the armchairs, but Zack remained standing. Finally he asked, "Mama, can I sit by the window?"

"That's a good idea, Zack," said Grace. "Mary and I need to talk." She'd hoped he'd plug in to his cartoons. If he heard the words *police* or *detective,* things could get dicey. She relaxed a bit when he flopped down beneath the window and re-inserted his ear buds.

Mary came over and sat on the edge of her desk. "I know he doesn't like loud talking. Is this okay?"

Grace nodded. "Perfect."

"Okay. Here's the deal—the police need Zack to give his sample in their lab to keep the chain of evidence clean. But Cochran's willing to let him come through the back entrance, so it won't seem like he's going to jail. It's only a cheek swab, so it won't be nearly as traumatic as before."

"Will Detective Whaley be there? He just sends Zack into a panic."

"I can't control who's there. But Cochran promised to remind Whaley that he's got a special needs suspect. Shall we ride over together?"

Grace knew that Zack got nervous when strangers were unexpectedly introduced into his equations. "How about we take two cars and meet you there?"

"That's fine," said Mary. "I'll have Annette call Cochran's secretary and let her know we're on the way."

———

Zack remained calm, at least until they pulled into the Justice Center parking lot. Grace had hoped he would keep watching cartoons until they parked, but he looked up as they passed the black-and-white squad cars in front of the building.

"No!" he cried. "I don't want to go here!"

"Its okay, Zack," she told him as he hurled the DVD player at the dashboard. "It's not going to be like the last time."

"No! I'm not going!"

He unbuckled his seat belt and started fumbling with the door handle as she sped to the back of the building. Careening sharply into a vacant parking space, she tried to get a grip on him. "Listen to me! We have to do this. We don't have any choice!"

"Smackertalker! Smackertalker!" he bellowed, batting at her with his hands.

She fended off his blows, wanting to scream. She was afraid to give him another Abilify, but if he went inside the building like this, they would tase him or put him in jail. Taking a deep breath, she grabbed his chin and pulled his face toward hers.

"You remember Caillou? On TV? Remember how Caillou always trusts his teacher? Even when he's scared?"

Zack just looked at her.

"Well, today you need to be like Caillou, and trust me. I know you're scared. I know you hate those policemen. But this won't be like it was before. They won't hurt you. That lady Mary Crow promised me that."

"I want to go home!" yelled Zack.

"I do too. And we will. But first they need to rub a Q-tip on the inside of your cheek. It won't hurt." Grace prayed she was right; prayed there wouldn't be fingerprints and mug shots.

"How long will it take?"

"Five minutes." Again, she lied. She had no idea how long this would take.

"That's all?"

"Yes, honey. I promise."

He sat forward in the seat crying, rubbing his forehead on the dashboard. She watched him, looking at the strong arms that might have, in a different life, thrown a football or escorted a girl to a prom or even held a baby of his own. She was reaching to touch his shoulder when someone tapped on her window. She turned. Mary Crow was standing there.

"Ready?" she asked.

Grace held up one finger and turned to Zack. "Come on, Zack. We need to go. Mary Crow is waiting."

He lifted teary eyes toward Mary. For a moment Grace couldn't tell what he was going to do, then he wiped his nose and said, "Okay."

They got out of the car and followed Mary to the back entrance of the jail. Though Zack shuffled his feet like an old man, he came more or less willingly. When they got to the lab, Mary opened the door. Grace's heart sank. Buck Whaley was sitting on a stool, chatting with a girl in a white coat.

"Well, look who's here," he boomed. "Ol' Zack Collier and his mama. And Ms. Mary Crow, herself."

"Put a lid on it, Whaley," Mary warned.

Grinning, he rose from the stool and stepped toward Zack, putting a hand on his shoulder. By police brutality standards, it was nothing. By Zack's standards, it was horrific.

"Mama!" He shrugged off Whaley's hand and turned to Grace, tears again streaming. "I want to go home!"

"What are you cryin' about now?" asked Whaley. "I'm just trying to get you on that stool. Boy, I think you're puttin' on an act. I think you been puttin' one on for years."

"Detective!" Mary stepped between Zack and the beefy cop. "My client is a special needs case. You need to proceed accordingly."

"Shut up shut up shut up!" Zack screamed. "Quit smackertalking!"

Suddenly Zack pushed away from them both. Mary went flying into Whaley, the top of her head banging into his face. The two of them stumbled, knocking over the stool. The lab technician yelped. As blood began to spurt from Whaley's nose, he reached for his Taser. All at once a tall, skinny man appeared in the doorway. He wore jeans and a blue dress shirt, and his dark hair was curly and flecked with gray.

"You don't need to Taser him!" The man stepped in front of Zack. "Just quit yelling. He's got hypersensitive hearing."

112

Whaley pushed Mary Crow to one side and pointed his Taser at the stranger. "Who the hell are you?"

"Next in line for a swab, Detective Whaley," the man said calmly. "Name's Adam Shaw."

"Adam!" Zack flung his arms around the man's shoulders. "You came back!"

"I sure did, buddy," said Adam Shaw, still keeping his eyes on Whaley. "Just to see you."

For a long moment, nobody moved. Then Whaley turned to Mary Crow, one great paw trying to staunch the blood streaming from his nose. "Can you control your client, Ms. Crow?"

"I can control him," said Grace, "if you'll just speak softly and not touch him. He's terrified of you."

"As well he should be." Whaley reholstered the Taser and glared at Adam Shaw. "Since you two have this little bromance going on, I'll just watch while you work this out. But I need DNA from both of you."

Grace took Zack's hand. "Come on … "

"Wait." Adam turned to her. "Let me go first. Zack can watch. We'll show Detective Whaley we're not afraid of him."

"Yeah," said Zack, thrilled to have an ally against the cop.

The lab tech handed Whaley a box of tissues, then filled out a new sheet of paperwork. As Adam took a seat on the stool, she donned a pair of latex gloves and pulled a long swab from a paper wrapper. She stepped over to Adam, but spoke to Zack in a soft voice. "Okay, Big Guy. You watch what I'm going to do. Your buddy's going to open his mouth and I'm going to rub the inside of his cheek with this. After that, it'll be your turn."

Adam opened his mouth as Zack watched the procedure. After the lab tech sealed up the swab in a sleeve, Adam grinned. "Piece of cake, Zack. You won't even feel it." He hopped off the stool. "Now you sit here and I'll keep an eye on Detective Whaley."

To Grace's amazement, Zack complied. He got on the stool and opened his mouth wide, as if he were at the dentist's office. The lab tech saw her chance and quickly swabbed the inside of his cheek. Thirty seconds later, she was finished.

"Good job, buddy!" Adam gave Zack a high five, then turned to Whaley. "We should be done here, according to my attorney."

"You are done here," said Mary. "I am an attorney."

"Then come on." Adam grabbed Zack around the shoulders. "Let's go."

The pair walked out the door. They brushed against Whaley, who was standing there holding a tissue to his nose. He started to say something, but Mary pointedly cleared her throat, her eyes hard on his. Aware of her presence, he said no more, but closed his mouth in a thin, angry line. Grace and Mary walked past him. When they got out into the hall, Whaley slammed the lab door shut behind them.

Grace leaned back against the wall, weak with relief. "Dear Lord," she whispered to Mary. "Are you alright?"

"Just disgusted. I've never been that close to Buck Whaley before."

"I'm so sorry," she apologized. "Zack didn't mean to hurt you. Whaley just scares him so."

"He scares me too." Mary rubbed the spot where her head had connected with Whaley's nose.

"Zack panics when he's scared. Or frustrated. Or just doesn't understand what's going on. Thank God for Adam Shaw."

Mary watched the man who'd saved the day, now laughing with Zack. "He's one of the old neighborhood kids, isn't he?"

Grace nodded. "His parents sent him away after they found Teresa. I don't think he's set foot in this county since. I was flabbergasted when he walked in."

"Zack seems pretty glad to see him."

"Zack adored Adam. Devin and Butch could be mean to him, but never Adam."

"Well, like you said, thank God for Adam," said Mary.

Grace pulled her car keys from her purse. "I'd better get Zack home. I can't thank you enough for this, Mary. If you hadn't been here, I know Whaley would have put Zack in jail."

"I was glad to help, Grace. I'll call you when they get the results of this test."

"How long do you think it will it take?"

"It's hard to say. Newer, more solvable cases take precedence."

Grace gave a little shudder. "That's what I was afraid of."

"I know it's hard to wait," said Mary. "Unfortunately, that's just the way the system works."

"It's not the system I'm afraid of," Grace replied. "It's all the people out there who still think Zack killed that little girl."

THIRTEEN

ADAM SHAW WATCHED AS Grace Collier's battered SUV drove pulled out of the parking lot, Zack waving wildly from the passenger seat. "Bye, Adam!" he yelled so loudly that a couple of people turned to look. "I'll call you!"

"Okay," Adam called softly, saluting Zack with one hand.

So that's Zack, he thought as the Dodge disappeared in traffic. *Fifty pounds heavier, but not a day older inside his head. What must that be like?* he wondered. To have your mother drive you everywhere, to still get caught up in cartoons. It was bizarre, yet there was an innocence about Zack that touched him. As ardently as his mother had hugged him, Zack's embrace had somehow been more freely given. The big boy/man had been truly glad to see him.

"Wow," Adam whispered. "All these years, and for him, nothing's changed."

After that, he headed back inside, looking for Detective Whaley. He found him, still in the lab, trying to staunch his bloody nose with a wad of cotton.

"What do you want?" asked Whaley, his voice both muffled and nasal.

"I figure you guys are going to want a statement, so I'd like to give it now. I'm helping my folks move and may not be in town much longer."

Whaley looked at him as if he were joking, but then decided he must be serious. Adam followed him to an interview room and sat down to yet again tell what happened that afternoon, to the best of his recollection. They'd played, then Devin brought out a deck of marked cards that he'd stolen from his brother. They'd tried to get the girls to play Bottom Up, but they'd gotten mad and gone home. Soon everybody went home.

"This doesn't shed any new light on things," Whaley grumbled when he'd finished.

"I have no new light to shed, detective."

"Okay." Whaley shrugged. "We'll be in touch if we need to talk again."

After that, Adam left, threading his way through the crowded Justice Center parking lot. He'd parked at the end of one row, where a man was leaning against his mother's Toyota, writing something on a long pad.

"Hey!" he shouted. "You can't give me a ticket! I'm here on police business!"

The guy looked up but kept on writing. Adam ran toward his car, angry. As he neared the guy, he saw that he wasn't a cop at all—just some dude wearing blue trousers and a light blue shirt. Still, he had his foot planted on the back bumper of his rental, making notes about something.

"What's the problem?" Adam asked the man. He looked to be in his late twenties, with sandy hair and glasses.

"No problem." He looked up from his writing. "Are you Adam Shaw?"

"I am."

"Then you're the guy I've been waiting for."

"Waiting for? Why?"

He pulled an ID from his shirt pocket. "John Cooksey, *Hartsville Herald*."

Adam stepped back, feeling like an idiot. He should have seen this coming. The *Hartsville Herald* was always hungry for news about Teresa Ewing.

"I've got nothing to say."

"Really? Don't you want to give your side of the story? You're the only one who ran way."

"No comment." He brushed past the guy, key fob in hand.

"You sure? You might come off as less of a coward if you, like, said something."

He unlocked the car, angry but also mindful of his father's sternest maxim. *Say nothing. Not to anyone. Not the cops, not the press, not to anybody. Ever.* He got in the car and lowered the window. "Here's my comment," he said.

The guy moved closer, ready to write. "What?"

"Get the fuck out of my face, asswipe."

The reporter looked surprised. Hurt, even. "Seriously? That's it?"

"You got it."

"Okay, Shaw. Don't say I didn't warn you."

Adam put the car in reverse and backed up so fast that Cooksey had to jump to keep from getting run over. He tore out of the parking lot angry, wondering if everybody did think he was a coward. Maybe it was time to go visit his old pals and find out. Turning left, he headed back toward town. All he had to do was cross his back yard to see Butch Russell, but Devin McConnell was a little different. He remembered his mother saying that Devin had taken over his dad's used car lot. He drove past their old school, farther past a new crop of fast-food places, then he saw it—Tote-A-Note Used Cars. The same manic-looking leprechaun was perched on the roof, the same shamrock-green balloons bobbed in the air. Adam had to smile. Once they were watching TV on Saturday morning, and Big Jim McConnell had come on in a car commercial, wearing a little green hat and pummeling car price tags with a huge plastic shillelagh. Mortified, Devin had immediately re-named his father's business Tote-A-Turd, and called his father the biggest shit of all.

He turned in, parking in an empty space marked *Customers Only*. Toyota Corollas, Subaru Foresters, a couple of old Saturns were lined up in front of small office, where other cars were parked behind a tall chain-link fence. Though the cars out front were clean, he could tell by the rusty wheels and clouded headlights that their best miles were behind them. They reminded him of dogs at the pound, tails wagging hopefully at everyone who passed their cage. *Pick me!* he imagined the Saturn saying. *I'm loyal. Reliable. I've got another hundred thousand miles if you'll just keep my oil changed!*

As he got out of his car, a fresh pang of guilt struck him. He'd had a good life, a privileged life. He would never be stuck in Hartsville, selling junkers from a building with a dwarf on top. He hesitated a moment, wondering if Dev might punch him if he went inside.

Certainly he had reason to. Then he thought, *so what?* If taking a punch would clear the slate, then he would walk out with a black eye. After all this time, it seemed a small price to pay. And besides, they could hardly call him a coward if he took a hit like that.

He took a deep breath and headed for the office. He pushed open the door and stepped inside a dark, paneled interior that smelled of cigarettes and disinfectant. When his eyes adjusted to the dimness, he saw that the same desk took up the same space, except that instead of Big Jim McConnell, Devin McConnell was sitting there, poring over some kind of notebook with a white-haired guy. The two were nursing liters of Foster's Lager, and Devin looked as Adam had imagined him—bulked up with muscle, ink-black hair falling onto his forehead, one green eye wandering while its partner stayed straight.

"I'm sorry, buddy." Devin stood up, swallowing a burp as he shifted into salesman mode. "I didn't hear you drive up. What can I help you with?"

"Dev?" He took a step forward. "It's me. Adam—Adam Shaw."

For a moment, Dev looked at him as if he didn't remember who he was. Then, as his errant eye briefly converged with his good one, the corners of his mouth drew down. "Well, I'll be damned. Chicken Little Shit has returned."

The white-haired man looked up over his shoulder. This time Adam was the one who stared. It was Butch Russell. His red hair had gone white and a tonsure of pink scalp was beginning on the top of his head. His boyhood chubbiness had become an adult-sized paunch and the inside of his forearm was tattooed with an array of religious symbols—an ankh, a cross, a Star of David.

Butch squinted at him. "I saw you at your house yesterday."

"I'm helping my folks move. And giving a DNA sample."

"You do that at the police station, Adam," said Devin. "Not here."

He looked at them and realized that they hated him too much to even bother with a punch. Better that he just say what he had to say and leave. "Look, I don't know what you've heard, or what my parents have put out there. But leaving wasn't my call. I woke up one morning and got in the car to go to school. Instead, my father drove me to the airport. 'You're getting a new life,' he told me. 'Don't fuck it up.'"

He paused, and took another deep breath. "So I just wanted to come by and say—I don't know—say I'm sorry, I guess. I know you hate me and I don't blame you. But I did want you to know that I would have stayed if they'd let me."

Both men looked at him with hard faces. There was no more he could say, no greater apology he could make. He turned to go. He was halfway to the door when Devin spoke.

"You know what my parents made me do?"

Adam turned, shook his head.

"They put me in house arrest. Until I turned seventeen, I only went to school and church. No baseball. No car. No girls. Nothing but my shitty brothers and mass at St. Boniface."

"What happened when you were seventeen?" asked Adam.

"I ran the fuck away. Forged some signatures, joined the army."

"Wow," Adam said, impressed.

Devin rubbed the back of his neck. "I fought in the Gulf War. Got married, got divorced. Then my dad died and left me this lot. I guess he felt bad about treating me like a damn criminal for all those years."

"Do your brothers still live here?" Adam's memory of Dev's house was of many children, squirming around the floor, ubiquitous as dust bunnies.

"Hell, no," he said. "They took so much heat for being related to me that they all moved to Florida. Took my mother with them, thank God."

Adam ventured a few steps closer, turned to Butch. "How about you?"

He checked his watch, which covered the lower half of his ankh tattoo. "Until forty-seven minutes ago, I was a security guard at the college. My boss called me in this morning. I thought it was my annual review. Instead, he told me they were letting me go."

"That sucks," said Adam. "Did they give you a reason?"

"Said it didn't look good to have a murder suspect working campus security." Butch held up the newspaper. "We all made the front page. *Case reopened, killer never caught, all suspects to give new DNA.*"

"I saw a reporter at the police station this morning," said Adam. "I told him no comment. Then I almost ran over him."

"Too bad you missed." Dev slowly crushed a beer can. "You know, it's always the same for us. We think it's over, people have finally forgotten. Then every couple of years, it all comes back, like a case of the clap. Cars take root on this lot, Butch loses another job, and for what? Nothing! I've got two little girls—one's in the seventh grade, same as we were back then. What's she going to think when nobody will hang out with her because they think her daddy's a murderer?"

Adam had no children—had no interest in children. He turned to Butch. "You have kids?"

"No," said Butch. "You?"

Adam shook his head. "Never been married. Never had kids."

"Too busy living the good life, huh?" Dev's tone was bitter.

Adam remained silent. He could not deny it. He was living a good life, or at least a much better life than these guys. He felt sorry for them, but he wouldn't for one second trade his life for either of theirs.

"So who all was down there this morning?" asked Butch.

"Whale-Ass. Zack and his mother and their attorney."

Dev sat up straighter. "Zack's got an attorney?"

"A woman," Adam replied. "Whaley started ragging Zack. He freaked out and pushed her right into Whaley's face. Gave him a nosebleed."

Butch giggled. "I bet Whaley went nuts."

"He went for his Taser but didn't pull it," said Adam. "I think having that lawyer there scared him. She must be good."

"What was Zack like?" asked Devin.

Adam frowned. "Don't you ever see him?"

"Not if I can help it," Devin replied.

"He's a head taller, fifty pounds heavier. Otherwise, he's still about twelve."

"God, he must be a monster," Butch said. "Did he have his Barbie dolls with him?"

"Not that I saw." Suddenly Adam felt protective of Zack. He'd been genuinely happy to see him—the Teresa Ewing mess had not altered his affection.

Dev cracked open another beer. "So what did the cops do this time? Draw your blood? Pluck out your pubic hair?"

"Just a cheek swab," said Adam. "No big deal." He looked at them. "Aren't you guys going down there too?"

"I've got cars to sell," said Dev. "I can't take a break from my job like you can."

"And I gotta start looking for a new job," said Butch.

"Guys, it looks better if you just go and do it. If they have to serve a subpoena, it makes you look guiltier."

123

Dev's gaze narrowed. "And Mr. Fancy Photographer couldn't look guilty, could he?"

Adam realized then that there was no bridging the gap between them. Their resentment was too deep, their bitterness too ingrained. "Whatever," he said, taking a step toward the door. "I'd better get going. Nice talking to you."

Butch started to offer his hand, but then dropped it awkwardly to his side. "See you around," he finally muttered.

"Come back any time, Chicken Little Shit," Dev called, rearing back in his chair. "You get tired of the jet set, Butch and I and the ghost of Teresa will be right here, waiting."

FOURTEEN

AFTER GRACE AND ZACK left the Justice Center, Mary Crow drove back to her office. Though it had not been her first time to accompany a suspect for DNA testing, it was the first time she'd delivered an autistic adult. That Zack Collier had bloodied Buck Whaley's nose and avoided jail was remarkable. Whaley prided himself on being the heavy hand of justice—he would have tased and thrown anyone else into jail on an assault charge. But Zack Collier had gone home with his mother. Maybe Cochran really had talked to Whaley. Or maybe Whaley had thought better of bullying a compromised suspect in front of so many witnesses.

Still, she thought as she pulled into her parking space, *Zack Collier is a real wild card.* Huge, yet childish. Smart, according to Grace, but totally unable to cope with the frustrations of real life. He'd shoved her and Whaley as if they were ragdolls, yet he'd been gentle as a puppy with his friend Adam.

"Jeez," she whispered. She couldn't imagine living through forty minutes of that kind of behavior, much less forty years. However pouty and hateful Lily Walkingstick had been, things had never gotten that bad.

She parked her car and walked toward Main Street. She should go back to the office and work on the squabbling Burtons, but the morning had left her feeling off-balance. So instead of turning into Ravenel & Crow, she walked down three more storefronts to HairTwister's Style Salon. As she neared the little salon, she stopped, stunned. Her campaign signs—the incredible ones Grace had designed—plastered the front window. She couldn't believe it. Quickly, she opened the door. Ross and Meilani, the younger operators, were working on two old ladies. Juanita Wolfe, the owner, looked up from sweeping hair cuttings into a dustpan.

"Mary!" called Juanita. "How do you like the front window?"

"It's amazing! When did you put these up?"

"Some woman came around this morning, asking if I'd take one. I told her I'd take ten. This town needs a Tsalagi woman in office."

"*Wahdoe*," Mary thanked her in Cherokee. Juanita was one of the few tribe members who ran businesses in Hartsville. "I really appreciate it, Juanita. I'm the underdog in this fight."

Juanita laughed. "So when weren't we Cherokees underdogs?"

"Good point," said Mary. "Hey, do you have time to work me in?"

"Come sit down," said Juanita. "My next appointment's not till noon."

Mary settled into Juanita's station. As she clipped a warm towel around her neck, she asked, "So what does the next DA want? A bright pink Mohawk?"

"Just a trim." Mary looked in the mirror. Her straight, black hair had just begun to touch her shoulders. "No more than an inch."

126

Juanita fluffed up Mary's hair. "Whoa," she said, fingering a spot on the top of her scalp. "Girl, you've got a goose egg."

"Collided with a shelf this morning," she said, unwilling to admit that her head had connected with Buck Whaley's nose.

"That's what they all say." Ross winked at her from the next station. "You've just been out having too much fun."

Mary laughed. "Can't slip anything by you, Ross."

Juanita turned the chair around and began washing Mary's hair. The warm, sudsy water felt wonderful, and Juanita expertly avoided the tender spot on her skull. Mary could have happily sat there for the rest of the day, but Juanita quickly had her upright and looking into the mirror again.

"So how've you been?" Juanita asked, starting to shape the wedge Mary had worn for years.

"Busy," said Mary. "Speeches, lunches, the whole campaign thing."

"Are you still lawyering, or did you put your day job on hold?"

"No, I'm still taking cases."

"Hey, Miss DA—what's your take on Teresa Ewing?" asked Ross.

"Who?" Mary played dumb, wondering what the street talk was about Teresa Ewing.

"The little girl who got killed so long ago. Haven't you read today's paper?"

Juanita handed Mary the paper they'd all apparently been reading. The headline blared in massive type: NEW EVIDENCE IN TERESA EWING CASE. She scanned it quickly. Jerry Cochran had downplayed the story, warning everyone that it was a slim lead at best, but the paper had run with the news, giving new readers a brief history of the case, then listing the "Salola Street Gang" and Two Toes McCoy as the last surviving suspects. She returned the paper to Juanita and sighed. Grace's worst nightmare really was coming true.

"Well?" said Ross. "Who do you think did it?"

"I don't know," replied Mary. "I was in the fourth grade at the time."

"Ooooh," said Ross. "Just like Teresa. Did you know her?"

"No. I went to public school. She went to Hartsville Academy."

"I was teaching English at Hartsville High when that child was murdered," said the old lady in Ross's chair. "I never saw anything like it. Everybody was combing the bushes for that child—all the clubs at school, the football boys. A psychic said she was at the bottom of Santeetlah Lake. And then they found her under that tree, which had been searched fifty times, at least. It just didn't make any sense!"

"That's because that big retarded boy killed her and hid her," chimed in the old woman in Meilani's chair.

"He had a funny name—Zeb, I think," said the first woman.

"Zachary," corrected her friend. "Zachary Collier. He raped and killed that child, then he carried her to his house. His mother put the little girl's body in their freezer and kept her there for a month. She didn't want her boy going to prison for the rest of his life."

"I heard something else," said Ross, rolling his client's cottony hair. "That the mother slept with Logan to keep him from arresting the boy."

Meilani's client went on, speaking with great authority. "I don't know about that. But I do know that my late husband's cousin Steve worked for Simpson's appliance company. That Collier woman ordered a new freezer right after they found that little girl. Steve delivered it and picked up the old one. He said that old freezer was horrible—full of bloodstains and it smelled like rotting meat."

Ross shuddered. "Did he call the police?"

"No. He said he was afraid to get involved. And then the boy's father just up and goes to Canada!"

128

"He couldn't take it anymore," said Meilani's client. "Didn't seem to bother the mother too much. She's still living here with that maniac, though I heard she keeps him locked up behind a fence."

"There you go, Mary," said Juanita, her scissors snipping around Mary's right ear. "Your first case as DA will be to convict that Collier kid."

"I guess so." Though Mary tried to smile, the alacrity with which these people had convicted Zack of murder and Grace of a cover-up sickened her. "Just remember—everyone's innocent until proven guilty."

"Oh Lord." Meilani's client glared at Mary with disgust. "You must be a liberal."

"I'm just an attorney, ma'am," Mary replied. "Sworn to uphold the Constitution. It guarantees due process, even for autistic people."

The talk then veered to autism, about one autistic man who could do calculus in his head but could barely talk; somebody else had heard of an autistic teenager who was good as gold until the day he woke up and killed his mother with a butcher knife. By the time Juanita finished, Mary had an inch less hair and a whole new appreciation for the powers of rumor and innuendo.

"I'm sorry if they jumped on you," whispered Juanita as Mary paid for her haircut. "People still have strong feelings about Teresa Ewing. They really want to hang whoever killed her."

"I do, too, Juanita," said Mary. "But I want to hang the right person."

———

Mary nodded at Meilani and Ross as she left, but was glad to step out into the bright sunlight. Though HairTwister's abounded in lights and mirrors, today it felt dark inside. She knew gossip always swirled around a murder case, but those old women at HairTwister's had made Grace Collier sound as conniving as a spider.

"Well, hello there, Mary," a voice called from behind her. "We were just talking about you."

She turned. George Turpin stood there, Harvey Pugh beside him. The Tweedledum and Tweedledee of the courthouse crowd, today in seersucker suits and striped ties—the summer uniform of certain Southern gentlemen.

"Those are terrific signs," said Turpin. "Really a fresh take on the usual red, white, and blue stuff."

"Thanks," Mary replied. "Grace Collier did them."

Turpin's mouth curled in a smug grin. "That's what we heard. She's such a talented gal. Too bad about her son."

"What about her son?" Mary wondered what Turpin was implying.

"Oh you know. All that Teresa Ewing business, right now with the election coming up." Turpin rocked back slightly on his heels.

"It's a shame," said Mary. "Takes everyone's attention from the larger issues."

"So it does. Well, I'm glad I got a chance to compliment you on your signage."

Again, Turpin smiled.

"See you at the Republican Luncheon."

Mary watched as the two men continued on toward the court-house, feeling a thrum of nervousness inside. That Turpin would try to make political hay over the Teresa Ewing case, she had no doubt. Probably he would paint all those boys-grown-to-men with a broad brush of suspicion, paint himself as the keeper of law and order, and paint her as a defender of child killers, working to help guilty people weasel out of the punishments they deserved.

Suddenly the absurdity of it all struck her. She was running for DA while representing a man everyone suspected of being a murderer. Probably, she should quit the case right now and pass Zack off to some other attorney. But Grace had worked on her campaign, believed in her message, was becoming her friend. Could she now turn Zack over to someone else?

"No," she decided, staring at her own campaign signs. "He hasn't been charged with anything. He's given his DNA. He's entitled to counsel as much as the next person."

And though that was true, she knew it wouldn't be enough. With Teresa Ewing, people didn't care about due process. People just wanted justice, with a huge dollop of vengeance thrown in.

Once more turning away from Ravenel and Crow, she walked to the offices of the *Hartsville Herald*. Though she hated to go to the paper since Ginger had left, she needed facts about Teresa Ewing's murder. If Turpin did make Zack Collier a campaign issue, she would need more reliable information than beauty shop gossip. Opening the door to the *Herald*, Mary put on her friendliest smile.

The prune-faced Ruby Potts looked up from the reception desk, no doubt aware that Mary would ask for something that would require some actual work on her part. "Well, Ms. Crow. Haven't seen you in a while. What can I help you with today?"

"I need something from the morgue."

"The morgue's online now. Everything from January 1, 2002."

"I need something from February 1989."

"Oh." Wearily, Ruby Simmons got out a pencil and note pad. "What items are you interested in?"

"Everything you've got on the Teresa Ewing murder."

The woman gave a weak, mewing laugh. "You going to solve that one now?"

Mary nodded. "I'm sure going to try."

FIFTEEN

JERRY COCHRAN RE-TOOK HIS position in front of the white board, thinking strangely of his father. Richard Cochran had spent his working life in front of a chalkboard, teaching organic chemistry to undergrads who hoped to become doctors. He would come home with chalk dust on his trousers, elated when the lightbulb finally gone off in some student's head. "We don't have to worry about Mr. Stevens transferring to law school anymore," he would tell his mother as he kissed her hello. "He finally figured out that pKa values are related to weak acids." Though Cochran smiled at the memory, he wondered what his father would think of him standing with a blue marker in front of a bunch of cops. *Your father would be so proud of you,* his mother always said. He liked to think she was right, that he was doing something that would please his old man.

He turned to face his own small class—a group of policemen ready to discuss what they'd learned about Teresa Ewing. Rob Saunooke leaned forward in his chair, the eager beaver of the class. Victor Galloway stretched his long legs forward, funny, but also observant and analytical. Buck Whaley sat sprawled, wheezing for air, his nose blooming like a red flower in the middle of his face. He reminded Cochran of a football player who'd taken a bad hit for the team.

Cochran looked at Whaley. "Did Maxine finally bean you with her frying pan?"

"Your pal Mary Crow did this," said Whaley, full of hurt.

"She hit you?" Cochran knew the two had a history, but he never dreamed Mary would plant a fist in Whaley's mug.

"Her retard client freaked out and pushed her into me," Whaley explained. "The top of her head caught my nose."

"Did you book him?"

Whaley waved his hand, as if a fly were buzzing around his face. "It's no big deal. You monkey with an ape, you take your chances."

Cochran assumed it had gone no further—certainly he would have heard if it had. "Well, I hope you feel better. File your injury report."

Whaley nodded.

Cochran turned to the board. "Gentlemen, this is the latest from Winston. Good DNA on Saunooke's cigarette butts, but it doesn't match a soul in the database. Marginal DNA on the underwear—they're going to do more tests to see if they can get a readable sample, and it could take a while."

"Are you shitting me?" Whaley's red nose grew redder. "They can reconstruct dinosaurs from a chip of bone, but they can't read a little girl's panties?"

"So they say." Cochran saw the keen disappointment on the men's faces. "But it's not over yet. We've still got more sampling to do."

"Who?" asked Saunooke.

Cochran looked at his notes. "Zack Collier and Adam Shaw complied Tuesday. Two Toes is already in the system. Lawrence Russell and Devin McConnell were no-shows. We still need a cheek swab from them."

"I told Russell's mother he needed to come downtown," said Whaley, "but I think she was on planet nine from outer space. That is one crazy old bird."

"Who had Devin McConnell?"

"I called him," said Whaley. "Said he'd come down, but I guess he lied."

"Okay, that takes care of the DNA." Cochran looked at Saunooke. "Did you interview Two Toes?"

Saunooke nodded. "He said he hadn't been near the tree, though he knew exactly why I was there.

"How did he know that?"

"He said the wind told him," replied Saunooke. "I imagine he just reads cops pretty well."

"He probably heard it from Janet Russell," said Whaley. "She's got a picture of Two Toes, along with a bunch of other freaks, standing in front of a teepee."

"Are you sure it's Two Toes?"

"I'd know those filed-down fangs anywhere," Whaley replied.

"Did you ask her about it?" said Cochran.

Whaley nodded. "Living under that tree has gotten in her head. Two Toes conducts healing retreats—sweat lodges, vision quests, that sort of shit. He's helped her make peace with the tree."

"Does she know Two Toes is an ex-con? Out on parole?"

"She said Two Toes had a vision in prison that led him to doing this work ... that as long as he did it, he would never be locked up again."

"Good grief." Cochran turned to Saunooke. "Did Two Toes tell you this?"

"No. Mostly Two Toes just wanted me gone. But he does live in a trailer, surrounded by teepees."

"I didn't think you Cherokees did teepees," said Galloway.

"We don't. Two Toes put them up for his clients. They pay to go there and be cleansed."

Whaley snorted. "Yeah, cleansed of their money by somebody crazier than a shit-house rat."

Saunooke, reticent in the face of Whaley's bluster, said nothing.

Cochran turned to the board. "Well, this is interesting. Janet Russell getting spiritually cleansed by Two Toes McCoy. Wonder how Butch figures in all this?"

"I don't know," said Whaley. "But I'll go find out."

Cochran shook his head. "I want you to take McConnell, Whaley. He hasn't responded either. Saunooke can trace the Two Toes–Janet–Butch connection." He looked at Galloway. "Victor, I've got a real good one for you."

Galloway leaned forward. "What?"

"The old guy—Wilkins—said there had been a powwow in Cherokee the weekend after the girl was murdered. He's got a theory that the killer could have been some itinerant worker on the pow-wow circuit."

"And you want me to see if there's a connection between pow-wows and murders?"

"Right. You might find a pattern."

"That was a mighty long time ago."

Cochran shrugged. "It's a small needle in a big haystack, but you SBI guys have resources I don't."

"I'm on it," said Galloway.

"Okay." Cochran put his marker down and looked at his men. "Gentlemen, this thing has gone the way I'd feared it would. Lots of papers being sold, lots of people speculating on who did it, lots of grumbling about why we stupid cops haven't been able to arrest anybody. I would consider it an achievement of the highest order if we could clear this case and let Teresa Ann Ewing rest in peace, for good. Any questions?"

No one spoke.

"Okay, then. Be careful, and let me know what you find out."

He watched as they filed out the room, Whaley shouldering his way through the door as if he were carrying a football, Saunooke lighter on his feet but hard on Whaley's tail. How many cops, he wondered, had gone out the door with the same orders to find Teresa Ewing's killer? It would be a miracle if his crew could nail down this one—then he really would think he'd done something to make his father proud.

SIXTEEN

BUCK WHALEY LEFT COCHRAN'S meeting eager to get back in his car. Not that he was particularly inspired by Cochran's little pep talk about the Teresa Ewing case—he'd ridden on that roller coaster too many times before. Mostly he was pissed that two of his four suspects had basically given the finger to his most polite request for their DNA. He couldn't say for sure if Butch Russell's nutcase mother had given him the message, but he had spoken with Devin McConnell on the phone. The little asshole had assured him that another DNA sampling would be no problem and he would come down to the Justice Center immediately.

"Which was total bullshit," Whaley said as he turned on to the highway. "Just another tick mark on Devin McConnell's long list of mistakes." He'd pulled up his jacket days ago. Several DUIs, a couple of domestic calls, and his wife once had a restraining order issued against him. McConnell ran on high-octane booze, just as his parents had. How he'd managed to hang on to that stupid car lot,

Whaley couldn't imagine. But he had, and not by going out of business and changing his sign every six months.

"Must have inherited his father's gift for blarney," muttered Whaley.

He drove through town, the sun glittering off the bumpers of parked cars. Campaign signs had begun to pop up in store windows. Lucy Keil for the statehouse, Cecil Earp for City Council. When he stopped for a light he noticed several eye-catching signs for Mary Crow—green and blue with a funny little crow sitting on top of her name. He shook his head. If Mary Crow won the DA's race, he didn't know what he would do. She would fill the courthouse with female attorneys and probably make Cochran bust him down to traffic.

"Maybe that would be my sign," he said. "Pack up Maxine and get the hell down to Florida. Work security for some fancy golf course in exchange for greens fees."

The light changed. He rolled down Main Street, then out past the mall and the fast-food shops. As he crested a hill, he saw the Tote-A-Note car lot on the left, its bright green balloons bobbing in the sun. He turned in and parked behind a row of late model sedans, their prices splashed in yellow paint across their windshields. As he got out of his car, he noticed a man in jeans, washing a white Prius. Something about him looked familiar, but he couldn't place him. He'd gotten to the age where a lot of faces blended together—one guy in church looked a lot like another guy he'd run in on a D&D. "Devin here?" Whaley called.

"Inside." The man glanced up, doing a double-take at Whaley's nose. Suddenly Whaley recognized him. No longer redheaded and wearing a security guard's uniform, but a balding, white-haired guy and a blue Carolina T-shirt. "Lawrence Russell?"

He gave a sheepish nod.

"Come with me." Whaley held up his badge. "You and me and McConnell need to have a little chat."

Reluctantly, Russell turned off his hose and trudged toward the office. Whaley followed him, his hand resting on his service weapon. Russell he'd always pegged for industrial-strength stupid. McConnell was the true loose cannon.

Russell opened the door, Whaley behind him. The interior of the office was dim, paneled in dark fake wood that held the stink of old cigarette smoke. Devin McConnell was sitting at a desk, sighting down the barrel of a Ruger 10/22, gun oil and a rag in hand.

"You get that Prius washed?" he asked, without looking up.

"He got interrupted," Whaley said before Butch could answer.

Devin sat up straighter, his wandering eye veering over Whaley's left shoulder. "Oh," he said, rosy spots blooming in his pale cheeks. "You."

"Yeah, me. I was expecting you a couple of days ago, down at the jail." With the flat of his hand he cuffed Butch on the back of his head. "You, too, Captain Jinks. Or didn't your mommy give you the message?"

"She gave it to me, but I've been busy," Butch said. "I saw you looking in my room without a warrant."

"I didn't need one. The high priestess of Cosmic Vibrations practically dragged me in there." He frowned at Butch. "You know, Einstein, if you've got something to hide, you need to tell your mother not to invite cops into your crib. That just ain't smart."

"Then that should tell you that I've got nothing to hide," Butch replied.

"Yeah, well, we'll see." Whaley turned to McConnell. "What's your excuse, McConnell? You said you'd be down at the jail just as soon as you could. You were so sweet on the phone, butter wouldn't melt in your mouth."

"I got busy, too," said McConnell. "Then I forgot."

Whaley walked over and picked up McConnell's rifle. "Well, I guess we'll just have to figure out a way to put DNA at the top of your to-do list." He raised the gun and drew a bead on Butch's head. "What would work for you, Russell? Some overnights in jail? Away from Mommy?" He turned the gun on Devin. "Should I march you out in cuffs when you've got some customers in this shit hole you call a car lot?"

Devin glared at him, his bad eye going nuts. "We've got rights, Whaley. I've got a lawyer. He says until I'm charged with something, I don't have to give you guys squat."

"Your lawyer must have one of those online degrees, then," said Whaley. "If you're a suspect in the murder of a child, there's not a judge in North Carolina who wouldn't jump to sign a warrant for your DNA."

McConnell shrugged. "Show up with a warrant, and I'll come down there."

Whaley lowered the rifle. "Are you sure? If I have to go to Judge Wood for this, I'm pretty sure my pal Cooksey at the paper will get wind of it. Then you two will go from regular suspects to uncooperative suspects. Wonder how many of those crates you'll move off your lot after that?" He turned to Butch. "And you might get a job doing parking lot security at Walmart." He laughed. "They don't pay well, but all the fat, crazy freaks on YouTube shop there. You might have some fun."

Butch swallowed hard. "Don't give my name to the judge. I'll come down there."

Whaley turned back to McConnell. "How about you?"

McConnell shoved a clipboard across the desk. "I've got two cars coming in this afternoon. I'll be there tomorrow."

Whaley looked at a bill of sale from a car auction in north Georgia. For once, McConnell seemed to be telling the truth. "Okay," he said. "I'll give you a break. But if I come to work tomorrow and find that you haven't had your mouths wide open in that lab, I'll have a warrant with your names on it before lunch."

Both men remained silent. Whaley laid the rifle back on McConnell's desk. "You two need to realize that this time, we're clearing this case. Somebody is going to jail for Teresa Ewing's murder."

———————

Whaley walked out the door. Butch went to the window and watched as he got back in his Crown Vic and cruised slowly out of the lot. "He's just like a great white shark," he whispered.

"What did you say?" asked Devin.

"I said Whaley's like a great white shark. You know, like in *Jaws*. He just swims along, biding his time, and then chomp! Some poor bastard gets bitten in half."

"Shut up," said Devin, trying to put the scope back on his rifle. "Whaley's more like a great white idiot."

"I don't think so." Staring out the window, Butch stuffed his hands in the back pockets of his jeans. "He's gonna get us this time."

Dev tightened a screw on the rifle's scope. "They're just bluffing, Butch. Like always."

Butch turned. "Dev, I used to read forensic magazines at work. The science is light years past what it was back then. They can get DNA from half-eaten pizza crusts now."

"So?"

"They're going to get us. They've found something with our DNA on it."

"The fuck they have!" cried Dev. Suddenly he stood up and hurled the can of gun oil across the room. It splattered across a poster of Miss Monster Truck, a bikini-clad blonde who sucked one finger while straddling a giant tire. "They haven't found anything in twenty-five years, and they sure as hell aren't now!"

"Dev," Butch said softly. "You know what we did."

"Yeah, but they don't." Dev got up from and started walking around his desk, like a big dog on a short chain. "Anyway, I know something we can do to make sure they never know."

"What? Blow up the police station?"

"We double back, like a rabbit. Send them in a different direction, away from us."

"How?"

"Come up with a story. Cry, pretend that we've been tortured by our guilty consciences. We should have done this years ago, we'll say. But we were scared. We were kids. We didn't want to be snitches."

"And what do we tell them?" asked Butch.

"Do you remember what you told them before?"

"How could I not? I've only told it about five thousand times."

"We'll tell them exactly the same thing. Only we'll add a new part. A part we were too scared to tell before."

"And say what?"

"I don't know," said Devin, pacing faster. "Maybe we could pin it on Mr. 'Please Forgive Me' Adam. His life has been a whole lot cushier than ours since Teresa died."

"He's too smart, Dev. His parents would get him a good lawyer and get him off."

Dev kept circling the desk. "Then how about Two Toes?"

Butch shook his head. "I'm not messing with Two Toes. He's one sick fuck."

"Your mother pals around with him."

"My mother's as crazy as Two Toes. Why do you think I keep all those guns in my bedroom?"

"You know who that leaves, then," said Devin.

"Yeah." Butch gazed at the floor. "Zack."

Dev walked over, scooped up the can of gun oil, and glared at Butch. "Quit standing there, looking like such a sack of shit! Zack was always in on everything we did."

"I know."

"He didn't have to be," said Dev. "We didn't have a rope around his neck, dragging him along."

"But it wasn't like he had any say-so in anything," cried Butch. "He did stuff because we did stuff. He didn't know any better."

"Fuck that, Butch." Dev held the gun oil in his hand, staring at it. When he finally spoke, his voice was soft. "Anyway, what would it matter, in the long run?"

Butch frowned. "What do you mean?"

"He's got no life now, and none ahead of him. His mother's what—sixty? In ten years or so she'll be dead and he'll have to go into some home anyway."

"So you think we should put him in prison now?"

Dev brushed a shock of black hair from his forehead. "I'm saying it wouldn't be that big a deal. They'd put him in Naughton—that's a crazy house, not a prison. His mother could visit, but she wouldn't have to put up with the dumb fuck anymore. We'd be, like, doing her a favor."

"I don't know, Dev." Butch lowered his gaze to the floor. For a long moment, neither of them spoke, then Dev went over and put a hand on Butch's shoulder.

"Listen to me. We've got a chance to end this for good. Tomorrow, when we go to give DNA, we ask to give a statement. We don't lawyer up, we don't do anything except tell them what most of them already think anyway."

"That Zack did it?"

Dev nodded.

"What about Adam? He likes Zack."

"So what? It's our word against his. Maybe we can put Adam in it too."

Butch looked at him, tears making his blue eyes look even bluer. Dev squeezed his shoulder. "Buddy, it's a Get Out of Jail Free card. Nobody would ever whisper about us again. They'd give you your badge back. People would buy cars off this lot. Everybody would call us heroes. Men who finally had the courage to come forward and tell the truth."

Butch wiped his eyes. "Yeah, like we're real heroes."

"Heroes take chances," said Dev. "If we don't take this chance, Teresa Ewing's going to haunt us for the rest of our lives."

Butch's chin quivered. For a moment he said nothing, then he said, "I don't know, Dev. It seems awfully risky."

"Grab a chair, Butch. We'll sit down and see what we come up with. If it's no good, then we'll forget all about it."

"No shit?" Butch sounded about ten years old.

"No shit, buddy." Dev slapped him on the back. "Come on. Let's get busy."

SEVENTEEN

GRATEFUL THAT THE DNA ordeal was over, Grace spent much of the day running errands with Zack. As they bought birdseed and turpentine, toilet paper and toothpaste, Zack strung more words together than he had in the past six months. The whole time he talked about Adam. He wanted to call Adam, he wanted to go swimming with Adam, he wanted to invite Adam over for dinner.

"I don't know his phone number," said Grace truthfully.

"292-3617," said Zack. "Butch is 297-2600. Devin is 292-4282."

As always, she was amazed at his memory. Phone numbers from his childhood, license plates on out-of-state cars he would see only once. It was a remarkable part of his brain. She used to think he might have a future in computers, back when she thought he had a future at all.

"Can I call him, Mama? Please?"

"Maybe when we get home." Again, she thought of the tall stranger. Once he'd hugged Zack, she recognized the boy inside the man—the up-turned, almost lupine eyes, the slightly nervous laugh, his wiry height. She wondered if Adam had ever gotten to play basketball in New York. He and Zack had shot hoops for hours, his adolescent voice cracking as he bragged that he was going to play for Dean Smith at Chapel Hill. If only he would come over and visit Zack, just once. It would mean so much to him.

Finally they headed home. She'd crested the hill before their house when she saw a small red car parked in front of their house. She frowned, growing tense. Strange cars on her street were never a good sign.

"Who's that?" Zack rolled down his window to get a better look.

"I don't know," she said, trying to keep her voice light.

She pulled up to the car. A sandy-haired man sat behind the wheel. Grace was about to ask if needed help when he pointed a camera at them. The flash went off like lightning, making them see stars. Her heart sank. A reporter. The second wave of Teresa Ewing invasion had arrived.

"Owww!" cried Zack. "All I can see is spots!"

"I know, honey. We need to go inside as fast as we can."

She sped forward, hoping to get the garage door up and then down before the reporter could catch them. But the young man was fast. He was on their tail, barreling up the drive right behind them. As the garage door opened to allow her SUV inside, the young man pulled up so close she didn't dare reclose the thing. Before she could unbuckle her seat belt, he was inside the garage, digital recorder in hand. She turned to Zack and handed him her Duke baseball cap, repeating the instructions Cecil Earp had given her so long ago.

"Put this on, Zack. Go inside. That man may yell questions at you, but don't answer him. Do not say a word."

"I can't see, Mama!" Zack fisted his hands, held them against his eyes.

"I know, honey. My eyes hurt too." *Dear God*, she thought, *all I need is for Zack to have a meltdown in front of the press.* "Look at me." She turned Zack's face toward hers, put a cool hand on his cheek. "If you stay quiet and go upstairs, I'll let you invite Adam to dinner."

"Really?"

She handed him her cell phone. "You have to go inside first."

He got out of the car. Pulling the cap low on his forehead, he walked with downcast eyes up the steps to the kitchen door, the reporter shouting questions at him.

"Hey, Zack, I hear you went downtown today. Did you give the police some DNA? How did that go? Did the cops ask you any questions? Did you see any of your old pals from Salola Street?"

Grace got out of the car. When the reporter realized he was getting nowhere with Zack, he turned to her.

"How about it, Mrs. Collier? Are you looking forward to your son being exonerated for Teresa Ewing's murder?"

Grace stopped at the top of the steps and turned to him. "The only thing I'm looking forward to is you getting off my property. I'm giving you ten seconds, then I'm calling the police."

"A lot of people think your son killed that little girl," he called. "You might generate some sympathy for him if you ... "

Grace went inside the kitchen and locked the door. She waited, listening. He called out a couple more questions, then a moment later she heard a car start. She went into the living room and watched as the red car backed out of the driveway and turned west, toward town.

"Round one to the Colliers," she whispered with a grim smile. She knew there would be more. This man would come back, or they would send other, more experienced reporters to badger them. They would accost her in the grocery store, wait for her at work, snap

148

photos of Zack through their privacy fence. She guessed it sold a lot of papers for them. All she knew was that it frightened her son and made his already small world even smaller.

––––––––––

Zack had Adam on the phone two minutes after the reporter had pulled out of the drive. To Grace's astonishment, Adam accepted Zack's invitation. Her son put the phone to his chest and asked, "What time should he come, Mama?"

"Seven o'clock," Grace replied. "And tell him if he wants beer or wine, he'll have to bring it."

Zack relayed her message to Adam, then clicked off the phone. "He's coming," he said, jumping up and down. "And he's bringing some beer."

"Then we'll have to hurry and get ready," said Grace. "You go sweep the patio and I'll think of something we can have to eat."

Zack hurried outside while Grace inventoried the kitchen. Normally she didn't keep much food in the house—she'd come home too many times to find that Zack had eaten the cabinets bare. Still, she had flour and yeast, tomato sauce and cheese. They could add some green peppers from the garden and some sausage from the freezer and have a pretty decent pizza. She was good at pizza. It had been one of Mike's favorite meals.

She mixed up the dough and went outside to pick some ripe peppers. As she walked between the rows in her garden, she peered through the fence, half-expecting someone to be pointing a camera at her. She didn't see anyone, but she knew eventually, they would come. They always did.

By seven she'd chopped her peppers and punched down the dough. Zack had set the table, and was watching a tape—some unknown family having a pool party, singing "Happy Birthday" to a little boy named Landon. Zack was enthralled, but when the digital clock over the TV read 7:15, he came into the kitchen.

"Where's Adam, Mama?"

"He'll be here, honey. People don't usually come at the exact minute."

He went back to his video, returning to the kitchen at 7:25. "He's still not here, Mama."

"I'm sure he's just running late, Zack. Go watch your video a little longer." She rolled out two large circles of pizza dough, now beginning to keep an eye on the clock herself. 7:30, then 7:35. Where was Adam? Had he decided not to come? Had Richard Shaw forbidden him to come?

"Don't be stupid," she told herself, working the dough to the edges of the pans. "Adam's a grown man. He can go where he pleases." Still, she worried. Had he gotten a better offer? A date with some girl? She wouldn't blame him if he had, but Zack would be crushed. He would cry for days.

She heard the recliner squeak in the den, then Zack came in again. "It's 7:45, Mama."

"I know, Zack." She wiped her hands on her apron. "Why don't you give Adam another call? Find out what's up."

She knew that was risky; if Adam didn't answer, or if Adam blew Zack off with some excuse, she could forget about pizzas. The rest of her night would be spent keeping Zack from punching new holes in the walls. She held her breath as he made the call, then she heard a car pull in the driveway. She looked out the window, half expecting the reporter, but a white Toyota pulled up. As she watched, Adam emerged, a grocery sack in his arms.

"Never mind, Zack," she called, weak with relief. "He's here."

———————

Adam came in full of apology for being late. "I would have been on time," he said, putting the beer in her refrigerator. "But my dad tripped over an old weed eater and sprained his ankle."

"That's too bad," said Grace.

Adam shrugged. "It's not serious, but it'll slow the move down a lot."

"How long will you be at your mom's?" Zack asked.

"Don't know, buddy," said Adam. "But we can hang out when I'm not helping at home."

"All right!" Beaming, Zack gave Adam a high five. "Just like we used to."

"Yeah." Adam gave a wistful smile. "Just like we used to."

———————

Grace put the pizzas in the oven while Adam and Zack tossed a salad. They lit citronella candles and dined on the patio. Zack still ate as he had when he was twelve, filling his plate with more pizza than salad, stretching the stringy cheese out from his mouth like a tightrope. Adam ate like a New Yorker—folding the slice into a wedge, and eating in neat, quick bites. "This is really good," he said.

She laughed. "Even by New York standards?"

"Actually, by Brooklyn standards. The best pie men live in Brooklyn."

"I know you're a photographer, but what exactly do you take pictures of?" asked Grace.

"I'm what they call a trek photographer. I go on expeditions and safaris. Mostly with spoiled rich people, but sometimes on scientific expeditions."

"That's incredible, Adam," said Grace. "Have you done anything Zack and I might have seen?"

He named a couple of outdoor magazines. "When I'm not shooting CEOs overcoming hypoxia, I've gotten some pretty incredible still shots. The aurora in Iceland, the moon coming up over K2."

Grace laughed. "I guess Pisgah County feels pretty sedate, compare to all that."

He gazed at the bubbles rising in his beer. "I don't know that I'd ever call Pisgah County sedate."

"I guess not," she said. "Salola Street sure looks like a war zone."

"Feels like one, too," he said.

"Oh?" She sensed that he wanted to say more, but Zack suddenly rose from the table. "I'm gonna go watch a video," he announced.

Adam looked up. "My mom says you bought some of our old ones."

"With all my grass money," Zack said proudly. "Fifteen dollars."

"Are you watching any of ours now?"

"No. This is Landon's birthday party," said Zack. "Landon and Lydia."

"Friends of yours?" asked Adam.

"No. Just people."

"Maybe I'll come over and watch some of our old ones with you, sometime."

"Awesome," said Zack, shuffling back inside the house.

Grace watched her son walk through the kitchen and turn on the TV in the den. "I guess you can see not much has changed here."

He took another sip of beer. "I went to see Butch and Devin today."

"Really." She checked to make sure Zack was out of earshot. "I heard Butch works security at the college, but I never see him."

"He just got fired. Devin scrapes by with his dad's used car lot." He looked at her, his eyes serious. "Teresa Ewing has turned them into very bitter men."

"I can see why they might be."

"They hate my guts for leaving. They hate—"

Suddenly they heard a *whirr* and a *click*, from the other side of the fence. Adam turned toward the noise, then jumped up to stand between Grace and the fence.

"Get back inside," he said softly. "There's a photographer over there."

"Where?"

"Behind me, shooting through the fence. I'd know the sound of a shutter snapping anywhere."

She hurried to the kitchen, Adam behind her. When they were safely inside, he locked the door and pulled down the shade. "In New York getting your picture in the paper is a big deal. Not quite the same here."

"Welcome home," said Grace. She went to the living room window, Adam following. They saw nothing beyond fireflies, but a moment later they heard a car drive off in the difference.

"And so it begins again," said Grace wearily.

Adam looked at her. "What?"

"The whispers, the pointing. Reporters hounding us. People driving by, gawking at the house. I just hope that's all it is."

"What do you mean, *all*?"

She put her palm against the cool glass of the window. "The last time I had to replace this window twice. I had a rattlesnake in my mailbox and I had to pay two hundred dollars to have the word *maniac* sandblasted off the driveway." She gave a bitter smile as Zack laughed loudly from the den. "I truly believe that if certain people ever caught my son out by himself, they would kill him."

"That's a shitty way to live," said Adam.

"Yeah, it is."

He stood straighter, suddenly full of new energy. "Look, I can help you with this. Secure your place a lot better than it is now. How about I come over first thing tomorrow?"

"Thanks, but you've got to help your own family."

"No, I want to." He ran a hand through his hair, the same gesture he'd made when he was twelve. "I feel like I need to, I don't know, make it up to you."

"But you don't owe us anything."

"I owe all of you something," he said. "For once, I need to be a part of this."

EIGHTEEN

WHILE ADAM SHAW WAS bidding Zack and Grace good-bye, Mary Crow was sitting at her kitchen table, poring over the old newspaper articles she'd printed a few hours earlier. In 1989 the paper had been photographed a page at a time, so reading the Teresa Ewing stories was like opening a time capsule. Tiananmen Square was the news of the day, along with a new cartoon show called *The Simpsons* and rock group named Milli Vanilli. Mary smiled, remembering how she'd loved Bart Simpson, then she turned to a picture spread on Teresa Ewing's murder. The paper showed pictures of the house, a diagram of Teresa's last movements, then several photos of Teresa— costumed as an orphan in a production of *Annie*, dressed in a junior cheerleading outfit, and the last school photo of her ever taken. Though the little girl was pretty, with dark curls framing a pale, heart-shaped face, what caught Mary's attention was her eyes. They conveyed a look both of promise and daring—a wink without winking. Mary had seen that look before, but usually in women far older than ten.

She scanned the article for quotes about the girl. Her teacher called her *imaginative* and said that she'd wanted to be an actress. "She was a lot of fun to be with," said a classmate named Ben. The principal of her school said she was full of life, and everybody liked her. "Boys and girls both," he added.

And yet somebody had bashed in Teresa Ewing's skull, and all that life and brightness along with it. It was beyond awful, the murder of a child.

Mary stared at the article, surprised at the depth of her own reaction. She'd prosecuted a boatload of homicides in her career, had seen the horrors that occasionally touched children. Yet something about Teresa Ewing tweaked a different chord inside her. She was trying to figure out what it was when the ringing of her phone split the silence of the room. She jumped and grabbed it.

"Mary Crow."

"Mary? This is Emily." On the phone her campaign manager was as direct as she was in person.

"Hey, Emily. Did you see all the signs in HairTwister's today?"

"They look great, but that's not why I called. I've got to tell you, Mary, I'm a little stunned."

"Stunned?" Mary wondered if she'd heard the woman correctly. What had she done to stun Emily Kurtz? Her big adventure for the day was giving Buck Whaley a nosebleed.

"I understand that you're representing Zack Collier in the Teresa Ewing murder case."

Mary had been half expecting this call, but she was still curious how the news had gotten out. "Where did you hear that?"

"From Harvey Pugh, Turpin's campaign manager. He could barely talk for laughing."

Mary remembered her earlier encounter with Turpin and Pugh. That must have been why they both looked like two fat cats who'd just chomped a canary. "Well, Harvey got it right. I'm representing the Collier boy."

"Seriously?" Emily's tone was acid.

"Yes."

"Mary, you're running for DA—to prosecute crime. How can you possibly square that with defending someone accused of the most infamous murder in the county?"

"Zack hasn't been accused of anything, Emily. He's only a suspect, one who's cooperating fully with the investigation. I wouldn't be much of a lawyer if I couldn't handle that."

"But don't you see how bad this will look? Pugh was practically orgasmic over this."

Mary shuddered at the image of Harvey Pugh having a sexual release. "Look, Zack Collier's entitled to the best representation he can muster. And don't forget that his mother designed every bit of our campaign publicity. What was I supposed to say when she called? 'Sorry, Grace, it won't look good if I represent your son'?"

"But couldn't you have gotten her another lawyer? David Loveman or Julie Burkhart?"

"Grace couldn't afford them. She would have been at the mercy of the public defender's office. This is no case for a kid just out of law school."

"But what if you win the election? Could you indict a former client?"

"If I were the DA and had a case, I could and would. Then I would recuse myself. Change the venue to Asheville or Charlotte, where another prosecutor would take over."

Emily sighed. "Look—I know how much we owe Grace. She was on board with us from the get-go. And I admire your loyalty. But you've got a real shot at this office, Mary. I'd hate to see you blow it by getting sucked into the Teresa Ewing quagmire."

"I realize that. But it's just not in me to leave Grace in the lurch. Anyway, I'm going to take a new tack in this case."

"Then please tell me you're getting a co-counsel. Couldn't your partner, Ravenel, step up?"

"No. Ravenel only defends things with feathers and fur. Listen, I've just read every shred ever written about Teresa Ewing. I think if I dig deep enough, I can figure out who killed that girl."

There was a long silence, then Emily spoke gently, as if she were addressing someone delusional. "Mary. Do you realize how crazy that sounds? People have been trying to solve this case for twenty years."

"But this is the first time I've ever looked at it," Mary replied. "Sometimes a cold case needs a new pair of eyes."

————

They went a few more rounds, then Emily clicked off in a huff. Mary stared at the phone, wondering if she'd just had the briefest political career in the history of North Carolina. She understood Emily's position, but she also knew she couldn't just drop Grace and Zack to better her chances at George Turpin's job. That wasn't what Judge Irene Hannah had taught her. She took another look at her Teresa Ewing notes, then she went into the kitchen and uncorked a bottle of Malbec. Maybe the Chilean grapes grown in 2009 might lighten her mood. She was letting the bottle breathe when her doorbell rang, loud and somehow angry sounding.

"Oh God," she whispered, wondering if Emily Kurtz had driven over to harangue her further. But when she checked the peephole, she saw Victor standing there in his soccer uniform, a white 1 emblazoned on his red jersey. She opened the door.

"Hey!" she said, standing on tiptoe to kiss him.

"Where were you?" He marched past her into the living room. Though he was fully dressed for soccer, he'd taken his cleats off and was pattering around in flip-flops.

"Here," she said, puzzled. "Where was I supposed to be?"

"My game?"

She looked at him, his black hair still wet with sweat, his face splotchy red with either exertion or anger. Then she remembered. Tonight was his big game. His club, the Rangers, were playing their arch rivals, the Growlers. She was supposed to have met him there.

"Oh Victor, I'm so sorry," she said. "I came home and got involved in something else. I just totally lost track of the time." Somehow that sounded better, she decided, than telling him she just forgot.

He let fly a stream of angry Spanish, then switched to English. "What other thing did you get involved with? I was going to introduce you to my friends. Everyone was going to McDougal's after the game."

"A murder," she replied, irritated by his anger. She'd never missed any of his games before. "And speak English. Don't go all Ricky Ricardo on me."

"What murder?"

"Teresa Ewing."

He frowned. "What do you have to do with that?"

159

"I'm representing one of the boys who was, and apparently still is, a suspect."

"But I thought you were working on an estate. And running for DA."

"I'm doing that too."

"No wonder you forgot something as silly as a football game."

"I'm sorry," she apologized again. "I meant to come; I just got involved in the old newspaper articles."

He walked over to the dining room table and looked at the stack of old clippings. "So who are you representing?"

There was no point to keep secret what everybody else in Hartsville knew. "Zack Collier. The autistic man Whaley likes."

Victor stared at the papers for a long moment, then turned to her, his expression unreadable. "You looked at my files, didn't you? The other morning when I was taking a shower."

Mary swallowed hard. She was guilty—he'd caught her in her one small transgression. "I just wondered if DNA reports had gotten any more comprehensible than when I was working your side of the aisle. That was the only thing I looked at."

"Then how do you know who Whaley suspects?"

"Because I've talked to Zack Collier's mother. Whaley's harassed that boy for years. Plus I saw Whaley down at the police station today, when Zack gave his DNA. He was practically salivating."

"But you looked at my case files," Victor repeated, paling beneath his tan. "Do you know how much trouble that could get me in?"

"Zack Collier wasn't my client then, Victor. He wasn't my client until later that day, when Grace called me. I haven't been at your apartment since then. And I certainly wouldn't look at your case files now."

"But we talked about that case. You asked me about going to Winston-Salem. I told you about the underpants the dog dug out from under the tree."

"I remember you talking about the old detective," said Mary. "You told me Cochran wondered if he'd planted those underpants."

He looked at her as if he'd caught her naked with another man.

"Victor, I haven't done anything unethical here," she cried. "Just peeked at a few incomprehensible DNA panels. I have no inside information on what you might have against Zack Collier. I didn't even know who Zack Collier was at the time."

He said nothing.

She lifted the stack of papers. "These clips from the morgue have told me far more than your DNA report. Whaley liked Collier. Logan arrested the kid, only to have Cecil Earp blow that up in court. It was a circus!"

He looked at her another moment, then shook his head. "I can't believe you read my files," he said softly. "You, of all people."

"What do you mean by that?"

"Because I thought if you were anything, you were honest."

"Victor, I am honest. If I weren't, I wouldn't be telling you this now. I would have kept quiet or said, 'Why no, Victor, I didn't look in your files.' And then I would have made love to you like crazy just to make sure you forgot all about it. *That's* dishonesty. What I did was just nosy. Go to the law board with a complaint if you want."

He shrugged, the big white 1 on his jersey suddenly looking alone and forlorn. "I don't want to go to the law board. I want to go home."

He walked toward the door. Mary dropped her clippings and hurried after him. "Seriously, Victor? You're leaving over this?"

"Yes," he said as he opened the door. "I guess I am." He gave her a brief smile, then he was gone, his flip-flops tapping angrily as he walked away.

NINETEEN

ADAM LEFT THE DINNER party earlier than he'd planned. He'd hoped to coax Zack into watching some of his old home videos, but Grace had been adamant about getting her son to bed by ten. "It's our routine," she'd explained, as she pulled Zack away from the birthday party video to give him three big pills and a glass of chocolate milk. "He goes to sleep early, and I get a couple of hours to myself. At seven tomorrow morning, it all begins again."

Wonder how she stands it? he thought as he drove home, the headlights of his car slicing through the darkness. The same schedule, every day, year in year out. No trips, no time off, not even much company, judging by the dust on their beer glasses and her frantic search for a bottle opener. Just Zack's caregiver and regular visits from Detective Whale-Ass.

"I couldn't do it," he whispered in admiration. He needed movement, new people and places, the feeling that he was reaching for something just beyond his grasp. He doubted he could last a day in Zackworld.

And yet he needed to visit Zackworld regularly, at least until he could get his videos back. Zack had purchased pieces of his childhood that he wasn't willing to give up—certainly not to a man entranced by the birthday partying of children he'd never met.

He turned onto Salola Street, then into his driveway. Nobody much had ever waited up for him—in New York his Aunt Jean had gone to bed early, and nobody gave a shit about him at boarding school. Yet tonight a light burned in their kitchen. His mother, no doubt. Pouring all of her stored-up maternal emotions over him as if he were sixteen instead of thirty-nine. He parked the car and let himself in the back door. As he guessed, Leslie Shaw was sitting at the kitchen table in a pink bathrobe, polishing off a bottle of Zinfandel as she squinted at a crossword puzzle.

"Hey, sweetheart." She looked up, bleary-eyed. "How was Zack's?"

He shrugged. "Funny. Pathetic. A lot of things."

"Did you get your tapes?"

"No. Zack had thrown them in a big box with about a hundred others. He was too caught up in some kid's birthday party. Grace says he can watch the same tape for weeks at a time."

She tilted her head, as if she'd misheard him. "Grace says?"

"Yeah, Mom. Grace. Zack's mother."

"When did you start calling her Grace?"

"Tonight. What was I supposed to do? Go over there and say 'Please, Mrs. Collier, may I have some milk with my cookies?'"

"Of course not." Flustered, she took a swallow of wine. "I'm sorry. I guess I still think of you as a little boy."

"Whatever." He opened the refrigerator and looked for another beer. "How's Dad's ankle?"

"Hurting. He's in bed, icing it. You won't forget about the shed, will you? He's depending on you to clean it out."

"First thing tomorrow." He opened an IPA as his mother rose from the table.

"I'm going on to bed," she said, lurching over to give him a hug. "It was good of you to visit Zack. You're kinder than I am."

"I hope it's less weird the next time," he said.

She stifled a burp. "You're going back over there?"

"I want those tapes, Mom. They're important to me."

"I'm so sorry I sold them. I can still call and explain that it was a mistake."

"No, I can take care of this."

"You be careful with those people, Adam," she warned. "I know you like them, but I think they're trouble."

He leaned against the kitchen sink as his mother shuffled down the hall. The sound of a late-night talk show briefly reached his ears as she opened her bedroom door, then the door closed and silence returned. As he sipped his beer his thoughts returned to Grace Collier. He'd had a monstrous crush on her the summer before Teresa died. One afternoon he'd cut through the woods in back of the Collier house and seen Grace swimming naked in their pool. Zack, he guessed, had gone somewhere with his father. With his heart thudding he'd dropped to the ground and slithered behind a tree. Through the branches he'd watched Grace dive cleanly into the deep end of the pool. Half a minute later she emerged from the shallow end, sleek as a seal, her light brown skin gleaming. Then she turned and he saw her in full—high, firm breasts, a flat stomach, a lush vee of dark pubic hair. It was the first time he'd ever seen a naked woman beyond the pages of a magazine. He'd felt the air go out of his lungs as his penis pressed into the ground so hard it hurt. A moment later he came in an expulsive rush that left him weak and shaking. Until that day, Grace had been nothing more than Zack's mother. From then on, she became something else entirely.

"And now I call her by her first name," he whispered, thinking of how many times he'd replayed that swimming pool scene in his head—at his aunt's house when he was scared, at boarding school when he was lonely. Even today, when he was between women in New York or sharing a tent with some rich old farts, Grace Collier was the default lover of his dreams.

"You're really fucked up," he said as he finished his beer. "But so is everybody else here on Salola Street."

———

Adam woke up early, jarred to consciousness by the roar of construction equipment. He pulled the bedcovers over his head and tried to go back to sleep, but it was pointless. The grinding roars and shrill beepings went on unabated. He got up and pulled on his jeans, headed for the kitchen. He couldn't imagine how his parents slept through all the racket, but when he passed their bedroom, their door was still shut.

He poured a cup of coffee and gazed out the kitchen window. He could see the crown of the old oak tree as it presided over the mayhem below. On the other side of Butch's house, a bulldozer was about to shove a mound of dirt out of the way. Two men in white hard hats watched, studying the blueprint rolled out between them. Soon those same bulldozers would come over here and start leveling this place. The thought of it made him smile.

He ate a bowl of cereal, grabbed a plastic trash bag, and walked to the shed through dew-slickened grass. He was glad to be assigned this task alone. The shed had been his refuge when he was a kid, and he wanted to dismember it slowly savoring what memories he had.

It stood at the back corner of the lot, under the shade of a tulip tree, now nearly consumed by wild honeysuckle and Virginia creeper. It had been a potting shed, built by the original owners of the house. His family had used it as a storehouse for various items—toys that he and Mark had lost interest in, sleds awaiting snowfalls, his father's huge, state-of-the-art wheelbarrow. As he neared adolescence he'd claimed the shed for himself, setting up his camera there and using it as a set for his movies—an ersatz log cabin where he and Devin fought off marauding Cherokees (Butch and Zack), then a Transylvania hut where Teresa and Shannon fled screaming from Zack, who was supposed to be Dracula, but who acted more like Frankenstein, chasing them with stiff, outstretched arms while he growled like a dog.

Now he was amazed at how small the shed was. The brown paint had flaked off the clapboards years ago and its single window was covered in thick dust and spiderwebs. Climbing steps that felt spongy with rot, he turned the white metal knob and pushed open the door. The dank smell of mildew engulfed him like sour breath. He stepped inside, stomping his feet, in case any snakes had taken up residence. When nothing slithered away, he moved to the center of the dim space and looked around. The huge old wheelbarrow stood in one corner holding a flat basketball, a dog bed their old Lab Izzy had used, and a couple of tennis racquets with broken strings. To the right of the wheelbarrow were three dates scrawled on the wall in white chalk. *Cdt. Hartley, 2-15-89, Cdt. Boyer, 2-24-89, Cdt. Hartley, 3-1-89.* As he gazed at the scribblings, the hair lifted on the back of his neck. Those were the dates the police had searched in here, looking for Teresa.

"Cadets," he whispered, remembering how they'd turned out everybody who'd ever worn or hoped to wear any kind of public servant's uniform. "Cadets from the police academy searched this shed three times."

He stared at the notations a moment, remembering how scared he'd been back then, how even though he hadn't wanted to leave, he was secretly glad that morning when his father turned toward the airport instead of his school. "If I had a kid, I'd do exactly the same thing," he whispered. "Nobody deserves to be bullied like that."

He stepped over and with the side of his hand, wiped the chalk marks off the wall. Even though the shed would be kindling in a few weeks, he wanted those marks gone forever.

After that, he opened a plastic trash bag and began taking stuff off the shelf that ran along one wall. He dumped in a petrified box of Miracle-Gro, an old can of white enamel, a glass jar full of old fuses. He was working his way down the shelf, dumping everything in the bag when his fingers curled around a dog-eared paperback. *Cupid's Arrow*, read the title, above a picture of a man and a women in bed. *An Illustrated Guide to Sexual Pleasure.*

A curious thrill went through him, as if he'd run into an old friend at some foreign airport. He opened the book, finding the photographs of the naked man and woman who'd instructed him—who'd instructed all of them—in their youth. He saw that the man's penis, which at the time had seemed impossibly large, was now not much bigger than his own. The woman had dark nipples, big as silver dollars. She reminded him of a translator he'd once slept with in Nepal.

He flipped through the book as they'd done so long ago, marveling at all the positions—the man doing it doggie-style, the woman with her feet waving over the man's shoulders, and most eye-popping of all, the woman sucking the man's penis while he tongued her twat. Somebody (the printing looked like Shannon's round, girlish hand) had drawn all through the book, pointing arrows at the models in the most amazing positions, giving them the initials of people they knew. AS + JM—that would be he and Jennie Mason. DM + MCF was Devin and Mary Catherine Frensley, a girl he claimed to hate. BR (Butch) had TE (Teresa Ewing) sitting in lap, his hands on her breasts. Only someone had later added *NO!!!!! HE'S TOO FAT!!!!* in bright pink marker.

"Those cadets really fucked up," he whispered, "if they searched this place three times and didn't find this."

He started to toss the book in the trash bag, but stopped. If that prick reporter was snapping shots through Zack's fence, what would keep him from going through their trash? The whole county would go crazy if a sex manual with Teresa Ewing's initials in it surfaced now.

He brushed the dust from the little book and put it in the back pocket of his jeans. He could take it up to the house and when his parents went out, burn it in the fireplace.

"Or I could do something else," he said aloud, taking the book from his pocket and smiling at the photographs they'd found so fascinating. "I could keep it. Maybe show certain pages to Butch and Dev. Let them know I've leveled the playing field a little bit."

TWENTY

"ARE YOU SURE YOU won't need me to come and get you?" Ginger Cochran asked as she pulled up in front of the Justice Center. She wore a big shirt and horn-rimmed glasses and her red hair was gathered in a ponytail, high on the back of her head. It was a bookwormish schoolgirl look that Cochran found incredibly sexy.

"No, I can get a lift over to the garage." Jerry turned to smile at Chloe, who sat in her car seat, chewing a teething biscuit. "What are you two up to today?"

"Chloe's going to Mommy's Day Out," said Ginger.

"What's Mommy going to do?"

Ginger smiled at him over her glasses. "You won't like it."

"You're getting a tattoo."

"No."

"Your nose pierced?"

"No."

"Then it must have something to do with Mary's campaign."

"Bingo," cried Ginger. "You're not the sheriff for nothing!"

170

Cochran sighed. Officially, he was supposed to have no opinion in elections—certainly no opinion in a race that would affect his office so profoundly. And though he had not publicly expressed his views at all, he could not say the same of his wife. She had been Mary's fiercest supporter since the get-go—making calls, raising money, advising Mary on what to say to the press. Though Ginger had tried to be discreet, her actions would likely turn his already cool relations with Turpin into permafrost if the man remained in office.

He looked at her. "If you really want to help Mary, go down to the paper and tell them to stop those newsfeeds about the Ewing case. They aren't making my job any easier, and Turpin's going to start calling her out for defending that Collier kid."

"I can't make a miracle, sweetheart. The *Herald*'s box sales are up and their website traffic's through the roof." She reached over and ran her fingers through the hair on the left side of his head. "You've got a gray hair!"

He looked in the rearview mirror. "I'm surprised I don't have more between you, Chloe, and this Teresa Ewing stuff."

"Poor baby," said Ginger. "Come home early tonight. We'll put Chloe to bed and I'll give you a massage."

Smiling at the prospect, he kissed Ginger good-bye, then leaned back to nuzzle Chloe's bare foot. "See you two girls later."

He got out of the car and watched them drive away. In that moment he was a happy man; happy that they were his, happy that at the end of the day, he would return to them. Whistling, he started walking toward the side door of the Justice Center when he heard someone call him.

"Sheriff!"

He looked around to see Louise, his new secretary, bustling out the front door. "Hey, Louise." He noticed a rare look of excitement on her long, slightly horselike face. "What's up? Somebody set off the smoke alarm in the jail?"

"I was going to text you, but I saw Ginger pull up," she said, breathless. "One of those boys—those men—who came to give DNA in the Teresa Ewing case, wants to make a statement."

"Which one?"

"Devin McConnell," she said. "And he'll only talk to you."

———————

Ten minutes later, Cochran entered the interview room that held Devin McConnell. Though he and Devin were close to the same age, he had seemed younger. He'd dressed up, misbuttoning a white dress shirt and crookedly knotting a green tie. He reminded Cochran of a kid sent to the principal's office, waiting to plead his case.

"Mr. McConnell?" Cochran nodded. "You wanted to talk to me."

"Yeah," he said, working a piece of gum double-time.

"Have you today been advised of your rights?"

"I signed the paper."

"Do you want an attorney? We can get you one if you can't afford one."

"I don't need a lawyer. I—I just need to put an end to this."

"An end to what?"

"Teresa Ewing."

"Okay." Cochran turned and nodded at a camera in the corner of the room, giving the signal to start the machine rolling. "Just so you'll know, we're recording this."

He shrugged. "I figured as much."

"So what do you want to tell me?"

"I, uh, I—" Devin coughed, his forehead shiny with sweat. "I want to clear something up. Something that happened a long time ago."

"Okay."

"That last afternoon—that last afternoon that Teresa was alive—Butch Russell and I saw something."

Cochran opened the file. "And what was that?"

"Well…" Devin continued to fidget in his chair. "We'd been playing. I'd borrowed some marked cards from my brother. We were trying to get the girls to play Bottom Up, but we pissed them off and they went home all mad. Then Two Toes McCoy appeared."

Cochran looked up. "Appeared?"

Devin shook his head. "I don't where he came from. We just looked up, and there he stood. Mad as hell."

"What about?"

"I don't know. He started giving us a lot of grief about the tree … that it was holy to his people, and not a place for little white boys to play cards. He pulled out a knife." Devin brushed his hair back and gave a weak laugh. "It seems pretty lame now. But back then, I was scared. I thought he might cut us up."

"Go on," said Cochran.

"Well, anyway, Two Toes threw his knife at the tree. It landed right over Zack's head. We all just took off running. Everybody went home as fast as they could. I didn't realize until later that I'd left my gym lock behind."

"Your gym lock?"

"Yeah. We had to clean out our lockers every Tuesday night and leave them open for inspection. If you didn't have your lock the next day, you'd be in trouble." He sighed. "Junior high is just so fucking stupid, you know?"

Cochran grunted, thinking of his own miserable days in seventh-grade gym.

"Anyway, I had to get that lock. I didn't want to go back to the tree by myself, so I called up Butch to come with me. He didn't want to go either, but I made him."

"How much time had passed when you decided this?"

"I don't know—maybe half an hour."

"And how did you make Butch go with you?"

"I told him he had to. You know, we were tight—better friends than with Adam or Zack." Devin cleared his throat. "It was almost suppertime, so we both hurried out of our houses and sneaked back up to the tree, in case Two Toes was still there."

"Then what?"

"We got to the opposite side of the tree and dropped down to the ground. We heard a noise, like something hitting the ground really hard. I thought maybe something had fallen out of the tree. A second later, I heard someone crying. I knew that wasn't Two Toes, so I looked around the tree." He looked at Cochran and swallowed hard. "I saw somebody tall, carrying Teresa over his shoulder."

"How tall?"

"I don't know—not Michael Jordan tall, but taller than Butch and me."

"How was this tall person dressed?"

"Jeans, and a dark sweatshirt with the hood pulled up."

"Who was crying? Teresa or the person carrying her?"

"I don't know. I guess it was more like a whimper than a cry."

"Was the hooded person a man or a woman?"

"I thought it was a man. It looked too big to be a woman."

"Were they white? Black? Cherokee?"

"I couldn't tell. It was almost dark and honestly, I was looking more at Teresa."

Cochran didn't blink. "Where did this person appear to be going?"

"Toward Zack's house."

"Did Teresa look conscious?"

Devin shook his head again. "Teresa looked dead."

"What did you do then?"

"I ran the hell home. So did Butch."

"What about your gym lock?"

Devin looked surprised at the question, then shrugged. "I forgot all about it. Nobody gave a shit about the gym lock after that, anyway. Everybody was too busy looking for Teresa."

For a while Cochran studied his notes. Then he said, "You know, Mr. McConnell, you could have saved the police a lot of time if you'd included this in your original statement."

Devin's bad eye rolled toward the ceiling. "I know I should have. But I was scared shitless."

"Of what?"

"Of being a snitch, of getting in deeper than I already was. Everybody had gone crazy. Cops were questioning us night and day, my old man was beating the crap out of me, people were saying we'd gang-raped and killed her. Hell, I wasn't even sure of what I'd seen. For a long time, I thought maybe I'd dreamed it."

"But now, suddenly you're sure?"

"I'm sure I saw a tall person in a hooded sweatshirt carry that girl off. I'm sure I heard someone crying. I'm sure Butch Russell saw and heard the same thing I did."

"But not Adam Shaw?"

"If Adam Shaw was there, I didn't see him."

"And you didn't actually see anyone kill Teresa Ewing?"

175

"No. But someone who looked was as tall as Zack found her and carried toward his house."

"Why do you think he would do that?"

"Because he's Zack," said Devin. "Because he wouldn't have known what else to do."

TWENTY-ONE

JACK WILKINS WAS SITTING at the counter of the Waffle House when his pal Irving slid onto the stool next to him.

"I see you're back to your usual today." Irving glanced at Jack's half-eaten hamburger and French fries. "Loading up for the Geezer Invitational?"

"Not this year. How about you?"

"Playing partners with Ray Mears. How come you're sitting out?"

"Too many chores at home," said Jack, "with the new dog and the chickens."

"Aw, tell him the real reason, Chief." Linda came by and poured Irving a cup of coffee.

"What?" Irving blinked at the two of them through his thick glasses.

"Haven't you heard the news?" Linda reached for the paper that someone had left on the counter. "Chief's cold case has just gotten hot. He's the man!"

Jack glanced again at the paper he'd already read twice. The headline trumpeted—Teresa Ewing Murder Reopened. A reporter named John Cooksey rehashed the case, complete with old pictures of him and Buck Whaley—both of them looking earnest, determined, and incredibly young. He flinched at the bushy blond sideburns he'd worn back then. He'd thought they looked dashing, but really they just looked silly. How kind Jan had been not to mention it.

Irving pushed his glasses up on his nose and devoured the story. "They've really got new suspects? After all this time?"

"They just found some new evidence," said Jack, trying to tamp down Irving's enthusiasm. "Same old suspects—only now they're men instead of boys."

"I remember that Salola Street gang," said Irving. "Crazy kids. One was, what, retarded?"

"Autistic, according to the paper," Linda chimed in. "They're the really odd ones. I've got one who comes in here with his family. Sits in that back booth, orders the same thing every time."

"Ha!" Irving poked Jack in the ribs. "A burger and fries?"

"As a matter of fact, yes. But the autistic kid goes crazy if it isn't *exactly* the way he wants it. Tomato on the plate instead of the bun, fries all lined up like logs. I'm telling you, those autistics look normal, but they're a few bricks shy of a load upstairs."

Jack suddenly thought of one of his chickens, Tallulah. The other hens considered her odd and had pecked her mercilessly, the dominant hen Sequoia leading the charge. Then one morning Tallulah got fed up. She flew at Sequoia like a rooster, feet forward, as if she had spurs. The two had quite a dustup, but afterward, none of the chickens ever messed with Tallulah again. Too bad that autistic kid couldn't beat up the people who talked about him.

"So, you think they'll get him this time?" asked Linda.

"Who?" Jack was still thinking about Tallulah.

"The retarded boy!"

"I don't know that he's guilty. I'm retired, remember? Right now I know as much about this case as you two." Which wasn't exactly true. He knew considerably more about this case, and kept checking his phone in hopes that young Sheriff Cochran or even Buck Whaley would call him and ask him to consult on it. But his phone had remained silent, except for this John Cooksey, who'd started pestering him yesterday.

"Well, it'll be interesting to see what happens," said Irving. "Personally, I never thought the retarded kid did it, anyway."

"You did the last time we talked about it," said Jack.

"No, I really always thought it was that Cherokee guy."

"Two Toes McCoy?"

"Yeah. He did yard work in that neighborhood. I think he was hanging around, saw the girl, and grabbed her."

"And then hid her for a month and brought her back?" Linda pursed her lips, skeptical.

"Sure," Irving insisted. "The Cherokees can hide anything they want to in these mountains."

Jack tucked back in to his hamburger, leaving Irving and Linda to debate the merits of Two Toes as the murderer. He'd just dipped his last French fry in his ketchup when his cell phone rang. He hoped it might be the sheriff, but John Cooksey's name appeared on the screen. Disappointed, he switched off the phone. He wasn't going to spin his wheels talking to some idiot reporter.

He finished his burger and got up from the stool, leaving eight dollars under his plate, the price of his meal and the two-dollar tip. "I'll see you guys later," he said. "I've got things to do."

"Let me know if you ever want to play golf again," Irving said, sounding wounded.

"I will." He clapped his friend on the shoulder. "Good luck in the tournament. Hope you take home the trophy."

He walked out into the parking lot, feeling as if he were in limbo. Before he'd gone over to that old tree, golf had been an enjoyable pastime—walking outdoors, navigating the perils of old age with his friends. Now trying to flail a tiny white ball into a distant hole seemed ridiculous, a waste of time insulting to the hours remaining in your life. Better to read. Better to watch his chickens. Better to figure out who killed that little girl.

He got in his truck. Lucky, who'd curled up in the passenger seat, woke up and wagged his tail. He gave the dog a pat as he turned on his engine. It was only when he'd pulled back out on to the highway that he realized the twitching had returned to both his thumbs.

————

He stopped at the hardware store to get a bag of chicken feed, then he headed home, Lucky leaning out the window, the wind blowing his ears back like furry brown wings. He turned into his driveway, ready to drive over to the chicken coop when he saw a black Miata parked in front of his house, the driver's door open.

"Cooksey," he whispered. "The little twerp must have found out where I live."

He drove slowly toward his house, wishing Lucky would leap out of the truck barking and snarling. But so far the dog had greeted everyone he'd met with wiggling delight. Jack doubted he would greet this Cooksey character any differently.

He pulled up beside the Mazda. "At least pretend to be a watchdog, Lucky," he told the dog as it jumped to the ground and ran over to the little sports car, his tail wagging.

Jack approached the car more slowly, waiting for the reporter to emerge and start peppering him with questions. Instead, a good-looking woman sat behind the wheel, her hair as black as the car. Cooksey must be taking a different tack, he decided. Sending one of his female cohorts to charm information out of him.

"Can I help you?" Jack asked neutrally.

"I'm trying to find Detective Jack Wilkins." The woman looked up from greeting Lucky. Her eyes were the kind of mottled hazel that could shift colors. Gray to green and even to gold, maybe.

"You found him."

She got out of her car. "My name is Mary Crow. I was wondering if you'd talk to me about the Teresa Ewing case."

"I told your pal Cooksey I had nothing to say."

She frowned. "My pal Cooksey?"

"Honey, I'm a veteran at this. I know all the tricks. Cooksey sent you out here to pump me."

"I'm sorry. I don't know anyone named Cooksey."

"From the *Hartsville Herald*? His byline was all over the front page this morning."

She reached for her purse, handed him a business card. Dark blue letters on a light green card spelled *Mary Crow, Attorney at Law. Tsalagi clients welcome.* Somewhere in his head, a faint bell of recognition chimed.

He returned her card. "If you welcome Tsalagi clients you must be representing Two Toes."

She shook her head. "Zachary Collier, actually. The one everybody thinks is guilty."

"And you want me to tell you he's not?"

"No, I just want to talk to somebody who was there. Stump Logan's dead and Buck Whaley would rather dance with the devil than talk to me."

He laughed at the notion of Whaley dancing with anything. "So that leaves me to help get your client off the hook."

"Sir, I'm not sure that he doesn't belong on the hook," she replied. "But I believe he's entitled to a fair trial. Thanks to Mr. Cooksey, that grows less likely by the minute."

He shrugged. She did have a point—certainly most of the people at the Waffle House were ready to string Collier up. He frowned, trying to place her. Then it came to him. "Aren't you the girl who defended that eagle trainer a couple of years ago?"

She nodded. "I was Nick Stratton's counsel."

"And that crazy Cherokee boy, a few years before that?"

"Ridge Standingdeer was also my client."

He gave a soft whistle. "You must have a real appetite for uphill climbs."

She laughed, and in an instant went from attractive to gorgeous. Something about her smile made his heart skip a beat. "Let's just say I have a soft spot for the unjustly accused."

"And a hard spot for the guilty?"

"Oh yes." Instantly, that gorgeous smile turned cold. "I take being guilty personally."

Though he knew it was crazy, knew he was being an old fool dazzled by a pretty woman, he decided to talk to her. Cochran and Whaley certainly weren't interested in anything he had to offer. He'd have to be careful of what he revealed, but at least he'd be kind of in the game again. It would be a nice break from watching chickens all day.

"Then come on in the house," he finally said. "And I'll tell you what really happened the night Teresa Ewing vanished."

TWENTY-TWO

GRACE WOKE UP LATE, the colors of her quilt glowing bright in the morning sun. Sleepy, she checked the clock beside her bed. 8:32—much later than her usual wake-up time. Had Zack awakened her in the middle of the night? Had something bad happened? No, she realized as her memory sharpened. Though a photographer had ended it badly, last night they'd had a party with Adam Shaw.

"Unbelievable," she whispered as she got out of bed. "After all these years, Zack has a friend."

She brushed her teeth and threw on jeans and one of the shirts she wore for her classes. No need to button the wrists today, she thought, looking at her arms. Zack hadn't grabbed her in a week. Considering all that they'd been through lately, that in itself was a miracle.

Tiptoeing into the hall, she opened his door. He slept, snoring, surrounded by his stuffed animals—Smiley the dog, Tigger the tiger, and some unnamed gray thing that had once been a toy kitten. Usually she woke him up before she went to work, but today she decided to let him sleep. Yesterday had been an ordeal for him, with the cops and the DNA, and the reporter. Who knew what today might bring?

Quietly, she made a circuit of the house. No photographers were lurking around the back fence, and the front yard was equally calm—cardinals flashing red at the bird feeders, two squirrels arguing in the maple tree. Distantly, she heard a car approaching. Dreading to see who might pull up, she waited. To her great relief, Clara's yellow Bug turned the corner and chugged up the driveway.

"Thank God," Grace whispered. She hurried into the kitchen and poured two cups of coffee. She was tempted to pretend this was just another ordinary day, but she knew Clara needed to know what was going on. Strangers—police, reporters, maybe even the FBI—might come asking for Zack. She opened the back door just as the girl was about to knock.

"Good morning." Smiling, Grace offered her a cup of coffee. "Two sugars, cream, and a little cinnamon, right?"

"Thanks." Clara took the coffee, her brown eyes wide. "Is Zack still here?"

"Of course," Grace replied, surprised by the girl's question. "Why wouldn't he be?"

Clara held up a copy of the *Hartsville Herald*. The front page dripped with news of Teresa Ewing. "I thought he might be in jail."

Grace's mouth went dry as she skimmed the stories.

"It's all about that murdered girl," said Clara. "They said Zack played with her. He was the only one they ever arrested."

Grace felt a sudden dizziness. She tried to explain. "Clara, Zack was fifteen then. The police questioned him for hours back then, yelled at him. He would have said anything to make them be quiet. You know how he gets when people talk too loud?"

She nodded. "Smackertalking."

"The police smackertalked for hours. He didn't know to ask for me or his father." Grace brushed her hair back from her forehead, desperate to reassure the girl. "Look, I know this looks bad, but you've worked with Zack for two years now. Do you honestly think he could kill somebody?"

Clara considered the question. "He can get upset pretty fast."

"Have you ever felt afraid of him?"

She stared at her coffee. "Sometimes he scares me," she finally admitted. "But I've never thought he was going to kill me."

"He never would kill you, Clara. He didn't kill that little girl."

"But is it dangerous here now?" Clara asked softly, the slightest trace of a Spanish accent returning to her voice. "I mean, are the police going to come here?"

"I honestly don't know," Grace said. "Why? Is that a problem?"

Clara swallowed hard. "I'm afraid of the police. When we lived in Miami, they took my brother out on our driveway and aimed a gun at his head. They screamed at him, yelled that he was a drug dealer. Turns out they had the wrong house, but they still almost gave my mother a heart attack."

Grace said, "I don't think they'll come back today. But I understand if you'd rather go home." She held her breath, praying the girl would be brave enough to stay with Zack for at least one more day.

Clara gave a deep sigh. "No, it's okay. You need to go to work, and I need this job."

"Then let's say this—if any strangers come by, close the drapes and don't answer the door. If the police come, call me. If anybody starts vandalizing the yard, call me."

Clara frowned. "Vandalizing?"

"Throwing paint on the driveway, destroying the mailbox. Stuff like that happens when the paper runs a story about Teresa Ewing."

"So, what should I do with Zack? Today we usually swim at the lake."

"Just keep him here," said Grace. "Have him fill the bird feeders and clean his room. This weekend he spent all his money on some new videos. He can watch those."

Clara smiled as Grace reached to give her a hug. "I can't tell you how much I appreciate your staying. You've got the emergency number. Call if anything happens—I'll keep my phone with me today."

———

Grace hurried on to the college. Though her first class was a long one—a three-hour landscape course—at least it was outside, away from her studio. If Clara had read about Zack in the paper, then so might Dean Ferguson or Alice Richards, the chair of her department. She always felt as if she were skating on thin ice with the administration; even though she got excellent critiques from her students and her classes had waiting lists, Zack's situation made her keep short office hours and skip most faculty meetings. Alice Richards never missed a chance to comment on her absences. "I'm so sorry," she would say. "I completely forgot about it." Alice always smirked, as if she knew Grace was lying.

Grace met her students at the door of her studio and led them to a small creek that bordered one edge of the campus. An old, vine-draped stone bridge spanned the stream, making the setting both romantic and challenging. "Concentrate on the reflective quality of water," she told them as they set up their easels. "And remember, you'll have to work quickly. The sun is moving, so your light and dark values will move as well."

Keeping her cell phone on vibrate, she walked from student to student, suggesting a darker shade of paint here, correcting an error in perspective there. Though she tried hard to concentrate on her teaching, it was difficult. Like the dragonflies that darted over the water, her thoughts kept careening first to Zack, then to Clara, then to the faceless, lab-coated scientist who would determine if her son's DNA was on those underpants. Just when she'd decided the class would never end, the students began folding up their easels, done for the day. Grace followed them back up to the arts building, relieved that she'd gotten no calls from Clara or any questions about the articles in the paper. *Maybe it'll just die down this time,* she thought. *Maybe some new war or epidemic will break out and everybody will forget about stupid little Teresa Ewing.*

She had just unlocked her studio door when Alice Richards bustled around the corner, a sheaf of papers in hand. Though it was eighty degrees outside, she wore a red wool beret with a ceramic zebra pin attached to the front. Alice's hats were legend; Grace always figured it was her attempt to look arty, as opposed to actually having any artistic talent herself.

"Grace!" Her pudgy face widened in a smile. "I was hoping to catch you. Have you got a minute?"

"Sure," Grace said weakly, knowing that her having a minute was not up for discussion. "Come on in."

She entered her studio and flipped on the overhead lights. Alice followed and closed the door behind her. "I need to speak with you before your next class."

"Okay." Grace's stomach grew queasy. Alice's pale blue gaze was friendly and yet sharp.

188

"Grace, I read the paper this morning. I knew you had a special needs son, but I had no idea he was a suspect in a murder investigation."

Grace fought a moment of panic. "He w-was one of several children who were questioned, Alice. I can promise you that he is innocent."

"You can promise me?" Alice's brows lifted, as if Grace might reach in her purse and pull out Zack's airtight alibi, wrapped up in a bow.

"He's not that kind of boy. He's not a killer." She knew her words sounded ludicrous. Osama bin Laden's mother had probably said the same thing.

"Of course he's not," Alice gushed, full of empathy." But the thing is, I'm responsible for making sure that our faculty members don't reflect poorly on the college."

Grace felt as if she were free-falling from an airplane. Was Alice going to fire her? Right now, before her still life class?

"I know this must be an incredibly stressful time for you. Would you like to take a leave of absence until all this is settled?"

Grace knew she couldn't quit working. She had bills to pay, medications that Zack's Medicaid did not cover, and now the ongoing services of Mary Crow. "I'd really like to stay on. This Teresa Ewing business will blow over. It always does."

"But can you teach effectively? Not be distracted?"

"Absolutely. It's what I do—what I love." She was about to explain that she'd just hired a new model for her anatomy class when her cell phone rang. It was the siren-sounding ring, the one she'd assigned Clara; the girl only called when the shit hit the fan. "Excuse me," she blurted, dreading what news the call might bring. "I need to answer this." She turned her back to her boss and spoke in a hushed voice, "Clara? Is everything okay?"

"I don't know what to do!" Clara sounded nearly hysterical. "Zack went out to fill the bird feeders and found dead animals all over the yard."

"He found what?"

"Squirrels, rabbits, all bloody. He ran back inside, crying, then he started beating his fists against the walls. I've never seen him like this!"

"Dead animals upset him, Clara. Give him a Valium and let him watch a video."

"There isn't any more Valium ... the bottle is empty. Zack! Noooo!"

Grace heard a crash, then a scream. "Clara?" she cried. "Clara, are you okay?"

There was a rustling sound, then Clara came back on the phone. "He just tore up one of your paintings."

"Don't worry about the painting." Grace turned, trying to think of what to tell Clara when she saw Alice Richards quietly letting herself out the door. "Wait, Alice," she called, "I'm just having a little emergency at home."

Alice flashed her dimpled smirk. "Don't worry about a thing! We'll talk later. After your emergency's over."

Grace watched her leave, knowing that her job was probably walking out the door with Alice, but there was nothing she could do about that now. Now she had to get Zack under control. "Clara? Are you still there?"

She heard another crash, then Clara spoke again. "I'm here."

"Listen," said Grace, "pop him some popcorn and turn on his videos. I'm going to call his prescription in to the pharmacy. I can't leave now, but I'll get somebody to come over with the medicine."

"Okay," Clara said, her voice shaky.

"I'll come straight home as soon as I can."

"Okay."

"Don't worry, Clara. Everything's going to be fine."

She disconnected the call and began scrolling through her numbers to find someone to help. She didn't have many friends, and none had ever been to her house when Zack was having a meltdown. She was going through her contact list when an idea occurred to her. Adam Shaw! Zack had used her phone to call him yesterday. Could she presume upon him again? Would he be willing to help Zack out once more?

She didn't know, but she had to ask. In five minutes her next class would start filing in the door. With shaking fingers, she punched in his number. "Please let him answer," she whispered. "Please let him help us one more time."

TWENTY-THREE

FOUR HOURS AFTER THEY began, Jerry Cochran had Devin McConnell sign his statement. "Thanks for coming in," he said. "Too bad you didn't do it a couple of decades sooner."

"Better late than never," replied Devin.

"Don't leave town," Cochran said flatly. "We may need to talk further."

Cochran escorted him to the front entrance of the Justice Center, watching as he left in a late model red Mazda. Then he pulled out his cell phone and texted Whaley. INTERVIEW RM 1 NOW. By the time he got a cup of coffee and made his way upstairs, Whaley was waiting.

"What's up?" The detective slurped something from a giant Dunkin' Donuts mug.

"Come watch this."

They went to the control room, where Cochran cued up Devin McConnell's interview.

"He came in this morning for his cheek swab," said Cochran. "Then said he wanted to give a statement, but only to me."

Whaley laughed. "Little shit's too scared of me."

"Have a look at this," said Cochran. They sat at a table, and watched as Devin McConnell gave the latest version of the afternoon Teresa Ewing died. Cochran had the thick case file spread out on a table, trying to corroborate the points of the story as Devin went along. Whaley sat motionless, ignoring his cold drink, his eyes focused on Devin. After he went through his first recounting of the story, Cochran turned off the monitor.

"It's just four more hours of the same," he said. "The guy didn't wobble at all."

Whaley leaned back in his chair and made a sucking sound with his straw.

"What do you think?" asked Cochran.

"He's lying."

"How do you know?"

Whaley snorted. "Because his lips were moving. Hook him up to a polygraph. You'll see."

"Whaley, you need to—"

"Devin McConnell is the biggest liar of that bunch. Zack Collier's an idiot, and Butch Russell's only a couple of IQ points smarter than a tree stump."

"What about Adam Shaw?"

Whaley shrugged. "He gave a statement right after his cheek swab. His story hasn't changed. The girls went home, the boys stayed longer, playing with that deck of cards. Two Toes showed up and they all scattered. Adam claims he went home, which his mother corroborated."

"That's not the strongest alibi I've ever heard," said Cochran. "My mother would probably say the same thing."

"Still, I'm guessing McConnell cooked up this new, improved version with Russell. They were both over at the Tote-A-Note lot yesterday."

"Oh?"

"Russell lost his campus security job, so now he's McConnell's detail man. I went over there to remind McConnell that we needed his cheek swab and saw the two of them."

"So you're thinking Russell's going to come in and give a statement similar to this?"

Whaley chuckled. "I would put a year's supply of donuts on it. Maybe not today, but tomorrow, or the day after, Russell will come in for swab and then say he wants to make a statement, probably only to you."

"Why me?" asked Cochran.

"'Cause you were what—ten when Teresa Ewing died? You don't know this case like I do. Nobody does, except Wilkins."

"But why hang this on Collier now? They could have done that decades ago."

Whaley shrugged. "Something about those panties is making them nervous. Or maybe they're just fucking tired of always being the ones whose names come up in the news feeds. McConnell's got a couple of kids, old enough to surf the net now. I imagine he'd rather not have it out on Facebook that their pop might be a murderer."

Cochran sighed. "You know, for three seconds I thought we might be making some headway."

"Welcome to the brotherhood of Teresa Ewing," said Whaley. "All of us suckered in by leads that go nowhere, clues that turn out to mean squat. It'll drive you crazy, if you let it."

"Is that what happened to Wilkins?"

"Hamburger Jack was sketchy for a while, but I think he's okay now." Whaley stuck out his hand. "How about it? Are we on for the donuts?"

"Sure," said Cochran. "Though I think this is one bet I might lose."

Whaley laughed. "All I can say is it's gonna get interesting when the DNA report comes in."

———

"So what did he say? How did he act?" Butch Russell shredded his napkin into small bits, a nervous habit left over from the seventh grade, when his dreaded English class met immediately after lunch.

"I did most of the talking, Butch. I was giving a statement." Dev McConnell dragged a French fry through the puddle of ketchup on his plate. They sat at Mike's Grill, a place noted for its patty melts and cheap beer.

"But did he believe you?" Butch reminded Devin of a chipmunk, with fat cheeks and tufts of hair fuzzing up over his ears.

Dev remembered Cochran's cop-cold eyes, the way he made him go over the story for hours. They didn't quit until well past noon. "I don't know. He asked me a lot of questions."

Butch reached for another napkin to shred. "Like what?"

"What Two Toes said, what Adam said, what Teresa said."

"What did you say?"

"The same story we've told since day one." Dev took a swallow of beer. "Butch, the only thing different is what we added yesterday. That's the only thing you have to worry about."

Butch gazed out into the parking lot, where two men in denim jackets pulled up on chromed-up Harley hogs. "Didn't he ask why you didn't say anything before now?"

Dev nodded.

"What did you tell him?"

"That we were scared."

"What else did you say about me?"

"I said we were best pals. I needed to get my gym lock. I asked you to go with me back to the tree because we were scared of Two Toes."

"Your gym lock?" Butch frowned, as if this detail were part of a complicated algebra equation. "You didn't say that yesterday."

"So what?" Dev looked around the restaurant to make sure no one was sitting nearby. "Write this down, shit-for-brains. I made you go back to the tree with me. We sneaked up on the tree, to make sure Two Toes wasn't there. We heard a noise. Then we looked around and saw a tall man in a dark hoodie carrying Teresa toward Zack's house. She looked dead."

"What about Adam?"

"Forget Adam, Butch. I don't know where the fuck he was. He isn't part of this story."

"But won't they ask?"

"Yes," said Dev, fighting the urge to stuff French fries up Butch's nostrils, "they'll ask. You say you don't know. It's okay. Nobody has the whole picture. Nobody remembers everything in exactly the same way."

"I don't know." Butch shook his head. "I think I ought to put Adam in there somewhere."

"No!" Dev slammed his fist down on the table. "You put Adam in there and we're dead men."

"But..."

"Butch, Adam is real smart. If he finds out that we put him in the story, it'll piss him off and he'll figure out a way to frame us. You've lived next to his parents all your life. You know what they're like."

"Yeah." Butch stared at his little pile of shredded napkin. "I guess I do."

"Okay, then. You need to stick with what we've already worked out. Don't add anything, don't leave anything out."

"I'll go down there, then. Ask for Cochran."

"Wait a minute—I thought that was the way to go yesterday. Now I'm not so sure."

"What do you mean?"

"If you go in there and do exactly the same thing I did, it's going to look like we worked it out beforehand. That's not good."

"But you said it would look better if we both volunteered the story when we had our cheek swabs!" he cried. "Now I'm sitting here looking like I'm hiding something."

"I know, I know. Let me think a minute." As Dev took another swallow of beer, he realized he might have laid too heavy a load on Butch's brain. Already the guy was close to freaking out. Adam would have been better to partner up with. He could have handled Cochran like a pro. But it was too late now. If he left Butch out at this point, he'd blow it for both of them.

"Just wait and see what they do," he finally said. "If they call you in, then we'll know they've bought the story. If they don't call you, then just go give your DNA. There's no point in your going through hours of saying the same if they aren't going to believe it."

For an instant Butch looked relieved; then his brows drew together in a new frown. "So I have to just sit here and sweat?"

"Don't think about it," said Dev. "You'll just make things worse."

Butch had just opened his mouth to say something when suddenly his phone rang. He dug it out of his jeans and answered it. "Yeah," he said to the caller, a moment later. "I can do that. No problem at all."

He clicked off and looked at Dev. "That was Sheriff Cochran. He wonders if I'd be willing to give an interview when I give my DNA."

"Damn!" Excited, Dev gave a fist pump. "It's working, brother. It's fucking working!"

"Yeah," Butch said weakly, his already pale complexion now the color of paste. "The thing is, Cochran also thinks I need a lawyer."

TWENTY-FOUR

MARY CROW LOOKED AROUND the small bedroom that served as Jack Wilkins's office and smiled. In the course of her career she'd visited a number of retired detectives. Every one of them had a bedroom or a den devoted to their glory days—pictures that traced their ascent from trim young patrol officers to paunchier plainclothesmen. Jack Wilkins was no different. His room was decorated with a number of photographs and commendations in one corner, including a shadowbox frame that displayed a gold star of a badge, seemingly from the days of Wild Bill Hickok.

"That's an interesting memento," she commented as Wilkins brought two mugs of coffee from the kitchen. He carried them on a tray, with paper towels for napkins and a little plate of Oreo cookies.

"That was my granddad's." He put the tray on the desk. "He was the sheriff of Fargo, North Dakota."

Mary turned to the tall, lanky Wilkins. "Fargo, like in the movie?"

"Yeah. He predated the movie by nearly a century, but he was just as Swedish. Just as no-nonsense."

"So if your family's from North Dakota, how did you wind up so far south?"

"Joined the army, got stationed at Fort Bragg. Liked the fact that North Carolina had four seasons instead of North Dakota's two."

"When did you start working on the Pisgah County force?"

"1989. I worked up to detective in Fayetteville, then came here as a lateral hire."

The year after Mama was killed, thought Mary. He wouldn't have been on that case at all. She looked again at the framed star, bright against a black velvet background. "Well, I'm sure you've made your grandfather proud."

"I've tried." Jack stared at the badge for a moment, then turned to Mary. "So what do you want to know about Teresa Ewing?"

"Everything," she replied. "Except what's in the paper."

He laughed. "Defense lawyers usually thrive on the crap in the paper."

She looked at him, serious. "Before I came here, I was a prosecutor in Atlanta. They used to call me Killer Crow. I won every capital case they assigned me."

Jack frowned. "Then how did you wind up working the dark side of law?"

"I came back here for a prosecutor's job that mysteriously vanished the moment I walked into George Turpin's office. I'd spent a lot of money moving up here, so I figured I'd better practice some kind of law."

"And you started defending criminals just to aggravate Turpin?"

She laughed. "Mostly I do wills, house closings, property disputes. Since I can't prosecute killers, I occasionally defend people I think are wrongly accused. Some are women, some are Cherokee. Almost always, they are poor."

"Sounds like you've got some skin in the game."

"My mother was Cherokee. And the victim of a homicide," she said flatly. "So yeah, I guess I do have some history there."

At that point Jack must have decided she was okay. He opened his files and spread them out, making little piles of paper across his desk, on his sofa, and finally on the floor. As the dog lay sleeping in the kitchen, they went through each pile, studying the crime scene photos, reading transcripts of the suspect interviews, going over the coroner's report. The sight of Sheriff Stump Logan's scrawl on some of the pages made Mary recoil inside, but she tried to put her hatred of Logan aside and regard his observations as those of just another law officer doing his job.

"There's an awful lot of confusion in this case," Mary said as they read through the reports. "The coroner first said she'd been dead for three weeks. Then he said she'd died just hours before they found her under the tree. Then he reversed himself again."

"I think the coroner was high on formaldehyde," said Jack. "He resigned his office about six months after his last report. But he was only part of the crazy stuff swirling around this case. We had calls from Arizona, Florida. One man said he'd seen Teresa on the boardwalk in Atlantic City, New Jersey. That was hard on her parents. All that hope, then nothing."

"But when was she killed, exactly?"

"Ultimately, they decided she died the day she went missing." Jack frowned. "You ever hear of a Cherokee guy named Two Toes McCoy?"

She laughed. "He was notorious when I was a girl. I haven't heard anything about him lately."

"Then old age and his parole officer must have slowed him down some. Back in '89, when Two Toes wasn't in jail, he did odd jobs in

Teresa's neighborhood. Yard work mostly—pulling up poison ivy, grubbing out ditches. All the kids knew him—if he was sober and in the right mood, he would tell them stories about that old tree."

"*Undli Adaya*," said Mary. "The tree that saved the tribe."

"Yeah. Well, Two Toes had worked for Norah Ferguson that afternoon, cleaning out her gutters. I floated the theory that maybe Two Toes had abducted the child. Hid her on reservation land. Kept her, killed her, then brought her back."

"Did he have an alibi?"

"Oh all his friends swore he was with them. You know how that goes."

Mary shrugged. "Anybody else look good?"

"Arthur Hayes, a sophomore at Western, who's since died. Lived in a basement apartment at 912 Salola. The campus cops had busted him twice for peeping outside the girls' dorm, plus he had a couple of indecent exposure charges."

"He sounds at least as good as Two Toes," said Mary.

"He did. Plus he had a car and could easily have hidden a little body for a month. "

"So what took him out of the running?"

"Nothing, really. Claimed he was studying at the library. We could neither confirm nor deny that. Nobody had security cameras back then."

"So if you had two viable adult suspects, why did you guys come down so hard on these kids?"

"Honestly?"

She nodded.

"The newspaper ran with the kid angle. Somebody said they were playing strip poker, games that were getting way out of hand."

"Was that true?" asked Mary.

He handed her one pile of interviews. "Not the day she died. All the kids said the boys asked the girls to play that last afternoon. Shannon Cooper and Janie Griffin refused immediately and went home, apparently in a huff. Everyone said that Teresa lingered behind and talked to the boys some more."

"So she played strip poker?"

"No. The boys said Teresa went home. They stayed there looking at the deck of marked cards until Two Toes showed up and ran them off."

"And my client confirmed this as well?"

"Mostly your client said, 'I want to go home' over and over. We never got any good information out of Collier."

"But how does he figure in the whole case?" she asked.

"We liked him because he was older—fifteen, as opposed to ten or twelve. A young buck where the others were still boys."

"What do you mean?"

"I observed them take the DNA samples. Zack Collier had a man-sized penis and pubic hair. None of the others were that well developed."

"But Teresa hadn't been raped."

"That's not to say somebody didn't *try* to rape her."

"And maybe got frustrated because they couldn't and smashed her head in?" Mary thought of all those holes Zack had put in the living room wall.

"Possibly," Jack replied. "Or maybe she screamed, and so they hit her to make her be quiet. Collier had some kind of super-sensitive hearing."

"Okay," said Mary. "But any of the boys have done that. Ten- and twelve-year-olds can have erections."

"True." Wilkins walked over to the stack of papers that described the suspects. "But not many twelve-year-olds can lug seventy-eight pounds of dead weight and hide it someplace."

"What from I've seen of Zack, he would have needed help too. He's not exactly a logical thinker."

"But don't forget he weighed a hundred sixty-two pounds," said Jack. "And he had parents who protected him. His father went on French leave a couple of years after this girl's death."

Mary frowned. It was again hard to hear that the cops suspected Grace Collier of abetting her son in murder, but she knew that's what good cops did—looked at a crime from every possible angle.

"I wish I could see this scene, you know, like it was back then," she finally said, looking at all the piles of paper spread out before them.

"Then let's go up there," said Jack. "I've got to go to the post office anyway. Follow me and I'll show you exactly how things were on Salola Street that day."

TWENTY-FIVE

ADAM WAS PUSHING THE big wheelbarrow out of the shed when his phone rang. Before he answered, he checked the number. A local area code, but not his parents. Wondering if Butch or Devin were cooking something up, he accepted the call. A breathless voice greeted him.

"Adam? This is Grace—Grace Collier."

"Hi, Grace," he answered. surprised. "What's up?"

"I'm so sorry to call you, but I've got an emergency. Zack's caregiver called, frantic. She says Zack found some dead animals in our front yard and he's having a bad meltdown. I can't leave my class right now—I was wondering if you could possibly go by Bell's Pharmacy and pick up a prescription for him? I know this is a huge favor to ask, and I'll be happy to pay you."

"No need to pay me, Grace," replied Adam, liking the way her name felt in his mouth. "I'm glad to help. Is Bell's Pharmacy still on Keener Avenue?"

"Yes. Downtown."

"I'm on my way," he said, rolling the wheelbarrow up against the shed.

"Bless you, Adam." Her voice cracked. "I can't thank you enough."

———

He told his parents he was going out and drove over to pick up Zack's prescription. "Holy shit," he said, reading the label on the bottle. "This stuff would knock out an elephant." *But maybe that's okay,* he decided. *Maybe if Zack passes out, I can find my old tapes. When he wakes up he'll never miss a dozen out of the hundred he's got in that box.*

Half an hour later, he pulled up at Zack's house, parking beside a yellow Volkswagen that sported a faded Obama sticker on the rear bumper. He went to the back door, just as he'd done the night before. He was lifting his hand to knock when a young, dark-haired woman cracked it open.

"Are you Adam?" she whispered. He could only see a sliver of her face, a smear of pink lipstick at the corner of her mouth.

Nodding, he held up the little sack from the pharmacy. "I've got Zack's medicine."

"Thank God." She unchained the door and opened it wide. "Come in. He's in the living room."

Adam stepped past her. "What's this with dead animals?"

"They're all over the front yard. Zack found them when he went to fill the bird feeders." She rubbed her arms. "Then he just went nuts."

"I'll go talk to him," said Adam. "I've known him a long time."

He went into the living room. It looked as if a small tornado had vented its fury within the walls. End tables were overturned and paintings hung crooked on the wall. Zack paced in front of the window, mumbling to himself in a constant, low tone. He kept shaking his head, as if trying to erase the memory of the dead animals. His heavy footsteps thudded as he stomped up and down the room. Adam stared, slack-jawed. He'd never seen him like this before.

"Hey, buddy," he called softly. "What's going on?"

Zack turned. His eyes were flat black orbs. Tears streamed down his face. "They're dead! They're all dead!"

"Who's dead?" Adam asked, keeping his distance from this hulk of a man. Zack was a half a head taller and probably had seventy pounds on him.

"The animals."

"What animals?"

Zack pointed to the window. "Out there!"

Adam grew curious. "Can I go have a look?"

Zack did not reply. He just gave a long sniff and continued his pacing.

Adam crossed the room, stepping over a shattered lamp and one of Grace's oil paintings, torn from its frame. He let himself out the front door and scanned the yard, looking for the animals Zack was talking about. At first he saw nothing but Grace's flowers, a riot of purples and yellows. Then, as he stepped off the porch and walked toward the bird feeder, he found them. Positioned like the numerals on a clock, were a dozen little carcasses. Squirrels, mostly, with a couple of rabbits and some mangled thing that might have once been an opossum. All were laid on their backs, their fur stained red with blood. Though the opossum thing looked like roadkill, all the rest had bullet holes, either in their chests or their heads. No wonder Zack had gone crazy. This was sick. Butch and Devin came immediately to mind.

He heard the door open behind him. He turned to see Zack coming down the porch steps, hiccupping with sobs.

"See?" he said, triumphant. "I told you so."

"I know, buddy," said Adam. "Somebody did a real bad thing here."

"But why?" asked Zack, his forty-two-year-old chin quivering. "The squirrels didn't do anything wrong."

"I know. Some people are sick jerks." Again, Adam thought of Devin and the rifle leaning in the corner of his office. He'd said he wanted Zack to take the fall. Maybe this was part of his plan—scare Zack bad enough to confess to anything. He stepped in front of the animals, trying to hide them from Zack's view. "I brought some medicine for you. How about you go take it and I'll bury these little guys."

Zack shook his head. "I want to help."

"Take your pills first," he said, trying to speak with Grace's tone of authority. "Then you can help."

Zack stared at him darkly for a moment, but then said, "Okay."

Adam waited until Zack went inside to take his medicine, then he walked over to the garbage. There he found two pairs of work gloves and a shovel. He grabbed some newspapers from their recycle bin and returned to the front yard. Zack was waiting for him.

"Take your pills?" asked Adam.

He nodded. "Clara gave me two."

"Good." Adam handed Zack the newspaper. "Let's wrap these guys up. Then we'll dig a little grave for them in the back."

"Can we have a funeral?" the big boy-man asked.

"Sure," Adam said, wondering if Zack had gone totally off the rails. "If that's what you want."

———

Somehow, Grace managed to start her next class. She set up an uncomplicated scene of peaches spilling from a fruit crate on a blue checked tablecloth. Her older students could have fun with the old-fashioned label on the crate and the folds in the material. But even the rookie painters would see the vivid relationship between the orange of the peaches and the blue of the fabric. It wasn't the tableau she'd planned, but neither had she expected Zack to find a bunch of dead animals in their front yard.

Again she worked her way around her students, trying to concentrate on her teaching. Just when she thought she might scream from the not knowing, her phone vibrated with a new message. Everything's okay, wrote Clara. Zack and Adam are having a funeral. The notion of a funeral shocked her, then she remembered how distressed Zack got over the smallest animal's passing. A funeral might help him deal with this, she decided. Adam had probably suggested it.

Silently, she offered a prayer of thanks for Adam Shaw. He'd saved the day yet again, maybe even saved her job in the process. As far as she was concerned, whatever duty he felt he'd shirked when Teresa died, he'd made up for many times over.

Keeping an eye out for Alice Richards, she taught her class, correcting drawings and offering suggestions on color and composition. When the students began to clean their brushes, she felt a weight lift. *Now*, she thought as they packed up their supplies, *if I can just get out of here with my job and my sanity.*

When the last student left, she gathered up her things and turned off the lights. She half expected Alice to be waiting for her in the hall, termination papers in hand, but she saw only students, ambling to and from classes, hooked up to their smartphones. As she walked toward the faculty parking lot, she passed two girls who pointed and started whispering, but she ignored them. Stares and whispers did not bother her; she'd gotten used to them years ago.

A half hour later, she rolled up in her own driveway. To her surprise, Clara's yellow Bug was gone, replaced by Adam's white Toyota. A new panic gripped her. Where was Clara? Had she quit? That would just be the horribly perfect end to a wretchedly imperfect day.

She pulled into the garage and hurried into the kitchen. The house was silent. She went down the hall to Zack's bedroom. The door stood open; she peeked inside and saw a tangle of sheets, but no Zack. Returning to the kitchen, she glanced in the living room. Someone had made an attempt to straighten up the wreck Zack had made—the furniture was mostly in place and only a couple of paintings were beyond re-hanging on the wall. But everything was just so silent. Zack liked things quiet, but not tomb-quiet like this. She wondered if they were even there. Had they all gone somewhere in Clara's car?

Running to the den, she searched the last room in the house. There, she found the reason for the strange silence. Zack lay asleep on the couch, his mouth gaping open. Adam sat at the television, headphones on, watching an old videotape.

"Hey!" she said softly, switching the overhead light on and off. "I'm home!"

Zack didn't move, but Adam leaped to his feet, startled and looking somehow guilty.

"I'm sorry," said Grace. "I didn't mean to scare you!"

"It's okay." He gave a nervous laugh, his face pale. "I didn't hear you come in." Quickly, he turned off the VCR. "Zack fell asleep, so I decided to watch some tapes." He looked at the box overflowing with old cassettes. "I'm trying to catalog them for him."

"Where's Clara?" asked Grace.

"I told her she could go home," Adam said. "She was pretty upset."

"Did she say she'd be coming back tomorrow?" Grace imagined the girl calling DSS, asking her supervisor for another case. *Please ma'am, I'd like a client who hasn't been accused of murder and doesn't try to tear the house apart.*

He nodded. "She said she would."

"Thank God." Grace slumped against the door, knees wobbly with relief. "I don't know what I'd do if she quit." She looked at Zack, sprawled on the couch, now beginning to snore. His meds, thank God, were working.

"He had a pretty rough day too," Adam reminded her.

"I guess we all have." She turned her gaze from Zack to Adam. "Would like a drink? God knows you've earned it."

He gave his funny, one shoulder shrug. "I've got time for one."

They went into the kitchen, and Adam opened one of his beers from the night before while Grace uncorked a bottle of Cabernet. She found a can of cashew nuts in the cupboard and poured them into a bowl. As they sat at the kitchen table, she broached the subject she hadn't even wanted to think about. "Tell me about the animals."

He pulled out his cell phone, pushed it across the table. "Have a look."

She looked at the picture he'd taken. A circle of little creatures, arranged around the bird feeder like the monoliths of Stonehenge. Sacrificed to some god she couldn't imagine. As she handed his phone back, her eyes welled up.

"Zack and I buried them in the back yard," said Adam. "He wanted to have a funeral."

"Zack wanted to have a funeral?"

He nodded. "He recited something. It sounded like Cherokee."

"The Twenty-third Psalm," said Grace. "My mother taught him that before she died. It's the only Bible verse he knows." Sighing, she

211

rubbed the nape of her neck. "I think we may be in for a bad stretch here."

"How so?"

"You've been here what—two days? Already we've had a bullying detective, a pushy reporter, a sneaky photographer, and now some creep dumping dead animals in the front yard."

He took a swallow of beer. "Bully, Pushy, Sneaky, and Creepy. Sounds like four of seven evil dwarves."

"I imagine we'll have more than seven before it's all over. As long as little Teresa keeps selling papers, Zack and I are fair game for every nutcase in the county."

"And the police don't help?"

"I call them, but we aren't exactly high priority."

He frowned at his beer, then said, "Do you have a smartphone?"

She nodded. "Two months ago I got the latest model from Cupertino. It makes calls and takes great pictures. That's about as far as I've gotten with it."

"Let me see it. I might be able to rig something up for you."

She handed him her phone, told him her password. As she sipped her wine, she watched his slender fingers fly over the touchscreen, with an expertise that would always elude her. She was old-school, growing up with rotary phones and black-and-white TV sets that only showed three channels.

"You call Mary Crow a lot?" he asked.

"I have lately."

"And Bell's Pharmacy?"

"Them too. Why? How do you know?"

"I'm looking through your recent calls."

He continued his clicking while she poured herself another glass of wine. When she'd drained half of that, he gave her phone back. "Punch that little button there," he told her.

She did. All the numbers she called regularly appeared—Clara, the drugstore, Mary Crow, and the Pisgah County Police. "What did you do?" she cried.

"I made you a favorite list," he explained. "So you can call these people faster."

"Cool!" she cried. "I never knew you could do that. Thanks!"

He drained his beer. "I guess I'd better get going and see what my parents have added to my to-do list."

"Listen, I can't thank you enough for all your help," Grace said. "If it hadn't been for you, I would probably have lost my job."

"No thanks necessary," he said. "Do you teach again tomorrow?"

"No, not till Friday."

"Then I might go see Devin McConnell. I've got an idea he may have had something to do with these animals."

"Oh leave him alone, Adam. He's a scary guy. He and Butch both."

"Devin doesn't bother me," he said, his tone bitter. "Neither does Butch. A thousand things scare me more than those two guys."

TWENTY-SIX

WHATEVER ELSE JACK WILKINS might be, he wasn't the washed up old codger of a cop that Victor had described. As Mary followed him back into town, she noted that he even drove like a cop—straight, sure, and about twenty miles over the posted speed limit.

"Hope he's still got some friends on the force," Mary whispered as he zoomed into the entrance of Lone Oak Acres. "He'll need them if he keeps driving like this."

Construction had ended for the day, so Wilkins pulled up at the far end of the park that now surrounded the old tree. The developers had landscaped a long oval of common space with the tree at one end and a silly-looking Victorian bandstand at the other. Mary felt an odd sense of grief for the old tree. Though she doubted that it had ever saved the Cherokees from any Spaniards, it stood strong and noble, reflecting a vital part of her people's spirit. Surrounding it with band shells and eco-friendly cottages seemed demeaning, like putting a party hat on an elephant.

She got out of her car and walked over to Wilkins, who was standing next to his truck, rolled up map in hand. The dog wagged his tail as she approached. "Want to go have a closer look?" Wilkins asked.

"Sure."

"Then I'd better hook Lucky up," he said, reaching in the truck for his leash.

They went over to the tree. Mary had a vague memory of coming here once, with Jonathan, to see if they could spot the Spanish helmet hidden somewhere in the branches. She never found it, but back then she was far too busy gazing at Jonathan to have much interest in an old piece of armor. Still, as they drew closer to the oak, her sense of awe grew. The leaves broke the sunlight into small twinkling emeralds dancing among the dark limbs.

"They found Teresa Ewing there." Wilkins unrolled his map on the ground. "This is a survey, drawn in 1985." He pointed to a mark toward the right margin. "The tree's here. A wet spring had eroded several little caverns beneath it. Neighborhood kids hid out and played here for years." He pointed to a slight depression between two huge roots of the tree. "They found Teresa there. Everything intact except her skull. I'll never forget it."

"Who owned the tree then?"

"It was in the back of Albert Wood's two-acre lot. Mr. Wood was eighty and crippled, so he wasn't a viable suspect." Wilkins pointed over Mary's shoulder. "The Ewing house was over there, across from Devin McConnell's house. Everybody's back yard ended at this tree." He pointed in the other direction. "If that mound of dirt wasn't in the way, you could see Adam Shaw's and Butch Russell's houses. Janet and Butch Russell still live there, as do the Shaws, though they sent Adam to live with a relative in New York."

"He's back now," said Mary. "I met him yesterday."

Wilkins frowned. "Really?"

"I went with Zack Collier for the DNA test. Adam came in right behind us."

"Wow," said Jack. "Things must be hopping down at the station."

Mary turned in a slow circle. "So where was the Collier house?"

"Two doors down from the Shaws." He pointed to a churned up chunk of earth marked off with stubby orange stakes. "Grace sold it and moved after her husband left. For a long time it was a rental. Now they're going to build something new on the lot."

"Let's walk over there. I'd like to see what the tree looks like from there."

They went over to the flattened piece of earth that had once been Zack and Grace Collier's yard. It was impossible to tell what their house had looked like back then.

"So how far were they from the tree?" asked Mary.

He looked through another folder he'd brought with him. "Sixty yards."

"So you guys think Zack got mad, killed her, then ran back home with her, where his parents helped him cover it up?"

"Whaley thought that. It was dusk. Most people were sitting down to supper. The kids roughhoused a lot with Zack Collier, because he was so much bigger than they were. If anybody had seen him carrying Teresa, they would have thought they were playing some kind of game."

"That's quite a theory, Detective."

"I know." He gave her a hard look. "And it's still the one people like best."

Lucky began sniffing the ground, pulling Wilkins toward the bushes at the back of the lot. "Come on," said Jack, stumbling after the dog. "I think he needs to pee."

Mary followed the pair over to a thick undergrowth of weeds. With intense focus, Lucky sniffed every bush, inhaling whatever information was there. Finally after several moments, he lifted one leg against a patch of pampas grass. Mary was about to comment on how discerning Lucky was in his urinating when Jack touched her arm.

"Don't say anything. Just turn real slow and look up at the tree."

She did as he told her. At first she saw nothing—then her eyes caught a motion behind the tree. Someone was walking down the pile of dirt between the tree and the Shaw house. She saw that it was a man, long-haired, wearing jeans. She could also tell the stranger was schooled in the old Cherokee way of walking, heel to toe, all tracks in a single file. And yet something about his gait didn't look right—even walking slowly there was a hitch to his stride.

"That's Two Toes McCoy," whispered Jack Wilkins. "Kneel down and let's see what he's up to."

They crouched down, hiding behind the weeds, Lucky between them. As they watched, Two Toes made his way down the pile of dirt and over to the tree. He walked not stealthily, but with quiet purpose. When he reached the tree, he dropped to his knees and lifted his arms to its huge expanse of branches. Mary could hear the faint sound of a chant rising high and ghostly, raising gooseflesh on her arms. Then, abruptly, Two Toes grew silent. He sat like a statue for a moment, then he began to dig beneath the tree. A moment later Mary saw the flash of a long knife blade as he held up something, cut it, and plunged it into the hole he'd just dug. He re-sheathed his knife, made another open-arm gesture to the tree, and got to his feet. Quicker than Mary thought possible, he was walking back up the pile of dirt, stepping in the footprints he'd already made.

"I'll be damned," Wilkins whispered as Two Toes crested the dirt pile and disappeared down the other side.

"I thought he would look different, somehow," said Mary.

"Different?"

"Where I grew up, everybody thought he was the devil. I figured he'd have horns and a tail, at least."

Jack laughed. "He's getting old. His tail's probably fallen off." He squinted at the tree. "I know that tree is significant to your history. Is it also an object of worship?"

"We aren't Druids, Detective."

"I meant no disrespect, but you've got to admit, what Two Toes did was strange."

Mary nodded. "It did look like some kind of ritual."

Wilkins nudged her with his elbow. "Let's go see what he buried."

With Lucky between them, they made their way back to the tree.

"Shall I see if he's still up there?" asked Mary. "He did have a pretty big knife."

"Good idea." Wilkins handed her the leash. "Take Lucky. He can pull you up that mound of dirt."

Mary took the dog and followed Two Toes's trail. It led to the top of the mound and then disappeared in the grass of the Russell back yard. She saw no car or motorcycle awaiting an owner—just two parked bulldozers waiting like huge yellow beasts, eager to chew up the remaining three houses. She and Lucky went back down to the tree.

"If he's up there, he's hiding," said Mary. "There's no sign of him."

"He might have gone back to the reservation." Wilkins pointed to the thick, dark woods a few hundred yards away. "Quallah starts there, and it's honeycombed with old trails. That's what made him such a good suspect. One minute he'd be cleaning gutters on Salola Street, the next minute he'd vanished into the woods."

Mary said, "I guess they called him a witch for a reason."

"Well, let's see what the witch just buried."

They knelt down. Two Toes had swept the earth between the tree roots free of all traces of his activity. If Mary and Wilkins hadn't seen him, they would never have known anything had been buried here.

"Here." Wilkins unfolded a pocket knife. "It might be better if you dig."

Mary looked at him, surprised. "Why?"

"Because you're Tsalagi. I'm just an old white cop from St. Paul."

Mary laughed, but then she realized that Wilkins was expressing his respect—for her people and for this tree.

"Okay," she said, accepting the knife as seriously as he'd offered it.

She dug slowly in a circle, a foot in diameter, careful not to disturb what might be evidence. The earth was grainy, damp, and smelled of iron and humus. Half an inch down, she found the lacy skeletons of decaying leaves. Beyond that, a few moldy acorns, then, suddenly she uncovered a small brown pile of shredded tobacco.

"That's it." Wilkins leaned over and took a big sniff of the stuff. "This hasn't been here twenty minutes." He sat back on his haunches. "And it looks just like what was in the sandwich bag that Lucky found."

Mary knew all about what Wilkins and his dog had dug up from Victor. She also knew that revealing that knowledge could get Victor in huge trouble, so she played dumb. "What sandwich bag? What are you talking about?"

"I came over here last week, just to revisit the place before it changed for good. A cop was taking Lucky here to the pound when he got a vandalism call on those bulldozers. He let the dog loose to pee,

219

and Lucky got a whiff of an old sandwich bag. He dug it up, and a pair of girl's underpants was inside. That's what got the case reopened."

"And tobacco was also in the bag?" asked Mary. Victor hadn't mentioned that detail.

"Yeah. Shredded, like this. For cigarettes, instead of pipes or cigars." He looked at her. "Don't Cherokees use tobacco in religious ceremonies?"

"Historically," she replied. "But it was smoked, to waft upward, like a prayer. I've never heard of anyone burying it in the ground."

"Maybe Two Toes is trying to commune with a spirit that didn't make it to heaven," said Jack. He withdrew an old-fashioned linen handkerchief from his back pocket. "Anyway, this could be new evidence. If this matches the sandwich bag tobacco, then Two Toes will have some explaining to do."

Quickly, Mary took a pinch of the stuff for herself.

"Hey!" Wilkins said. "That's tampering with evidence."

"I'm not tampering with it," she replied. "I'm just taking a little for myself, in case I need my own analysis of it."

Wilkins snorted. "To get your guy off the hook, Counselor?"

"To give my client the best defense I can provide, Detective."

TWENTY-SEVEN

"THE THING IS," SAID Harvey Pugh as he placed his coffee cup on George Turpin's desk, "Your numbers are flat."

"Flat?" Turpin looked up from the chocolate croissant he was eating for breakfast. "What do you mean flat?"

Pugh pulled a red folder from his briefcase. "According to Effective Government Research, your numbers have moved less than one percent since the campaign kickoff." He handed Turpin the report. "Read this."

Turpin put his pastry down and opened a folder of pages filled with graphs and statistical projections. He thumbed through it, unable to make any sense of the squiggles and lines. "Harvey, I've got court in thirty minutes—just tell me what this means."

"These pollsters have determined that your voter base is male, white, fifty years and older. Traditional conservatives who don't want change."

"What's so bad about that?"

"Nothing, except that even among your base, you're not getting any buzz. You're just one great big yawn to voters who used to turn out for you big-time."

"Don't tell me they've gone over to that little simp Prentiss Herbert."

Pugh shook his head. "Herbert was dead right out of the gate. But look at this." He flipped to a three-line graph. "According to their research, *this* is who people are talking about."

Turpin did a double-take at the page, then gaped at Pugh, horrified. "Mary Crow?"

"Mary Crow." Pugh turned to yet another page in the report. "People like her story—a Cherokee girl whose mother was murdered, who then goes to law school so she can fight crime. George, if they held the election today, Mary Crow would cook you."

"But she's never run for anything in her life," said Turpin. "When she filed she had two hundred dollars in her war chest."

"But she's got that Poli Sci class from Western working for her. You could have had those kids working for you, but you wouldn't even meet with the professor."

"He said he just wanted them to see how an election works. What good would that have done? They can't even vote here."

"No, but they can organize. And post on Facebook and Twitter and Instagram. Mary Crow has six hundred and seventy-two friends on Facebook. You're only listed on the county government page."

"Well, then get me a fucking Facebook page! And some friends!"

"I will, but you've got a worse problem than Facebook."

"What?"

"Your track record on the governor's domestic violence act. Mary Crow hammers you with that every chance she gets."

"It's a crappy piece of legislation," Turpin insisted. "It does not treat both parties fairly."

"George, you've taken sixty-six percent of accused females to trial and only twenty-five percent of men—"

"The women won't press charges! They're afraid they'll get beaten up worse if they do. I've begged every one of them to stand up to their abusers, but they're too scared. If the State has no witnesses, the State has no case."

"You should have made a better effort, George. Mary Crow's talking about establishing a safe house for such cases."

"I didn't give anybody a free pass. Most of the male cases were alcohol related. I made sure AA meetings and anger management courses were part of their pleas."

"But couldn't you have done a little more for the women?" Pugh held his hands out, helpless. "Given them a little protection?"

"I did the best I could!" Turpin slammed the report shut. "This office isn't exactly rolling in money!"

Pugh shook his head. "Mary Crow's got a good argument, George. And you handed it to her on a platter. If you lose this election, it'll be on this issue—perceived unfairness."

Turpin sat back in his chair, loosened his tie. The tips of his ears glowed a vivid pink. "Can we turn this around, Harvey? Or should I start packing up my office now?"

"Right now female voters consider you soft on domestic violence. Change that and you might get some traction."

"At every luncheon I say how Mary Crow's defended two men, both accused of murdering women."

"And Mary comes back with how they were both innocent."

Turpin continued. "And now she's even defending Zack Collier, the man everybody thinks killed Teresa Ewing."

Pugh said, "And that, George, is the silver lining to this grim little cloud."

"How so?"

"Remember who designed all of Mary Crow's signage?"

"Of course I do. Zack Collier's mother, Grace."

"What?" Turpin's jaw went slack.

"So here's our new game plan, from now until November." Pugh flipped to the last few pages of the report. "We hammer home the fact that right now you're gathering evidence to solve the worst crime ever committed in Pisgah County, while Mary Crow is defending one of those suspects in that murder! The suspect's mother even works for her campaign! A District Attorney is supposed to prosecute criminals, not defend them!"

"Harvey, she'll come back with that everybody's-innocent-until-proven-guilty chestnut."

"Then, you soften a little. Say Mary's a capable attorney, say her heart's in the right place, defending the son of a campaign volunteer. But ask the hard question—would she be willing to indict this man? A former client, the son of a friend? And if she indicted him, could she then prosecute a client she's just defended?"

Turpin shrugged. "All she has to do is recuse herself. Convene a grand jury and if they indict, she changes the venue. It's uncommon, but it's not that big a deal."

"I know that. You know that. But Fred at the hardware store doesn't. Neither does Frances, the clerk at the drugstore. You've got to make old Hardware Fred and Drugstore Frances think that Mary Crow defends child killers, that she gives her criminal friends special treatment, that her campaign is full of shady characters who know a lot more about Teresa Ewing than they're telling."

Turpin stared at his croissant, remembering when former governor Carlisle Wilson had stood in almost the same spot as Pugh and threatened to out him as a pedophile. Though it was totally untrue, he knew in the community it would have blotted his name until the day he died. The memory still made him shudder. "It's ugly, but I guess I can do it."

"You need to do one more thing too," said Pugh.

"What?"

"Keep the Teresa Ewing pot simmering."

"What do you mean?"

"Sit on your evidence. Even if those underpants come back clean, tell the press it's still an active and ongoing investigation. When their questions get specific, punt. Say you've got new information but you can't reveal it at this time."

Turpin sighed. "Wouldn't it be wonderful if Zack Collier's DNA would turn up on those underpants?"

"If it does, fall on your knees and thank sweet Baby Jesus for saving your ass," said Pugh. "Then get the hell up and call a news conference."

Turpin finished Pugh's sentence with a smile. "And put a torch to every hope Mary Crow will ever have of becoming DA."

"That's the name of the game," Pugh replied.

Two miles from the courthouse, in the lab of the Justice Center, Butch Russell sat with his mouth open.

"This won't take a minute," said the lab tech, a young black woman whose name tag read Shauna. "Much easier than a trip to the dentist."

Butch thought of the dentist as Shauna rubbed the long-stemmed Q-tip on the inside of his cheek. Dr. Miles was his dentist, though he couldn't remember when he'd last been. "Miles for Smiles" was his slogan. "Spit for shit" could have been Shauna's.

"Okay," she said, as she put the swab in a little bag. "All done."

"Where do you go to see Sheriff Cochran?" Butch asked. His mouth was so dry he was surprised Shauna had gotten any kind of DNA out of it. "I've got an appointment with him."

"I'll call his office," said Shauna. "They'll send someone down to get you."

Butch sat, nervous, his palms sweaty as she spoke on the phone. Labs had always made him jittery—his doctor's lab when he was little, with all the hypodermic needles lined up like small, glittering missiles. Back then, the worst that would happen was a penicillin shot in his butt. Now, who knows what they could hang on him, with his DNA in the system. He jumped as Shauna hung up the phone.

"Someone will be down in a minute."

He closed his eyes, feeling as if he were about to plunge off a cliff. Why had Devin's addition to the Teresa Ewing story sounded like such a good idea? Now it seemed ridiculous—a fairy tale not even the dumbest cop would believe. He couldn't even remember half of it. And why had he let Dev talk him out of a lawyer? His mother could have gotten him one—she'd saved her money from the house sale like a squirrel burying nuts. A chill went through him. He was getting in way over his head. He needed to get out of here—come back when he had a lawyer, or at least a better recall of Dev's newly revised version of events. He stood up and was halfway out the door when he heard a deep voice call his name. He turned, then his heart stopped. His worst nightmare stood before him. Detective Buck

Whaley in full sail, Taser on one side of his belt, a box of donuts in his hand.

"Hey there, buddy." His voice boomed down the hall. "I was just coming to get you."

Butch didn't know what to say. "I was g-going to talk to Sheriff Cochran."

"He got called away at the last minute. But since you're just giving a statement, I can take it."

Butch swallowed hard, considering his options. Leaving would make him look as if had something to hide. But could he get through a statement with Whaley glowering across the table?

"It's no big deal, Lawrence. Your pal Devin did the same thing, a couple of days ago. Come on. I've got a dozen crullers and a pot of coffee brewing. This shouldn't take long at all."

"Well, okay." Butch eyed the donuts. "I-I guess I've got time for that."

"I thought you might." Whaley grinned.

———

Whaley took him not far down the hall, to an interview room with a desk, several chairs, and a mirror. Butch guessed the mirror was two-way and that other officers would be observing this session. Whaley told him as much, several moments later, when he again read him his rights and asked if he wanted counsel.

"Just so you know"—Whaley pointed to a camera in the corner of the room—"we're recording this."

Butch sat down, numb, trying to remember what Dev had told him to say.

"Okay, then." Whaley took the seat opposite and shoved the box of donuts toward him. "Let her rip."

He took a chocolate cruller, then started to repeat the statement that seemed encoded in his DNA. He and Dev and the others often played around the tree, and that afternoon they had tried, without luck, to get the girls to play Bottom Up. Then Two Toes showed up, threw a knife, and told them to get lost—the tree didn't like white kids playing around it. As he talked Whaley listened, seemingly more interested in his apple fritter than Butch's story. By the time he got to the new part, Whaley was licking sugar off his fingers.

"W-what I want to add is this. After Two Toes ran us off, I went home. A few minutes later, Dev called, begging me to go back up to the tree with him." He stopped. For an awful second couldn't remember why Dev was supposed to have called—then it came to him: a gym lock. "He said he'd left his gym lock up there and he'd have to scrape gum if he didn't have it on his locker the next morning."

Whaley chuckled amiably. "I remember having to scrape gum a couple of times. Wasn't much fun."

"So we went back up there. We were looking around for the lock when we heard a noise. We hid, 'cause we thought it was Two Toes. But then when we peeked around the tree, we saw a tall man in a black hoodie, carrying Teresa over his shoulder."

"Carrying her where?" asked Whaley.

"Up toward Zack's house."

Whaley frowned. "Anything else?"

An electric current of panic zipped through him. Had he forgotten something? Some vital detail that would turn Dev's malarkey into the gospel truth? He didn't know. He couldn't remember.

"I don't know." He shrugged, embarrassed, helpless. "It was a long time ago."

"Sure was," Whaley agreed. "Why don't we go over it again. You might remember something else."

"The whole thing?" His voice cracked like a girl's.

"Just from when Dev called you to help him find his lock."

———————

For three hours Whaley made him tell the story, stopping him at different places. *Did he have a snack after school that day? Was his mother at home? What was he doing when Dev called him to go back up there? What TV show was he watching?* He blurted out answers fast, barely thinking. Though Whaley remained pleasant after he'd asked him the same questions, two and three times, it became hard to remember what he'd said before. As Butch's sweaty shirt began sticking to the back of the chair, Whaley finally seemed satisfied.

"Lawrence, I really appreciate your coming in," he said. "It must feel good to get this off your chest."

"Yeah," he breathed, feeling as if he'd crossed some invisible finish line. "It does."

"There's just one thing I can't square up, though."

Butch felt his bowels turn to water. "What's that?"

"My brother's kids went to Pisgah Junior High, just a grade behind you."

"Oh yeah?"

"They didn't have gym lockers at Pisgah Junior High. They didn't get gym lockers until Pisgah High."

Every cell in his body seemed to freeze. "Are you sure?"

"I called the old superintendent of schools. Pisgah Junior High didn't even have a gym until 1997."

229

Butch shook his head, desperate for an answer. "Maybe it was one of his brother's gym locks. All I know is what Dev told me. He was really scared about losing that lock."

"That's probably it," said Whaley. "Those McConnell kids were a real scary bunch."

TWENTY-EIGHT

"FINDING ANYTHING?" JERRY COCHRAN peered into the office Victor Galloway was using while he looked for a powwow–roustabout–homicide connection.

"Now some tribe's having a powwow about every ten minutes," said Victor. "Then there didn't seem to be a national circuit."

"So no carnies, traveling from reservation to reservation?"

"No. In '89 they set up regionally. A few in the southeast, a few up north. More west of the Mississippi. Most of the crime associated with them was petty stuff—larceny, DUIs. You know, party time crime." He sat back in his chair. He had dark circles under his eyes and stubble on his cheeks. "I feel like I've picked through lint for about three days."

"Want to get some lunch?" asked Cochran. "I'm waiting for Whaley to finish up with Butch Russell."

Victor shrugged. "I'm not all that hungry."

"Then walk with me," said Cochran. "You look like you could use some fresh air."

Reluctantly, Victor shut down his computer. They left the Justice Center and walked the mile into town. The day was already hot, the traffic heavy with cars sporting out-of-state tags.

"Looks like the tourists are here big-time," said Victor.

Cochran laughed. "They'll come until the leaves fall, then it's back home before it snows."

"Can't say I blame them for that," said Victor.

"I suppose. I kind of like winter here. Ginger actually got me up on skis a couple of times last year." Cochran turned to him. "Before I forget—she wants to have you and Mary over for dinner. I didn't want to say anything at the office."

At first, Victor didn't reply. Then he shook his head, glum. "That's really nice of you guys, but Mary and I aren't together anymore."

"What?" Cochran looked astonished. "How come?"

"Let's just say I was an asshole," Victor replied, "and leave it at that."

They went to Cecilia's, an Argentine-French restaurant that had a lunch counter that overlooked the street. Victor decided to eat after all and ordered tamales. Cochran followed suit. As they waited they sat on tall stools and watched the town going about its business—a beer truck making a delivery to Mick & Mack's, people getting fishing lures at the outdoor shop. Cecilia had just brought them their tamales when the beer truck pulled away from the curb, revealing HairTwister's Style Salon, its front window plastered with MARY CROW FOR DA signs. Cochran risked a quick glance at Victor, who gazed at the window wistfully.

"You want to move over to a table?"

"It's okay." Victor shrugged, unwrapping his tamales. "It's not like I don't see Mary Crow signs every day."

They spoke then of other things—how well cute little Chloe Cochran was walking, how Victor's soccer team was playing, whether Atlanta's new quarterback would be any good. Though Victor kept up his end of the conversation, his responses were more dutiful than engaged, as if he were really thinking about something else. Cochran could sympathize. Every time he and Ginger tied up, he felt as if some inner gyroscope had gone slightly off-kilter and the sun wasn't going to rise in quite the same way until he made it right again. As he finished his lunch, he turned cautiously to Galloway.

"You know, Victor, sometimes you can just stumble into asshole-hood, before you even know it. I do it pretty regularly with Ginger."

"Oh yeah? What does she do?"

"She calls me out. Ginger has no trouble expressing herself."

"So you fight?"

"We argue. Sometimes at top volume. Then we make up, and go on."

"This thing with Mary is a little different," said Victor.

"How so?"

"After this fight, she apologized to me, wanted to talk things over. I was the one who walked out."

"Ugh." Cochran winced. "That is bad."

"I know. I can't believe I did it."

"Well, I'm the last guy to give advice, but why don't you go over to the flower shop and buy Mary a rose?"

"You don't understand," said Victor. "I said some terrible things…"

"Then that's all the more reason to go," said Cochran. "Mary's a great girl; you make a great pair. Admit that you were an asshole. Apologize and promise never to be an asshole for the rest of your life."

Victor turned tired brown eyes on him. "You think?"

"I've known Mary since the ninth grade. She's the fairest person I know."

"Fair as in blind justice?"

"Fair as in justice tempered with mercy."

For the first time, Victor laughed. "That's good to know."

Cochran got up and left a twenty-dollar bill between their two plates. "You do what you want, buddy. Lunch is on me."

"Thanks."

Victor watched as Cochran strolled up the street. He gazed at Mary's campaign signs in the beauty shop window for a long moment, then he took a deep breath. "Okay," he whispered. "Here goes nothing."

He did exactly as Cochran advised—bought a single red rose at the florist's and walked toward Mary's office. While waiting for the traffic light to change, he almost lost his nerve—what if she was busy? What if her secretary Annette wouldn't let him see her? Or worse, what if she did see him and wouldn't accept his apology? He would feel like a fool. But then he looked up into a cloudless blue sky that seemed to stretch forever and thought, *You've got to try. Otherwise you'll grow into an old man wondering how differently your life might have turned out if you'd only apologized to Mary Crow.*

The light changed. He took a deep breath and crossed the street, feeling slightly silly. He went up the stairs that led to Ravenel & Crow and opened the door. He expected to see Annette, but Mary was sitting at the front desk, searching for something in a file drawer. She looked up when he came in.

"Victor!" A slight smile turned up the ends of her mouth.

He hurried over to the desk, before his courage evaporated. Her eyes were that amazing gold-to-green-to-gray color. "I don't know how to say this, except to say it. I was an asshole the other night. I had no right to say what I did. You are a person of honor, the best person I know." He gulped and stuck out the rose. "I—I love you. I hope you can forgive me."

She looked at him for what seemed like forever, then she stood up and walked around the desk to face him. "Of course I forgive you," she said softly. "I'd forgiven you before you left my apartment."

"Then we're friends again?" He needed to ask, needed to be sure.

"No, Victor," she said. "I'm friends with Jerry Cochran. Friends with my nitwit partner Ravenel. With you, I'm something else entirely."

He pulled her to him. "I was hoping you'd say that." He bent down, kissed her, and in an instant, the world went right again.

———

The world, however, was not so right at Tote-A-Note Used Cars. Butch Russell sat in Devin McConnell's office, trying hard to hold back tears.

"It was the gym lock," he cried. "The fucking goddamn gym lock. We didn't have lockers until high school, Dev. You got it wrong."

"I'm telling you it's not that big a deal," Dev insisted.

"I'm telling you it is! They got Timothy McVeigh for a missing license plate. It's the stupid details that get people in trouble. They'll know we made this up!"

Dev walked over to the window, scanning the parking lot for customers. There were none, and the few he'd had lately looked harder at him than any automobile. It occurred to him that he might make more money selling photographs than cars—for ten bucks you can have your picture taken with a real live suspect in a real live murder investigation.

"Listen to me!" Butch slammed his fist on the desk, jarring him back to reality.

Dev turned back to his friend. "You did the right thing, Butch. Maybe it was my brother's gym lock. He was in high school. Maybe he was going to beat the shit out of me if he found out I'd taken it. Maybe after spending most of my life with cops in my face, I just fucking forgot the details of the gym lock."

"God, I wish I'd never listened to you." Butch buried his face in his hands. "My mom always said you were trouble."

Dev strode over to Butch, grabbing him by the shirt. "Get a grip, you fucking little Nellie. It's no skin off your nose about the gym lock. You didn't know anything about it, except what I told you."

"But now Whaley knows we cooked this up." Butch's forehead glistened with sweat. "I could see it in his face."

Dev fought the urge to punch Butch out. "No, he doesn't, Butch. Not if you just shut up and stick with the story."

"I don't know what I'm going to do, except call a lawyer," Butch said miserably.

Dev pushed Butch away and walked over to the poster of Miss Truck Tire in her skimpy bikini. He couldn't afford a lawyer; he could barely afford to keep the lights on in his office. If Butch bailed on him, he'd be up shit creek. Then he remembered a trick he'd learned early on, from his brothers.

"You know what we need, Butch?" he asked dreamily.

"What, other than a million dollars and a good attorney?"

"We need a diversion."

Butch's laugh edged toward hysteria. "You want to go play slots at Harrah's?"

"No." Dev turned back to him. "Did you ever really piss your mom off when you were little?"

"I don't know. Maybe. Probably."

"Well, I was in trouble most of the time when I was a kid. My brothers and I would make some mess, and really get creamed for it. Then we figured out that the best way to hide a mess was to make a much bigger mess. A huge mess. Then my mom would get torqued up over the big mess, that she wouldn't even notice the little one."

"So what do you want to do? Blow up the police station?"

"No, stupid. It can't be illegal. And it's got to tie in with this fucking murder." Dev stuffed his hands in his pockets and started pacing around the office. He made slow turns, considering the possibilities. He'd come to the window that overlooked the lot when he saw a red Mazda pull up. For an instant his heart leapt at the thought of a customer, then a familiar figure emerged from the car. John Cooksey, from the *Hartsville Herald*.

"Oh shit," he whispered. "Here comes Cooksey."

"I'm getting out of here." Butch leapt up and headed for the back door. "See you around, Dev."

"Wait!" Dev cried. "I just had an idea. I know how we can create a diversion that will knock everyone on their ass."

"What's that?"

"Wait till Cooksey comes in here, and find out."

TWENTY-NINE

MARY GOT DRESSED SLOWLY, studying her reflection in the bathroom mirror, wondering if she should put on more make-up. Today had been the first time a man had used the L word since she'd lived with Jonathan Walkingstick—two years, ten months, and three days ago. Victor had looked as surprised to say it as she had been to hear it, but he did not go on to qualify his statement, omitting the usual bromides about taking their relationship to the next level (which reminded her of an escalator) or building a future together (which connoted carpentry). He'd simply said "I love you" and stood there looking so hopeful and terrified that she almost cried. She would have been thrilled with a simple apology. His proclamation of love had caught her by surprise.

"I hope he won't be weird tonight," she said, brushing her cheeks with blusher. "Hell, I hope I won't be weird tonight." After several days of no communication at all, it was a pretty big leap to go from being broken up to being in love.

The doorbell rang. She hurried to living room and grabbed her purse. "No shop talk," she reminded herself as she headed to the door. "Nothing about the campaign, nothing about Zack Collier, and not a word about Teresa Ewing." Though Victor had taken the first step to bridge the gap between them, she knew the span was still fragile, the new threads that reconnected them still easily broken.

She opened the door. Victor stood there, taller somehow, wearing a dress shirt and tie. For a moment she wondered if her funny, goofy Victor had morphed into a more staid and serious suitor, then he smiled his old smile as he leaned down to kiss her.

"Ready?" he whispered.

"Where are we going?"

"Drinks. Dinner. Then maybe we could stop by Finnegan's on the way home."

She knew where this was going. "Soccer game?"

"Argentina versus Brazil," he said. "But we don't have to stay long," he added quickly.

"You're on," she said. "Wouldn't miss it for the world."

———

Five hours later, after champagne, dinner, and a soccer game that went through two overtimes and ended in a shoot-out, Victor grabbed Mary for a passionate kiss. Everyone in Finnegan's was kissing somebody, while on the big-screen TV, Argentine soccer players collapsed in joy as they defeated Brazil 3–2. Across the street, a more somber crowd was leaving Mick & Mack's—Brazil fans who'd lost because their goalie screwed up.

"Victor!" cried Alejandro Rodriguez, who was weeping with joy. "We did it!"

"*Sí, amigo.*" Victor slapped Alejandro's upraised hand. "It's a miracle. Now, on to those dirty Germans!"

Laughing, Mary moved out of the line of fire. Though she did not yet appreciate all the nuances of soccer, she adored Victor's enthusiasm. If a game made him this happy, then she would do her best to become a fan. He had, on more than one occasion, sat through some of her tennis matches without complaint. Besides, it was fun to be in a bar where everyone was jubilant. She watched as Alejandro waddled to the bar and announced a round of beer for everybody in an Argentine jersey. Then another man got up and announced a round of beer for everybody, regardless of what they were wearing.

Victor looked at her through the throng of people and pointed at his empty beer bottle, asking her if she'd like another. She nodded. Why not, she figured. Argentina didn't beat Brazil every day. Neither does a good man tell her that he loves her.

Salsa music came on the sound system; two couples started a conga line. Finnegan's wasn't set up for dancing, but she doubted Jerry Cochran would be enforcing any ordinances tonight. Someone had opened a window, allowing a breath of cool night air inside. She moved closer, away from the main crush of the celebration. As she did, she felt the thrum of her cell phone in her pocket. She pulled the thing out and looked at the screen. She'd missed four calls from Emily Kurtz, each a single minute apart. Finally Emily had resorted to text: EMERGENCY! CALL ME ASAP.

"Jeez," Mary whispered. "What now?" She punched in Emily's number. She answered on the second ring but sounded as if she were speaking from the other side of the planet. From every third or fourth word Mary could understand, she gathered that the paper had put some kind of Teresa Ewing video up on their website.

"I'm downtown," Mary shouted above the din. "But I'll go over to my office and watch it there."

She clicked off her near-useless phone and looked for Victor. He was making his way toward her carrying two bottles of beer. She hurried through the crowd, remembering her earlier vow of no sensitive subjects broached tonight. She didn't want to risk spoiling what had been an incredible evening, and yet she couldn't just tell him she was leaving, going to her office to work.

"Dos Equis with lime." He handed her the beer. "From the most interesting man in the world."

"Thanks." Grabbing his hand, she pulled him to the door, where the decibel level allowed nominal hearing. She took a deep breath—knowing she had to be honest with him. Law and elections and defendants were as much a part of her as the Argentine soccer team was of him. "I just got a call from Emily Kurtz. The paper's put out some kind of Teresa Ewing video. She says it's really important."

He did not blink. "You want to go look at it?"

She nodded. "I can go to my office. You stay here, with your friends."

"No." He shook his head. "I want to come with you."

————

They walked, hand-in-hand, to Ravenel & Crow. The night was soft, Victor's hand was warm, and the magnolia tree that bloomed in front of the Baptist church made the night air heady and sweet. Though Teresa Ewing's murder seemed as distant as the stars, Mary knew it wasn't. There was, according to Emily, quite a surprise awaiting her on the Internet.

She unlocked the door to the building and walked up to the second floor. Her office was dark, illuminated only by the moonlight shining through the high, arched windows. Half a block away the courthouse stood on the hill, its gold dome shining in the darkness.

Victor gazed at the handsome old building. "So where's your office going to be?"

She went to stand beside him. "Right now Turpin's on the third floor, in the back. I'd like that corner office in the front."

"Why there?"

"One set of windows overlooks the town. The other set looks south, toward the rez."

"Your mother's home." Victor put his arm around her.

"My home too," said Mary softly. "If I win, I don't ever want to forget where I came from." She leaned against him a moment longer, then she turned. "Come on. Let's see what Emily's so upset about."

She switched on her computer. Victor sat down in her chair and pulled her on his lap. Together they watched the *Hartsville Herald* logo fill the screen, then a headline appeared above a video. "Teresa Ewing Witness Breaks Silence."

"What the hell?" Victor sat up straighter.

"I don't know," said Mary. She clicked on the play button. John Cooksey came on the left side of the screen, sitting across someone cast in shadow. It was impossible to tell if it was a man or a woman, young or old.

"Did you see Teresa Ewing on the last afternoon of her life?" Cooksey acted as if he were interviewing someone on *Sixty Minutes*.

"I did." The person's voice had been altered, making it sound mechanical and slightly drunk at the same time. "We were playmates."

242

"Could you tell us what happened that last afternoon?" asked Cooksey.

The strange voice went on, recounting much the same story she'd heard from Jack Wilkins. Seven of them playing under the tree, the three girls went home, then Two Toes McCoy ran the boys off. *This is a setup*, thought Mary. But then Cooksey went on.

"That's pretty well documented," Cooksey acknowledged. "What makes your story different?"

"I went back," said the voice. "Later. I left something there and had to find it."

"And what did you see then?"

"I heard someone crying. I couldn't tell who it was, so I peeked around the tree. I saw someone carrying Teresa Ewing over their shoulder, toward Zack Collier's house."

"Did you recognize this person?"

"No. It was dark. But I could tell they were big—bigger than the rest of us."

"And was Teresa Ewing crying?" asked Cooksey.

"No. Teresa Ewing wasn't moving at all."

The interview went on for a few more exchanges. The voice claimed to be scared, claimed to have run home only to find later that Teresa had gone missing.

"Why didn't you tell the police this at the time?"

"I was scared. I knew we'd been done something bad, asking the girls to play strip poker. The cops were in my face all the time anyway. I figured if I told them anything else, it would just make everything worse."

The video stopped then; the show was over. So far, no comments had been left on the site, so Mary turned off the computer.

"Who do you figure that was?" asked Victor.

"I'd say somebody who wants to frame either Zack Collier or Two Toes McCoy," she replied. "Which brings Adam Shaw, Devin McConnell, and Butch Russell to mind."

"That's just what I was thinking," said Victor. "But you've got to wonder—why now, after all these years?"

She nestled down in his arms. "Maybe your SBI report's making somebody nervous."

"I know you're representing Collier, but why did Emily want you to look at this tonight?"

"Because she wants me to dump Collier. She heard that Turpin's going to make it look like my campaign is full of criminals who I'll go easy on if I get in office."

He kissed her behind her ear, raising the most pleasurable goose-flesh. "So what are you going to do now?"

"What time is it?"

He shifted, looked at his watch. "12:47."

"First thing tomorrow I'll call Grace and tell her she may get more baseball bats aimed at her mailbox. Emily, I'm sure, will call me."

"And you'll reassure her that you're not going easy on any criminals?"

"I will never go easy on a criminal."

He nibbled her earlobe. "Then, would you like to go easy on me?"

She shifted in his lap. "What did you have in mind?"

"Right now. Over there, where the moonlight comes in those windows. I can look at you and you can look at that office you want so badly."

"Are you being sarcastic?"

"No." He stood up, lifting her in his arms. "I want it for you too. I think it is the only thing that will make you truly happy."

"I can think of one other thing," she whispered as he carried her over to the window.

"No need to worry about that," he said. "That, I've got covered."

THIRTY

THE FIRST BAT HIT Grace's mailbox just after sunrise. She was asleep and dreaming when three sharp *blam*s made her sit up in bed, her heart thumping. At first she thought it was her usual chase nightmare, then a car roared off, tires squealing. By the time she got out of bed and ran to the front window, the mailbox was in pieces, all over the street. When she heard a second car approaching, she hurried outside and stood on the front porch, hands on hips, daring the driver to whack the remains of it. A low-slung black coupe rolled past her house slowly, as if reconnoitering her property. But the driver must have seen her and recognized her challenge. He gunned his engine and roared off down the road.

Something has happened, Grace thought. *Something bad.* She went back to her bedroom and dialed Mary Crow.

"How bad is it, Grace?" Mary said immediately, as if she'd been expecting her call.

"Two drive-bys already. The first destroyed my mailbox. I went outside and scared the second one away. What's going on?"

"The paper posted an interview with one of the Salola Street gang on their website last night. Now somebody's re-posted the thing on YouTube."

"The Salola Street gang?" Grace cried. "One of those boys?"

"One of those men, now. But they never showed the guy's face on camera and his voice was distorted."

"But what did he say?"

"Nothing new, until the very end. Then he claimed to have come back to the tree and watched a tall person in a dark hoodie carry Teresa Ewing toward your house."

Grace went cold inside.

Mary continued. "It sounds fabricated, plus it's too vague a description to be of any use in court, so don't worry about that. But things could get dicey out there. I was just going to call you."

"I see." Grace opened her blinds to keep watch on the front yard.

"Have you got any relatives you could visit for a couple of weeks?" asked Mary.

"No." She gave a bitter laugh. "The people who would welcome me would not welcome Zack."

"Even in an emergency?"

"You know the word *oolundeeha?*"

Mary translated the Cherokee. "Crazy."

Grace said, "My great aunt Junebug calls Zack *egwa oolundeeha*, Big Crazy. She's afraid of him. Throws salt over her shoulder every time she sees him."

"And there's nowhere else you could go?"

"My parents are dead, and my two brothers live in Alaska."

"Okay," said Mary. "I'll ask Cochran to up his patrols out there. But be careful, Grace, and keep a record of what goes on. The world isn't short of crazies these days."

"No kidding." Grace replied, giving a heavy sigh. "It's not like this is anything new."

For a moment she sat on the bed, angry tears welling in her eyes. Then she blinked them away and padded into the den, to the computer. First she watched the video on the paper's website, then she watched it again on YouTube. Though it was impossible to tell which of the Salola Street gang was talking, the idea of some coward hiding in the shadows, implicating her son relit her anger. She found her cell phone at the bottom of her purse and punched in Adam's number.

"Were you the one on that video?" she spat, shaking with rage.

"Huh?" he asked, his voice husky with sleep. "What are you talking about?"

"Go look at the paper's website," she said. "Or just search Teresa Ewing on YouTube."

She clicked off the phone and made some coffee. By the time she'd poured her first cup, he called her back. "It's Devin."

"How do you know?"

"His speech pattern. Plus he's always tilted his head funny—probably because of his goony eye."

Suddenly she wanted to cry, to scream. "But why say all this now? Does he not realize how much evil this brings down on our heads?"

"He's scared, Grace. Whatever new evidence the police have must be making him very nervous."

"So of course he implicates Zack."

"He actually just implicated somebody taller than he was. It sounds like he's desperate to blame anybody but himself."

"Do you think he killed Teresa?"

"I don't know," said Adam.

She gave a deep sigh. Though talking to him had dissipated her rage, she was now exhausted, at only 7:13 in the morning. "Well, thanks for talking to me. I'm sorry I woke you up."

"You didn't really think that was me on the video, did you?"

"No. I was just angry. And I didn't have anybody else to call."

"I would never do anything like that, Grace. Not to you, not to Zack, not to anybody."

———

After that day, there was nothing to do but slog through. Hillview Haven sent her a nice letter, thanking her for her interest, but saying that they did not consider Zack a good fit for their program. Hardly surprised, Grace kept on teaching, relying on Clara to take care of Zack. Adam, whose parents had hit a plumbing snag with their new home in South Carolina, visited most afternoons, helping Zack catalog his vast collection of videotapes. Grace slept poorly at night, one ear attuned for a footstep outside her window, a car rolling up her drive. Every morning she woke at dawn to search the front yard for dead animals. Her landline began ringing constantly. Afternoons, a group of little girls would call and ask for Zack. The first time Clara handed him the phone, one of the young callers pretended to be Teresa Ewing speaking from the grave. It scared him so badly that he cried. After that Clara started screening the calls, telling the girls off in rapid Spanish.

At night the calls were for her. Most of them were stupid, but one caller frightened her. Always it was eerie, whistling music playing, then a gravelly whispered *I'm coming for you, Grace. You and your fucked-up son.* The voice was male, younger than her fifty-eight years, his accent distinctly Southern. A couple of times she was tempted to say, "Go fuck yourself, Dev!" But she had no proof that it was Devin McConnell. With her luck it would be John Cooksey, who would then put her on YouTube, or Twitter, or some other stupid site where teenagers could make fun of an old woman using the F word.

Ultimately, painting saved her. She had her upcoming show in Asheville, and when she wasn't teaching at the college or checking the front yard for dead squirrels, she holed up in the little mudroom off the garage and worked on her canvasses. Entering a world of color and light was like diving in a pool of warm water. As long as she kept a paint brush in her hand, the accusations and hatefulness seemed distant and far away.

Finally one afternoon she lined up all her canvasses and signed them with the GC monograph she'd used throughout her career. Twelve landscapes, representing a year of work. Before, she'd hoped to make enough for a weekend at the beach. Now, all her money would have to go to Mary Crow.

She studied the paintings another moment, then called down to the den, where Adam and Zack were watching videos.

"You guys up for a road trip to Asheville?"

"Sure," yelled Zack, excited.

"If you two will help me get these canvasses up there, I'll take you out for dinner afterward."

"Can we go to the restaurant with the hat?" asked Zack.

"Yes," she replied. "Casa Lupe it is."

———————

With her available manpower doubled, they got the van loaded quickly. Two hours later, she stood in the Gallery L'Atelier, talking with Sue Creason as Adam and Zack brought the canvasses. The coil of nervousness in her stomach loosened as the no-nonsense, spiked hair Sue enthused over the paintings.

"Grace, these are just amazing," she gushed. "I don't know how you do it." She glanced at Zack, who was carrying a huge landscape to a far corner of the exhibit space and lowered her voice. "I heard you had some trouble in Hartsville. That little girl who was killed years ago."

"We've had some tough days," Grace admitted. "But we're getting through them."

"Well, it doesn't show in your work," said Sue. "We won't have a bit of trouble selling these. You have any preference about how we hang these?"

"Any way so they sell like hot cakes," said Grace. "I need the money."

———

After that they were done. As promised, she drove them to a Mexican restaurant north of Asheville. Usually, the floppy black sombrero was reserved for people celebrating their birthdays, but she whispered to the manager that her son was autistic, and wearing the hat would mean a lot to him. A few minutes later Zack was sitting at a corner table, the sombrero casting a shadow over all their food. Grace ordered a pitcher of beer and sat back, happy. It had been a good day. She'd finished her paintings, Sue was confident that she could sell them, and Zack was sitting with his best pal, Adam. *Maybe the worst is over,* she thought. *Maybe the phone will stop ringing and the cars will stop driving by and the DNA test will exonerate Zack, forever. Then you can get back to your regular, everyday troubles.*

———————

They finished at Casa Lupe's and drove home. It was dusk when she pulled into the driveway, fireflies twinkling over the front yard. She was tempted, for a moment, to check the yard for dead squirrels, but she decided she could do that in the morning. Better to get Zack inside and settled down for the night. They'd all had a big day. Zack hurried into the house, eager to watch a final video before bed. She followed him, assuming that Adam was right behind her, when he called her name.

"Grace," he said softly, looking up at her from the bottom of the steps. "I didn't want to say anything at the restaurant, but I'll be leaving tomorrow. We've gotten everything loaded and Dad says the plumbing at the new house is working fine."

"Oh," she replied. His words took her by surprise. She knew he was only here temporarily, but she'd grown accustomed to having him around. "I'm happy for you, Adam, but Zack and I will miss you terribly."

He smiled. "I wanted to ask you the best way to say good-bye to—"

Before he could finish a scream came from inside the house. "Nooooooo!" Zack screamed. "Not them!"

Grace turned and raced up the stairs, Adam following. Zack was standing in the doorway of his room, hands flapping like wings, tears streaming down his cheeks.

"Something happened, Mama!" He pointed into the room. "Something bad!"

She looked where just hours ago he'd had bird paintings on the wall, stuffed animals piled on the bed, Barbie dolls arranged in some kind of tableau only he could understand. Now the room was a wreck. The bird paintings had been sprayed with black paint. All the stuffed animals had been decapitated, their heads grotesquely re-arranged on different bodies. But the Barbies were the most disturb-ing—someone had arranged them in sexual positions. One doll's head was between a prone one's legs; another doll's face was on her breast while another straddled her face. The fifth stood propped against the wall, apparently observing the whole scene.

"Jesus," Adam whispered. "Who the fuck did this?"

"I don't know," replied Grace, feeling shaky inside.

"Let's get it cleaned up," said Adam, moving toward the Barbie dolls.

"No." Grace touched his arm. "Not yet. I want Mary Crow to see it first."

THIRTY-ONE

Emily Kurtz was the one who inadvertently received Grace's urgent calls to Mary Crow. She was sitting in the back of the Lions Club dining room, listening as the candidates for District Attorney spoke to the gathered Lions. Mary had left her purse and phone in Emily's keeping, and the campaign manager gave an inward groan when she saw Grace Collier's name appear on the phone screen. *Every candidate has a fatal flaw,* she remembered one of her political science professors saying. *It's your job to figure out how to hide it.* Misplaced loyalty was Mary Crow's flaw. She doubted it would take George Turpin to figure that out.

As it turned out, not long at all. Mary had just given her basic pitch for more transparency and equal justice in domestic abuse cases when Turpin took the microphone.

"Ms. Crow, how can you talk about cleaning up the DA's office when you have so much dirt among your own campaign staff?"

"Excuse me?" Mary turned to face the man. Though Emily could tell he'd caught her off-guard, Mary's expression revealed nothing.

"I think you need to put your own house in order before you tackle the courthouse," Turpin went on. "One of your clients is a murder suspect, and his mother is on your payroll. Seems to me that's lying down with dogs and getting up with fleas."

The audience gave a low murmur. Emily bit her lip as she waited for Mary to respond. Smiling, Mary addressed her opponent as she might a jury—friendly, but oh so firm.

"Mr. Turpin, unless you have some inside information from the sheriff's department, I don't believe any of my clients have been indicted for murder."

Turpin tried to speak, but Mary went on. "Let's not be coy, though. I'm assuming you're speaking of Zack Collier, who is among several suspects in the Teresa Ewing case. His mother Grace volunteered to design my signage over six months ago. She has never been on my payroll. Unlike yours, my campaign's run mostly by volunteers.

Again, Turpin started to respond, but Mary didn't give him the chance. "What's more distressing about your question is that it makes me think you've fallen victim to rumor." Mary turned to the audience. "If Mr. Turpin's planning on building his cases from clips on YouTube, I've got some great footage of a Skunk Ape I'll send his way."

The audience roared. Emily released the breath she'd been holding. This time Mary had nicely dodged the DA's bullet this time, but she knew Turpin would bring up Zack and Grace Collier again. It was just too sketchy, and neither he nor Pugh were rookie politicians.

The meeting lasted another twenty minutes. The candidates restated their positions one final time, then started to work the crowd. Emily noted with relief that the knot of people around Mary equaled the knot around Turpin. Like a wallflower at a dance, Prentiss Herbert stood by the speakers table alone, courted by no one.

255

When everything finally ended, Mary came over to retrieve her purse. "How many votes did I lose tonight?" she asked, a thin line of worry between her brows.

"You may have gained a few," said Emily. "You responded well under pressure. And you were funny. Voters remember funny."

"The bastard really blindsided me with that question about the Colliers."

"You'd better get used to it, then. I guarantee he'll use it next time, and he'll use it better."

Mary shrugged. "It won't change anything. Zack's my client, Grace is my friend."

Emily held out Mary's phone. "Speaking of your friend, she's called three times."

"Did you answer any of them?"

"She's not my client," Emily replied coolly. "And I wish to God she wasn't yours."

———————

An hour later, Mary turned into Grace's driveway. Every light blazed inside the house, giving it a strangely festive look. She parked beside a car she did not recognize and hurried up the front steps. Just as she was about to ring the bell, Grace opened the door. She looked in shock, as if she'd just walked away from a bad wreck unscathed.

"Come inside," Grace said, her voice wobbly. "You need to see this."

Mary followed her into the living room. Distantly, she heard a television and the sound of male laughter. "Zack's friend Adam is here," explained Grace. "He and Zack are watching videos."

"Adam Shaw? The other suspect at the DNA test?" Mary remembered the slender man who'd stepped between Zack Collier and Buck Whaley.

"Yes. He's been a godsend to us these last couple of weeks."

Mary shrugged as they walked down the hall. It was nice, Mary guessed, that the boys could still be friends. Jack Wilkins had told her the other families on Salola Street hadn't spoken to each other in years.

"This afternoon Adam and Zack helped me take my paintings up to Asheville," said Grace as she led Mary down a short hall. "When we got back, we found this."

She opened the door to a bedroom. Clearly, it was Zack's—though the décor was dolls and stuffed animals, it smelled of soiled sheets and unwashed man. But the room had been trashed—pictures on the wall had been sprayed with black paint, the stuffed animals lined up on the bed with their heads gruesomely rearranged. A big yellow dog had the tiny head of a pink rabbit; the plump body of a brown teddy bear wore the small green head of a turtle.

"Whoa," Mary whispered.

"Look on the floor," said Grace.

Mary turned. At the foot of Zack's bed, someone had constructed a bizarre tableau of Barbie dolls, all in sexual poses, legs spread wide, arms above their heads. Mary felt the hair lift on the back of her neck. She turned to Grace. "Are you sure Zack didn't do this?"

"No. I came in here about five minutes before we left for Asheville, to get him a clean shirt. His room was messy, but not like this." She leaned against the door, defeated. "This is new. Not like the other stuff."

Mary frowned. "Other stuff beyond your mailbox?"

"Phone calls night and day," said Grace. "Dead animals arranged in the yard."

"Dead animals?"

"Squirrels and rabbits, mostly. Some are roadkill, but most have been shot. The worst day we found a dozen posed around the bird feeder. Adam can show you a picture of that."

Mary couldn't believe what she was hearing. "Jeez, Grace, why didn't you tell me?"

"What could you have done? The people come at night. Occasionally I hear their footsteps in the driveway, but by the time I look out the window, they're gone."

Mary tamped down a flash of anger. Grace was a lot smarter than this. "Did it ever occur to you to call the police?"

Grace backed up a step. "And have Detective Whaley come over here? No thanks. That's why I called you. Somebody needed to see this, but not the cops."

"Yes they do, Grace. Now." Mary flipped out her phone and started to call Jerry Cochran.

"Wait!" Grace grabbed her hand. "Please don't call them. This room is the one place Zack feels totally safe. If the police come in here in the middle of the night, he won't sleep for months."

"Grace, there could be fingerprints on these dolls—evidence pertinent to the Ewing case. The cops need to know what's been going on out here."

"Couldn't you just take the dolls to the police station?"

"No. Is that his pal Adam's Toyota in the drive?" asked Mary.

Grace nodded.

Mary dug in her purse and pulled out a twenty-dollar bill. "Give Adam this and have him take Zack to the late show at the

Brew N View," said Mary. "Then he won't be here when Jerry Cochran comes."

———

Two hours later, Jerry Cochran had Grace Collier sign the complaint she'd made. He'd taken pictures of the room, bagged up the Barbies, and studied the little notebook Grace had whimsically titled "How I was Driven Crazy, Volume 4." The current vandals, Jerry determined, had jimmied the lock on the back door to gain entry to the house. How they knew the house would be empty for several hours was up for grabs.

"Is Adam Shaw always with you when these incidents occur?" asked Cochran.

Grace nodded. "He was today, when we went to Asheville. Mostly, he's helping his parents get ready to move."

"Does he come here often?"

Mary noticed Grace stiffen slightly. "He comes by evenings, to watch videos with Zack. Look, Sheriff, stuff like this happens every time the paper runs a story about Teresa Ewing. Adam Shaw hasn't been in Pisgah County since he was a kid."

Cochran made a note and went on. "Any other people come here on a regular basis?"

"Only Clara Perez, Zack's hab-tech."

Cochran frowned. "Hab-tech?"

"A caregiver, provided by the State. She watches Zack during the week, while I teach. She's worked here two years.

"You have her phone number?"

"Please don't call her, Sheriff. She's a sweet girl, and Zack loves her." Abruptly, Grace teared up. "If you start investigating her, then she might quit. It's almost impossible to find good people to work with autistic adults. Most of them just camp out in front of the television and eat Cheetos all day."

Cochran nodded. "I understand." He checked his notes, then closed his notebook. "We'll take these dolls for evidence and bump up the patrols along this road. In the meantime, I urge you to get an alarm and an unlisted phone number. Put a good dead bolt lock on the back door and a floodlight for your front yard."

Grace sighed. "I moved out here because I thought we'd be safe. I guess I was wrong."

"You never know what goes on in some people's minds," said Cochran. "I wish I could tell you otherwise."

———

Mary followed Cochran as he returned to his car. "What do you think?"

"Friend to friend?" replied Jerry.

"Of course."

"If I were you, I'd get them both out of here. None of my squads can get out here in under thirty minutes, and this could get ugly."

"That's exactly what I was thinking," said Mary. "Do you have any idea when the DNA report might come in?"

"I call Winston every day. They say soon." He opened his door, slid in behind the steering wheel. "You know, I've never seen anything like this case. It happened when we were in grade school, but people act like the girl died yesterday."

She thought of the years of anguish she had endured, before she found out who killed her mother. "I guess an unsolved murder just sticks in the collective craw."

"I know it sticks in Whaley's. Probably Jack Wilkins's too. The whole thing is like trying to catch smoke. Every time you think you've grasped a clue, it vanishes. Unless we get a hit from the DNA, I don't think we'll ever solve this one."

"God, I hope that's not the case," said Mary. "Grace and Zack deserve some kind of closure."

"Don't they all?" Cochran replied. He turned the engine on. "You be careful, okay?"

"*Tsutshintasti*," she answered in Cherokee.

She watched him go down Grace's driveway, the taillights of his Camaro squinting a demonic red in the darkness. When she returned to Grace's house, she found her sitting on Zack's bed, her hands shaking as she tried to match the right animal torso with its proper head. Mary came in and sat down beside her.

"Grace, we need to talk."

"I've got to get these things back together," she said, tearing off a strip of gray duct tape. "Zack sleeps with them at night."

Mary put her hand on Grace's, stopping her frantic restoring of the toys. "Grace, you and Zack need to relocate. It's dangerous for you to stay here. Sheriff Cochran said so."

"We've been over that before, Mary. I've got nowhere else to go."

"I might have a place for you."

Grace looked up from the stuffed rabbit. "Where? Jail?"

"A cabin. It's part of an estate I'm settling. I'm going to call the owners and see if they're agreeable to having you and Zack stay there."

Grace shook her head. "You don't understand, Mary. I don't have any extra money and we can't do cabins, anyway. We need electricity. Indoor plumbing. A TV Zack can watch his tapes on."

"It's got all of that," said Mary. "And the heirs don't need the money."

"Why don't they want to use it themselves?

"Because it's in Rugby, Tennessee. The absolute middle of no-where." Mary picked up the head of a penguin. "Pack up your stuff. I'm calling them tonight, when I get home. I'm pretty sure they won't mind."

"But what about my job?" Grace cried. "And Clara's job? She needs to work too."

"Call in sick. Use some vacation days. Tell Clara this is just until the DNA results comes back."

"And when will that be?" she said, growing angry. "How long will our lives be in this limbo?"

"As long as the lab in Winston takes, Grace."

"I don't know." Her hands trembled as she held the little rabbit. "I don't know what to do anymore."

Mary took the toy from her grasp. "Grace, these are dolls. With some tape and thread, we can fix them. Next time, it might be you and Zack. You two won't fix so easily."

For a long moment Grace just stared at the rabbit, then she gave a great sigh. "Okay. I've got two weeks of vacation, plus some sick leave. I guess we can go for a little while."

"Good," said Mary. "There's just one thing you've got to remember. You can't tell anyone—not Clara or Adam or anybody—where you're going."

Grace suddenly gave a wild laugh. "Crazy is where I'm going, Mary. And everybody knows I'm pretty much already there."

THIRTY-TWO

FOR THE FIRST TIME in years, a middle of the night phone call awakened Jack Wilkins.

He grabbed the phone automatically, barking, "Wilkins," just as he had when some gunshot or stabbing would get him out of bed. But instead of a police dispatcher, Mary Crow's voice came over the line.

"Jack? I'm sorry to wake you up, but I need your help."

"What's wrong?" he asked, flattered that she'd thought of him.

"Some thugs are coming down pretty hard on Grace and Zack Collier."

"Oh?"

"Somebody broke into their home and demolished Zack's bedroom. Decapitated all his stuffed animals and arranged his Barbie dolls in a kind of sex scene."

Wilkins cringed at the notion of a grown man having Barbie dolls at all, but he pushed the thought aside and refocused on Mary Crow. "Did they call it in?"

"Yeah. Jerry Cochran came out and promised to up the patrols."

"Then how can I help you?"

"I have an idea that somebody's trying to scare Zack Collier into a confession. People have battered their mailbox, put dead animals in their yard, and they're getting phone calls. Little girls call Zack during the day, pretending to be Teresa Ewing. A man makes threatening calls to Grace at night."

"Did she tell Cochran all that?"

"She did, but she didn't want to. She's afraid of the cops. According to her, Buck Whaley comes over, hassles Zack every month or so."

Wilkins frowned. "And you think Whaley's behind all this?"

"No, no," said Mary. "But I think that whoever's doing this to the Colliers knows a lot about Teresa Ewing's murder. If we can find them, we might finally learn the truth about what happened."

He stretched the shoulder that always stiffened when he slept. "So what do you need from me?"

"I just called in a favor from some other clients of mine. I'm relocating the Colliers to some of their property tomorrow morning. I want you to find out who's doing these things while they're gone."

Wilkins thought of the hours and days and years he and the rest of the department had devoted to this case. "I'm sorry, Mary, I can't work to exonerate Zack Collier. It would be like, I don't know, betraying my friends."

"But you'd be trying to find out who's stalking a fifty-something woman and her autistic son. That's a crime, right there. Anyway, if my idea holds water, then you just might be the one to crack this case."

He looked at the red numerals glowing on his clock radio. 1:23. He hadn't been awake at this hour in years. It made him feel not sleepy, but youthful—as if the universe had reversed itself and was giving him another shot at catching the person who killed that child.

"Okay." He grabbed a pen and the crossword puzzle book he worked every night, ready to write in the margin. "Tell me when and where."

That had been six hours ago. Now it was just past dawn and the smell of coffee was wafting in from his kitchen. It was time to get up. Not to tend chickens or play golf, but to go somewhere and do something with meaning and purpose. He shaved and dressed, fixed the dog a bowl of kibble and himself a bowl of bran flakes. Then he let the chickens out of their coop, gathering four eggs in the process. After that, he went into the room that served as his office. Slowly he opened the lap drawer of his desk and pulled out his PI license. Though he hadn't carried it for two years, it had not expired, and his ID photo still looked more or less like him.

"Who knew?" he whispered, glancing at his picture of nine-year-old Teresa Ewing. "All this time, and it's still you." He closed the drawer and wondered if he ought to get his Smith & Wesson. At first he thought, no, he was too old for fireworks. But then he changed his mind and grabbed the gun. You never knew when you might need protection, and these days a lot of nitwits sported their Second Amendment rights locked, loaded, and ready to go.

He strapped on his gun then zipped up the light tan jacket he wore on the golf course. As he headed for the back door Lucky followed him, tail wagging, bright eyes hopeful of inclusion. Jack had planned to leave him shut up in the kitchen with food and water, but then he changed his mind.

"Come on, boy," he said. "You dug up the first clue in this old case. Maybe you can dig up the next one today."

He drove to the address Mary had given him. Grace Collier's house was a modest rancher, set back off a county road at the end of a gravel drive. Not totally isolated, but definitely out of the way to those unfamiliar with the area. The front yard was lush with flowers and bird feeders; a tall privacy fence hid the back yard from view. Jack saw Mary's Miata parked near the garage, so he pulled up beside it. Leaving Lucky in the truck, he walked to the front door. Grace Collier answered his knock. He recognized her dark Cherokee eyes and high cheekbones right away. Though her hair was still black and her olive skin unlined, her mouth was drawn, and she looked at him warily.

"Hi, Jack." Mary suddenly appeared behind Grace. "Did you have any trouble finding us?"

Before he could answer, Grace spoke. "You came to see us before, didn't you," she said softly. "With Whaley. When we lived on Salola Street."

He nodded. "Yes ma'am. Whaley and I were partners then."

"Did they bring you back on duty?" Grace's tone was bitter. "Just to question us again?"

"I brought Detective Wilkins here, Grace," Mary explained. "He's retired from the force, working for me as a private investigator. I'm hoping he can figure out who's been harassing you, while you and Zack are away."

Grace snorted. "Oh sure. And just for fun maybe he can plant some new evidence."

Jack was surprised at the woman's cynicism, then further surprised when Mary Crow came to his defense. "That's uncalled for,

266

Grace," she said, her voice like a knife. "You've hired me as your attorney. You have to trust that I'm doing the right thing."

"*Hadi.*" Grace folded her arms across her chest.

Jack listened as they went for a couple more rounds in what he assumed was Cherokee. Mary Crow's eyes flashed as she spoke, and it occurred to him that she'd be the last person he'd want to tie up with in court. Finally she stepped back as Grace Collier nodded at him. "Please come in, Detective Wilkins," she said. "Forgive my rudeness. I just don't have a very good history with the Pisgah County Sheriff's Department."

He smiled. "I understand." He started to say something more— that he knew Whaley could be a jackass, that he'd ridden her son way too hard then and had, apparently, continued to do so, but then the boy himself came into the living room, dripping from a shower, with only a skimpy towel around his waist.

"Who's here, Mama?" Zack asked, turning wide eyes on him. Jack marveled at how little the boy had changed. Where his own sons had put on muscle and grown out of their baby fat, Zack Collier had just turned into a bearded version of his fifteen-year-old self. There was little muscle tone in his arms and his fingers had dimples where knuckles should have been. Despite all that, Jack could see that had he been normal, he would have been as striking as his mother.

"You remember Mary, don't you?" Grace hurried toward her son. "She's going to take us on a vacation. Her friend Mr. Wilkins came along with her."

"Is he going on our vacation too?" Zack eyed him suspiciously as his mother herded him out of the living room.

"No. I need you to pack up your videos and your animals and put on some clothes. We're going to leave soon."

"But I don't want to leave! I want to … "

"Zack, we talked about that this morning. Some very nice people are letting us use their cabin."

Mary and Wilkins stood in the living room as their voices faded down the hall.

"That's Zack in a good mood," Mary told him. "It's a whole different ball game when he gets mad. Most of these paintings are covering holes he put in the plaster."

"Don't they have places for people like him?" he asked.

"According to Grace, very few that welcome adults with anger-management issues."

Jack nodded, remembering Whaley's pet theory—that Zack Collier had killed Teresa Ewing and Grace had covered it up. In a way he couldn't blame her—what parent would want to see their only, damaged child spend the rest of their life in the criminal ward at Naughton Hospital?

He turned to Mary. "Why don't you show me where all this bad stuff's been going on?"

She took him on a brief tour of the yard—pointing out where the dead animals had surrounded the bird feeder, showing him the remnants of the shattered mailbox.

As they returned to the front porch, he pointed to a series of small holes in the side of the house. "Grace ever mention these?"

Mary peered at the line of small dots. "Bullet holes?"

He nodded. "Looks like from a .22. Probably from a rifle, fired from the street."

"Wonder why they didn't aim for the window?" asked Mary.

Wilkins shrugged. "Bad aim, crappy rifle. Who knows?"

"Let's just keep them to ourselves," said Mary. "Grace may not know about them and it would be just one more thing for her to worry about."

They went back inside the living room, where Grace had left her diary on the sofa. Mary picked it up and handed it to Jack.

"'How I Was Driven Crazy, Volume 4'?" Jack had to laugh. "At least she hasn't lost her sense of humor."

"Everything's in there—dates and times of footsteps in the driveway, crank calls at night. Even little cartoons that illustrate every incident."

"If these calls are coming in on a landline, I can tap that here in the house. Phone records would take a subpoena."

Mary was searching for a phone when Grace came back in the room.

"I've gotten Zack loaded up," she announced, looking at Mary. "We're ready to go any time you are."

"Grace, have you got a landline?"

"In my room." She led them to her bedroom and pointed to an old white phone on the bedside table. "Why?"

"I can record whoever's calling you," said Jack.

"How nice." Grace gave another sardonic smile. "Our whole lives will be open for inspection."

"Not really," he replied, feeling both sympathy for and irritation with this woman. "Just the parts Ms. Crow wants me to inspect."

Mary stepped forward. "Remember Grace, you need to trust me on this."

She gave a reluctant sigh. "Okay. I'll leave my house keys on the kitchen table. Mary, we'll be waiting for you in the car."

She feels violated, Jack thought as he watched her leave her own bedroom. *Probably thinks I'm just another cop, trying to nail her son.*

He frowned at Mary. "Your client doesn't seem exactly thrilled with any of this."

"I don't care," Mary replied. "My client needs to do what I tell her." She shouldered her bag. "I'll leave you to it, Jack. I'll give you a call tomorrow."

"You have a weapon?"

She laughed. "You sound like my boyfriend."

"Well, do you?"

"My old Glock Nine," she said. "In my glove compartment."

"Keep it with you. You never need it until you need it, and then you need it big-time."

"Now you really do sound like Victor."

He smiled at the woman he was growing to like. "Then I'll take that as a compliment."

THIRTY-THREE

GRACE FOLLOWED MARY CROW west on I-40, snaking through the Appalachian Mountains. Zack wept for the first hour of their trip, not understanding why a detective was at their house and Adam had not come over to say good-bye.

"Adam moved his parents to South Carolina this morning," Grace explained. "And Mr. Wilkins is a friend, not a policeman."

"He is too a policeman." Zack turned his tear-stained face toward hers. "He came over after Teresa died. He wore a red tie. His badge was number 311."

She looked at him, stunned. His recall was quirky, but amazing. Sometimes she wondered what she would find if she truly plumbed Zack's memory, though she'd long ago decided it was better not to try.

"Mr. Wilkins is going to take care of our house while we're on vacation," she told him, the lie sour at the back of her throat. "And Adam told you good-bye last night."

"He still could have come over this morning," he muttered, staring miserably at the lush green foliage passing by.

Grace gave a heavy sigh. Not only did she have someone from the enemy camp occupying her home, now Zack was alone again. It would be hard for him to go back to just quarterly outings with the Autism Society. For once in his adult life, he'd had a real friend who'd visited almost every day. They would both miss Adam a lot.

They crossed over into Tennessee, stopping once for hamburgers, then once more at a flea market, west of Knoxville. "Zack wants to look for videos," she explained, calling Mary on her cell phone. "Trust me, it's better if we do."

"No problem," said Mary. "I can return some calls while you two shop."

They pulled into the flea market parking lot. While Mary stayed in her car, Grace trailed Zack as he scoured the market for old videos. As she watched him, her thoughts went back to the detective who was now probably perusing everything from her underwear drawer to her old check stubs. The anger she'd felt when he'd shown up at the door again raced through her veins. How dare Mary Crow invite a stranger to come and stay in her home! And why had she, Grace, even called Mary Crow in the first place? She could be in league with the police after all. Planting evidence against Zack and then defending him at a murder trial might be a big boost for her political career. Hot tears came to her eyes as she watched Zack, absorbed in the video selection. Maybe she just ought to tell Mary that they were heading west, and she would return with Zack only if he was indicted. She was about to go back to the parking lot when someone touched her arm.

She looked over her shoulder. Mary stood there, smiling. Grace started to cry.

"What's the matter?" Mary asked, surprised.

Grace shook her head, unable to speak. She was too confused, too upset. Why were men calling her at night? Why were little girls calling Zack during the day? Who had wrecked Zack's room? Why had she ever confided in this light-eyed woman? She and Zack could have handled everything, by themselves. They'd done it plenty of times before.

"Come over here." Mary grabbed her hand, led her over to a little snack bar.

"Wait—Zack won't know where I am!"

"Go sit down," said Mary. "I'll take care of Zack."

Grace took a seat at the counter. She watched as Mary went over and touched Zack's arm, pointing to where she sat. Then she gave him some money from her purse, and whispered something in his ear. He nodded, then returned his attention to the tapes.

"What did you tell him?" asked Grace when Mary came back to the table.

"I told him we'd be right here. To take his time with the videos and to come over when he'd finished." Mary smiled. "I also gave him ten bucks, which he seemed particularly pleased with."

Grace had to laugh. "Zack doesn't understand a lot of things, but *money* he gets."

Mary sat down beside her. "Now. Why were you standing in the middle of this flea market with tears running down your cheeks?"

Grace took a deep breath. She liked Mary, but she also feared Mary. "You want to know the truth?"

"I always want to know the truth, Grace."

"I'm having second thoughts."

"About?"

"This. Everything." She gulped. "Mostly, I'm just not comfortable with Jack Wilkins in my home. I remember what he was like back—back when Teresa was killed."

"What?"

"Oh he wasn't as mean as Whaley. He just looked at us as if we were scum. Zack remembered him too."

"He had a murder case that was eating away at him, Grace. Eating away at all of them. They were crazy to find that child's killer."

"I suppose." She pulled a paper napkin from the dispenser and dabbed at her eyes.

"Did he look at you that way this morning?" asked Mary.

Grace shook her head. "No. This morning he just looked old. And sad."

"Teresa Ewing has been as much a cancer on his life as it has on yours and Zack's," Mary said softly. "It's the one case he's never cleared. He nearly had a breakdown over it."

"Is that why you brought him to my house? So he could solve the case and die a happy man?"

"Of course not. I brought him because I believe he can find out who's harassing you. He's not a cop anymore. He's working for me. Anything he learns at your house is privileged information. Inadmissible in court."

"But he was Whaley's partner," cried Grace. "Whaley would plant evidence—I know he would. What makes you think Wilkins wouldn't too?"

"Because the only thing Jack Wilkins is interested in is the truth. He's not out to burnish his arrest record anymore." Mary reached

274

for Grace's arm. "Let me ask you a theoretical question. In your heart of hearts, do you think Zack could have killed Teresa Ewing?"

Grace looked at Mary. Her eyes seemed to bore inside her head, as if seeking whatever truth hid there. "Ninety-eight percent of me says no."

"And the remaining two percent?"

Grace hesitated, afraid to give voice to the cold, silent fear that had lurked in the shadows of her heart. She looked at Zack, happily flipping through the videos, then at Mary, sitting across from her, her face as unreadable as the Sphinx. Then she took a headfirst plunge into truth. "The other two percent doesn't know."

Mary nodded, unsurprised. "That's what I thought."

"But you don't think it's terrible that I wonder at all? His own mother?"

"No. People love their children, regardless. Whatever they might have done."

———

Ultimately, Grace decided to continue to the cabin Mary had arranged for them. She'd already cashed in her vacation chips with Alice Richards, so she figured they might as well take advantage of it. They exited the interstate at a little town called Harriman and drove northwest on a two-lane road, through mountainous country where thick stands of Sycamore trees bordered narrow, rushing creeks. Zack laughed at a miniature Statue of Liberty that beckoned the huddled masses into a restaurant; every mile or so they would pass a different Baptist church. Grace was beginning to fear they would spend their vacation behind some discount store at a country crossroads when they came to the town of Rugby. It looked different from the outset—a settlement of old-fashioned clapboard cottages with cedar shake roofs. Most were painted in somber colors and stood behind moss-covered picket fences. They seemed Old World, as if they'd been transplanted from the British Cotswolds. Men with croquet mallets and cricket bats would have fit right in.

Zack looked up from his video game. "Where are we?"

"Where we're going to stay," she replied.

"What's here?"

"I don't know," she said, wondering what Mary had gotten them into. "But they call it Rugby."

Following Mary through the town, they turned down a bumpy side road, then drove into thick green forest. Zack removed his ear buds and rolled down the window. A moment later, he said "I hear a wood thrush, Mama."

"That's great honey," she said instinctively ducking as low hanging branches slapped against the windshield. "You might see a lot of birds here."

She followed Mary another hundred or so yards, then the road—or, really, the path—ended in front of a dark brown cottage with a screened in porch. Mary got out of her car, grinning.

"This is it. I'll go see if the key works."

Grace watched as Mary went to unlock the door. The cabin looked so quaint that she feared it might have oil lamps and a wood stove. Mary opened the door of the screened porch, then a moment later, she beckoned them inside.

They got out of the car and went onto the porch. Zack plopped down in a wooden swing that hung from the rafters while Grace followed Mary into the living room. There a long sofa faced well-stocked bookcases that flanked a stone fireplace. Beyond that was a small kitchen outfitted with new appliances. Two bedrooms opened off a short hall, a bathroom between them. As rustic as the place appeared, it had central air conditioning and electricity that powered everything from a convection microwave to a Jacuzzi.

"Wow," said Grace, as they walked through the little house. "This isn't like any cabin I've ever seen."

Mary laughed. "It's certainly not like the one I grew up in."

Grace returned to the kitchen. On one wall was a sliding glass door that led to another room with louvered glass windows. In one corner sat a huge TV with some kind of gaming console already attached. Grace walked over and drew back the drapes. The back yard was similar to theirs at home—a shady lawn with a bird feeder, bordered by woods. Only here the woods were different. Here the woods would be more correctly considered wilderness.

"That's the Big South Fork National Forest," said Mary. "125,00 acres. Goes all the way into Kentucky."

"How do you know so much about this?" asked Grace.

"I've been working on this estate for months. This little cabin and a hunting camp near Jackman, Maine, are what this family is squabbling over. I could quote you acreages and rights-of-way until the cows came home."

"I had my doubts about this," said Grace. "But with a giant TV, bird feeders, and those woods, Zack will feel right at home."

"According to my client, there's a church, a library, a café, and several bed-and-breakfast inns," said Mary.

"Where can we get groceries?"

"Carson's General Store. A mile down the main road."

"What if we need a doctor?"

"Call the Clear Fork Volunteer Fire Department. They'll get here the fastest."

"Okay, then." Grace smiled. "I guess we'll unpack."

———————

Zack unloaded the car. Grace got the groceries she'd brought from home stashed away in the kitchen. As Zack began to fill the bird feeder, Mary gathered up her purse.

"You're leaving?" Grace sounded surprised.

She nodded. "Emily's booked me into a campaign appearance with the United Methodist Women tomorrow. She called me while you guys were at the flea market."

"Can I at least fix you a sandwich to take with you?"

"No, thanks." Mary smiled. "I'll just grab something in Knoxville. Listen—my clients tell me cell service is sketchy here, but you can always get a signal at the grocery store. How about I call you with an update every day at one in the afternoon?"

"That would be great," said Grace. "Zack and I will make it an outing."

Mary smiled. "If there's an emergency or you need to get to a landline, there's a neighbor—a Reverend Steele—who lives a couple of hundred yards down the road."

Grace nodded, then swallowed hard before she spoke. "Mary, if you get the test results back with Zack's DNA, don't send the cops, okay? Just call me at the regular time and say we need to come home."

"Okay. Just remember, Grace: if you run, they'll only hunt you down."

"I know," she said. "I promise we're not going to run away."

"Good." Mary gave her a hug. "Then hopefully I'll see you soon."

"In *Usuhiyi*," Grace said softly.

"In the Twilight Land?" Mary laughed. "Surely before then. Call me if you need me, okay?"

Grace nodded. "*Wahdoe*, Miss DA. Travel safely."

THIRTY-FOUR

At dusk Jack Wilkins pulled his truck into Grace Collier's driveway. After Mary and Grace took off, he'd gone back home. He read Grace's illustrated diary, took an afternoon nap, then fed the chickens, the dog, and himself. That done, he returned to the Collier house. He planned to stake out the place and see if any of the harassment Grace had written about would recur. He knew it might be a fool's errand, but such was the nature of stakeouts. At least he had a whole house to move around in, instead of the front seat of some cramped patrol car.

Punching the remote he'd taken from Grace's kitchen drawer, he opened the garage door and eased his truck inside. Her clutter was not the typical array of rakes and garden tools, but easels, a molding joiner, and blank canvasses awaiting paint. He noticed someone had painted cartoon-like owls on the windows, and wondered if Grace had done that to maintain her privacy. If so, it fit in with his plan nicely—his truck would not be visible to anyone peering in the windows. To anyone driving by, it would look like Grace and Zack were in for the night.

He made a quick reconnoiter of the house—the tape he'd placed high on the front and back doorjambs remained in place—nobody had entered the house in his absence. As he let Lucky out for a final pee, he noticed no new bullet holes by the front door, nor any more dead squirrels. As robins hopped on the lawn, it looked like a normal house on an ordinary summer evening, on an ordinary country road. Only the ghost of Teresa Ewing had a way of turning the commonplace into something sinister.

He called Lucky inside and turned on the lights that Grace Collier said she left on—the porch light over the front door, the TV in the den, a light in her bedroom until around 11:30, which, according to her, was her usual bedtime. As he turned on that light, he paused to look around her room. Compared to his wife's stacks of books and family photos, Grace Collier's furnishings were almost Spartan—a bed and night table, a dresser, and a desk. Two framed pictures sat on the night table. In one an older Cherokee couple smiled stiffly at the camera. In the other, Grace and a man held baby Zack between them. Mike, Jack remembered. The husband who bailed. When they'd checked him out back in '89, he'd had not one but two girlfriends he was hiding from his wife. Jack lifted the photo and examined it more closely. He could see the resemblance between father and son—Zack might have his mother's coloring, but those downcast eyes were his dad's.

He replaced the picture and walked over to her desk. A school calendar lay open, her classes for the fall already written in. He sat down and eased open her lap drawer. It held pencils and pens and a lumpy eraser that looked like a wad of gray putty. When he reached to open her file drawer, it did not budge. She had locked it.

"Wonder what she keeps in there?" he whispered. He looked at the drawer. He knew he could jimmy the lock in five seconds, but she would know it the moment she sat back down here. His snooping was what she feared; it was also the very thing Mary Crow promised wouldn't happen. And yet here he stood, tantalized by a locked drawer. Had Grace Collier hidden evidence there for a quarter of a century? Some damning wisp of paper that would allow him to call that young Sheriff Cochran and say, "I know who killed Teresa!"?

"You're getting as crazy as Whaley," he whispered. "If she's clever enough to pull off that kind of cover-up, she wouldn't keep the evidence in her bedroom."

Forgetting about the drawer, he went into Zack's room. His bed was unmade, and his bath towel lay in the middle of the floor, topping a pile of cast-off clothes. On the wall hung clever caricatures of various birds, now blackened with spray paint. What stuffed animals remained among his bed sheets were missing their heads. Wilkins felt suddenly uncomfortable, as if he were looking at something both grisly and intimate.

"Come on, Lucky," he said to the dog. "Let's get out of here."

———

After dark he closed all the drapes, maintaining the charade that Grace and Zack Collier were at home. He moved Grace's landline telephone to the den, where he and Lucky settled down in front of the TV. Though he changed the channel from cartoons to a baseball game, he kept everything else the same. He opened the thermos of coffee he'd brought from home, muted the ball game, and started to listening to the house—familiarizing himself with the rattle of the air conditioning, the groan of the refrigerator as it began a new cycle. He was growing accustomed to the sounds when the telephone erupted with a loud ring. He jumped, almost grabbed the thing, and barked his name, then remembered—he was Grace tonight. He let it ring three times, then lifted the receiver to his ear. At first he heard only scratchy static, then a hoarse male whisper came through. "*What are you doing Grace? Waiting for me? I've been watching you. Coming to see you soon.*"

Jack remained on the phone, listening for any background noise. There was a kind of piping, calliope sound, then the caller hung up.

He took out his notepad and scribbled down the time and the caller's exact words. His voice was raspy, his accent Southern. If he was at all smart, he was using a burner stolen from some stranger in Cleveland or Omaha, who was probably cursing the bastard who'd lifted their smartphone. Still, it did prove one thing: Grace Collier had not lied about the phone calls.

"Okay," he whispered to Lucky, "wonder what else is going down tonight?"

Waiting for the next phone call made him edgy, so he tried to concentrate on the baseball game. It was a defensive battle, 2–2 in the eighth inning, the Pirates coming to bat. Both teams were so far out of first place that the managers were playing rookies, no doubt hoping they would gain some experience along with their new, Amish-looking beards. Jack yawned as the dog hopped up on the couch beside him. He wondered if he ought to make him stay on the floor, but given the mess in Zack's room, he imagined far worse than Lucky had been visited upon this couch.

He stared at the screen, the game droning on. His eyelids grew heavy as the eighth inning turned into the ninth, then the tenth. He watched, dimly, as the Pittsburgh catcher conferred with the pitcher, then he started dreaming about baseballs—fast balls, sinkers, then people tossing them like Frisbees. When one came straight at his head, he ducked, startling himself awake. He blinked at the TV set. The baseball game had ended; now some football player was yakking about new helmets. The dog, though, no longer sat beside him. Lucky was standing at the door, sniffing at the threshold. For the first time ever, Jack heard him growl. Something was on the other side of that door.

Jack froze, watching the door as intently as Lucky. Slowly the doorknob began to turn. First to the right, then to the left, both times stopped by the lock. Jack reached for his gun.

He got to his feet and crept to the door, careful not to jostle the curtain the covered the window. Pressing his ear to the crack, he listened. Somebody was walking along the deck; he could hear the squeak of the floorboards. It sounded as if they were moving toward Grace's bedroom.

Grasping his gun, he hurried down the hall, Lucky at his heels. Grace's bedroom had two windows, so turning off her light would let the intruder know he'd been spotted. Pressing himself next to the window on the backside of the house, he risked the barest peek behind the edge of the closed blinds. He couldn't see much—just the tops of the zinnias, growing to the corner of the house, and the dark yard beyond. Then he heard a soft, muffled thump, as if someone had jumped off the deck. Holding his breath, he peered into the dimness. For a moment he saw nothing, then a shadow fell across the tops of the flowers and moved to the corner of the house.

Quickly, he crossed the room to Grace's other window. As Lucky jumped on her bed, Jack pressed his finger to his lips. Amazingly, the dog seemed to understand the need for silence. Together, they waited, Lucky staring at the window, Jack listening, his finger on the trigger of his gun.

He heard nothing for so long he thought the intruder might have gone back to re-try the door in the den. Then, he heard something scraping against the window screen. Whoever was out there was standing no more than a foot away, on the other side of a thin pane of glass.

Jack clicked off the safety on his gun. If whoever was out there tried to come in through the window, he would shoot them. Flat out, no questions asked.

His gun raised, he listened. An owl hooted in the distance; katydids sawed to raspy crescendos. For a moment he wondered if the trespasser had sensed him and retreated into the darkness. Then he heard the soft scratch again, this time against the window screen, followed by a whispery, "Grace?" It reminded him of the voice on the phone—male, Southern, of indeterminate age.

He clutched his pistol. He heard another long scratching noise, then suddenly a car horn blasted, loud. Rapid footsteps scuttled through the gravel, toward the front of the house.

He raced out of the bedroom and into the hall. Just as he turned into the living room, the front window exploded. He dived for the floor as shards of glass rained down on him like needles. When they finally stopped pinging on the furniture, he crawled to the window frame. He peered out to see a car by the mail box, a dark figure running toward it. With the bottom of the shattered window providing cover, he fired three rounds. The first one missed, while the second one ricocheted off the back of the car. The third, though, was gold. It hit the runner, who gave a high scream, and fell. Jack raced to unlock the front door, hoping he could take out the car, but the punk he'd hit got up again. Limping to the car, he dived in the passenger seat. By the time Jack could take aim from the front porch the car had cut its lights and taken off, tires squealing, as it made a U-turn in the middle of the road. He emptied the rest of his clip, but he didn't think he hit anything. A black car with no lights on a dark country road was a tough target.

He stayed on the porch, his heart thudding, listening as the sound of the car's engine grew fainter, then faded away. They won't come back tonight, he decided. They weren't expecting quite so warm a welcome. Holstering his gun, he walked back inside the house. To his horror, Lucky lay among the broken glass on the floor.

"Aw, no!" Jack cried, hurrying over to him. "Not you," he whispered. "Please not you." The dog was still breathing, but unconscious. Jack ran his hands over his body, searching for wounds. But his fingers touched no blood—only a few small shards of glass from the window. Jack wet a paper towel with cold water and wiped Lucky's mouth and eyes. Slowly he revived, trembling and shaking his head as if he had something in his ears. Jack checked them for glass, then he realized that he'd fired his weapon right beside the dog. Lucky was probably in shock from the loud report, his ears no doubt ringing from the blast.

"I'm so sorry, buddy." Jack held the dog close. "I should have kept you in the other room."

After a few moments Lucky perked up enough to lick Jack's face, but he would come no farther into the living room. Probably just as well, Jack decided. Shattered glass covered everything, and the window was a gaping hole into the night sky. For now, he would hunker down and wait for them to come back. If he and Lucky were still alive in the morning, he'd go looking for a black sedan with a bullet hole near the left rear fender and a creep running around with a big bandage on his ass.

THIRTY-FIVE

IT WAS ALMOST MIDNIGHT when Mary returned to her apartment. Wilkins wasn't answering his phone, so she'd grabbed a late supper with Victor. Afterward she'd invited him to her place. It was the first time he'd been there since their argument and she was nervous, as if her living room might hold bad karma for the two of them. "Would you like a beer?" she asked, remembering the three bottles still lingering from his last visit.

"Sure," he said.

She fished two of the remaining bottles out of the fridge and returned to the living room. "I've got to speak at the UMW breakfast tomorrow," she told him as she sat down on the sofa beside him.

He frowned. "The United Mine Workers?"

"United Methodist Women. Emily booked me in at the last minute. I suspect their scheduled speaker cancelled."

"I didn't know the Methodist Women were into politics."

"I don't think they are, necessarily," she said. "But Emily sees everyone as a potential vote. I'm surprised she doesn't have me handing out bumper stickers at the Burger King."

They clicked their beer bottles together and stretched their legs out on the coffee table, staring at the unlit gas logs. Victor again wore his flip-flops, the sandals that had made such an angry sound as he'd walked away before. Mary knew from some of her more wrathful clients how insidiously the embers of old arguments could rekindle into flames, so she decided to tackle the unbroached subject of work head-on. As deeply as she cared for Victor, if they couldn't speak freely about their jobs, then they had no real future together. She turned to him.

"So how's it going at the SBI?"

"They're sending me to the Body Farm at the end of the month to study maggots. I'll be in Tennessee for a couple of days." He took a swallow of beer. "How about you?"

She paused, wondering how much she could say and not start everything all over again. "Actually, I've just come back from Tennessee."

"The Body Farm?"

"From someplace else. I relocated Grace and Zack Collier there."

He looked at her seriously, his playfulness gone. "What for?"

She told him about all the things going on at Grace's house—the harassing phone calls, the dead animals, and last night, a home invasion.

"Does Cochran know about this?"

She nodded. "He advised me to relocate them himself."

"Were the Colliers scared?" he asked, carefully not asking where exactly she'd taken them.

"Very scared. But neither of them wanted to leave."

"How come?"

"Grace didn't want to take off work. Zack thrives on routine—same people, same things every day. They seemed satisfied with their new location, though. It has all the bells and whistles they need." She pressed the cold beer bottle against her cheek and gazed at the dark fireplace, remembering her trip to Rugby. "Grace said the strangest thing when I left."

"What?"

"See you in *Usuhiyi.*"

"Where's *Usuhiyi?*"

"It's Cherokee—means the Twilight Land."

Victor laughed. "Is that anywhere near the Twilight Zone?"

"No, it means west—the place where Cherokees go when we die." She frowned. "You don't think she might be planning murder/suicide do you?"

"Sounds more like she might go west in her car," said Victor. "Doesn't she have an ex-husband somewhere out there?"

"Colorado," said Mary. "And two brothers in Alaska."

"That's about as west as you can get," he said. "I hope she doesn't lam out on you."

"I warned her about that. She gave me her word she wouldn't." Mary grew quiet, considering the possibility of returning to Rugby and finding Grace gone or, worse, dead. "Anyway, she seemed more concerned about what Wilkins would do in her house while they were gone."

"Wilkins?" Victor's brows lifted. "Wilkins, the old nutcase?"

She nodded.

"I'm sorry, I must have missed a paragraph here. What's Wilkins doing in Grace Collier's house?"

"I hired him as my investigator. He's staking out the place to see if he can find out who's behind all this harassment."

"Oh darling." He flopped back on the sofa and looked at the ceiling. "Why? What's wrong with Jack Wilkins?"

"Whaley's given me more of the skinny on Wilkins. The Teresa Ewing case drove a pretty big wedge between him and reality."

"What do you mean?"

"According to Whaley, as the months passed and they kept coming up empty, Wilkins got obsessed—wouldn't eat, couldn't sleep, started spending his paycheck at the liquor store. They finally made him take a medical leave. That's why Whaley has ridden Zack Collier so hard—he thinks eventually he'll crack and admit to the murder. Then Wilkins can die knowing they finally solved the case."

"But he acts like a regular old man. Pictures of his grandkids, golf clubs in his garage."

"Have you seen his war room?"

She nodded. "I've seen all his Teresa Ewing files."

"Didn't you wonder why the former lead detective would show you, a defense attorney, his old files?"

"I told him I'd been a prosecutor," she said. "Nine capital cases, nine convictions. He seemed impressed."

"I'm sure he was. But I'm also sure he was using you. That old fart would give his left nut to be back on this case. Probably his right nut as well, if he could collar somebody for that crime."

"But…"

Victor went on. "Did he tell you about his wife?"

"Yeah. She's in Minneapolis, helping their daughter with a new grandchild. She's coming back as soon as the daughter gets back on her feet."

"Well, part of that's true," said Victor.

"What part?" asked Mary.

"His wife's in Minneapolis, but she won't be coming back."

"Why not?"

"Because a couple of years ago she got fed up with Wilkins. It was as if a ten-year-old dead girl was the other woman in their marriage. Finally she went back to her family. Permanently."

Mary sat there, bewildered. Had Whaley been telling the truth? Had Wilkins touched the third rail of police work and gotten brain-fried for his trouble? She couldn't say; she didn't know. She looked at Victor. "You know what's weird about this?"

"Everything is weird about this," he replied. "But what specifically?"

"Whaley wants to hassle Zack Collier into a confession to save his old partner. I think the real killer or killers are hassling Zack Collier into a confession to save themselves. Everybody's drawn a bull's eye on Zack Collier, for totally different reasons."

"I think it's the same reason," said Victor.

"What?"

"Because he's the scapegoat. The guy's different; different scares people."

She turned to him. "I hate to admit it, but sometimes Zack scares me. I've seen the bruises he's put on Grace's arm."

"What are you going to do if his DNA comes back on those underpants?"

"I'll start working up a defense. Even if his DNA does show up, it still doesn't mean he killed her. It's circumstantial evidence."

"And then we're back to square one."

She laid her head back on the sofa. "Crazy, isn't it? The murder that can't be solved."

He put his empty beer bottle on the coffee and scooted closer. "I want to tell you something."

"What?"

"I'll do anything I can to help you. Whatever I'm working on, I'll always be with you—always on your side, win, lose, or draw."

"Thank you," she whispered, thinking that not once had Jonathan Walkingstick ever said such a thing to her. She wrapped her arms around Victor and pulled him close. The back of his neck felt gritty with dried sweat and when she kissed him, he tasted like salt. He took off his shirt, then he took off hers. They slid to the floor, making love in front of the fireplace. His body and his warmth made Grace and Zack and George Turpin and even the United Methodist Women seem insignificant; they were problems that might plague her tomorrow, but they were now just distant gnats hovering, waiting to assail her in the morning.

THIRTY-SIX

THE UNITED METHODIST WOMEN turned out to be a captive audience. Neither Turpin nor Prentiss Herbert showed up, so Mary had the microphone to herself. She gave her ten-minute stump speech, then for the next half hour she fielded questions. Most of the ladies were polite and interested, asking her about concealed carry prosecutions and hiring more women in the DA's office. A few, though, kept grilling her about why she was defending the retarded man who killed Teresa Ewing. "Everybody knows he did it," said one woman whose flowered dress gave her bosom the look of low hanging melons. "You seem like such a nice girl ... I don't know why you'd want to defend somebody like that."

"Because everyone is entitled to the best counsel they can get," Mary explained. "That's fundamental in American law."

"That's why rich people get off and poor people go to jail," said another woman.

"But what if you win and he gets arrested?" asked Melon Bosoms. "Will you just let him go?"

"No ma'am," said Mary. "Should I win, I'll convene a grand jury. If they return an indictment against Zack Collier, I'll recuse myself, which means a different prosecutor will take the case and Zack Collier will have to get a new attorney."

"Well, he'd better get a good one," someone else grumbled. "All I know is it's about time he paid for what he did."

A few minutes later, the meeting ended. Though even Melon Bosoms stood and applauded, Emily Kurtz just shook her head. She stood and waited for Mary to make her way through the crowd, to the back of the room.

"You had every one of these women," Emily said pointedly. "Until—"

"Until they asked me about Zack Collier." Mary finished Emily's sentence.

Emily shrugged. "I counted twenty-two votes in your column until the Z-word came up."

"And how many votes did the Z-word cost me?"

"Every woman over fifty. Maybe a few of the younger ones too. And from here on out, it'll only get worse. Turpin and Pugh aren't going to give you a free pass on this."

Mary's temper flared. "Then why don't we get some people to ask Prentiss Herbert what his conviction record is? Or how many female attorneys are currently working in Turpin's office? Or why Turpin allows men to plead down in domestic abuse cases while he prosecutes the women big-time?"

"I can find the figures," said Emily.

"Then find them. I'm sick of being blamed for representing a compromised man who hasn't even been charged with as much as jaywalking!"

They parted then, each angrily striding off to opposite ends of the parking lot. Mary got in her car, amazed at how quickly politics could spoil her mood. After a wonderful night with Victor and a great start with the Methodist women, she was back trying to dig out of the endless hole Zack Collier always put her in. Even worse, she'd only gotten Jack Wilkins's voicemail since yesterday morning. After hearing Victor's assessment of the man, she was beginning to wonder about the wisdom of hiring the old detective. If that arrangement blew up in her face, she could kiss the DA's office good-bye forever. She pulled out of the church parking lot and turned south. It was time to go out to Grace's and find out what Wilkins was up to.

She saw him the moment she pulled into Grace's driveway. He was standing, talking to a man in green work clothes. For a moment, she felt foolish about her concern, then she saw that the two men were surveying what had yesterday been Grace's front window. Now it was a just jagged, gaping hole covered from the inside by a pink flowered sheet that rippled in the wind. She parked her car and hurried over to them.

"What on earth happened?" she asked Jack, whose face was speckled with what looked like a hundred tiny shaving nicks.

"An interesting night," he said, recounting the phone call, the attempted entry into the kitchen, then someone scratching on Grace's window screen.

"What happened next?" asked Mary.

"Something spooked them. A car horn honked, I heard footsteps, like someone running. I got to the living room just as somebody shot out the front window."

"Are you okay?"

"Just a few cuts from the glass shards. I returned fire, striking an older sedan above the right rear tire and I winged one individual, who proceeded to escape in the car."

"Damn, Jack!" cried the glass man, who was short, bald, and had the name *Daniel Boone* embroidered on his dark green work shirt. "If you'd hit that gas tank them intruders would have been barbecued."

Jack laughed. "I guess my aim isn't what it used to be."

"Did you get a plate number?" asked Mary. "A description of the guy you shot?"

Jack shook his head. "It was too dark, too far away."

"You're not a-wanting bulletproof glass in this window are you?" Daniel Boone interrupted, eager to get to work.

"No," said Jack. "But put the regular stuff in fast. I want to be ready if they come back tonight."

"Hold on, Jack." Mary took his arm. "Let's go talk about that."

————

They went inside, to the kitchen. Mary fixed a pot of coffee, though Jack acted as if he had gone through several pots already. He paced around the kitchen with his gray hair sticking up in little tufts, his face looking as if it had barely escaped the death of a thousand cuts.

She handed him some coffee. "Did you call the cops last night?"

"No, I called them this morning. They said they'd send someone out."

"Did they?"

"Not yet."

"Why did you call someone to fix the window before the police could file a report?"

"Because I know where those reports wind up. I need to get going on this, but I didn't want to leave the house without a front window. Boone's an old buddy of mine, so I called him." He took a slurp of coffee. "His crew will have everything fixed up in a little while."

Mary sat down across from him. "What do you mean, you've got to get going on this?"

"Find those bastards. I've got a pretty good idea who they were."

"Who?"

"Russell, Shaw, and McConnell. The three remaining boys-to-men members of the Salola Street gang."

"Shaw left yesterday for South Carolina. He's helping his family move."

"Even better. That leaves just Russell and McConnell."

She frowned. "I would agree with you, Jack, except these guys are close to forty. Broken windows and crank phone calls smack of somebody just out of juvie."

"But don't you see—these boys have never grown up! They're stunted. Teresa Ewing's murder messed them up for life."

"What do you mean?"

"Look at them—Russell still lives with his mommy, McConnell can barely keep his daddy's business afloat, and Shaw is a vagabond photographer. They don't think like grown men! They figure if they can scare Zack with Barbie dolls and beheaded toys, he'll cop to Teresa. He did it once before."

Mary didn't know what to say. Though a possibly off-his-rocker cop had come up with a theory that made a good deal of sense, she still had her doubts. "But don't you think this could be the next generation of stupid redneck kids, out to raise a little hell?"

Jack shook his head. "Teresa Ewing is ancient history to the teenagers slamming mail boxes today. I doubt any of them have even heard of her."

"You're right." Mary did the math. "Most of the people who care about Teresa Ewing are well over forty years old."

"I think if I just put in a little legwork, I can catch them." Jack's blue eyes almost sparkled. He reminded her of an old hunting dog that had caught the fresh scent of a rabbit in the field.

"I'm sure you could, Jack. Unfortunately that's not why I hired you. You're supposed to keep this house secure. Let the police take over now."

He shook his head. "I can't. They already think Teresa Ewing drove me over the edge." He put both hands on the table and leaned toward her. "Don't you see? This is probably my last shot at proving I'm not nuts."

She studied him, tired and eager, young and old, all at once. "Okay," she said, not knowing what else to tell him. "See what you can find out. But be back here by dark, alright?"

"No problem," he said, starting for the door.

"And answer your cell phone, Jack. I called you about fifty times this morning."

He blushed, as if he'd gone outside with his fly unzipped. "Sorry," he told her. "I guess I'm still not used to carrying a damn telephone around in my pocket."

———————

Jack left Mary and Daniel Boone and drove toward town. He knew a PI license wouldn't get him all the information he needed, so he pulled over at a gas station and called his old partner, Whaley.

"I need you to look something up for me," he said after they'd gone through their usual list of complaints—Whaley carping about the police department, him griping about his bad leg. "I'm playing dick today."

Whaley laughed. "You say you're playing with your dick today?"

"May as well be," said Wilkins. "Listen—I need you to find out if anybody showed up at the hospital last night with a gunshot wound."

"What kind of gunshot wound?"

"A .45, fired from thirty yards away."

"That's a pretty serious hole, Jack." Whaley was no longer laughing. "You haven't gone all Dirty Harry, have you?"

Jack gave him the short version of what had happened the night before. He said he was aiming at the car when he hit the guy running away.

"Yeah, right." Whaley's tone was sarcastic. "Where were you?"

"Honeysuckle Lane. Out near the county line."

There was a long silence. "Jack, are you working for Mary Crow?"

"I don't have to tell you that."

"Jack, there are only three houses on Honeysuckle Lane and the only one that gets dispatch calls belongs to Grace Collier, who happens to be a client of Mary Crow."

"Okay," said Wilkins. "I'm working for Mary Crow."

"What the fuck for?" cried Whaley. "She's representing that Collier bastard."

"I don't care who she's representing," Wilkins replied. "What I'm doing is figuring out who killed Teresa Ewing."

"Oh Jack." Whaley didn't bother to hide his disgust.

"You guys at the station haven't come up with anything," said Wilkins. "Humor me, Buck."

For a moment he heard only silence—he knew Whaley considered him nothing more than an old cop who couldn't let go. But Whaley owed him. Years ago he'd "lost" the breathalyzer test that put the still-on-duty Whaley way over the legal limit for driving under the influence. Whaley later admitted that he owed Jack his career. Today he was calling in his debt.

"Okay," Whaley finally said. "What time did all this go down?"

"Shortly after midnight. I think the wound would have been buttocks or back of the thigh."

"Ouch," said Whaley. "That's a gift that keeps on giving. He'll never sit down in quite the same way."

"My heart bleeds. I only grazed him—he managed to scramble back into the car."

Whaley chuckled. "And I bet his jockeys looked like fudge pie. You get a make on the vehicle?"

"A not-too-new sedan, black, I think."

"Okay, buddy. You got it. I'll call you back if I find anything."

"Thanks, Buck. I guess we're square now."

"Don't take this any further, Jack. You're not wearing a badge anymore."

———

Jack clicked off, wondering if he should go pay Devin McConnell a call. The little shit would know Whaley on sight. Him he'd likely forgotten—he would be just another faceless senior citizen come to tire-kick with his dog. He drove through town under a low-hanging sky that promised rain. He turned down Main Street, passed the Burger King, then saw the green Mylar balloons floating against the sky.

"Good old Tote-A-Note," he whispered as he pulled into the turn lane and put on his blinker. "Hasn't changed a bit."

He parked beneath the faded leprechaun that leered from the roof. When Teresa was killed it was Hartsville's only used car dealer, and Big Jim McConnell advertised on the TV station out of Asheville, batting down high prices with a plastic shillelagh. He smiled at the memory—his kids used to watch TV on Saturday mornings and laugh harder at Big Jim than they did at Bozo the Clown. But as funny as the guy had been on the tube, he'd grown dead serious when they started looking at Devin for Teresa Ewing's murder. He sentenced the kid to house arrest, making him permanent babysitter to his houseful of brats. It was harsh, even by the time's stricter standards, which made him wonder if Big Jim knew more about Devin's activities than he ever admitted.

He got out of the truck, rolling the windows down to give Lucky some air. He strolled toward the first rank of cars, parked facing the highway. All were sedans, mostly Japanese imports in shades of gray and silver.

He ambled around the lot, waiting for Devin to emerge from the little office. When, after five minutes, nobody had come out to sell him some lady-driven number with only a hundred thousand miles, he walked over to the office and tried to open the door. It was locked. He stepped over and looked in the window. The lights were off, the desk stood vacant. Nobody was working at Tote-A-Note today.

"Okay," he whispered. "So much the better for me."

Whistling, he strolled around the office, to the back fence. Padlocked and concertina-wired, it enclosed old, rusted vehicles destined for the scrap heap. He saw a red Ford with a number 9 painted on its side and a black Subaru that looked as if a boulder had fallen on it. Then, backed up behind the office, he saw a dark gray Corolla.

Though mud covered most of the body, it was several cuts above the other specimens in this lot. He walked over to the far side of the fence to check out the passenger side of the car. He hoped to find blood smear, or even a bullet hole. Instead all he saw was a regular old Corolla, its rear bumper bashed in.

He gave a disgusted snort. "I should have known this wouldn't be easy."

He stepped back, trying to avoid an oil slick when suddenly the loud *brrrppp* of a siren caught him totally off-guard. As Lucky began barking furiously, he turned to see a police cruiser just inches from the back of his truck, its light bar flashing. Immediately, he lifted his hands, figuring someone had made a prowler call. Then the passenger door of the cruiser opened. Buck Whaley emerged.

"I thought I might find you here," Whaley called, draping his fleshy arms over the door.

"You son of a bitch." Jack lowered his hands. "You almost gave me a heart attack."

"Yeah? Well, you almost gave me one, saying you might have put a slug in someone's ass."

"Did you find out who?" asked Jack.

"Possibly," said Whaley. "Get over here and we'll talk about it."

THIRTY-SEVEN

"You think he's armed?" whispered Saunooke, who sat watching Jack from the driver's seat.

"He's got a Smith and Wesson .45 in a shoulder holster," Whaley replied as Jack came toward them.

"Shouldn't you disarm him?"

Whaley looked at the young patrolman as if he were an idiot. "He's not going to shoot me, Saunooke. He's after the Salola Street boys. You stay here while I go talk to him."

Whaley left the cruiser and walked toward Jack's truck. The dog in the front seat leaned out the window barking, snapping at him as he drew closer. Then Jack came over and patted the dog's head. Immediately, he started trying to lick Jack's face.

"Quite a watchdog you've got there," said Whaley.

"He wasn't until you drove up," Jack replied. "Your siren must have scared the shit out of him too."

Whaley shrugged. "I had to get your attention somehow." He looked at the lump under Jack's jacket. "You carrying?"

Jack allowed him a brief glimpse of dark brown holster just under his left arm. "Just my old pal."

Whaley frowned. "Don't you think you're too old for this?'

"There's no statute of limitations on murder, Buck—on either side of the coin. Did you find out anything about my bullet wound for real, or were you just trying to make an old man faint?"

"Nobody with their ass shot up is in any hospital around here. That made me think maybe it was just wishful thinking on your part. Then I remembered something."

"What?"

"When I was wrangling the very reluctant Salola Street boys into giving their DNA, I found McConnell and Russell sitting right in that office, thick as thieves. I put the fear of God into them, and they complied with the DNA right quick. But a few days before that, I'd gone over to Russell's house looking for him. His holy roller mother invited me inside. While she was yakking about how much psychological damage we'd done to her precious son, I saw a picture of her and Two Toes McCoy."

"Janet Russell? With Two Toes?"

Whaley nodded. "Wearing robes, at some kind of retreat. She said Two Toes was a great healer—spiritual as well as physical." He smirked. "Now I know you don't think I'm the sharpest knife in the drawer, but if my little boy came home with a bullet in his ass and I had a real chummy relationship with an Indian healer..."

"And your little boy didn't want to call attention to a gunshot wound," added Jack.

"Then I might take him up to Two Toes," Whaley finished. "Which is why I busted you with Saunooke, instead of by myself."

Jack peered at the squad car. "Why?"

"Because Saunooke's the only one who knows exactly where Two Toes lives."

"And you two are going up there to check it out."

Whaley nodded. "That's the plan. You need to go home now, Jack. Leave it to us."

Whaley watched as Jack Wilkins cocked his head, looking at the cruiser wistfully, as if he'd bumped into a long-ago lover who had no memory of him at all. "Take me with you," he said softly. "Just one last time."

"You know I . . ."

"Please. It's the last shot I'll have at this. I don't want to die with my life in pieces and not know why."

Whaley looked up at the leprechaun on top of Devin McConnell's office, mostly because he didn't want to see the look in Jack's eyes. He could lose his badge for involving a civilian in a police operation; yet he would have lost his badge years ago if Jack hadn't covered for him. Jack must still be pretty damn good with a gun and though Saunooke was a good man, he was also a young man, untested in many ways. What would it hurt to have Jack with him? Nobody would ever know, unless Two Toes blew all their brains out. Then it wouldn't matter anyway.

"Okay," he finally said. "But this is it."

"I know," Jack whispered.

———

In the parking lot they conferred with Saunooke, who told them they'd never catch Two Toes unawares. "He's got all these dogs," he told Whaley. "If they're tied up, they'll just bark like crazy. If they're not tied up, they'll eat you alive."

"We can shoot the damn dogs," said Whaley. "What else? What's the layout up there?"

"He's got a trailer in a little clearing, surrounded by some teepees. I imagine that's where he'd put somebody who was sick."

"How many teepees?" asked Whaley.

"I saw two. There could be more."

"Why don't we do this," suggested Jack. "Saunooke goes in as a decoy, sirens blaring, gets the dogs all crazy, and asks Two Toes if he's seen McConnell or Williams." He looked at Whaley. "You and I can sneak around and check out those teepees. If we find either one of those guys, we can bring 'em in on suspicion of criminal mischief at the Collier home."

"That's pretty shaky ground, Jack," said Whaley.

"Well, it gets them cooling their heels in jail until you can drum up something better. Lucky dug up those underpants in July—now it's almost September. I've seen faster DNA tests come back on dinosaurs."

Whaley couldn't help but laugh. "No offense Jack, but are you sure you're up to playing commando? Run around peering in teepees?"

"Don't worry about me." Jack eyed Whaley's rotund stomach. "I'll be fine."

———————

So they started off, Saunooke and Whaley in the cruiser, Jack and Lucky following.

"You do know to keep your mouth shut about this, don't you?" Whaley asked Saunooke.

"I do."

"If it gets ugly up there, you take care of Jack. He may be old and crazy, but I don't want anything to happen to him."

"Yes sir."

Saunooke drove deep into the reservation, turning where the old woman had told him weeks before. When the pavement ended, he continued down the trail of mashed-down grass that tunneled through the forest. At the end of the path, where the RIGHT PATH RE-TREAT sign arched over the road, he stopped.

"If you want to reconnoiter those teepees on foot, you should start here," he told Whaley. "Two Toes's trailer is about a hundred yards that way." He pointed to the left. "The teepees are set up around it."

"Okay." Whaley opened the passenger door. "Let's switch cars. You take Jack's truck and tell Two Toes you're here unofficially, that you got a tip about him and the vandalism at the Collier house. It might piss him off so bad that he'll give up Russell and McConnell. At any rate, it'll be a good way to keep him occupied while Jack and I check things out."

"You got it."

Whaley and Saunooke went back to the truck and explained the plan to Jack. The old man got out of the truck, leaving Lucky with a pat on the head. As he handed his keys to Saunooke, he said, "If anything happens to me, give this dog to Mary Crow. Tell her I said to take good care of him. His name is Lucky."

"Don't worry about the dog, *enisi*. Worry about yourself."

"*Enisi*?"

"Grandfather," replied Saunooke.

Jack laughed. "Good luck to you, too, junior."

The two older men took off through the trees while Saunooke headed toward Two Toes's cabin. A quarter mile up the ridge they heard dogs barking wildly, as if they were within seconds of tearing something to pieces.

Wilkins just hoped it wasn't Lucky.

They kept going in the direction Saunooke had told them, Whaley breathing hard, Wilkins feeling the climb in his bad leg. When they got to a break in the foliage, they looked down at the trailer. They had a perfect view—Saunooke had cleverly angled the truck around so that his back was to the dogs. Two Toes was facing Saunooke, unaware of them on the rise behind him. All six dogs had hushed, but they kept their eyes riveted on Two Toes. Whaley only hoped that the rope that tethered them held fast.

"Smart boy, that Saunooke, turning Two Toes away from us," whispered Wilkins.

"He might have a future," Whaley admitted. He scanned the perimeter of the trailer. "I count three teepees. How about you?"

"Me, too," said Wilkins. "You want to split up or take 'em together?"

"Together. It doesn't look like anybody's in them, but I like backup when I'm dealing with Two Toes."

"Lead on, then. And hurry. That Saunooke won't be able to stall him forever."

The teepees circled the back of the trailer, roughly fifty feet apart. Wilkins and Whaley drew their weapons as they approached the first one. Tall, straight poles were covered in white canvas painted with red symbols that could have been either stars or swastikas. Wilkins watched as Whaley crept up to the entrance and put his ear to the tent flap. For a long moment he listened, then looked at Wilkins and shook his head. Wilkins inched forward, slowly pulling back the tent flap. He peered inside but saw nothing except a stone-lined circle in the middle of the floor and a few blankets scattered around it.

He made a rolling motion with his right hand, their old signal for "keep going."

Whaley headed for the second teepee. They approached it as silently as the first. Decorated with the same red squiggles, it too stood as empty—holding a fire pit and few moth-eaten blankets. The third was the same, except someone had left a crumpled pack of cigarettes in the fire pit. Jack stooped inside to retrieve them. When he crawled out, Whaley was waiting.

"I think we've crapped out, buddy. Nothing here but—"

Suddenly Jack shook his head, pointing over Whaley's right shoulder. Through the trees they could see a thin plum of white smoke another twenty yards away. Immediately, they melded into their old team—Wilkins taking the lead, Whaley following. They crept up to a fourth teepee hidden in the woods. They stopped, listening for a word, a breath, a rustle from inside. Amazingly, they started to hear voices, loud and argumentative.

"Do you have to put that shit on me?" a male voice cried.

"Yes," replied a female voice. "Two Toes says it shrinks the wound without leaving a scar."

There was a moment of silence, then a scream of pain. "Jesus, it feels like a blowtorch! I don't know why you think fucking Two Toes knows anything about healing."

"You're the one who didn't want to go to the hospital," the woman warned.

"I wouldn't have needed to go to the hospital if you two had just stayed out of my damn room."

"Somebody had to pack your things before they bulldozed the house. You sure weren't."

"But did you have to bury my things under that tree? Couldn't you have thrown them the fuck away?"

Whaley locked eyes with Wilkins. This was huge ... more huge than they'd ever dreamed.

"I saw what it was! I was afraid to throw it away! If you bury a bad thing with tobacco, it can't harm you. You throw it away and its ghost haunts you for the rest of your life."

Whaley looked down at the ground and offered a silent prayer. *Please dear God, let them say the word* underwear. *That's all we need. Just one* underpants *and it will be all over for good.*

"They were a fucking pair of girl's panties, Mom. Panties don't have ghosts. They weren't going to follow anybody, anywhere."

They grinned at each other, then moved as one, smooth as old silk. Whaley through the door first, Wilkins right behind him, both pointing their weapons. Butch Russell was lying facedown on a blanket, Janet Russell putting some kind of foul-smelling poultice on his left butt cheek. Janet Russell shrieked, terrified, as Butch started flailing his arms and legs, like a swimmer on dry land. "Noooooooooo!" he screamed. "Nooooooo!"

Whaley tossed Wilkins his handcuffs. "Congratulations, detective. You do the honors and I'll call Saunooke."

Trembling, Wilkins grabbed both of Russell's arms and shackled them together at the wrist.

With his gun pointed at the terrified Janet Russell, Whaley punched the number that would connect him to Saunooke. The young officer answered a few seconds later, over a barrage of static.

"We need backup at a teepee about fifty yards behind the trailer," he told the young man. "We have two individuals in custody."

"What for?" asked Saunooke.

"The murder of Teresa Ewing."

THIRTY-EIGHT

THE FIRST DAY AT Rugby, all Zack did was pace around the little cottage and cry. He wept over his maimed toys, over the fledgling wrens they'd left behind in a nest in their back yard, over the fact that he wouldn't see Clara for a long time. Mainly, though, he mourned the loss of Adam, his one and only friend.

"I don't see why he couldn't come and *say* good-bye," he told Grace repeatedly.

"He did, honey. He told us his family was moving, and he had to help them."

"But he could have taken me with him," he said miserably. "I'm strong. I could have helped them. I helped Adam move a rug one time."

"You did?"

"Yeah. We put it in his dad's wheelbarrow."

Grace could just picture Leslie Shaw's expression if Adam had shown up with Zack, ready to help them move to South Carolina. It would have been laughable were it not so sad.

The second morning of their vacation Grace was standing on the back porch, staring into the thick woods that pressed up against their cabin. At first she felt as if she'd been condemned to an undetermined sentence in an upscale prison, but then, as abruptly as the sun appearing after a summer shower, she realized the one enormous difference between North Carolina and Tennessee. She and Zack had no history here. Nobody knew who they were or that they'd been accused of anything. They were as free as the birds that fluttered around that feeder, to go wherever they pleased.

The thought buoyed her, making her turn to her son. "I've got an idea, Zack. Go find that book on day hikes that we saw in the bookcase. You choose a hike, I'll pack a lunch, and we'll go exploring."

She expected him to balk, to insist on staying inside and watching his videos. But he surprised her. Excited, he got the book and found a half-day hike to a place called the Gentlemen's Swimming Hole. He packed a small knapsack with drawing paper, a pack of chewing gum, and a first-aid kit. Though it took them most of the morning to hike to the wide expanse of water that nestled between lush stands of hemlock and laurel, Zack jumped in and splashed away the rest of the afternoon, finally sunning himself dry on the boulders that edged up against the water.

That adventure set their vacation on a radically different course. From then on they hiked every day, exploring both the mountains and the little town. They learned that Rugby had been founded by an Englishman who'd wanted to create a "new Eden" for the second sons of the British gentry. Each day she and Zack made a circuit of the little village, nodding at people they were coming to recognize, always ending with a stop at Carson's General Store. Grace used its free Wi-Fi to keep in touch with Mary Crow, and Zack loved the old-fashioned pinball machine with its silver balls and red flippers.

One day they'd made their daily tour of the town and were going up the steps to Carson's when Zack asked a question.

"Can I call Adam?"

"I imagine he's back in New York, honey."

"But couldn't I call him? Just once? We never said good-bye."

She knew how important closure was to Zack. It had eluded him most of his life; he'd had too many people—his father, more caregivers than she could count—happily tell him "see you tomorrow" and then vanish forever. And Zack had been so good lately—no meltdowns, no hitting her, not even too many tears. Surely he'd earned one phone call to his friend.

"Do you know his number?" It was in her phone, but she tried for one last reason to deny him the call.

"212-555-0342," he repeated without hesitation.

"Okay. Here." She handed him her cell phone. "But you have to promise not to tell him where we are. It's a secret."

"I promise." He punched in the number, listened for a few moments, then handed the phone back to her. "Nobody home," he said, disappointed.

"He's probably on assignment," she told him, secretly relieved that Adam had not picked up. "You can try again tomorrow. Let's go get something to cook for dinner."

They went inside the store. William Carson, the owner, looked up from the cash register. He reminded Grace of an overgrown teddy bear—bushy gray hair and beard, but so tall that even Zack looked small beside him. Oddly, her son did not seem intimidated by William Carson. Grace figured it was because he always spoke softly and gave Zack plenty of space.

"Hey, Zack." Carson smiled, typically greeting Zack first. "How's it going?"

"Okay," he replied shyly.

"Here for your daily Internet fix?"

"Yes," said Grace. "But we need some groceries too."

"You came at the right time, then," said William. "I just got some Grainger County tomatoes in and fresh corn from Sunbright."

"Wonderful." Grace reached for a small basket. "I'll get Zack going on the pinball machine and do some shopping."

Carson watched her search for quarters, then said, "How about I give Zack a little job? He can earn a few bucks and pay for his own pinball."

"What kind of job?" asked Grace.

"I've got some boxes that need to be broken down and stacked up for recycling. Shouldn't take him more than about ten minutes."

She turned to her son. "Would you like to earn some money, Zack?"

He nodded, though he kept his gaze on the floor.

"Come on then," said William Carson. "Let's get busy."

As Grace watched, Zack trooped after William Carson into the back room of the store. A few minutes later she saw him flattening cardboard boxes, readying a pile for the loading dock. William Carson returned to the cash register, smiling.

"That was amazing," Grace said. "He's only ever earned money for cutting my grass."

"Makes them feel self-reliant," William Carson replied. "Getting paid to do something."

"Have you worked with autistic people before?"

"In my former life I taught teachers how to teach. Special needs students were a large part of our curriculum."

"How did you wind up here?'

314

William Carson smiled. "I came up here from Nashville for a long weekend and fell in love with the place. Shortly after I retired from teaching, this store went up for sale. I pounced."

"And you've never looked back?"

"Not once." His eyes crinkled up behind his glasses. "This truly has turned out to be a new Eden. For me, anyway."

Suddenly Zack appeared in the doorway. "All done," he said, grinning proudly.

William Carson went to check his work, then came back and opened his cash drawer, handing twelve quarters to Zack. "You did a good job," he said. "Maybe you can help me out again sometime."

Zack nodded, pocketing his wages and hurrying over to the pinball machine. As he started firing the silver balls, Grace checked her messages via Wi-Fi. None from Mary Crow, thank God. Then she took her basket and shopped for necessities—toilet paper and wine, a pound of bacon and some of the fresh tomatoes William had bragged about. After that, she headed to the cash register.

"Are you enjoying the Burton cabin?" asked Carson as he rang up her purchase.

Grace flinched—their location was supposed to be secret. "How did you know we were there?"

He grinned. "Just a little downside to Eden. The local gossip grapevine swings pretty wide."

She swallowed hard, suddenly nervous. "What else did the grapevine reveal about us?"

"That you're wealthy, from North Carolina, and that your son is ... different."

"It got two out of three things right," replied Grace.

"You're not from North Carolina?"

"No, I'm from North Carolina and Zack is different. But I'm about as far from wealthy as you can get. I'm a painter."

"Really?" He smiled, interested. "What do you paint?"

"Landscapes, mostly," Grace answered truthfully at first, then added a lie. "Which is why we're here. We're friends with the Burtons and I'm doing some painting, up in the forest."

"And you probably don't wish to be disturbed," said William.

She didn't know how to answer him—probably they shouldn't make friends with anybody up here, but some nights she would give anything to hear another voice besides the ones coming from Zack's videotapes.

"I've put you on the spot," William said quickly. "I apologize."

"No, it's not that. It's just that Zack doesn't deal that well with strangers."

"I understand."

"But don't please don't tell anybody that," she added. "People have been so friendly to us."

"How about I just don't add to the gossip one way or the other," said William. "And you and Zack can go at your own pace."

"Thank you," said Grace, grateful. "That would probably be best."

———

She paid for their groceries and they started the mile-long walk back to the cabin.

"I like Mr. Carson," said Zack, her two bottles of Merlot clanking together in his backpack. "He doesn't smackertalk."

"I know. He was nice to give you a job."

"I did a good job too," he added proudly.

"Yes, you did."

They walked down the main road, the sun warm on their backs. Zack spotted a turtle crossing the pavement and ran to move it off the road.

"Mama, can we stay here?" he asked when he returned to walk beside her.

"Where?"

"Here. In this town. We get to walk around. Go places. It's fun."

"I'm sorry, honey, but I don't think we can stay."

"Why not?"

"Because our home is in North Carolina. My job is there and Clara is waiting for you to come back."

"But I like it here better. Adam moved away; couldn't we move away too?"

She sighed, her own backpack suddenly growing heavy. What could she tell him? That life wasn't that simple? That teaching jobs were scarce and making a living as a full-time painter was virtually impossible?

"No, honey. We just don't have the money."

"So we'll have to go home?"

"Eventually." She suddenly wished she could tell him her dream instead of their reality. That the DNA on those underpants would be someone else's, and they would go home to find that people had forgiven him for being different, forgiven her for trying to protect him from the viciousness of rumor. But she doubted that would happen—hate was a hard habit for people to break. But what not even Zack knew was that if his DNA showed up on those underpants, they would not be going home at all. They would walk up to Carson's store one last time. She would buy chocolate milk and chocolate ice cream and make a big milk shake with it. Then she'd empty all the bottles of tranquilizers she'd brought into it. Then she and Zack would curl up in front of that fancy TV and fall into one final, deep sleep as they watched videos of other people's lives, where husbands remained true, boys grew into healthy men, and little girls like Teresa Ewing weren't allowed outside after dark.

THIRTY-NINE

VICTOR GALLOWAY WATCHED THROUGH the two-way mirror as Butch Russell squirmed in his chair, trying to find a comfortable position to sit in. He'd been transferred to the Justice Center from the hospital, where he'd been treated for a gunshot wound to his left buttock and blood poisoning brought on by Two Toes McCoy's herbal remedy.

"Did you tell him that the DNA test came back inconclusive?" Victor asked Buck Whaley, who stood beside him.

"Nobody's getting that information," replied Whaley. "Word from the boss."

"Cochran?"

Whaley looked at him as if he were stupid. "Turpin."

"But that report came in days ago," said Victor. "I gave it to Cochran myself."

"Turpin's put out a gag order." Whaley turned his attention back to Russell, who fidgeted as if fire ants were hatching in his trousers. "Anyway, it gives us a little more leverage if nobody knows we don't have shit."

Victor frowned. "Did the other guy ever turn up? The used car guy?"

"Saunooke and Riley brought him in yesterday, from Florida. He'd been hiding out at his mother's."

"Cochran told me Two Toes buried the underpants."

"Two Toes was helping his disciple Janet pack up to move. They found the panties hidden in the back of Butch's closet. Janet freaked out, realizing that her precious baby might be a killer. Two Toes had to slap her to calm her down. Finally he told her he would take care of them."

"But why bury them?"

"Something to do with his loony religion. He told her it would make peace with the tree, since that's where we found the girl. The sandwich bag was from Janet Russell's kitchen, the tobacco from Two Toes's pack of smokes."

"But how did Butch Russell get them in the first place? Did he kill the girl?"

"He says he didn't, but he did finally admit that they were playing strip poker. Teresa agreed to do it, but only if they got rid of Zack Collier. She was afraid of him."

"What then?"

"Teresa had just lost her underpants when Two Toes showed up and started throwing his knife around. The kids grabbed their clothes and scattered. Russell and McConnell snatched Teresa's panties as they left."

"You're kidding."

"According to Russell, McConnell took them home. Then when the girl went missing and things got serious, he gave them to Butch for safekeeping."

Victor frowned. "And Butch kept them for twenty years?"

"He was scared to get rid of them when the case was hot. After that, he got all weird and paranoid about them. He admitted he'd jerked off into them a couple of times. I'm guessing McConnell probably had too. That's why they freaked when this blew up again. Russell knew the new DNA techniques are light years beyond the ones in '89."

"So they needed a scapegoat and chose Collier," said Victor.

Whaley gave a weary sigh. "Einsteins, they ain't."

"Has Russell fingered anybody for the murder?"

"The only thing Russell says it that it wasn't him. That's the one part of this stupid story he's never waffled on."

————

Victor walked out of the Justice Center, frustrated. He'd had cases wash out before—key witnesses had been scared out of testifying, or the definitive piece of evidence simply wasn't there. But for Turpin to keep this pot boiling just so he could get some votes didn't seem right. He had little knowledge of politics, but he realized Mary was on to something when she kept talking about transparency in the DA's office.

He got into his car and pulled out onto Main Street. Mary had mentioned that she had another luncheon appearance today, but he couldn't remember where. She'd done the Methodist Women and the Chamber of Commerce—what was it today? He closed his eyes, then it came to him. The big Baptist church that stood in the shadow of the courthouse. Bag lunch with the candidates. He drove east, parked in the lot behind Mary's office, and walked the two blocks to the church.

At the back of the building, a number of cars were parked around a door covered with a green canopy. He went over and let himself inside the building, where he heard distant laughter, then applause. He followed the noise down a hall and through some double doors. Suddenly he was standing in the back of a large auditorium where about thirty people sat listening to Mary and Turpin and Prentiss Herbert. He caught Mary's eye, then took a chair in the back of the room. The stumping went on as usual—Mary talking equality in domestic violence prosecutions while Turpin thunderously accused Mary of defending child-killers and hiding suspects to avoid questioning. As the DA hammered away, Victor grew angry. He wanted to stand up and say, "You're full of shit, Turpin. You know you don't have the goods in the Ewing case. Why don't you just shut the fuck up?"

But he knew that would certainly cost him his job and probably make things worse for Mary. If his father, a former Golden Gloves champ, were describing this DA race, he would say Mary was swinging hard, trying to land a knockout punch, but Turpin's little jabs were scoring points with the voters. Prentiss Herbert hadn't even answered the second bell.

Finally it was over. Mary shook hands with her opponents and slowly made her way over to him.

"Agent Galloway." She smiled as if she hadn't seen him in weeks instead of this morning, in bed. "What a nice surprise!"

"Can we go up to your office?"

"Sure." Her smile faded. "Why am I thinking you don't have good news?"

He shrugged. "It just depends on how you look at it."

———

They hurried up to her office. Ravenel was gone and it wasn't Annette's day to work, so they had the place to themselves.

"Don't tell me." Mary gave an edgy laugh. "You're going back to Rosaria."

"Who?"

"That girl tattooed on your back."

He shook his head. "Don't be ridiculous. This is much more important than Rosaria."

"Then you're going back to Atlanta. They offered you an undercover job in Narcotics."

"I'm not going anywhere, Mary."

"Then what, Victor? I've never seen you look this way."

"Remember our talk, when we agreed that there were certain things about our jobs that we couldn't share?"

"Of course I do."

"Well, I need to share this. It may get me in big trouble, but I don't care."

"What?"

"There's no DNA that links Zack Collier to that crime. There's no DNA linking anybody to it. It's contaminated and inconclusive. Turpin's sat on that information for a week and will probably continue to sit on it until after the election."

She looked at him, incredulous. "Are you kidding?"

"The report came in last Monday. I didn't tell you because I assumed you'd hear it from Cochran. Today I found out that Turpin put the clamps on everybody."

"Are you sure it's inconclusive?"

"Absolutely. Now, I'm going to break the rules again. Do you want to hear Butch Russell's version of what happened that afternoon at the tree?"

"Of course I do."

He told her what Whaley had gotten from Butch Russell—the strip poker game minus Zack, Two Toes's arrival, the kids fleeing, Devin and Butch stealing and keeping the underpants. She listened, not missing a beat of what he said. When he finished, she stared at the rug, frowning. Then she spoke.

"So when Teresa dropped off that casserole, she probably didn't have her underpants on."

"Not if I remember the timeline right."

Mary leaned forward. "So maybe after she delivered the food, she went back to the tree to look for them. That's where she ran into whoever killed her."

Victor nodded. "Which now looks like to me like either Two Toes or your boy Zack."

"Only we'll never know," said Mary.

"Not from those underpants."

"But how did they wind up under the tree twenty years later?"

"Janet Russell and Two Toes were packing up Butch's room. Janet found them stashed in his closet and went nuts. Two Toes got rid of them for her."

"And buried them," Mary whispered, remembering the strange little ceremony she and Wilkins had witnessed. She leaned against the edge of her desk, staring at her mother's tapestry. Then she said, "What time is it?"

He checked his watch. "One twenty-seven."

"Maybe I can still reach Grace." She reached for her phone. "She goes to some grocery store that has Wi-Fi. If I have news, I'm supposed to call her at one."

Mary punched in the number, waited for Grace to answer. When she didn't, Mary put the phone on speaker and looked for the neighbor's number, thinking she'd call him. But then she remembered she'd told Grace he would show up only if the DNA test was bad. For the first time in two weeks she had good news for Grace, but no way to tell her. She hung up the phone, disgusted.

"I've got to go over there," she told Victor. "If I leave right now, I can get there by late afternoon. I can tell Grace the news and get back here by midnight."

"That's a pretty intense trip," he said. "Is there no other way you can reach her?"

"None that wouldn't scare her to death. Anyway, if the rest of my life was hinging on a DNA test, I'd appreciate knowing the results as soon as they came in."

He stepped over and kissed her. "Can I come with you?"

"Better not," she told him. "Her son's kind of dicey around cops." She wrapped her arms around him, loving the way he felt next to her. "Victor, I can't tell you how much I appreciate this. And I promise you, nobody will ever find out where it came from."

"I'm not worried about that. But I am a little worried about you taking off for the Twilight Land. Especially with that Collier kid there."

"The Twilight Land is in Rugby, Tennessee." She laughed. "Now I have no secrets from you at all."

"You take your gun, okay? And come over to my place when you get back."

"You'll be awake?"

"Awake and waiting," he whispered, his breath tickling her ear.

———

She changed from her beige linen suit into shorts and sneakers and started driving. Traffic was heavy, with carloads of flatland tourists heading into the mountain coolness. She crossed into Tennessee behind a battered Ford with South Carolina plates, two children sticking their feet out the back windows. When she got to the little town of Newport, she pulled into a liquor store and bought a bottle of champagne. Though the DNA test had not exonerated Zack, neither had it nailed him as a child killer. She figured that alone was worth a glass of bubbly.

She inched through five o'clock traffic in Knoxville. As the sun became a fierce orange ball on the horizon, she turned north. Two hours later she finally arrived at the little cabin that had so divided the Burton family. It nestled under the tall pines serenely, like a child blissfully unaware of the custody battle swirling around it. Mary pulled up beside Grace's SUV, grabbed the champagne, and hurried to the front door. She knocked loudly, thinking Zack would have the TV or the VCR up full blast, but she heard nothing from inside the house.

She knocked again. This time she thought she heard footsteps thudding to the door, then running away. "Grace?" she called, wondering if she'd caught Grace in the bathtub and Zack was too shy to open the door. "Grace, it's Mary Crow."

The door opened abruptly, as if Grace had been standing there the whole time. She looked at Mary terrified, a long-handled spoon in one hand.

Immediately, Mary realized what was wrong. Grace thought she'd come with bad news.

"It's okay." Mary held up the champagne. "The test came back inconclusive. They won't be arresting him on that evidence."

"Oh God." Grace dropped the spoon and held both hands to her cheeks. "I thought you'd come to get him!"

"No," said Mary. "I called you a little past one, but I missed you. They're learning more about what happened that night, but they still don't know who killed that little girl."

Grace started to cry. Mary stepped inside to hold her, then Zack wandered in from the den. "Mama?" he said, his voice full of concern. "Are you okay?"

Grace wiped her eyes. "Oh yes, sweetheart. I'm so much more than okay." She smile at Mary. "Set another place at the table, Zack. We're having company for dinner."

———

They ate in the living room, in front of the fireplace. Grace had fixed spaghetti, a Friday night tradition at their home. She lit candles and asked Mary if Zack might open the champagne. "Amazingly, he loves to hear it pop."

Mary handed him the bottle. Zack carefully removed the foil wrapper and wire, then wrenched out the cork with a single pull, laughing as it gave a loud pop. After Grace filled their glasses, Mary offered a toast. "To the future. Brighter than it was yesterday."

They ate then, Grace telling her about Rugby and all the hiking they'd done. Zack had lost ten pounds and had developed a remarkable sense of direction in the woods.

"Maybe it's his Tsalagi genes," said Mary, noting that both of them did look fitter than when she'd brought them here.

"He found this wonderful little waterfall, not on the maps," said Grace. "It's high—about twenty degrees cooler there, so we take our lunch when it's really hot. The cold spray feels terrific."

Zack shoveled his spaghetti in quickly, hunched over his plate, then asked to be excused.

"You want to watch your tapes?" Grace asked.

He nodded. "I just started one of Adam's."

"Okay, then. We'll be in here."

Zack took his empty plate to the kitchen. A few moments later the tinny, recorded voices of children came from the den.

"He'll watch his tapes awhile," explained Grace.

"You know, he doesn't seem to need nearly as much medication here, and he goes to bed a lot earlier."

"Maybe it's all the hiking," said Mary.

"But you know what's been the most wonderful thing here? Nobody knows about us. We don't have to stay hidden. Zack's even made friends with the man who owns the grocery."

"That's wonderful." Mary smiled.

They sat for a moment, listening to the birds outside and Zack's video from the den. Grace disinterestedly pushed some spaghetti around her plate, then she looked at Mary with sadder eyes. "This DNA report won't change anything for us, will it?"

Mary shook her head. "I'm afraid not."

"So we'll go back to our pretty little prison in Hartsville and live in limbo all over again."

Mary stared at the bubbles rising in her champagne. Grace had just voiced what she'd realized the moment Victor told her about the report. All this had solved nothing—Teresa Ewing's killer remained a mystery. "I wish I could say you're wrong, but you're not. Until they figure out who killed that girl, Zack and those other three men will remain suspects for the rest of their lives."

Grace was about to say something more when suddenly a high pitched scream split the night.

"No!" shrieked Zack, sounding like some wounded animal. "No! Stop it! No!"

Grace leapt up from the table. Mary followed. They raced through the kitchen and into the den. Zack stood in front of the television, his mouth square, both hands fluttering like trapped birds.

"Honey, what's wrong?"cried Grace.

"Teresa!" he cried, jumping up and down as he pointed at the screen. "I just saw Teresa get killed!"

FORTY

MARY AND GRACE TURNED to the TV screen. The picture careened wildly, topsy-turvy, light to dark, then it seemed to focus on a wall with peeling paint. The audio was a dragging sound, then a young male voice cried, "You shouldn't have laughed at me!" A dark thing obscured the wall for a moment, then they heard another scraping sound. After that, the screen faded to black.

"What are you talking about, Zack?" cried Grace.

He pointed at the screen. "Teresa! She was right there!"

"Can you rewind the tape?" asked Mary.

Hands flapping, he refused. "No! I don't want to watch it again!"

"You don't have to," said Grace. "Just rewind the tape for us. Then you can go in the other room."

He rewound the tape, but instead of leaving, he sat cross-legged on the floor with his eyes squeezed shut, his hands over his ears. Mary and Grace watched as Teresa, the dark-haired gamine, came on the screen.

"Which one do you want to do?" Her was voice was childish, but she sounded put-upon, as if she been talked into doing someone a favor. "I've got to get home for supper."

"Let's do the one where he puts it inside her," said the huskier voice off-screen.

"The missionary position," she said. "You swear you won't tell? I don't want Shannon and Janie to find out."

"I won't tell."

Whoever was operating the camera moved it back, getting a broader view of the girl, who flopped down on a plaid blanket and started unzipping her jeans. "And you promise to give me back my underpants?"

"I promise."

She sighed. "All right." She took her jeans off, then pulled her green jacket down to cover herself. "Okay. Now you take your pants off." She sat there, eyes bright, watching her companion with considerably more interest. Suddenly she started to giggle. "That's it?"

"Yeah," the deeper voice said gruffly. "What of it?"

"It doesn't look like the ones in the book."

"It gets bigger," he replied.

Laughing harder, she pointed. "It's not even as big as Butch's. You're like a baby!"

"Shut up!"

"Adam is a ba-by," she started to sing-song, her bow of a mouth curling in a mean little smile. "I'm gonna te-ell. I'm gonna tell Shannon and Janie and Marie and Miss Kalman, the math teacher!"

All at once her teasing stopped. Her eyes grew wide as her companion moved in front of the camera. Suddenly her face was obscured by an oversized blue-and-white football jersey emblazoned with the name SHAW above the number 15.

"Quit it, Adam," she squealed. "That hurt! Now I'm really gonna tell! My parents and the police!"

The picture became a blur of color and motion, Mary and Grace watched, horrified, as the pair struggled, fighting and yelling.

"Shut up!" said the huskier voice. "Just shut up!"

"Make me."

For a moment they heard nothing, then Teresa gave another vicious little laugh. But that laugh was cut short as a blur of an arm lifted once, then twice as number 15 brought something down hard on Teresa's head. Then he said, "Just try and tell now, Teresa. Just try and tell now!"

The tape showed a brief glimpse of Teresa's limp body, then it went into the wild, topsy-turvy picture they'd seen before. As it again faded to black, Mary and Grace stood there, stunned into silence.

"Oh my God," Grace whispered. "It was Adam."

"No kidding!" The words came loud—hard and fast as bullets— from behind them. They jumped, turned. Adam Shaw stood at the doorway to the kitchen, dressed in black, pointing a pistol straight at them. Mary recognized the weapon; a fifteen-round Glock. He could kill them five times over.

"Adam?" Zack jumped up from the floor. "How did you get here?"

Adam smiled at his old friend. "I've known where you were all along, buddy."

"You have?"

"Remember the day we buried those animals? I played a trick on your mom while you were watching cartoons."

Zack grinned, video forgotten. "What did you do?"

"I put a little spyware on her phone. I've heard about everything you've done—your phone calls, your hikes, your visits to Carson's grocery. You and your mom have a nice life up here."

"Is that a real gun?" Zack asked, more excited than scared.

"Yeah, buddy. It's real."

"You're not going to shoot any animals, are you?"

"No, all I ever wanted was to get that tape back. Now, I don't know what I might have to do."

"Don't get in deeper, Adam," said Mary. "Put the gun down, get a lawyer, and confess. You were what—twelve at the time? Better to have killed one as a juvenile than three more as an adult."

"I'm sure that's good advice, Ms. Crow. But I don't like the idea of prison, for any length of time." He turned to Grace. "I don't think you want to see Zack there, either."

"Zack didn't do anything to that girl," said Grace.

"He didn't kill her," Adam replied. "But he did help me get rid of her body."

"Zack?" Grace looked at her son. "What's he talking about?"

Zack stared at all of them, his jaw flaccid.

"Remember the rug in the shed, Zack? The one you helped me put in my dad's wheelbarrow?"

Zack nodded. "It was too heavy for you to lift."

"It was too heavy to lift. But it wasn't too heavy to push, once we got it in the wheelbarrow."

"You killed her, then rolled her up in the rug," said Mary. "Then you pushed her out to the tree."

"I had a new moon, the Cadillac of wheelbarrows, and I waited until two in the morning. It took me five minutes and nobody saw a thing."

"Teresa's body was in your shed the whole time?" asked Grace.

Adam nodded. "I couldn't believe they didn't find her. Still can't. I think they had rookies searching that shed."

"What are you going to do now?" asked Grace.

"Zack's going to give me that tape. Then we're all going on a hike. In the moonlight. We might even hear some owls."

"But it's my tape!" cried Zack. "I bought it with my own money!"

"It's a bad tape, Zack. It will give you nightmares."

Zack shook his head, stubborn. "No."

Adam pointed the pistol at Zack's chest. "Give it to me, you moron."

"I'll get the tape, Adam," said Grace. "Please just stop pointing the gun at him." She gave Mary a furtive glance, then walked over and knelt in front of the television. Fumbling with ejecting the video, she looked up at her son.

"Can you help me, Zack? My hands are a little shaky."

As Zack stooped down to help his mother, Mary realized that Grace was up to something. Mary stepped forward. She dared not look into the round, black gun barrel, but kept her eyes focused on Adam's, hoping to find some trace of rationality. "I'm telling you again, you don't need to do this. You were a kid back then, teeming with hormones and insecurities. On that tape Teresa comes across as a mean little flirt who threatened you with exposure, the worst thing imaginable for a pubescent male. She humiliated you. You got angry, wanted to hurt her back. There's not a man in America who wouldn't understand that."

His gun wavered slightly; she could tell she was getting to him.

"Hell, I'll even represent you. We'll go for a jury trial, ask for a change of venue, seat twelve men on the panel. Teresa's family is all gone. No weeping parent will be there to hold up her picture." She licked her dry lips, praying her voice would remain even. "I'll get you off, Adam. It'll be a slam dunk."

She watched the barrel of his gun sink lower. *Five more seconds,* she thought, *and I've got him.* "Only Pisgah County cares about that little girl. It's their great unsolved mystery. But even Pisgah County just wants to—"

Suddenly Zack sprang up from the VCR and barreled to the front door, the tape tucked under his arm.

"*Didagedi*, Zack," cried Grace. "Fast!"

The spell Mary had almost worked on Adam broke. He pushed her backward then leaped over the coffee table, hot after Zack. Grace lunged forward, managing to grab his ankle as he rushed by. Adam fell with a crash that jarred the cabin. He and Grace struggled on the floor, Grace desperately trying to wrench the gun from his grasp. But before Mary could help her, Adam shook free and scrambled after Zack, gun in hand. He tore out the door but stopped just past the screened porch. His old friend had vanished, taking the tape somewhere into the thousand acres of dark forest that surrounded the cabin.

He turned back to Grace and Mary, his gun gleaming in the dim light. "You stupid bitch," he told Grace as he wiped blood away from the corner of his mouth. "Get over there and sit with your counselor. You two are going to pay for this."

Grace came over and plopped down beside her. At first Mary thought Adam Shaw might put a bullet in both their heads, but he pulled a length of twine from his back pocket.

"Hands out, wrists together," he ordered.

Mindful of the Glock pointed at them, they complied. Adam tied their hands, then he tied them to each other with another length of rope around their waists.

"This is a trick I learned in Myanmar," he explained. "When they catch two thieves on an expedition, they tie them together. If one falls, the other goes too. Saves them a lot of time and energy, trial-wise."

When he had them bound to his liking, he pulled them toward the door. "Okay, Grace. Take me to Zack. Any tricks and you'll be dragging your dead pal right along with you."

Mary tried to remember all the things she'd learned from Jonathan, desperate to come up with some kind of plan. She did not recognize the Cherokee word Grace had used, but she knew that in the forest, at night, their best chance would be to outmaneuver Adam Shaw. "*Amaskagahi?*" She stared at Grace, praying she knew the word for waterfall.

Grace started to reply, then a knowing look flickered in her eyes. "*Amaskagahi.* That's exactly where we're going."

———

They left the cabin—doors open, lights on—and plunged into the forest. Though the aroma of cedar and the call of screech owls were familiar, this part of the Appalachians was new to Mary. The trails seemed rockier, the undergrowth thicker than in the woods at home. They walked in silence, Adam keeping up with them. After a steep, half-hour climb, the trail divided, encircling the top of a mountain.

"This seems like a pretty stiff trail for Zack," Adam said, his eyes gleaming feral in the moonlight. "You wouldn't be leading me away from him, would you?"

"This is where I told him to go," Grace said flatly.

She led them down the right prong of the trail. Distantly, they could the low rumble of water, a steam rushing far below them.

"What are you going to do when we find Zack?" Mary asked. She'd learned long ago that it was better to know what your enemy was willing to reveal.

"Get my tape back."

"Then what?"

"Another thing I learned in Myanmar," he said. "Bad accidents happen in the mountains, and nobody gives them a second thought."

No kidding, Mary thought, appreciating the man's spiteful cleverness.

They went on. The September moon was a bright white orb glowing through the black lacework of trees. The air went from chilly to cold, making them shiver to keep warm. As the rush of the creek grew louder, the trail ended, spilling them onto a rocky mountaintop, slick with icy wetness. On three sides the forest loomed; to their right a cascade of water spewed out of the rock face like a geyser, tumbling into the vast expanse of darkness below.

"Well?" said Adam. "I'm not seeing your boy anywhere."

"Zack?" Grace called over the roar of the waterfall. "Zack, are you here?"

They listened for his reply. All they heard was the water, pouring out of the mountain.

"Zack?" Grace called again. "You can come out now. Everything's okay!"

Again, Zack did not answer.

"He must have gotten lost," Grace said. "This is where I told him to come."

Adam looked at her for a moment, then a slow smile stretched across his face. "You're awfully calm, Grace. Considering your precious little boy could have taken a header off this waterfall."

"He knows to stay away from the edge," said Grace, her words frosty on the air. "He's not an idiot."

Mary noticed then that Adam wore only a T-shirt; he was shivering as badly as they were. If she and Grace could get the gun away from him, they might have a chance. Slowly she inched closer. As the gun in his hand started to shake, she took her shot. "*Hega*, Grace. *Asdawadega!*"

Jerking Grace toward her, Mary kicked at the Glock with her right foot. She caught Adam by surprise; the gun flew out of his hand and slid along the icy rock. Mary ran for it, dragging Grace along with her. She fell into Adam, catching him across his hips. As he and Grace fell down together, Mary lunged for the gun. It was wet and slippery as a minnow. Twice it squirted out of her grasp, her fingers pushing it farther toward the waterfall. Then she tried to hold her hand like a claw and clamp down on the thing. Finally it stopped sliding, trapped by her icy fingers. Never had any gun felt so precious. Clutching it tightly, she twisted to turn it on Adam, who was scrambling to his feet on the sleet-covered rock.

"Grab him, Grace!" Mary yelled.

Flat on her back, Grace struggled to flip herself over. She grabbed Adam's arm, but his momentum was too great. Suddenly all three of them were tangled together, sliding helplessly toward the waterfall.

Mary crawled toward them. Gripping the gun, she threw herself over Grace's legs, knowing her weight would either stop them or they would all die together. For a moment the hideous slide continued, then slowly it stopped, with Mary pinning Grace to the rock, and only Grace's tied hands keeping Adam Shaw from plunging over a waterfall.

"What now?" Grace's breath was rapid little puffs of smoke.

"I'll get his other arm," gasped Mary. "And pull him back on the rock."

"Where's the gun?"

"I'm aiming straight at him."

Mary crawled toward the edge and, with the gun in one hand, grabbed Shaw by the sleeve of his T-shirt.

338

"I didn't mean to kill her," he sobbed. "It was an accident."

"Too bad you didn't say that years ago."

Mary sat up, dug in her heels, and finally found purchase on the face of the rock. She and Grace pulled him back from the edge. His face looked ashen in the moonlight, his eyes huge as he stared down the barrel of his own gun. "What are you going to do now?"

"Get you back to Hartsville. I want everybody to find out who really killed that little girl."

Grace untied the rope that joined them. As Mary held the gun on Adam, Grace hog-tied him, hands and feet together behind his back. As she worked he glowered at Mary, his eyes dark pits of anger. "Zack never was up here, was he?"

"Zack is at Carson's Store, in Rugby," Grace replied. "*Didagedi* means 'glasses.' It's Zack's name for William Carson."

"They may not catch killers like this in Myanmar," said Mary as Grace started to untie her hands. "But it works pretty good for us Cherokees in Tennessee."

EPILOGUE

– Two Months Later –

"How are we doing?" Mary asked Emily Kurtz, who had commandeered Annette Henry's desk and telephone. Ginger Cochran was pacing around her office, cell phone at her ear.

"Hang on!" Emily held up one finger while listening to someone on the phone. She grabbed Annette's While You Were Out tablet and scribbled down some numbers. "Okay, thanks," she told the caller. "Talk to you later."

She turned to Mary, her eyes bright. "The Quallah vote went for you 80–20. The Hartsville vote looks good, maybe up by seven points. The 'burbs are still out."

"And that's Turpin's territory," said Mary.

"Maybe not this year," said Emily. "Bringing that Shaw guy in was pure gold. You know, Mary, I honestly thought you'd lost it when you said you were going to solve that case."

"Probably I had." Mary laughed. "Must have been the same day I decided to run for DA."

"Well, you may have to get used to that idea, honey. By the end of the night you might be moving your law books up to the courthouse."

"Don't say that!" Mary cried. "You'll jinx me."

"Okay, okay." Emily pushed her glasses higher on her nose. "Look, there's nothing to do here but bite your nails while we wait for the returns. Why don't you go down to HairTwister's? That's where your party is."

"I didn't think you were supposed to go there until you'd won. Or lost."

"No, go down there and enjoy yourself. I'm sure the press will be there—make nice with them if they want an interview."

Mary said, "Are you sure there's nothing I can do here?"

"No." Emily smiled. "Go and have fun. Ginger and I will keep you posted."

Mary started downstairs, then turned and walked into her office. Though no one was in there, the lights were on, making her mother's tapestry glow along one wall. Slowly Mary walked toward it, a thousand memories flashing through her mind. She and her mother swimming at Atagahi, her mother gathering ramps in the spring and telling her all the old Cherokee stories of how the world came to be. What a fine childhood that had been; how much it had given her then, and still gave her to this day. "Thank you, Mama," she whispered, running one finger along a silver thread that ran through the design. "I don't know what's going to happen tonight, but I'll always try to make you proud." She stared at the tapestry, then her gaze fell on a photograph on her credenza. She and her mentor Judge Irene Hannah at her graduation from Emory Law. "And you, too, Irene. I owe you both everything." She was reaching to touch the photo when someone knocked on the door. She turned. Victor stood there in a shirt and tie and a new haircut that made the hair on the top of his head stick straight up.

"You like my new do?" He grinned, turning his head from right to left.

"Yeah," she said. "Looks right out of *GQ*."

"Ross and Meilani are giving free cuts down at HairTwister's. Everybody who voted for Mary Crow gets one."

"Well, hey," said Mary, patting the tapestry a final time. "I'd better hurry down there and get a trim."

They waved at Ginger and Emily and headed for HairTwister's. As they made their way down Main Street they saw Turpin's election-night party in full swing at the Ridgeview Restaurant. Red and blue balloons decorated the entrance, and the place was crowded with people inside. By contrast, the party-goers at HairTwister's spilled out on to the sidewalk, drinking cider, showing off their free haircuts, and dancing to an old-time music band. To her surprise, Mary saw Grace Collier dancing with the man she'd called Didagedi.

"Look," said Victor. "There's Grace. Who's that guy she's with?"

"William Carson. She met him at Rugby. He's the one who called the cops when Zack showed up at his store."

"And preserved the evidence, I assume?"

"Carson couldn't quite make sense of what Zack was telling him, but he figured that tape was important. He locked it in his safe."

"And now he and Grace are a couple?"

"Grace says they're moving in that direction. I worked out a deal with my clients where Grace can stay at that little cottage—maintenance in exchange for cheap rent. And William Carson has given Zack a job at his store."

"That's a pretty sweet deal," said Victor.

"I can't think of any two people who deserve it more."

They plunged into the crowd at HairTwister's. Juanita had dyed her hair red, white, and blue and set up a long buffet line of refreshments—fry bread, squash, and barbeque made with Turpin's own special sauce. "You cooked Turpin's goose," Juanita cackled as she served Mary's plate. "So now he can do barbecue sauce full time."

"Juanita, this is amazing," said Mary. "There must be two hundred people here."

"I told you I'd give you a party if you won."

"But I haven't won yet."

"Shoot, after that Teresa Ewing business? Honey, Turpin should have thrown in the towel the day that story broke. I hear all the scuttlebutt around here, and that's all anybody talks about—how Mary Crow caught the man who killed Teresa Ewing, over in Tennessee."

Mary laughed. The gossipmongers who'd once turned Zack into a homicidal maniac were now making her sound like Davy Crockett. "Thanks for the support, Juanita, but don't say anymore about winning. I'm getting superstitious."

"You got it." Juanita grinned. "The TV people will call it any minute now, anyway."

She and Victor took their plates over to one corner of the salon and tried to eat, but it was impossible. Campaign workers, well-wishers from the tribe, and people she'd never seen before in her life came to congratulate her, to tell her they had a good feeling about this election. She'd managed to get one bite of barbecue down when she saw a tall, gray-haired man starting through the buffet line.

"Would you hold my plate a minute, Victor? There's somebody I need to speak to."

He sat down at a hair dryer while she dived back into the crowd. She made her way to the buffet line and tapped the man on the shoulder. "Jack?"

Jack Wilkins turned and stopped to give Mary a hug. "I'm so glad to see you. What a great night this is."

"Thanks, Jack. How are you?"

"Fabulous!" He grinned. "Hang on—I want to introduce you to someone."

She waited while he reached down the buffet line and touched a woman's shoulder. Smiling, she came to stand beside him. Like Jack, she had Swedish good looks—incredible blue eyes, amazing skin.

"Mary, I'd like you to meet another of your voters, my wife, Jan."

"Hello, Mary." Jan extended her hand and smiled. "Jack's told me so much about you."

For an instant, Mary didn't know what to say. She'd known of the rift between Jack and Jan, but only from other people. "I'm so glad to meet you. I understand you've been in Minnesota with a grandchild?"

"I have been." She stepped closer to Jack and patted his chest, a gesture affectionate and proprietary. "But now I'm back."

"I'm so glad to hear that," said Mary. "I know Jack missed you."

"I missed him, too," she replied. "But now we're both back. Together again."

Mary was going to say something else, when Ross stood up on a hairdryer.

"Here it comes, everybody. Watch for it!" He lifted a laptop over his head. The room grew quiet as an election update came on.

A pretty blond reporter gave the totals in Jackson and Swain Counties, then said, "There could be an upset in the making in Pisgah County, where Cherokee challenger Mary Crow has a slim lead over long-time District Attorney George Turpin ... "

Whatever the reporter said next was lost in the din. Jack and Jan both hugged her, then she was engulfed by the crowd. Grace and William Carson, Ginger and Jerry all came and threw their arms around her. As the old-time band struck up a version of "Carolina in the Morning," another pretty reporter shoved a microphone in her face.

"So does it feel fine to be in Carolina tonight, Ms. Crow?" she asked above the noisy celebration.

"Absolutely," said Mary.

"This was a hotly contested race. Should you pull off an upset, do you feel like you have the political capital to make serious changes in the DA's office?"

"I ran on transparency and a more equitable dispersion of domestic abuse cases," said Mary, trying to make herself heard. "If I win, I'll implement those changes immediately."

"Tell us a little about the cold case that you were so instrumental in solving. People are talking a lot about that."

"With a lot of luck, I helped the police in Morgan County, Tennessee, arrest this man. He's currently awaiting trial here, in the Pisgah County Justice Center."

"Should you win, do you intend to prosecute? Or are you going to recuse?"

Mary thought of the slimy way Adam Shaw had used Zack Collier, all of the damage he'd done to so many innocent people. She looked straight into the camera. "Absolutely I'm going to prosecute. To the fullest extent of the law."

The camera lights went off; the reporter disappeared into the crowd, no doubt buzzing across the street to interview Turpin. As more people milled around her, Mary felt someone touch her shoulder. She turned. A young man from Hartsville Florist stood there with three red roses in a silver vase.

"Mary Crow?"

She nodded.

"For you." He gave her the flowers and disappeared into the crowd. With a thought that Turpin might have sent her a poison-laced bouquet, she opened the card attached. When she read it, she gasped.

Utluhgwodi. Congratulations.

With *Jonathan* underneath.

She looked around the room. Was he here? Standing by the punch bowl? Waiting in some nook for her to notice him? She swirled around, searching for the face that she'd somehow been born knowing. It was not there. She hurried through the crowd and out to the sidewalk. More people were standing around, drinking cider and laughing. Again she searched for him by the storefronts, even in the parking lot across the street. But he wasn't there any-more than he'd been inside. And yet—he'd known about her, known about this night. How could that be? She didn't even know what country he was in. A teenager brushed past her, his eyes focused on the bright screen of his smartphone.

All at once, she felt like an idiot. Of course Jonathan would know what she was doing. Anybody with a cell phone could find out ex-actly what was going on in Pisgah County.

She walked away from the party angry, feeling as if she were being played by a ghost—a man who could not show his face, but who also could not leave her alone. Every time she thought she'd forgotten about him, something—garnets on her fence post, flowers at an election party—brought him back as real as if he stood in front of her. As she looked down a dark alley, she almost felt he was there—then suddenly, she realized he was. Not in the light and

346

laughter of her life, but in the shadows of her memory, the darkness of her regret. There, Jonathan Walkingstick would always be.

She turned. Across the street, HairTwister's glowed like a beacon. Music was playing, people were dancing. As she watched, another tall figure came out on the sidewalk.

"Mary?" Victor called, searching up and down the street. "Are you out here?"

"Over here." She lifted her hand. "Just looking at things from a different perspective."

He gave her a crooked smile. "Any better from over there?"

"Actually not," she said, hurrying toward him and all that he promised. "But everything looks incredible right where you are."

© Sallie Bissell

ABOUT THE AUTHOR

Sallie Bissell is a native of Nashville, Tennessee, and a graduate of George Peabody College. Bissell introduced her character Mary Crow in her first adult novel, *In the Forest of Harm*. *A Judgment of Whispers* is Bissell's seventh Mary Crow book (third with Midnight Ink). The first four titles in the Mary Crow series are available in print from Bantam Doubleday Dell and as e-books from Midnight Ink. Bissell is a Shamus Award nominee, and her work has been translated into six foreign languages. She currently divides her time between Nashville and Asheville, North Carolina, where she enjoys tennis and an occasional horseback ride. Visit Sallie on Facebook or at www.salliebissell.com.